— PRAISE FOR —
The Elements of the Crown

"The story is absolutely immersive from the beginning to its intriguing end; and with a fiery determination, Talise is someone you can't help but root for."

"The world building is fantastic, and the main characters draw you in and become like old friends."

"Kay has given us an exciting new world to enjoy and takes us on the journey of ups and downs with our main character. It is a little emotional and caused a bit of heartache, but I loved Talise's strength."

"I enjoyed being inside Talise's head as she learned ways to manipulate water, fire, wind, and earth with dazzling effect."

"A fantastic beginning to what promises to be an intriguing series. Talise has so much to gain and so much to lose, but her reasons for both are compelling."

"It's a really great premise, you've got fantasy, drama, friendship, heartbreak, it will keep you glued to the book. The writing is great, and the world building shows a lot of promise."

"The world we are introduced to is absolutely fascinating."

"The writing is appropriately detailed, the story well-plotted, and the world building is on point."

ALSO BY KAY L. MOODY

The Fae of Bitter Thorn

Heir of Bitter Thorn
Court of Bitter Thorn
Castle of Bitter Thorn
Crown of Bitter Thorn
Queen of Bitter Thorn

The Elements of Kamdaria

The Elements of the Crown
The Elements of the Gate
The Elements of the Storm

Truth Seer Trilogy

Truth Seer
Healer
Truth Changer

**Visit kaylmoody.com/kamdaria to read the prequel
novella, *Winds of Flame*, for free**

THE
ELEMENTS
OF THE
CROWN

THE ELEMENTS OF KAMDARIA

KAY L. MOODY

The Elements of the Crown
The Elements of Kamdaria, #1
By Kay L. Moody

Published by Marten Press
3731 W 10400 S Ste 102, #205
South Jordan, UT 84009

www.MartenPress.com

Cover by Angel Leya
Edited by Deborah Spencer

ISBN: 978-1-954335-05-9

Ice through the fingers;
Fire in the veins.

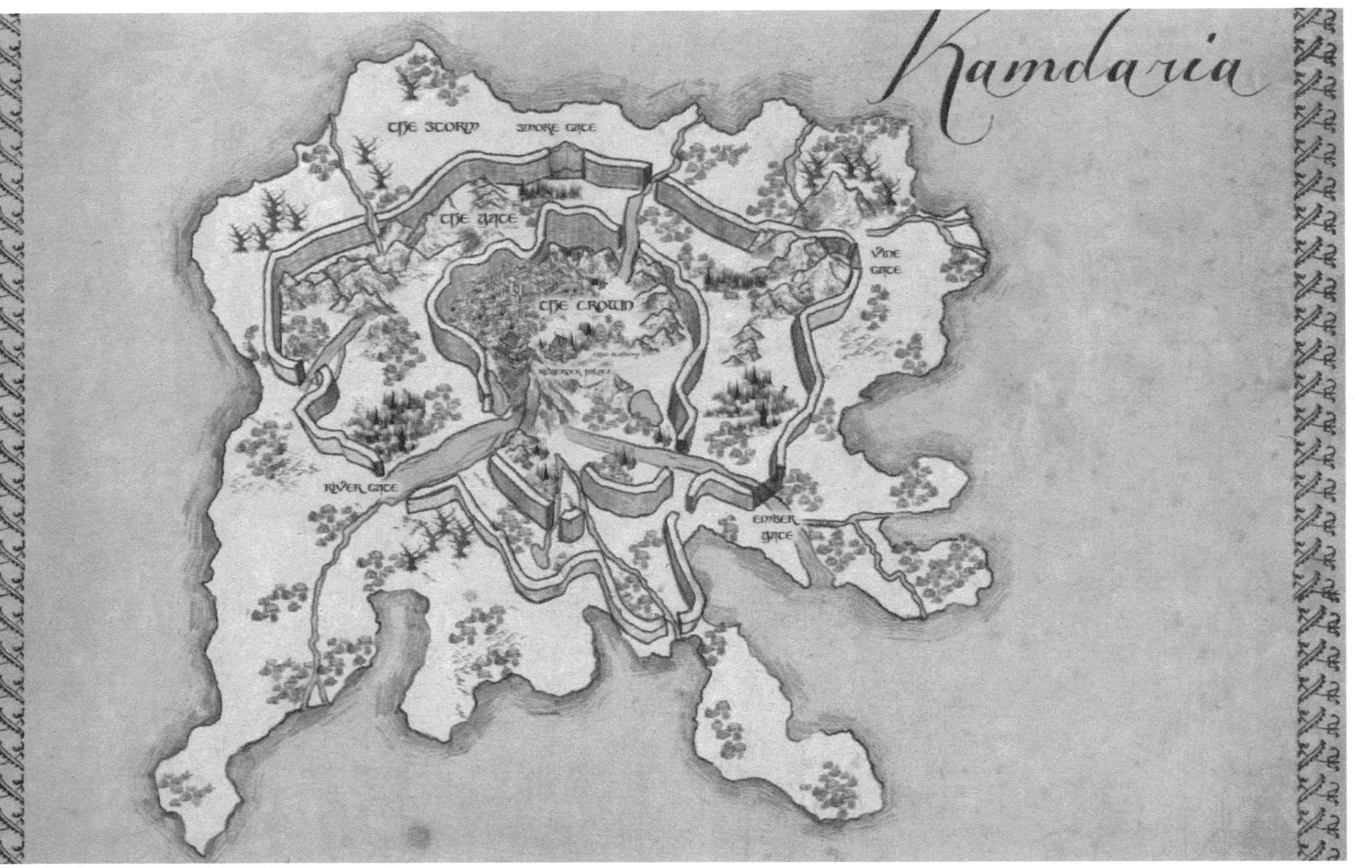
Kamdaria
THE STORM
SMOKE GATE
THE GATE
VINE GATE
THE CROWN
RIVER GATE
EMBER GATE

PART ONE

ICE CROWN

CHAPTER ONE

IT WAS AN HONOR TO train at the academy.

Talise recited the words to herself over and over again as she stood stiff-backed in the crowded deck of the riverboat. If chosen, she'd be ripped away from the home and family she loved. She'd leave behind the life she knew. All to train at the academy. An honor.

It didn't seem so great to her.

A stuffy, humid heat hung thick in the air of the lowest deck. The lowest deck had no windows, offering no sunlight and no view of the river to help with seasickness. Two small lanterns hung from the ceiling, each giving off a flickering glow. Whenever the boat jostled, several people were thrown off balance.

Marmie gripped Talise by the shoulders, tucking her into the corner where no one could hurt her. The top of Talise's head only barely reached Marmie's elbow, which meant she couldn't do much to free herself from the corner. Instead, she folded her arms over her chest and pouted. They'd been saving for this trip for months. Two years really. They had always known it would lead here. She always imagined it would be less stuffy and more exciting.

Most people from the outer ring of the continent—or the Storm as it was usually called—couldn't shape. Talise had the ability to mold and manipulate elements while most of her neighbors in the Storm could only worry about their next meal.

The academy would be safer than her harrowing and vicious life in the outer ring. She wanted to leave the Storm, but she didn't like the idea of being away from Marmie.

"Almost there," Marmie said, her voice like honey and sparkles. She looked down at Talise and gave her a smile that was meant to ease fears. It helped a little but not enough.

Especially because the riverboat jostled again, and a heavy-set man lost his balance, nearly toppling Marmie to the ground. Talise let herself be tucked behind Marmie's skirts after that. This time with no complaint.

She didn't understand why they had to ride in the lowest deck at all when both the higher decks had plenty of room. At least up there she could feel a misty breeze on her face and smell the wet soil.

Truthfully, she did know why they stood in the lowest deck. It was the same reason they didn't have enough food and couldn't learn to read. They were from the Storm. They were the lowliest members of the continent of Kamdaria: criminals, thieves, murderers.

Once people were sent to the Storm, they never left. Even if the original crimes had been committed ten generations earlier, people still never left the Storm. They never left because life in the Storm required crime.

It required stealing from trade wagons just so there would be a slice of bread for dinner. It required threatening guards so they wouldn't torment a neighbor. It required saving rainwater just so there would be something to drink after a day of labor.

Why it was illegal to save rainwater didn't make any sense to Talise. No one from the Storm could shape the water, so it was far from dangerous. It just seemed like another way to control the people. Another way to force people to commit crimes, which then forced them to stay in the Storm. Where they belonged.

People never left the Storm. Never. Especially not children who were seven years old.

Unless they got into the academy.

Talise sighed. Marmie had been saying they were almost there for the past twenty minutes. Maybe she'd be right at some point.

A toddler's sharp shriek broke through humid air of the deck. The mother looked mortified as she tried to appease her child with promises of what they would see once the riverboat stopped. Cherry tree blossoms and green-tiled buildings. Fresh air and gravel on the streets. Only small glimpses of mud instead of big mounds of it.

The toddler didn't find any of these satisfactory. The heavy-set man gave the mother a hard glance, and he wasn't the only one. Everyone shifted to move away from the child, but that only made him more upset. One man put his palms over his ears looking pointedly at the mother.

"Please Terreth. *Please*," the mother begged. "We are almost there."

The child looked more terrified by the minute as the bodies around him became angrier. His shrieking bounced from wall to wall while his little eyes filled with a well of tears.

As Talise watched the child, she tried to think of a way to help. Not for the sake of the other passengers. They could jump into the river for all she cared. But the child looked so frightened. He needed a distraction. Something fun.

Talise lowered her body until her hand hovered just above the floor of the deck. She'd been practicing hard, but even a little shaping still required her absolute attention. With narrowed eyes and a clenched jaw, she willed the dirt on the floor to rise into the air.

It took a minute, but soon, little dust particles rose up in a cloud. She clenched her jaw tighter. A cloud wouldn't do her any good. She needed enough dirt to make something the boy could see easily in the flickering light. Something he couldn't miss.

She narrowed her eyes even more. Her stomach tightened with anticipation. Finally, a solid clump of dirt broke apart, and the little dirt pieces flew up toward her hand. Now she had something she could work with.

Taking a tentative step out from Marmie's skirts, Talise shaped the dirt so it would hover above her palm. She turned her back to the other passengers and bounced her eyebrows up and down until she caught the boy's eyes.

When he finally looked at her, he was still shrieking. She gave him a crooked smile and looked down at the hovering dirt. Then, she bounced the dirt until it hovered as high as her head before it fell back down only a few inches above her palm.

The sour expression on the boy's face didn't relax, but the volume of his shrieking lowered. She did it again. This time she wore an expression of surprise as if the dirt bounced of its own accord, and she hadn't shaped it at all.

The boy quieted mid-shriek as his eyes opened wide. Now that she had his full attention, she shaped the dirt until it formed a long line. It didn't look much like the snake she was going for, but it was close enough.

She had to pull her stomach muscles in tight as she moved the line of dirt to look like a snake slithering. Again, it didn't look as neat as she wanted, but this was probably the first time in his life the boy had seen a citizen of the Storm shaping. He was more than mesmerized.

After the snake, Talise tried a bird. Her epic failure of that produced a giggle from the boy, who then clapped his hands and said, "More!"

Before she could think of something else to make, the riverboat floated to a stop. Talise made the clump of dirt bounce a few more times while the other passengers unloaded. When no one was left in the lowest deck besides her, Marmie, the boy, and his mother, Talise finally let the dirt fall to the floor.

"Thank you," the mother said, lowering her head so she could be eye level with Talise.

After Marmie poked her in the back, Talise remembered to respect her elder. Lowering her head in a short bow, she said, "You're welcome, but it was nothing."

"Are you going to be tested for the academy?" the woman asked.

After Talise nodded, the woman gave a smile so genuine it didn't seem possible for someone from the Storm. She wiped a bead of sweat off her forehead, leaving behind a short streak of dirt. "A shaper from the Storm," she said, shaking her head with disbelief. "I never could have dreamed of something so wild."

Marmie nodded to the woman and started nudging Talise forward. "Come. The testing begins soon."

"Wait," the woman said. "I just wanted to say how special you are. You made my son laugh when everyone else just scowled. And you're a shaper from the Storm. You'll change Kamdaria for the better, my dear. I'm sure of it.

CHAPTER TWO

TALISE'S HEAD BOUNCED RIGHT TO left as she tried to soak up her surroundings. They had arrived in the middle ring of Kamdaria—better known as the Gate. The streets were gravel just like the woman on the riverboat said they would be. There were no clouds of dust as people jogged past. A few people pulled wagons, but many of them had horses. Horses! Every so often, a stagecoach would fly past, and Talise's mouth would drop all over again.

The stores looked bigger than they did in the Storm as well. Shop keepers in the Storm were terrified of risk, so they only stocked the absolute necessities. Sometimes they didn't even have those, which meant their stores were even tinier and emptier than the ones here in the Gate. These stores had all sorts of items.

And everything was so clean. Marmie had scrubbed Talise's face a thousand times that morning and brushed her hair until her scalp seemed raw. Now Talise was grateful for the effort. She only wished her cotton dress were a little less weathered. The ugly patch near her hem seemed infinitely brighter in this light. At least it was clean.

Even the people seemed different. They didn't look so worn. So tired. They looked like they could think about something other than the hunger creeping at them from every side.

A man bumped into Marmie as they crossed the street. He looked apologetic at first until he saw the state of their clothes. He bared his teeth as he jumped away from them. A sharp intake of breath went through his teeth like a hiss.

He muttered under his breath, but the only word Talise could make out was *vermin*. Nobody liked people from the Storm. Even people in the Storm didn't like people from the Storm. Now that they had traveled to the Gate, everyone shot them angry glares and suspicious glances.

Marmie seemed oblivious to the entire interaction. Her eyes were set on a nearby building with unpainted walls and a gabled roof with cypress bark shingles.

When they arrived, Talise was ordered to sit on a nearby bench outside the building while Marmie went in and did the paperwork. Not that Talise minded. She was too busy soaking in more of the Gate. They weren't even in the inner circle of Kamdaria—also called the Crown—but everything already seemed a thousand times better than the Storm. There was so much water, so much vegetation, so much life.

Her eyes wandered when the sound of a wooden hammer rippled through the air. She took a few steps down the cobblestone path until she could see inside a courtyard that stood next to the building where Marmie was.

She recognized the scene at once, even though she had never seen anything like it in the Storm. A wooden podium stood at the back of the courtyard with an orange tree on the right and a cherry tree on the left. A man stood behind the podium wearing a red silk hat with a ball and tassel at the top. A judge. A woman sat on a chair next to the podium.

This was a trial. But not a regular trial, a card-marking trial.

The judge had two stamps on the wooden podium in front of him. Talise knew one of the stamps would be of a silver crescent moon and one would be a black *X*. Judging by the woman's face, the crescent moon stamp wouldn't be used today.

The woman clawed at her tunic hem as she chewed her bottom lip. She kept nodding and shaking her head in answer to someone's questions. Talise was too far away to hear the questions, and she couldn't even tell who was talking.

The woman began gulping and didn't seem to notice when her chewing teeth drew blood from her lips. All at once, she let out a gasp and her hands flew over her open mouth.

"Guilty!" The judge's booming voice erupted through the courtyard.

Jumping to her feet, the woman screamed, "NO!"

The judge sneered at her and glanced toward a wooden platform where a dozen people sat. The woman's family. It seemed the woman had five generations with her. Talise picked out a couple who must have been the woman's parents. Another man and woman who must have been grandparents. There were also a few people the woman's age, probably her siblings. And then, three adults who must have been the woman's children.

A son and his wife and then a daughter who looked barely eighteen. Most concerning of all was the baby, quietly sleeping in the son's arms. Since ID cards weren't given out until a child turned eighteen, any of the woman's children under eighteen wouldn't be present.

"ID cards out," the judge said, pulling one of the stamps off the podium. He held an ink pad in his palm, which must have been black.

"No!" the woman shouted again. "Please don't. Punish me. Punish me instead."

The judge turned on her as his eyebrows furrowed together. He spoke in a tight voice that was just loud enough for Talise to hear. "You dare question the laws of Kamdaria?" he asked. "It has always been obvious that we care for our children better than we care for ourselves. It is only fitting then, that our punishments should pass to our children as well."

"But they did nothing wrong." The woman had lunged from her chair and reached so desperately for the judge that two guards had to hold her back. "My son's baby is just a newborn. She won't survive winter in the Storm."

The judge whirled around to face the woman. "Then you will suffer knowing what fate awaits them and knowing your actions brought them there. That is the greatest punishment there is."

"Please, she's just a baby. *Please*. I beg you." The woman's face had been pressed into the gravel by one of the guards, but it did nothing to stop the words spewing from her mouth.

The judge ignored the woman as he traipsed over to the wooden platform where the family members sat. They all had tears streaming down their cheeks. One of the older women was convulsing as her body shook with sobs.

But none of them protested. They knew the laws of Kamdaria. The card system had been implemented centuries ago and since then, crime was almost non-existent except in the Storm. People could hurt themselves easily, but no one wanted to force their children and children's children to bear a punishment they themselves deserved.

A perfect system. Supposedly.

The son clutched his baby closer as he held his ID card out to the judge. A look of resignation paired with his dwindling tears. His wife wore no resignation. Instead she buried her face in a handkerchief and couldn't look as the judge stamped her card with a black *X*.

The barely eighteen-year-old daughter had eyes so wide someone could walk straight through her irises. She gasped when the judge stamped her card, as if it wasn't real until that moment.

When the son, his wife, and the daughter all had their ID cards marked, the judge waved at a nearby guard. "Take them to the docks immediately. A riverboat will be leaving for the Storm soon."

"Now?" the son asked. He gripped his wife around the waist with one hand and clutched his baby to his chest with the other. "Don't we get to say goodbye to our friends?"

"No," the judge said without a shred of sympathy.

"What about our things?" the wife asked. "We need the baby's sleeping mat and her books."

"Books?" The judge let out a laugh that shook through the courtyard. "Children in the Storm are not taught how to read. You'll get none of your things. You'll start life the same as everyone who has been sent to the Storm. With nothing but the clothes on your back."

"Mama," the eighteen-year-old girl called out. Her voice wobbled as reality seemed to hit like a brick on her vocal cords.

The wife began trembling. The son gripped his family more desperately, but he seemed to realize his grip wouldn't save anyone from anything now.

As if sensing their fear, the baby let out cry. When his family only sobbed in response, the baby cried harder.

"Talise."

Talise jumped at Marmie's quiet voice. "It's time for you to come in now."

Marmie spoke in a whisper with her eyes on the family that was in the midst of falling apart. She tugged Talise by the elbow, not taking her eyes away from the courtyard until they stood in front of the building where the testing would occur.

Just when Marmie touched the door handle, she turned to Talise with misty eyes. Her mouth quivered, but Talise already knew what she was going to say.

"I know," Talise said. She tried to set her jaw the way Marmie did when she had won an argument. It made Marmie look powerful. Talise needed some of that power now because Marmie's unspoken words were just as heavy as the scene in the courtyard.

Unless she sought an early death, Talise had to get out of the Storm. Honor or not, the academy was her only chance.

Chapter Three

THE ROOM SEEMED TOO HOT for the spring air outside. Maybe it was nerves or maybe it was the little balls of fire that would erupt from a hand every few minutes.

A woman guard in a yellow silk tunic and black belt ushered Talise and Marmie into a corner of the testing room. She didn't say it, but it seemed like the woman was trying to hide them.

Children about Talise's age stood in different parts of the room. One girl wore an expression coursing with excitement. One boy kept tapping his feet together before he would grab his mother by the waist and give her the world's shortest hug. But it would only be a moment before he did it again.

Another girl was showing off for some of the other children. She could shape two elements. All of them would be able to shape all four elements by the time they finished the first stage at the academy, but for now, shaping more than one element was impressive. The girl tucked her hair behind her ear before she moved a tiny pile of dirt and then blew off the top of it with air. The other children clapped in delight.

Scanning the room, Talise guessed she was one of the youngest children. She was only seven when most of them were probably eight. She was probably the thinnest too thanks to the Storm. If she weighed even a few pounds less, she would lose her ability to shape. She had lost it before.

Marmie went three weeks eating nothing but lemon water and breadcrumbs so Talise could have the extra food. Even when the shaping returned, Marmie took smaller portions so Talise could have more.

Another guard wearing yellow entered from the back room. He called a name from his leather-bound writing pad. Soon, a dark-haired child who looked a full year older than Talise bounded to the middle of the room. The child bowed to his elder.

The yellow-clad guard pointed to a pile of dirt. "If you can shape earth, please move the pile to the spot indicated."

The dark-haired child shook his head and the guard made a note in his writing pad. Then he said, "If you can shape water, raise the water from this bowl and put it back again."

The boy shook his head again and a note was made.

The guard pointed to the red and black brocade curtains on the window behind him. "If you can shape air, make these curtains dance."

The boy nodded, and soon the curtains were fluttering with sharp bursts that indicated shaping.

The guard made another note in his writing pad before he said, "If you can shape fire, produce a small ball of fire above your palm."

The boy shook his head, and the guard nodded as he made note in his pad. Then, the guard pointed to the back room. "Off you go. Say your goodbyes, and don't forget your personal effects."

The boy bounced over to his parents wearing a smile that must have hurt his cheeks. His parents clapped and gave him so many kisses, his cheeks were probably wet. They strapped a large sack on his back that looked almost as heavy as him.

Talise's eyes slowly trailed over to the small tote bag she had brought. It only had two dresses, some toiletry items, and a tiny pouch of money. When she scanned the rest of the room, her tote bag looked even smaller.

Biting her bottom lip, Talise sidled up to Marmie and squeezed her hand. "I don't want to go to the academy without you."

"I know, love," Marmie said with a gentle smile.

"Do I have to?"

Leaving no room for interpretation, Marmie said, "Yes dear, you have to." Then she added with a bit more kindness. "All the other children will be away from their families too."

"Where will you go?" Talise asked, bracing herself for the answer.

"I must go back to the Storm."

Even though she'd been expecting this, the words still jarred on her insides. "How will you survive? Academy training lasts ten years."

Marmie took her hand out of Talise's grip and wrapped it around her shoulders instead. She began tracing swirls into Talise's upper arm as she spoke. Her voice was even and sweet, telling the truth, but making it sound better than it was. "The first stage of training is only five years. You'll have to test again after that to get into the second stage. And you'll test again three years later. The third stage is only two years."

Talise nodded, wishing the years could go by as quickly as this day seemed to be going.

Marmie continued. "A child of the Storm is never allowed to leave the Storm unless he or she becomes Master Shaper. Getting into the academy isn't enough. At the end of each year, there's a competition. Based on the demonstrations during the competition, Emperor Flarius chooses one Master Shaper from the graduating class to work with him in the palace. You must become Master Shaper or else you'll have to go back to the Storm after your academy training."

"I know all that," Talise said jutting out her bottom lip. "I know what I have to do. But *if* I pass all the testing and make it through all three stages and win the competition and become Master Shaper…," she bit her bottom lip again, looking up at Marmie, "will you be able to move to the palace with me?"

"You already know the answer to that," Marmie said with the smallest wink.

Talise's stomach sank all the way down to her toes. She did know that already. She'd asked these questions a hundred times in the last few months wishing there was any other way. It didn't help her nerves at all.

Her entire future rested on the competition. How could she feel anything but anxiety skewering her muscles when so much depended on this?

Marmie met her eye and put two fingers under her chin. "You're the best shaper here." Then she shrugged with a tease. "Even if you weren't, they aren't testing how good you are at shaping. You only need to show that you *can*. Any child who can shape is welcome to the academy for the first stage of training."

Again, she knew all that, but it helped to hear the words anyway. Talise tucked herself closer to Marmie's side, wishing they had a little more time. Maybe just a few more days.

Mercifully, time went by slowly as the guards tested each new child, let them say goodbye, and then followed him or her into the back room to give more instructions about the academy. Hours passed by while more children were tested.

The other children were getting antsy, but not Talise. She drank up every last minute she had. When she felt brave, she'd ask Marmie to tell her a story or recite one of their favorite memories. Marmie always complied with a gentle smile and a reassuring lilt to her voice.

But even as one of the more boring days of her life, time still marched on. Soon, Talise was the only child left in the room.

The older guard entered and glanced around. Not noticing Talise at first, he checked with the woman guard. They whispered together for a moment until the woman guard pointed to the back corner where Talise and Marmie sat. The air seemed to grow hotter and thicker. More anxiety trampled through Talise as she tried to hold her head high. She wanted to be brave for Marmie. She knew what she had to do.

The guard nodded and went to his usual place in the middle of the room where he called out her name, almost with a grimace.

Talise walked over, pinching folds of her dress between two fingers before releasing them again. She took a deep breath when she reached the center of the room. After a quick bow and a long gulp, she looked up at the guard.

He stared down at her, surveying every inch of her tattered clothes. His eyes landed heavily on the bright patch near her hem. He looked back at Marmie and scoffed loudly. Slamming his writing pad shut, he looked at the other guard. "Tell them we're done here. They can take the children to the docks now."

CHAPTER FOUR

TALISE TOOK A STEP BACK while Marmie took a step forward. Talise clutched at her dress. All of the softness in Marmie's face hardened to jagged lines. Her cheekbones cut like knives. No more honey and sparkles. When Marmie spoke now, her voice was fire.

"She can shape. You are required to give her entrance to a training academy."

"Don't be stupid, vermin," the guard said as he peered down at Marmie. "*No one* from the Storm can shape. How did you even get enough money for the riverboat? Did you sell your hair?

He and the other guard glanced at each other before bursting into a fit of laughter.

Marmie reached for the frizzy ends of her hair, all uneven and dull. At the last second, she turned her hand into a fist and set her jaw. "Test her," Marmie said.

The guard began walking toward the back room, still letting out the whispers of a laugh.

Marmie stood in front of him leaving only a few inches between them. She crossed her arms over her chest and said more firmly, "Test her."

"Get out of my way," the guard said, brushing her to the side.

With such weak muscles inside her, Marmie staggered at the man's touch. She gripped him by the forearm to catch her balance and tried to steady herself.

Talise wrung her hands all around each other as she watched the pair of them. Perhaps the guard only needed to see that she was capable of shaping. Maybe she should just show him what she could do. But she feared disrespecting her elder. He clearly had a prejudice that ran deep. Would shaping get them into more trouble?

When Marmie steadied herself, she said, "The girl can shape. You must test her."

The guard moved to push her away again, but with greater force this time. To protect herself, Marmie grabbed his arm.

The guard ripped his arm from her grip. "You dare attack me?"

Even though it was clear an attack was far from her mind, Marmie narrowed her eyes. "I'll do whatever it takes to make sure this girl goes to the academy."

The guard moved so swiftly, Talise didn't realize he had Marmie by the wrist until he was already reaching for the wooden baton under his tunic. If Talise didn't do something, Marmie would be beaten. Her frail body couldn't handle a beating of any kind right now.

"Stop!" Talise shouted.

That only seemed to add fire to the guard's flame. He pulled the baton out while a hint of glee passed over his features. If she was going to do anything, clearly words would not be enough.

She took one glance around the room and did the only thing that seemed logical in the moment. Many people considered fire to be the most difficult element to master, so she lit a fire in her palm.

Thinking only of Marmie's safety, Talise took a fistful of the guard's tunic. "Look," she said as she forced him to turn around.

As his feet moved to face her, the tunic in her left hand collided with the flame in her right. Her eyebrows flew up her forehead as the silk fabric caught on fire. The guard let out a gasp that could have fluttered the curtains as much as air shaping.

Talise shaped away the fire in her palm instantly, but the damage had been done. The guard seemed too surprised, or angry, to react to his still burning tunic.

Though less than a second had passed, it felt like five hundred. Talise scanned the room, letting her mind whirl as it tried to find a way to fix this.

I'll never go to the academy now, she thought. *I won't even go back to the Storm. They're going to kill me here and Marmie too.*

She looked at the curtains. She could pull them down and suffocate the fire. No, she'd never be strong enough to rip them away. *Useless.* Her tote bag of dresses was closer, but the fire might be out of control by the time she got a dress out of it. *Also useless.* The bowl of water for shape testing would work. Her foot had already taken a step before she realized that even that would take too much time. The bowl was on the other side of the room.

Without a single thought about the consequences, Talise used her shaping to raise the water out of the bowl and splash it onto the guard's tunic. The fire was out, and it had only taken the longest three seconds of her life.

Before she could let out a breath of relief, the guard's mouth dropped. It looked more like surprise than anger this time, but now she was all too aware of just how wet the guard's clothes were.

The guard worked his jaw up and down as he looked from his shirt to the empty bowl and back to his shirt again. He touched the damp fabric as if daring it to be real.

But it was real. Talise's stomach sank. She had to do something. "I can fix it," she said. The words sounded so stupid as soon as they left her mouth. She turned her head to the ground, afraid to make eye contact. "Well, not fix it. At least not the fabric that got burnt. But I can help with the wet clothes at least."

The guard took a step away from her, his eyes widening every second.

Undeterred, she raised her hands until the palms were an inch over the wet fabric. Then, she shaped as much air as she could to blow against the fabric. If only she were a little better at shaping, she could just shape the water out of his clothes and back into the bowl. Instead, the air shaping would have to do.

The guard took another step back and grabbed both of her wrists. He stared down into her palms with his mouth gaping open. "You … you can shape three elements? How is this possible?"

"Four," Marmie said. Her breath was weak, but she was still on her feet.

The guard turned to her and shook his head.

Marmie stood a little taller and set her jaw. "Not three, she can shape four. Show them, Talise. Do the snake like you did on the boat."

Talise was back to pinching the folds of fabric in her dress. The guard was astonished? Not angry? Maybe he was still both, but the astonishment seemed to be winning at the moment. Would shaping something fancy get her into more trouble?

Marmie gave her a gentle nod, and the lines around her eyes softened to the face Talise knew.

With a gulp, Talise moved her hand toward the pile of dirt in the center of the floor. She pulled in her stomach muscles and tried to work past the anxiety threatening to smother her. As the little snake started to take shape, the woman guard took a step forward with eyes full of wonder.

"Of course she will have place at the academy," the first guard said as he touched the burnt hem of his tunic. "I've never seen a child with such advanced shaping."

The woman guard brushed a strand of hair behind her ear. "She shouldn't train at any of the academies in the Gate. She should go straight to the elite academy in the Crown."

Marmie gave a smug grin, but Talise's insides were bubbling over with excitement. "If I train there, will I finish sooner?" she asked.

"No," the first guard said as he opened his writing pad. "Training always takes ten years, but it will be more advanced at the elite academy. I'll have to write a special recommendation for you, but you should get in with no problem."

That wasn't exactly the news she wanted to hear, but it didn't take away any of her excitement. She did it. She was going to the academy.

"Say your goodbyes," the guard said, his eyes still on his writing pad. And with those words, all the excitement was sucked up and out of her body, leaving nothing but a pit in her stomach.

Marmie brushed the hair out of Talise's face as she set the strap of the tote bag on her shoulder. "Work hard," Marmie said.

"I'll write to you." Talise's lip quivered. "Every week."

Marmie brushed her thumb under Talise's chin, giving her a smile. "And I'll write to you. Twice a week."

"What if I forget your face?" Talise bit her bottom lip to keep it from quivering again. She knew she had to go to the academy. She knew she needed it. But why did it have to mean leaving Marmie? Why couldn't they go together?

"You'll never forget my face as long as you love me," Marmie said with a laugh.

"But what if I do?"

Marmie bent down to leave a soft kiss on Talise's cheek. With her head still bent, she whispered into Talise's ear. "You must try. You must promise that you'll do your best to become Master Shaper. You can't entertain any thoughts of rejoining me in the Storm."

It pained her more than anything else that day, but Talise knew what she had to say. She put both her hands on Marmie's cheeks and said, "I will try. In ten years, I'll be the best shaper Kamdaria has ever known."

CHAPTER FIVE

TEN YEARS LATER

MRS. DEW ALWAYS POINTED TO the slate board as if it held the key to life's mysteries. Talise preferred the academy lessons that included actual shaping. Mrs. Dew had taught them nothing but theory for the past month. It didn't seem very smart when the competition was only a month away, but Mrs. Dew had been the top instructor at the elite academy for twenty-five years. Her methods weren't up for debate.

Talise sighed and started shaping little bursts of air from her palm. The bursts reached just high enough to tickle her hair before they would fizzle out.

Mrs. Dew slapped her palm against the slate. "That is why you must never attempt to freeze water while you're shaping it. You'll give yourself hypothermia and your fingers could break clean off."

She emphasized the point by making some gesture with her hands. She was probably miming her fingers falling off, but since Talise sat in the back of the classroom, she couldn't tell for sure.

Talise pulled a letter from the front pocket of her school uniform. Her latest letter from Marmie. She traced a finger over her favorite paragraph, trying to carve the words into her mind so she'd never forget them.

Anyway, I'm sure you don't care about all that, but the point is it worked! I finally grew a flower in the Storm. I've learned a lot from living here, and the most interesting thing is this: without hope, people have nothing. They aren't happy; they don't live. But the smallest things can change that. You should see what this little flower has done to the neighborhood. It's like there's magic all around us now.

Magic. Talise loved that part. Marmie had never sent such a happy letter in the ten years since Talise had gone to the academy. Maybe it was just because the competition was so close. Talise knew Marmie never expected to live long enough to see Talise compete. But she had. Just like magic.

Talise had saved just enough money for a riverboat ride from the Storm to the Crown. Soon, Marmie would use it to travel to Ridgerock Palace for a temporary visit. Long enough to see Talise in the competition.

After several more slaps to the slate board, Mrs. Dew released them for lunch. Talise bowed to the portrait of Emperor Flarius as she left the room. His golden crown never seemed oppressive to her, but every so often, his eyes did.

Shrugging away the feeling, Talise went through the doorway to find Wendy.

Just outside the classroom, Talise bumped into a student whose eyes were on the ground. He had light brown skin and a thin mustache and goatee. He held his shoulders back with an easy confidence that usually came from those born in the Crown. Aaden. At least she thought his name was Aaden.

Earlier that week, all the top students in the final year of the third stage were combined into one class. Students from academies all over Kamdaria were now in one class at the elite academy, and Talise only knew a handful of them. Based on his demeaner, she guessed he came from another academy in the Crown.

"Sorry about that," Talise said as she passed him.

Aaden scowled as he trudged past her.

Rude.

Marmie would have scolded her for making such a harsh judgment. As Talise wandered down the hallway, she opened her mind to other possibilities. Maybe he was nervous about being at a new academy. Maybe he just needed a friend.

Talise finally found Wendy at the end of the hall. She was checking on a pastry in her school bag. "Just a little something to add to my lunch," Wendy said as she looked away with a smile. They walked side by side as they headed for the dining courtyard.

Luckily, the academy paid for their lunches or Talise might never have eaten. Marmie sent her money as often as she could. And Talise always sent it back, except when she was desperate. The academy also paid for her school uniforms. They spent so much time in training, no one ever realized Talise only had two dresses apart from her school clothes. Her other possessions were fewer than the fingers on her hands.

"Fish again?" Talise asked as she wrinkled her nose. Fish always reminded her of the Storm.

Wendy giggled and tugged her through the gate. "What do you expect when we live so close to the palace? Ridgerock Lake is full of fish."

Talise scowled, not caring if Wendy noticed how her feet were dragging.

Wendy did notice. She shot Talise a disapproving look before erasing it with a smile. "At least there's noodle soup to go along with it. You love the noodle soup." Her eyebrows teetered upward, begging Talise to agree.

Unable to stop herself, Talise let out a chuckle. "Yes, I do like the noodle soup."

Wendy always had a way of scolding without making it feel like a drudgery. Just like Marmie. Talise had been drawn to Wendy for that exact reason. Wendy was sweet and gentle like Marmie.

"And look," Wendy said, bouncing on her heels. "They're even serving the soup in the round bowls instead of the square. You love the round bowls."

Talise shook her head but let out another chuckle. "I don't love them. I just think they're easier to hold. And I only said that one time."

After receiving their food, Talise quickly scanned the courtyard for a place to eat. One end of the courtyard looked empty except for a single person. Aaden. Maybe she had been right about him needing a friend.

"Do you know him?" Talise asked, pointing to the lonely young man.

Wendy nodded. Of course she did. Wendy knew everyone. It was part of her charm.

"Aaden," Wendy said. "He's from the other academy in the Crown."

"Let's go sit with him."

Wendy's eyes widened, but she tried to smile the expression away. "I don't know him *that* well."

Talise started walking toward him. "Maybe he doesn't know anyone in the new class. We should be friends with him."

Wendy blinked and glanced around the courtyard. "Maybe he wants to be alone."

Talise gave her friend a sideways glance. Usually Wendy was the one who wanted to make new friends.

"Look, there's Claye over there. Let's go sit with him." Even with her hands full of dishes, Wendy managed to nudge Talise away from that part of the courtyard.

"What are you grinning about?" Wendy asked as she settled into the seat next to Claye.

His brown eyes looked bright with a joke that would probably befit a ten-year-old boy. "I just slurped my noodle the wrong way and it came out my nose."

"That's disgusting." Talise tried not to think about it too much or she wouldn't be able to eat anything at this meal.

Claye snickered, seeming to care even less than usual about her opinion. "And," he said rounding on Wendy. "Mr. Cobble confirmed that training the day before a competition can weaken your muscles."

Wendy stiffened before she shook her head firmly. "Only if you train too much. Surely, no training at all hurts more than it helps."

Talise idly put the spoon to her lips as Wendy and Clayed jumped into a deep discussion on which was best. They both had compelling arguments that had been picked apart in detail over the last year by every student in the final year of the third stage.

Right now, Talise was more captivated by the young man who stared at the ground and ate alone. So quiet. If he had so little to say, he must have had mountains of things going on in his head.

What secrets did he hold?

CHAPTER SIX

WHEN TALISE FINISHED THE LAST of her noodle soup, she pushed the plate of grilled fish over to Wendy and Claye. "You two share this," she said as she stood up.

She cleaned her soup dish at the washing station and watched Aaden as she worked. His neatly trimmed hair had been combed with precision. The black strands were so shiny, they gleamed in the sunlight. His clothes hung stiffer than hers, which could only mean his school uniform had recently been pressed.

He was definitely from the Crown then. Only someone from the inner circle of Kamdaria could afford such a luxury. She didn't know whether to be awed or angry by how casually he broadcasted his privilege.

Instead, she focused on the one thing she knew for sure. He ate his entire lunch alone. Someone like that must have needed a friend. She tried to smile with the same warmth Marmie had taught her as she headed his way. He stood up even before she got to him, as if eager to avoid any interaction. Hopefully, he only wanted to avoid her because he was nervous.

"I'm Talise," she said when she reached him.

Aaden gave her a short glance through the side of his eye. "I don't care."

She raised an eyebrow.

He began marching toward the washing station, and his body language didn't invite her to join. But she did anyway. Her lips twitched at the corners while she tried to decide if she should be offended or humored by his brash words.

Not funny, she finally decided. But maybe he only pushed her away because he was nervous. Attempting a friendly smirk, she asked, "Is that how you greet everyone?"

"No," he said with utterly no explanation at all.

They had reached the washing station now, and Aaden kept his eyes down as he scrubbed his dishes clean.

Everything in her told Talise to give up. This young man smelled like trouble and it wrinkled her nose even more than the grilled fish had. She wanted to walk away. She almost did when some of Aaden's washing water splashed onto her. It didn't seem like an accident.

But then she remembered Marmie and the Storm. She knew desperation when she saw it. It looked like anger when it was really fear. It looked like hatred when it was really sadness. *One more time*, she thought. *I'll try one more time to befriend him.*

Talise shaped the splashed water out of her clothes and back into the washing bin. "What's your primary?"

"Fire," Aaden said, putting as much heat into the word as an actual flame. He dropped his clean dishes onto the pile and whirled around to face her. "Just like you."

Such simple words. How did he make them sound like a threat?

Her lips parted as their eyes met. With his earlier words, he had pushed her away. Now, he practically begged her to respond. For once, she had no idea what to say.

How did he know her primary? What else did he know about her?

She opened her mouth to ask, but his eagerness for a response evaporated. He turned his back on her and said, "Leave me alone."

He stalked off with his shoulders hunched forward and a fist forming in one hand. For a moment, she almost followed him. His anger only made her think he was really desperate. For *something*.

The only thing holding her in place were those words he spoke that felt like a threat. *Just like you.*

If he was so quick to threaten, maybe it was because he felt threatened by her. Maybe he wanted the title of Master Shaper. Talise had been the top of her class for so long, she couldn't even remember what real competition felt like.

This, she thought. *It feels like this.*

TWO WEEKS LATER, Talise rummaged through the books in the library. All she needed was a book that classified the different wind types. If she could just understand where the different types of wind came from, it would be easier to shape air in the same way.

She almost rolled her eyes at the thought. Apparently, Mrs. Dew had been right about theory. It really did help with technique.

Biting her bottom lip, she opened another air book. She slammed it shut a moment later when it showed the same diagram the rest of the books showed. Air shaping must come from the lungs. She knew all that. It didn't help her understand wind any better.

The golden spine of another book caught her eye. The title looked promising. *Air Shaping Origins.* Before she could grab it off the shelf, a clatter from a nearby aisle caught her attention. She peeked around the bookshelf, expecting to see one of the younger students. Instead she saw Aaden.

She'd avoided him since their brief conversation. Not that it had been that hard. Aaden stayed away from her and everyone else. She learned that Wendy had already tried to befriend him and had failed as miserably as she had.

Aaden crouched over a painting of Ridgerock Palace that was supposed to be hanging on the wall. He glanced around from one end of the room to the next. Without thinking, Talise hid herself behind the bookshelf and then peeked out again.

Thinking he was alone, Aaden bent over the painting and ran a finger over the cherry trees standing like sentinels at the main gate of the palace.

After studying the painting, he did the unthinkable and pulled the painting from its frame. The canvas stretched as he rolled it up tight. He then stuck it into the jacket of his uniform.

Talise's mouth was still hanging open when he left the library. He didn't even bow to the emperor's portrait on his way out. Her brain was busy processing what he had done, but it didn't stop her feet from following. She put enough distance between them to not seem suspicious, but her ears were hyper aware of each of his movements.

He left the instructional building and flew through the gardens to get to the training building. She almost lost him when he made two sharp turns in the halls of the training building, but she found him again a moment later. He had settled into an empty training room that was a little smaller than the others. It stood in the back corner of the building. That, combined with its small size, meant hardly anyone used it.

Aaden had shut the door when he entered, but Talise managed to push it open slightly without his notice. He was too busy propping the painting up on a desk.

He traced his fingers over the cherry trees again. The pink blossoms burst out of the branches like little clouds of delight. He stared at the painting for so long, Talise was ready to give up and just tell Mrs. Dew how he had stolen the painting from the library.

Just when she lifted her foot to walk, Aaden took a step away from the painting and a fire burst out of his palm. The fire burned in a column, but little by little, bits of the column drifted away, and a tree began to form.

Fire sculpture.

When the tree was formed, it grew larger until it burned as high as Aaden's chin. Then, he stared at the tree like a mother coaxing her baby to eat. When his eyes narrowed, the branches of the trees seemed to shudder. He clenched his jaw and one branch seemed to grow small pustules.

As impressive as it was, that didn't seem to be what Aaden wanted. The fire vanished as he dropped his hand away and let out a groan. He kicked the wall twice and then did it again, all the way down to the pustules.

It didn't matter if he was doing what he wanted or not, fire sculptures were hard. His were detailed and looked as though they were alive. On his fourth try, one of the pustules popped open and a blossom appeared.

Talise gasped.

She couldn't help it. She had no idea he was attempting something so complex.

Aaden's tree vanished as he whirled around to face her. His lips were pressed to a thin line while a huff of air burst from his nose. He worked his jaw up and down as he shaped a fireball in each of his hands.

The balls flew toward her, and she leapt back with a yelp. One of the balls hit the cement wall, but the other hit the door right next to her arm. It was close enough that it burned her forearm.

Aaden glared at her as he formed two more fireballs in his hands. Not needing anymore encouragement, she ducked away and ran out of the building.

With the fresh air blowing on the burn, the stinging decreased. She went straight for the kitchen building, hoping to find some ice. Even with such a direct mission, she could barely focus on the burn.

Aaden's trees.

They were incredible, she had to admit it. And to emulate the same trees that stood in front of the palace was a stroke of genius. It was sure to catch the emperor's eye.

The reality settled into her, leaving her insides a writhing mess. Aaden had a chance of winning Master Shaper. Maybe a better chance than her. Who was she kidding, he had a way better chance than her.

Just like anyone from the Crown, he had everything he ever needed without even blinking. That's why most people from the Crown didn't care about becoming Master Shaper. They didn't need it.

But when someone from the Crown *wanted* to become Master Shaper, they did. End of story. Aaden probably had a personal shaping tutor that had been teaching him for years.

Talise had spent the past ten years keeping her promise to Marmie, training hard with the intent to win. She'd been the best for so long, she stopped worrying about the competition years ago. Everyone knew she was going to win. And still she never stopped training as hard as she could.

Now, all that hard work fizzled out in just one afternoon. All along, there had been someone just as good as her at the other academy in the Crown.

If she was going to win the competition, she needed to up her game.

Chapter Seven

THE LAST PARAGRAPH OF HER letter to Marmie seemed a little ridiculous. Truth laced every word, but that didn't mean she should send it. But what else could she say? Talise read through it one last time.

He did fire sculptures like I've never seen before. Somehow, he managed to get little cherry blossoms to burst out of the fire branches. I'll admit it, Marmie. I'm scared. I've tried so hard to win, but I think he's better than me. At least I'm not a child anymore. If I have to go back to the Storm, I'd probably survive now. And then I'd get to be with you again. That doesn't sound so bad.

Marmie would be angry. She'd scold and remind Talise of her promise, but none of that changed how Talise felt in this moment. Living in the Storm with Marmie really didn't sound so bad. Certainly not as bad as it did when she was a child. She was stronger now.

Shaking her head, Talise got a blank sheet of paper to start a new letter. She couldn't send something like that so close to the competition. Marmie would worry too much.

She had to say something else.

Talise stared at the blank paper for two and half minutes before she gave up. She added a quick, *Please don't worry. I'm still going to try.* to the end of the letter and shoved it into its envelope.

With the letter in hand, Talise left her room to find the nearest academy guard.

"Can you make sure this is sent tonight?" Talise asked the woman.

The woman nodded as she tucked the letter into a hidden pocket of her yellow silk tunic. "Any special instructions?" the guard asked.

"No." Talise smoothed the bottom of her uniform so she could avoid the guard's eye. Why did they always have to ask that? She stuffed a hand into her pocket, but it only reminded her of how empty that pocket was. No money for special requests. No money for extra pastries. No money for anything but survival.

Talise gulped as she turned away. How could she forget so easily the challenges of the Storm? She had been in the Crown for ten years, but the challenges still chased after her. They were little things like not being able to afford a pass to leave academy grounds. Never having anything extra beyond necessities.

But with all her necessities taken care of for ten years straight, it was easy to forget how bad things in the Storm were. Marmie had sacrificed so much to get her here. She couldn't let that sacrifice be in vain.

LATE THAT EVENING, Talise slipped out of bed still wearing her school uniform. She tiptoed out of her room and held her breath as she walked down a hall where one of the night guards patrolled.

The hall remained empty as Talise tiptoed down it. Just as she was ready to round a corner, she heard footsteps. There were punishments for sneaking around at night, but none of them were worse than losing the competition.

She tucked herself into a supply closet just as the footsteps came around the corner. Who was it? Did they see her?

Talise gripped her elbows. She tried to force herself to breathe, but her lungs seemed to think it would be more fun to hold her breath until she couldn't stand it another second. Just when she sucked in a loud breath, the door to the supply closet swung open.

Her hands flew into the air in defense. "I was just—" Talise's words cut off as she blinked. "Wendy? What are you doing here?"

Wendy's finger flew to her lips as she looked over her shoulder. "I was going to the bathroom," she whispered. "What are *you* doing here?"

"Um." Talise began rubbing a hand up and down her forearm. "I need to train for the competition."

Wendy let out a snort and a new pair of footsteps started coming from a nearby hall. Her eyes widened as she grabbed Talise by the wrist. "Come on," Wendy said, pulling her down the hall. "They always check this closet, but I know another place we can hide."

"How do you—"

"*Shhh!*"

Talise clamped her mouth shut until they were out of that hallway and in the guard's hallway. When Wendy's feet began to slow, Talise looked at her seriously. "This is the guard's hallway. Where the *guards* check in and get their gear and everything. We can't hide here."

Wendy smirked. "Yeah, but they only check in every hour on the hour. This place is empty the rest of the night."

"How do you know that?" Talise asked. She stared at her friend's gentle smile and innocent face. "How often do you sneak out?"

"What?" Wendy asked as she put a hand to her chest. Somehow, she managed to imbibe each of her words with a sweetness that jarred against the reality of the situation. "I never sneak out. How could you suggest such a thing?"

Talise could only respond with a disbelieving chuckle. "Then what are you doing right now?"

Wendy's ears turned pink as she looked down at the ground. "That's different. I had to go to the bathroom. I hate how they make us take a guard escort. I never sneak out for anything else." Her lips squished up into a knot as she looked at a nearby wall. "Well, sometimes I do sneak into the kitchens. But only because the headmaster forgets to feed the animals."

She looked up with a smile but then her ears turned pink again. Looking away, she said. "Oh. There was one time I didn't turn an essay in on time. But I finished it that night, so I snuck into the teacher's classroom and put my essay in the pile. But that was only one time."

Talise wanted to laugh hard, but since the guards were looking for them, she had to keep it to a quiet snicker. "How did you learn what the guards do at night? I can't imagine you sneaking out enough to find out." She cocked her head to the side. "Can you get us to the training building?"

Wendy nodded and glanced around a corner. She waved at Talise to follow her and then she said, "My brother, Cyrus, taught me everything. Do you remember when he was here a few years ago? He got into lots of trouble. Once he graduated, he thought he'd pass his legacy on to me I guess."

Another snicker escaped Talise's mouth, but she quieted it when Wendy put a finger to her lips. They were silent through a few more halls, and even more silent through the gardens.

When they reached the training building, they were so used to whispering, they didn't even notice that they kept it up.

"Why do you have to train anyway?" Wendy asked. "Everyone knows you're going to win."

Talise closed her eyes as she filled her palms with fire. When a cold chill swept into the room, she shaped more fire, but this time inside of herself. Why couldn't she do that during her demonstration? Shaping fire inside the veins was such a difficult skill, most students never learned it. Sadly, it wasn't flashy enough for a demonstration, not to mention Emperor Flarius would have no way of knowing fire actually ran through her veins.

Putting that thought aside, Talise focused on the fire in her palms. She shaped each of them to look like the long ribbons that were often used in air shaping demonstrations. "It's Aaden," Talise said.

Wendy settled into a corner of the room and pulled out a pastry she had hidden in her robe. At the mention of Aaden, her body shivered.

"He's going to do a fire sculpture for his demonstration. I saw him practicing. He's doing cherry trees, and he's going to make cherry blossoms pop out of the branches after he shapes the tree."

Whatever made Wendy shiver before seemed to float away. Her eyes went wide as she popped a piece of the pastry into her mouth. Then she shook her head. "Are you sure he's not going to make a tree that sort of looks bushy? He can't really make cherry blossoms pop out of the branches."

"He can," Talise said as she shaped the fire ribbons through the air. She moved them the same as people often moved colorful ribbons with wind shaping. The ribbons curled and weaved as if a wind danced with them. She chose this demonstration specifically because it used her primary element of fire, but also because it showed that she knew how to shape air.

Only someone talented with air shaping could understand the movements well enough to move fire in the same way. Except fire was harder to control. Many people in Kamdaria, the emperor included, believed fire was the most difficult element to master. This demonstration proved she could shape fire with skill, but it also showed off another element she knew well.

"That's incredible," Wendy said. "Cherry blossoms popping out of branches. *Fire* cherry blossoms. And fire branches. That's so cool."

"I know," Talise said with a frown. "And I have to beat him, so don't act too impressed."

"Sorry," Wendy said, softening her voice. She chewed her pastry slowly, watching as Talise shaped the fire around them.

Talise moved one of the fire ribbons to look like a tornado, spinning down until it nearly kissed the ground. With the other ribbon, she made it whip and whirl above her head in waves. Two completely separate motions moving simultaneously. It was impressive by anyone's standard. But was it enough?

"He's going to beat you," Wendy said. Her voice was so quiet, Talise almost didn't hear. She wanted to be angry, but Wendy's words had been uttered with such love, the anger left before it could settle.

Talise let her fires vanish before she dropped onto the floor. With her forehead buried in her palms, she said, "I've been training ten years for this. There has to be something I can do."

They sat in silence long enough to hear a changing of the guard in the courtyard.

"Make it dangerous," Wendy said.

Talise looked up as she raised an eyebrow.

Wendy nodded. "Aaden might beat you with the detail of his sculpture, but everybody loves a bit of danger. It will make you impressive in a different way, and it will make you memorable."

Talise's head bobbed up and down as she got to her feet. She shaped a long ribbon of fire and swirled it around like a tornado. When it got closer to the ground, she turned it back upward. Before she could reconsider, she held her arm out straight and let the fire ribbon twist around her arm. The heat brought a line of sweat to her forehead, but it didn't burn.

Slowly, she untwined the fire ribbon from her arm and let it twist around her leg. She had to keep the fire farther from her leg, so it didn't burn the fabric. The temperature inside her raised even higher, but it didn't stop her yet.

She raised both hands high above her head and clasped them together. Then she let the fire ribbon swirl around her entire body.

When she finally shaped the fire away, Wendy clapped with delight. "Now *that* was cool."

"It's pretty hot," Talise said, wiping the sweat from her forehead.

"Too hot?"

With a shrug, Talise said, "It has to be dangerous to be impressive, right?"

As Talise wiped another line of sweat from the back of her neck, she thought about shaping ice into her veins. The thought of Mrs. Dew's lesson stopped her in her tracks. She didn't need her fingers breaking off. Especially not before the competition.

But maybe she could pack ice in her pockets and rub them over her body after the competition. Except if she did that, the ice would melt in her pocket during the demonstration.

It didn't matter. She'd think of something and make sure she became Master Shaper. She'd have to tell Marmie the good news.

Chapter Eight

DAYLIGHT STREAMED IN THROUGH THE window of the training room as Talise worked to improve her technique. The competition was only a week away now, and she'd been training during every minute of her spare time. When the fire ribbons got too close to her body, it would raise her internal temperature just like a fever. But she needed that little bit of danger or else the demonstration wouldn't be impressive enough. She'd written another letter to Marmie all about her new plan.

This one would work. It had to.

She swirled a fire ribbon around her arm. When it reached her shoulder, she let the ribbon grow longer so it could then swirl around her torso, and down one leg. A cool afternoon air drifted in through the training room door, which felt nice on her heated skin.

Just when Talise made another fire ribbon spin around her from bottom to top, Mrs. Dew walked into the room. Talise hadn't snuck in this time, but the sight of her teacher still made her jump.

"Mrs. Dew." Talise stopped shaping immediately as she lowered her head in a quick bow. "What can I do for you?"

To her surprise, Mrs. Dew didn't answer. Her face remained stoic as she pointed toward the little stools in the corner of the room. One thing did seem different though. The muscles around her eyes looked heavy as if something weighed them down. It made Talise's hair stand on end.

"What is it?" Talise asked. "What's wrong?" Terror flashed through her, but the logical part of her brain tried to swat it away. Mrs. Dew always looked serious. That was her default. This expression was no different than usual. Still, something like doom seemed to settle into the walls. Something was wrong. Talise didn't know how she knew it, but she knew it.

Mrs. Dew only pointed to the stools again. Without waiting for Talise, she lowered herself onto the nearest one.

Terror gripped Talise by the insides, but she tried to squash it down. Mrs. Dew probably just wanted to see Talise's demonstration. She'd been going around to the other students giving advice.

No matter how much her brain worked, by the time Talise sat down across from Mrs. Dew, she knew this had nothing to do with her demonstration. A faint glisten of tears sat in the corner of Mrs. Dew's eyes.

At the same time, a lump appeared in Talise's throat. Her muscles suddenly couldn't be relaxed, no matter how she tried to soothe them. And when had she started breathing so quickly?

"What happened?" Talise asked.

"I just received word," Mrs. Dew said, suddenly staring at the ground. She gulped and held her lips together as if unable to force them open.

A rope of ice seemed to tighten around Talise's heart. Her breathing got deeper, and her muscles got tighter. How many seconds had it been since Mrs. Dew entered the room? Ten? Twelve? It felt like a thousand. Not a thousand seconds, but a thousand hours.

She knew what was coming. She *knew* it.

But how could she know it? Mrs. Dew hadn't said anything about it yet. This conversation could have been about anything.

Talise tried to force her mind to consider how ridiculous she was being. Tried and failed.

Her mind had no control now. She was being led by her thumping heart and the anxiety that seized her muscles. No longer able to calm herself, she held her breath waiting for Mrs. Dew's words.

"Your," Mrs. Dew said before she gulped again. "I just received word from one of the guards. Your…"

She paused again as if the words were too much. Too heavy.

Just say it, Talise thought. *I already know what you're going to say, so just say it.*

Mrs. Dew closed her eyes and turned away. "Shyna was found this morning by a neighbor."

Marmie.

"Apparently she's been sick the past few weeks."

Talise's seizing muscles were replaced by a cold, icy grip. No more thumping heart. It must have stopped. It had to have stopped. Because how could she be alive when Marmie…

"The neighbor was there the night before. He said she fell asleep. When he came back in the morning…"

"No," Talise said. It was all she could think to say. This couldn't possibly be real.

"She passed away in her sleep. She probably didn't feel anything at all."

"No!" Talise shouted. She jumped off her stool, but then standing there didn't feel any better. She had to do something. She had to move, or her muscles would explode.

The stool.

She kicked it over, but it wasn't enough. She threw it across the room, but that wasn't enough either. Grabbing the stool again, she heaved it at the wall. It needed to break. Something had to be destroyed. Something needed to break for the impossibility of this situation.

When the stool hit the wall, it bounced to the ground with barely even a dent. Talise let out a guttural scream and fireballs appeared in her hands. She didn't really mean to set the stool on fire, but at the same time, she did.

Soon, the wooden stool had burst into flames atop the cement floor. The wood cracked by the heat of the flames. Talise watched until the legs of the stools turned black.

And then she fell to the ground with her face in her hands and wept.

Sobs shook through her. The muscles inside had been weakened by the anxiety that gripped them. Her heart no longer beat, it only fluttered. For some reason, her eyes felt tired.

So tired.

"I'm sorry," Mrs. Dew said.

Her teacher had never been particularly comforting, but having her arm wrapped around Talise's shoulders felt nice. Not enough, but nice.

Mrs. Dew said nothing of the burning stool. Instead, she squeezed Talise's shoulders and let her cry as long as she needed.

It took longer than it should have.

"How did she die?" Talise finally asked. Her voice sounded like the croaking of a frog, but she managed to get the words out.

"In her sleep."

Talise nodded. "Yes, I know you said that, but what did she die of? Why was she sick?"

Mrs. Dew wet her lips as she looked away.

"Are a lot of people getting it? Is the sickness spreading? A fever? A cough? What?"

Looking at the ground, Mrs. Dew asked, "Do you know how most people in the Storm die?"

Blood rushed through Talise's ears as her heart pounded. Again, the world seemed to freeze while she was forced to deal with these awful truths. "Malnourishment," Talise whispered. The same thing that prevented people in the Storm from being able to shape was also the thing that usually took them away forever.

Mrs. Dew nodded, still unable to make eye contact.

They were both quiet, watching the flames around the stool turn to embers.

"I have to go to the funeral," Talise said. "I have to leave a mark on her gravestone." It was the only thing she could do now.

Since the time of Kamdar, the first emperor of Kamdaria, gravestones had been marked by the deceased's family members. The simple marks honored the person's life and acted as symbols for the love their family members held for them. The more marks a grave had, the more honored that person was considered to be.

Talise had just enough money to get to the Storm. Not enough to get back, but Mrs. Dew or the school might help with that. They allowed that sort of thing on occasion.

Maybe it was reckless to spend a day of traveling this close to the competition, but Talise didn't care. She needed this. She had to say goodbye. She had to leave a mark on Marmie's grave because hers would be the only mark the grave would bear.

"Of course. We have funds for you. I'll contact the city and find out when they plan to do the funeral."

"The city?" Talise looked up with a start.

Mrs. Dew nodded. "Yes, the city is doing her funeral." When Talise stared back at her, Mrs. Dew added, "She didn't have any family in the Storm, did she?"

Talise turned away as she wrapped her arms around her stomach. Shaking her head, she said, "No. She has no family in the Storm."

And whose fault is that? she thought.

Talise dropped her head into her palms and began crying again as if she had never stopped. At this rate, she might never stop.

Not until Marmie's grave bore her mark.

CHAPTER NINE

LETTERS.

They captured the essence of Marmie, but not the smell. They didn't hold the soft edges of her wrinkled skin or the few gray strands in her hair. How many strands of gray were there now?

Talise hadn't seen Marmie in ten years. When she first joined the academy, the one thing she feared most was forgetting Marmie's face. At first, it took no effort at all to recall her sparkly smile and gray eyes. The first few years, it was easy.

And then it wasn't.

Now she wondered if she had imagined that freckle under Marmie's right eye. Or was it her left? Had her lips been full or thin? She never thought to look when she was younger.

Marmie insisted Talise would never be able to forget her as long as she loved her. But she was wrong. She loved Marmie with more heart than she even knew was capable.

And she could barely remember her face.

Talise clutched the letters against her chest and breathed them in again, praying for even the hint of a smell.

Of course it never came. What *did* Marmie smell like? Now she'd never know. At the funeral, she'd smell like embalming fluid. That wasn't Marmie. All Talise would really get was to see Marmie's face again.

Her beautiful face that had sacrificed everything, *everything* for Talise to be here.

Why did fate have to be so cruel as to let Marmie see Talise get so close to the competition, but not close enough to win? Talise had bought Marmie a riverboat ticket so she could attend. If things had gone according to plan, Marmie would have had one full day of food and rest. It would have been the best she'd felt in years.

And now she was dead.

Gone.

Sand seemed to scrape down Talise's throat as she tried to swallow. She clutched the letters to her chest as she paced across her bedroom.

How was she supposed to compete like this? How could she focus now?

She swallowed again and brushed an errant tear from her cheek.

She just had to put a mark on Marmie's gravestone. If she could just leave a mark on the gravestone, then she could focus again. Why was Mrs. Dew taking so long to tell her when the funeral would be?

Talise's bedroom door opened a crack, and the letters flew through the air as she wrenched the door open. Her arms sagged at her sides when she saw Wendy in the doorway.

Talise turned away and tucked a strand of chin-length black hair behind her ear. "I thought you were Mrs. Dew."

"Why weren't you in class this morning?" Wendy asked.

Gulping seemed like a good way to subdue the frog in Talise's throat, but the sandpaper feeling only got worse. Considering how much she'd been crying, it made sense that her throat was dry.

"I had a, uh… personal…" Why was she trying to be brave in front of Wendy? Wendy was her friend. But maybe if she could be brave in front of Wendy, she could be brave in front of everyone else too. "A personal issue," Talise finished with a curt nod.

Wendy's face had fallen. All the lighthearted laughter in her eyes had been replaced by a shroud of black. "What happened?" Her voice came out higher than usual.

All of that Talise probably could have handled. But then Wendy touched her arm with fingers as cold as ice. In a voice barely above a whisper, she asked, "Marmie?"

The floodgates released and tears fell down Talise's cheeks in sheets before she could even nod. Gripping her arms tight around her stomach, she turned away. She felt foolish for crying, but she didn't know why.

The emotion boiled inside her until it was too much. She threw her body onto her bed and kicked her feet against the mattress as she sobbed. She felt like a child throwing a tantrum, but it didn't stop her. Nothing could.

Why did this have to be real? Why couldn't it be a fairy tale where she gained some magic power for going through a tragedy? In reality, all this gave her was the urge to curl up in a ball and never face the world again.

If she couldn't even keep her cool around her best friend, what chance did she have around the rest of her classmates? Around Mrs. Dew?

Around the emperor?

He'd never understand or forgive her for letting her emotions get in the way of shaping.

Wendy had sidled next to Talise. She stroked her hair and let her cry. Minutes passed without either of them saying a word. Or maybe it was hours.

All Talise knew was her shoulders still heaved with sobs, but no more tears fell from her eyes. Maybe she'd finally gotten too dehydrated. When the sandpaper coating her throat became unbearable, she sat up.

Wendy sat across from her on the end of the bed. Were those tear streaks on her cheeks too?

"I just," Talise said as she started twisting a chunk of her hair with both hands. "I just want to go to the funeral and put a mark on Marmie's gravestone. If I can just see her one last time, if I can just say goodbye, I know I'll be okay. I'll be able to focus on the competition and do my best like I promised her. I just need to put mark on her gravestone."

"When is the funeral?" Wendy's voice came out in a gentle wisp, floating on the air like an air shaping ribbon.

"I don't know. Mrs. Dew was supposed to find out, but she doesn't know yet. She said the city is taking forever to write back. Or maybe the letter got lost in the mail."

One of Wendy's eyebrows shot up for a brief moment before it fell back into place. It was such a small expression, but on Wendy, it spoke volumes.

"What is it?"

Wendy seemed to curl into herself. She shrugged her shoulders until they touched her earlobes. "I'm sure it's nothing."

Talise sat forward, grabbing one of Wendy's hands until it was tight between both of hers. "Please, Wendy. It's my…" Her throat seemed to choke up before the name could escape her lips. In a whisper, she finished, "What do you know?"

Wendy's eyes were full to the brim with tears. A light flush colored her cheeks as she nodded. Maybe she had been trying to protect Talise from the truth, but she understood now. Talise needed the truth more than anything.

"I think Mrs. Dew already knows when the funeral is. I heard her talking to another teacher. I don't know when it's supposed to be, but I think she's hiding something."

Talise clasped her hands over her mouth. Her stomach seemed to solidify into a knot with thousands of strands that grew tighter each second. "It's the same day. What if it's the same day as the competition?"

"They wouldn't do that," Wendy said, forcing her head side to side in sharp jerks. "They wouldn't wait that long to do the funeral. Especially in the Storm. Have you ever heard of them waiting an entire week to do a funeral?"

The knot in her stomach loosened one strand at a time. "No. No, you're right. Funerals in the Storm usually happen within three days." With those words, another strand came loose, allowing her to let out a breath. But then, it recoiled, and the knot seemed even tighter than before.

"But then why hasn't Mrs. Dew told me when it is? What is she hiding?"

"Maybe she doesn't want you to get distracted from the competition."

Talise let out a snort. "Too late for that."

"Is money a problem?" Wendy asked. Her eyes were focused on her fingers as she picked at her cuticles. "I have a little money in savings if you need a ticket."

It took everything in her for Talise to keep her mouth from gaping. This was not typical for their relationship. Wendy was from the Gate, so she always had more money than Talise. But even still, Wendy never had exorbitant amounts of money. At least not like people from the Crown.

Another frog settled into Talise's throat, though she couldn't figure out exactly why. "Mrs. Dew said the school might pay for the ticket."

Wendy let out an audible breath of relief that was probably meant to be silent. Her cheeks turned pink for a moment before her eyes narrowed at a spot in the floor. "Something weird is going on."

Talise nodded and crossed her arms over her chest. She wanted to scowl too but worried Wendy might think it was about her. For now, her scowling would have to stay in her head.

Wendy twisted her hands around themselves before she spoke again. "My brother told me he used to bribe guards when he wanted information. You know they hear everything. He told me who the trustworthy guards are, who can be bought, and who gives good information."

A light bloomed in Talise's heart for only a moment before it was snuffed out. "I can't. I only have enough money for my riverboat ticket. If the school doesn't help, I don't have anything extra for bribery."

"I wasn't suggesting you pay for it," Wendy said in a matter-of-fact tone. She grabbed Talise's wrist and pulled them both out the door before Talise could even think about protesting.

Wendy led them out into the gardens where they hid behind a particularly stiff bush. Prying a few branches apart, Talise looked through a small opening in the leaves.

A guard stood in front of a fountain wearing a uniform covered in wrinkles and dirt smudges. One of the older guards was talking to him, and the younger guard didn't like what he was hearing.

The moment the older guard stepped away, Wendy pulled them out from behind the bush and marched toward the younger guard. He didn't notice them at first because he was too busy grumbling under his breath and digging his toe into the dirt.

When they stood directly in front of him, he finally seemed to notice they were there for him. His toe stopped mid-dig as he looked up. He pasted on a cocky smile and shook his hair until it fell into his eyes.

But then, he saw Talise's face and everything in his expression changed. First his eyebrows shot up, and then he stuffed his hands into his pockets. After a tiny gulp, his cocky expression returned, but nothing about it felt natural now.

"Why did you make that face when you saw me?" Talise asked. "Did that guard say something to you about me?"

"No!" the guard said, a little too quickly.

Wendy placed a hand on his forearm, and his shoulders seemed to relax instantly. She turned her eyes downward so the only way to look at him was up through her eyelashes. "Do you know anything about a funeral for a woman named Shyna?"

The guard seemed mesmerized by Wendy's honey-sweet voice. After a brief blank stare, he shook his head and looked away. "No. I don't know anything about that."

Talise was ready to grind her teeth into dust, but Wendy seemed to welcome the challenge. She bit her bottom lip and touched the guard's forearm again. He was too busy staring into her eyes to notice she had retrieved a wad of money from her side pouch.

"What about now?" she said with a playful smirk.

He eyed the money for a long second but then looked back into her eyes. And then back at the money. Without warning, he took a step back and raised his hands in front of himself. "I'm straight now. I don't do that kind of thing anymore."

Wendy let out a soft sigh and reached back into her side pouch. This time, an even bigger wad of money lay in her palm. Even Talise's eyes widened at the sight of it.

"What do you know?" Wendy asked. She probably meant for her voice to sound serious and business-like, but she was too sweet for it. Instead, it sounded just as innocent as her.

The guard showed a moment's hesitation. After one last look into Wendy's eyes, he leaned forward, keeping his head bent low. "The funeral is scheduled for the week after the competition."

Talise's fingers curled into a fist. "Try again," she said. "That's two weeks away. They would never wait that long to do a funeral."

"I swear," the guard said, placing a hand over his heart while the other took the money. "I thought it was weird too, but they said they're doing some embalming thing so they can hold off until then."

Talise was still busy eyeing the guard, trying to decide if he was telling the truth or not, when Wendy said, "Thank you. You don't know what this means."

A sheepish smile grew on the guard's lips as he rustled his hair with one hand. Talise still didn't know if he could be trusted, but then again, why would he lie? Everything made sense now. Mrs. Dew didn't want to say when the funeral was because she wanted Talise to focus on the competition without worrying about it. They postponed the funeral to make sure Talise could be there.

It all made sense.

Even still, the curling knot of anxiety in her stomach only seemed to twist and tighten at the thought. Could she focus on the competition even with the funeral postponed?

CHAPTER TEN

THE CLASSROOM LOOKED NOTHING LIKE it usually did. The desks and chairs had all been pushed against the walls, so the floor was wide open. The students sat cross-legged at the back of the classroom.

Mrs. Dew and four other shapers from the Crown sat at a long table in the front. They each held a writing pad and kept whispering to each other. They didn't seem to be concerned in the least that their whispers increased the tension in the room by ten times. In fact, a few of them seemed to enjoy the affect they had on the students.

Pre-competition day.

Competition day was most important to Talise, but for almost everyone else, this was the day they'd been training ten years for. Mrs. Dew and the fellow judges would make notes on the demonstrations and those notes would ultimately help place the students into their future jobs. Plus, it gave anyone vying for Master Shaper the chance to see each other's demonstrations and alter theirs to better compete.

On competition day, the only judge would be the emperor. He would choose the best shaper as Master Shaper. Everyone already knew there were really only two students who had a chance at this.

But pre-competition day?

Everyone had a chance here. For everyone besides Talise and Aaden, today was the day their lives would be set. They had to show the very best of their skills, and they had to do it without throwing up.

Talise dug her fingernails into her knees, trying to keep her mind occupied with anything besides Marmie's funeral. She should have been more worried about Aaden and seeing his skills, but all she could see in her mind was Marmie's empty gravestone until Talise would be able to put one tiny mark on it.

One mark that would look so little compared to the life that Marmie had led. Her sacrifice and love deserved a hundred marks. The only thing Talise could do now was make her mark so intricate and detailed that it would be marveled by all who saw it.

Wendy jumped to the center of the room when Mrs. Dew called her name. Talise dug her nails deeper into her knees. She needed to focus on this demonstration. She owed it to Wendy to pay attention at least to hers.

Every time Talise's mind would wander to Marmie's grave, she'd press her nails in deeper. Her mind still fought to dwell on the grave even while Wendy asked for the classroom windows to be opened.

The other judges looked bored, but Mrs. Dew gave Wendy an encouraging nod. Wendy lifted her bow and a single arrow from the ground. She took aim before shooting, but her demonstration began after the arrow left the bow.

Wendy dropped the bow and put both hands in front of her, sending a rush of shaped air after the arrow. With the added air, the arrow was able to travel three times the distance it could have without it.

The judges were impressed.

Talise was proud.

But then the judges asked too many questions, especially one judge wearing red silk. He asked about the military application of her shaping technique, and Talise's head was filled with thoughts of Marmie once again.

When Aaden's turn came, she could barely keep herself from losing the food in her stomach. He had improved his cherry blossoms to perfection. Even from the back of the classroom she could see how beautiful they were.

Her stomach roiled and clenched as she watched. No amount of nail pressing would help her insides now. When she was called up to do her demonstration, she already had a headache and her skin seemed to be on fire.

She'd been practicing with so much fire lately, she didn't notice her internal temperature rising so much. But this time, she was pretty sure it was an actual fever, not from fire shaping. A stress-induced fever no doubt.

Maybe if she lost her lunch in front of the judges, they would let her do her demonstration another time.

They wouldn't.

She already knew they wouldn't. It wouldn't do her any good even if they did. Marmie's funeral was still an entire week after the final competition. How could she concentrate on anything before then?

She shaped her fire ribbons into the air and let them spin around her. Her veins protested at every second. Her temperature was rising much more than it ever had in practice. She gritted her teeth together and tried to think of something that would encourage her. She tried to think of Marmie's sacrifice and how she couldn't let it be in vain.

With a fire ribbon high above her head, an image of Marmie came into Talise's head so clearly, it was as if Marmie sat next to her. Talise remembered sitting in that little room where she'd been tested for a shaping academy.

Talise had asked if Marmie could come live in the palace after Talise became Master Shaper.

"You already know the answer to that," Marmie had said in a gentle tone. Her right eye had squinted, almost in a wink. The freckle under her eye bounced through the movement. So, the freckle *was* under her right eye.

For a moment, Talise's heart soared with relief. She could see the face with perfect clarity. It felt as though Marmie looked down on her, offering love and approval through her memory.

But then reality settled in again.

Marmie was dead. Gone.

Forever.

In that moment, everything fell apart. When the fire ribbon fell, Talise's shaping became jerky and rigid. Instead of falling in a swooping swirl, it looked more like a snake slithering down a spiral staircase, and not in a graceful way.

She managed to regain control when the fire ribbon reached her shoulders. She spun the ribbon around her body just like she had practiced all those times. But still, when the ribbon swirled around her ankles, she shaped it too close.

The skin over her ankle bone tingled with a burn, and the hem of her pants had probably been singed.

She didn't care.

She tried to; she really did. How could she be so careless with the competition so close? She needed to know if her demonstration was good enough to beat Aaden's.

But how could she care about anything when Marmie was dead?

Her senses seemed to sharpen at the thought of Aaden. He was an impressive shaper. She needed to beat him. All this moping wouldn't do her any good.

Talise lifted her chin in the air and attempted a smile at the judges. *Be brave*, she thought. *That's what Marmie would want.*

She ended her demonstration with one fire ribbon twisting around her arms and another twisting around her legs. They joined together around her waist only to sprout several new ribbons that shot out from her body like a firework.

The rest of the demonstration was flawless just like all of it should have been.

When Talise bowed to the judges, she noticed one of them was still gaping at her. Mrs. Dew looked smug as she glanced at that judge.

The walk to the back of the room seemed longer than it should have. It was made a little easier when Talise recognized a glint of fear in Aden's eyes.

Good. He deserved to be as worried as he had made her feel.

Wendy looked delighted when Talise sat down next to her. "Very cool," Wendy said under her breath. She paired the words with an encouraging nod.

That lifted Talise's spirits. Not a lot, but when she was feeling so low, a little made a big difference.

The judges began whispering as they compared their notes. Mrs. Dew had chosen Talise to go last because she knew it would be an impressive demonstration. Of course, it looked better for Mrs. Dew if one of her students won Master Shaper. That was how she kept her spot at the elite academy year after year.

The whispering among the judges lasted too long. Despite their years of studying patience and discipline, every single one of the students was fidgeting.

Aaden kept glancing over at Talise, but then his eyes would flick away, and he'd try to pretend like he had never looked.

His nervousness probably shouldn't have made her feel so good, but she couldn't help it. Whenever his eyes flicked, a shot of glee danced through her.

She did feel a *little* guilty, but this was for Marmie and Marmie wanted her to win.

After several more minutes of biting her bottom lip and checking the hem of her pants—which had been singed—the judges announced that they had made a decision.

The man wearing red silk stood from the judges table. He held a thick stack of papers which would determine job placements for all the students. With a good recommendation from pre-competition day, even someone from the Gate could get a job in the palace.

But not someone from the Storm. The only way someone could escape the Storm was by winning Master Shaper. Which meant Talise didn't care one bit about the stack of papers in the man's hand. She only cared about the words ready to spill from his mouth. Now she'd know once and for all if her demonstration was good enough to beat Aaden's.

"We are most impressed," the man began.

That was a good sign. Talise noticed the man wore a silver pin engraved with a miniature tornado. The silver pin meant he worked at the palace and the tornado meant air was his primary element. He wasn't a Master Shaper, or his pin would have been engraved with the symbols for all four elements.

Talise wracked her brain, trying to think if she knew of any air shapers from the palace important enough to come to pre-competition day. Like all the students, she had been disappointed that no Master Shapers had come. They usually had at least one for pre-competition day.

But still, this man had to have a high level of authority to be here.

General Gale Asato. It came to her suddenly as he opened his mouth to speak again. No wonder he had been so intrigued by Wendy's demonstration. He oversaw shape training for all military personnel, especially the royal guard.

"Never before have we seen shaping like we saw today. Mrs. Dew truly deserves a promotion after what she has helped you achieve."

Mrs. Dew's cheeks turned pink and General Gate gave her the barest hint of a wink. He licked his lips before he continued. "The winner for today was most difficult to choose. Not all the judges agreed on the same student."

He paused, seeming to hold his breath.

Just say it! With the added anxiety running through her, Talise suddenly remembered her fever. She wanted nothing more than to lie down. And to win of course.

"Aaden is our winner today."

Talise's mouth dropped open at the words. Wendy let out a small gasp. Mrs. Dew frowned at the table. Every pair of eyes in the room seemed to wander over to Talise. Claye gave her an apologetic look before he glanced at Wendy and shrugged.

The fever inside Talise seemed to explode through her skin while a deep shiver ran through every part of her body.

Her teeth rattled, and she had to clench them together. Tears threatened to spill over her eyelashes, but she managed to hold them back. The last thing she wanted was to start crying in front of the judges.

She probably would have held it together too. She was strong. She had been through a lot. Yes, Marmie had just died, and she was devastated. But still, Talise wasn't one to burst into tears with a roomful of eyes on her. She *could* have held it together.

Except then Aaden looked at her.

It didn't even matter what expression he wore because his stupid face was the reason the past ten years meant nothing. The reason Marmie's death meant nothing.

He dared to make eye contact, and she lost all semblance of control. Her body seemed to detach itself from her mind, so she had no control over it.

Springing to her feet, her legs propelled her out of the classroom, as far from Aaden as she could get.

Chapter Eleven

Talise hugged the wooden gate that separated the academy grounds from the palace graveyard. Without a pass, she wasn't permitted to leave the school grounds. And she'd never gotten a pass because she'd never had enough money.

From her spot behind the gate, she could just make out the marks on the late empress's grave. Isla Tempest Malksur Ruemon had one thousand three hundred and twelve marks on her grave. Talise had counted them all.

Many citizens of Kamdaria had come to her funeral and been invited to leave a mark on her grave. Marks were usually reserved for family members only, but as empress, Isla Ruemon was considered family to all of Kamdaria.

Talise couldn't bring herself to have bitterness toward the late empress. Isla had been murdered in cold blood after all. But why did Empress Isla get over a thousand marks when Marmie would only get one? One mark was a disgrace, even if it was an intricate one.

A crunch of gravel made Talise jump, but she relaxed immediately when she heard Wendy's voice.

"I thought I'd find you here."

Talise didn't have to wipe any tears before she turned around. Maybe rushing from the classroom had dried them all up. No matter how she stared at the graveyard, they stayed back, stealing the emotional release that tears usually provided.

"What did they say after I left?" Talise asked. She hoped Wendy wouldn't guess that *they* really just meant Aaden.

"Nothing," Wendy said in her usual timid voice. "No one said a single thing, and Mrs. Dew looked at them all really sternly in case they were thinking about it."

Talise tried to smile. She was grateful Wendy had come for her. She was even grateful Mrs. Dew had given stern glares.

"What does your recommendation say?" Talise asked.

Wendy's eyes lit up with a grin. "I've been recommended for military shape training. General Gale wants to work with me himself." Her smile looked too big for her face and somehow, it made her look even sweeter than ever.

"You deserve it," Talise said. Her words had never been more sincere, but that didn't stop her from choking up.

"Oh Talise," Wendy said, throwing her arms around her. "You're still going to win; I know you will."

Talise opened her mouth to speak. Sniffed. Felt tears welling in her eyes. And closed her mouth again.

Wendy hugged tighter, seeming to sense her distress. "You were just distracted because of Marmie's funeral, and it made you mess up in the middle of your demonstration. You'll be more focused on competition day. You're going to win. Then, when you visit Marmie's grave, you'll be a Master Shaper, and you can leave four marks on her grave. One for each element."

The tears subsided for a moment as Wendy's words sunk in. Talise had forgotten Master Shapers were allowed to leave four marks. That lifted her spirits slightly.

"Do you really think I have a chance?"

Wendy pulled away and nodded emphatically. "You only messed up because you were thinking about Marmie, right?"

"Yes."

"See? Then you still have a chance for sure. We all saw when you messed up. The rest of your demonstration was perfect except that one part. Even General Gale said the judges were divided on who should win. One competition day, the emperor is the only one who matters. As long as *he* likes your demonstration better, it doesn't matter what happened today."

Talise wrapped a hand around her elbow and pulled it close to her body. What if the emperor liked fire cherry blossoms more than fire ribbons? Talise was almost certain he would. Ridgerock Palace was known for its cherry blossoms and the emperor loved them. How could he appreciate dancing ribbons more than his favorite trees? The only thing he liked better than those blossoms was his crown.

"Your skin seems warmer than usual. Is that still from the demonstration?"

"Um," Talise pulled her elbow even closer to her body. "Yes," she lied. The fever inside her had been growing worse, but she chose to ignore it. If she didn't get some rest soon, it would become an even bigger problem. One she couldn't deal with at the moment.

"Come on. Let's get you to the kitchen so we can get some ice to cool your body."

Talise allowed Wendy to tug her along. As they walked, Talise glanced back at Empress Isla's grave. Even with over a thousand marks, it still looked sad. So many strangers had left marks that the ones from her real family members were impossible to spot. The memory of them seemed to be buried along with the empress herself.

The walk to the kitchen building seemed longer than usual. At first, Wendy's presence had been welcome, but now Talise wanted to be alone. Her mind was wrestling with too many things at once.

Could her fire ribbons beat Aaden's cherry trees? Did she even care when Marmie's death was so fresh? How could she not care when Marmie had died to get her this far? How should the mark look that she would leave on Marmie's gravestone?

Wendy's chatter kept interrupting her thoughts and each time it felt more intrusive. When they reached the kitchen building, she told Wendy to go on and get the ice while she stayed outside. She needed a moment.

What she really needed was for Marmie to be alive and all this to be a horrible nightmare, but Talise didn't think that would happen.

She pinched herself just to be sure. The pain brought a scowl to her face that only deepened when Aaden appeared in front of her.

He blinked as his chest rose and fell against his fire orange tunic. It took her a moment to realize why that seemed so strange. Aaden was out of breath.

He stared at her like he had found what he was looking for. And yet, his shoulders pulled back as if unsure whether being in her presence was what he really wanted.

She eyed him carefully, hoping her gaze would make him squirm like he had after her demonstration. Sadly, her gaze seemed to have no such effect on him. Even worse, he took a step toward her with his shoulders rolling forward.

"Your demonstration was impressive."

Talise curled her lip into a snarl and jerked herself away from him. "I don't need your pity."

Aaden let out a sigh and glanced over his shoulder at the instructional building. It may have been her imagination, but he seemed to focus on the window to Mrs. Dew's office.

When he turned back, he shrugged, and a look of resignation fell over his features. "Look, I'm glad I won, and you lost. I won't deny it."

Talise clenched her teeth as a hot anger boiled from her toes all the way up to her bobbed hair. "Is this your way of trying to make me feel better? Because if it is, you're failing miserably. And don't think I'm only upset about losing."

"I know."

This time, she took a step toward him. It took everything in her not to slap his smug face. She crossed her arms over her chest to keep them from acting on their own. "My Marmie died and I just want to put a mark on her grave, but the funeral isn't until a week after the competition. I'm having a hard time concentrating. It has nothing to do with you. *Nothing!*"

"Marmie?" His voice sounded hollow. When she braved a glance toward him, his face looked hollow too. Gray and ice seemed to spread through his skin as he looked at her. The question sizzled in his eyes, almost begging to be contradicted.

She turned away.

This wouldn't do at all. She liked being angry with him much better. As she had said earlier, she didn't want his pity. It only made her feel pathetic.

"There's something I think you should know," he said.

Before she could ask what he meant, he turned and waved at her to follow.

She glared at his back, trying to decide if she should. He was probably just trying to mess with her head. He was probably trying to ensure that she failed when they did their demonstrations for the emperor next week.

But a tiny piece of her, way down in her gut, trusted him. She planted her feet and scolded that tiny spark in her gut. What did it know? How could she trust him? *Him?*

Aaden kept marching on, and it became clear he wouldn't ask her again. If she wanted to know whatever mysterious information he thought she needed, this was her last chance.

The spark in her gut seemed to make the decision for her. She sprang forward, rushing to catch up with him.

He stopped directly under the window to Mrs. Dew's office. Pressing a finger to his lips, he pulled the window out so the sound from inside drifted out to them.

"What did you say to her exactly?" Mrs. Dew didn't sound happy. She wasn't the sunshine and roses type, but this seemed even more serious than usual.

"She doesn't know. I swear on the emperor, I didn't give anything away."

The owner of the second voice was harder to place. Talise recognized it but couldn't remember from where.

"I'll have your guard status revoked if you try to sidestep my question again!" Mrs. Dew shouted.

It wasn't until the guard replied that Talise finally placed him.

"I told her the funeral would be a week *after* the competition."

Mrs. Dew scoffed. "She would never believe that. She isn't stupid."

Talise's gut started thrashing inside her, pinging off all sorts of warning signals to her brain. Why *had* she believed it?

"I'm very convincing," the guard said, and she imagined that he wore a charming smile as he said it. "Trust me, she still has no idea."

"You don't understand what will happen if she loses. Talise needs to win." When Mrs. Dew spoke again, it sounded like her jaw was clenched. "If she finds out the funeral is the same day as the competition, she'll lose for sure."

The guard said something in reply, but Talise didn't hear it. She was too busy unraveling from the inside out.

The same day?

She pressed her back against the wall of the building as she sunk to the gravel. Her knees were pulled up to her chest, and her chin rested on top before she dared take a breath.

Why?

Why hadn't Mrs. Dew told her from the beginning? Why had the guard lied?

Why did Marmie have to die this close to the competition?

A shiver ran up her spine thanks to her fever. Anger jabbed her in the stomach, and then it stabbed her in the chest.

Aaden shifted on the gravel once he closed the window. She wasn't angry at him. How could she be when none of this was his fault?

But he was nearest, and the anger inside her was slamming against her insides, desperate to spring on anyone or anything.

"You disgust me." Her voice sounded more like the hiss of a snake than a human. "You only brought me here to make sure I'd lose."

Aaden looked mortified by the mere suggestion. It didn't matter if she didn't believe her own words or not.

"I hate you," Talise said, and for a moment, she did.

Aaden gave her one last glance before he stalked away. The glance held not even a shred of pity.

Her stomach dropped. Now her anger had nothing to latch itself to. This wouldn't do at all. This was too much.

People in Kamdaria said that life wouldn't give you anything you weren't capable of handling. But they were wrong. She'd seen it in the Storm and now she felt it firsthand.

All she could do was give up because this was too hard.

How could she possibly choose between Marmie's funeral and the competition?

♛

Chapter Twelve

IT DIDN'T TAKE LONG TO pack her belongings. Just one extra dress, a handful of toiletries, and a stack of letters from Marmie. Her tote bag had long since been lost, but a pillowcase worked just as well to carry her things.

She was running away.

Forget the competition. It had brought her nothing but anxiety anyway.

Hours had passed since the pre-competition demonstrations. Everyone let her go to bed with no idea that she was falling apart. But she knew she had to act now before she lost her nerve. The curtain of night would aid in her escape.

She pushed open her bedroom door and peeked out. Empty. With the bulging pillowcase over her shoulder, she crept into the hallway as silently as she could.

If she was caught off academy grounds and in the Crown without an ID card or pass of some sort, she would get arrested. Since she was under eighteen, she didn't have a card yet, but she didn't have a pass either.

Her only hope was to sneak off academy grounds, go through the palace graveyard to Ridgerock Lake, and then she'd swim through the river that ran through the Crown to the Gate.

Once she made it to the Gate, things would be easier. Security was more lax, and she had a little money. Just enough to get her to the Storm. She didn't remember exactly where their cottage had been in the Storm, but it would easier to find than Marmie's grave after she was buried.

Talise had been tiptoeing for the last two hallways. Now, she held her breath as she pressed her back into the wall. Two guards whispered just around the corner from her and all she could do was pray they weren't about to walk right into her.

One minute passed.

Then two.

The muscles in her leg began to cramp. She adjusted her feet and tried to think relaxing thoughts. Her flesh shivered at the prompting of her fever.

Her legs started cramping again.

Just when she was ready to give up, the guards stopped whispering and their footsteps sounded through the hall. Were they coming her way?

She let out a breath of relief when their footsteps got progressively quieter with each step. The guard's hallway was just around the next corner, and then she'd be off toward the graveyard.

Once outside, Talise used her pillowcase to wipe the sweat from her forehead. Fevers had always been her least favorite way to be sick. Her body began pulsing with anticipation as she walked. The closer she came to the edge of academy grounds, the more her stomach roiled.

She'd stopped looking over her shoulder now. This was happening whether her brain liked it or not. With one final glance back at the grounds, she hoisted her leg up on the gate and prepared to climb over it.

The sound of crunching gravel made her heart stop in her chest. Her eyelids dropped while the rest of her body froze.

Her only option now was to run. Whatever guard stood behind her would soon sound the alarm. Hopefully she'd have at least a few seconds to get to the lake. Maybe she could shape a fire onto the academy grounds to keep the guards from following her.

Just as she was about to thrust herself over the gate, a small voice froze her muscles again.

"Wait," the voice said. "Just wait, please."

Wendy. Not a guard.

Relief spread through Talise almost as completely as her fever. But no matter how relieved she was, her determination hadn't wavered. When she turned to face her friend, she didn't relax her grip on the gate. "You can't stop me," Talise said.

Wendy scrambled toward her, clutching her side and panting. "I'm not here to stop you." Wendy's voice was breathless yet resolute all the same.

It might have worried Talise if Wendy's previous words weren't busy needling through her mind. She tried to find sense in them, but none could be found. *Not* there to stop her? Maybe it was a trap. It didn't seem likely from someone like her gentle friend, but she didn't have the luxury of taking any chances. Clutching the gate even harder, Talise asked, "Why are you here?"

Wendy lugged a bag off her shoulder that seemed much heavier than Talise's. Tossing the bag toward her, Wendy said, "Did you even think to pack food? Isn't food scarce in the Storm? Like dangerously scarce?"

Talise caught the bag with her mouth half open. After fiddling with the knot, she peeked inside and saw her favorite fruits, breads, and a large pouch of dried meat.

Wendy shook her head and let out a sigh. "I would have packed some pastries, but I ate the last of mine a few nights ago. I haven't had time to get more."

Talise was still gaping at the bag of food. It was heavy but invaluable. The bread wouldn't survive her swim in the river, but the fruit and meat would. This supply could last her weeks. It could mean the difference between death and survival. She wanted to be grateful for Wendy's generosity, but apparently, she was still too stunned to speak. At last, she managed a quiet, "You're not going to stop me?"

Wendy ignored the question while she dug through her pockets. When her eyes lit up, she pulled a few paper packets from them. Each was labeled with painted pictures of vegetables. Suddenly sheepish, Wendy bit her lip as she handed the packets to her friend. "I thought you might need some seeds too. I don't know if the ground is rich enough in the Storm to grow vegetables, but some people live there, and they have to eat something, right? I figured it was worth a chance."

Now the emotion came. Talise's throat choked up as her eyes stung with tears. She opened her mouth to say thank you, but no words escaped. It took all her effort just to take the packets and hold them close to her heart.

They shared a glance, and it spoke more than all the words Talise had ever said in her life.

Wendy's eyes filled with tears as she threw her arms around Talise. They didn't speak, but they didn't have to. There was nothing to say except goodbye and goodbye was a horrible thing to say.

When Wendy pulled away, the finality of the decision started catching up to Talise.

Wendy grabbed a piece of her hair and twirled it around her finger. She always did that when she was nervous. Clearing her voice, Wendy said, "You know you can't come back, right?"

Talise's throat swelled.

Wendy's voice rose up a notch. "The competition will be over by the time you get to the Storm."

"I know," Talise said, but the surety in her voice was as much for her own benefit as it was for Wendy's.

"You *know*? Are you sure you know? Do you really understand what you're giving up?"

"I have to be there." This time, Talise's words weren't for anyone in particular. They were simply the words from her heart. The things her soul whispered into her bones.

"At her funeral?" Wendy asked. Her voice had risen again, and her lip trembled with each word. "You have to be at her funeral when she's already dead? You have to trap yourself back in the life she wanted you to escape?"

Talise gulped. Her soul had stopped whispering. Now it was listening to Wendy and Talise didn't like it one bit. "What about her grave? She won't have a single mark without mine. They don't keep grave records in the Storm. If I'm not at the funeral, I might never find her grave, and it will be bare forever."

"If you go," Wendy said. "You'll give up everything Marmie wanted for you. That's not what she would want. She wants you to have a life outside the Storm."

"Well, that's impossible now." Talise turned away as she said it, pulling her arms over her stomach. The frog in her throat made it difficult to speak, but somehow, she managed. "Aaden beat me. He's going to beat me again in front of the emperor. Why should I stay when I don't even have a chance?"

Now the truth came out. The truth she'd been hiding even from herself. She pulled her arms tighter over her stomach, wishing she could curl into them the way she used to curl into Marmie when she was scared. A single tear began trickling down her cheek.

"So, find a way to beat Aaden." Wendy didn't seem to have any sympathy for Talise's tear. "You still have three days. Make your demonstration more detailed or dangerous or something. Beat him like Marmie knew you could."

The words sounded nice. Inspiring even. But they weren't enough. Talise had made her decision. "I'm leaving," she said as she wiped away the tear.

Wendy tugged at Talise's elbow until they were facing each other. Wendy wore a frown as she stared at her friend. It seemed like she intended to change Talise's mind with her look alone. It wouldn't work. After a few seconds, Wendy seemed to understand. Her face slackened as a tremble shook through her bottom lip.

Wendy turned away and reached for another piece of her hair. In a whisper she said, "I won't stop you."

Talise's heart seemed to freeze. She breathed in and out just to make sure she still could. It was so much easier being defiant. But now Wendy gave her the responsibility of the decision. It was a heavy weight to bear.

Wendy was right. Talise knew she was right. A mark on a grave wasn't worth what she would have to give up.

But how could she leave Marmie's grave bare? Completely and utterly bare without one single mark. The idea slashed through her like a sword and her heart bled through her bones. It didn't matter what Marmie would have wanted. Talise couldn't live with herself if she knew Marmie's grave was bare.

She hoisted her leg onto the gate and ignored how her stomach sank. She ignored how her body shivered from a fever. She had to ignore it because she knew she wouldn't last long in the Storm with a fever.

But that didn't matter. Even if she only lived another week, it was worth it because Marmie would have a mark on her grave.

And then her own grave would be bare. Not Marmie's.

Talise's breath hitched as the thought of death shook through her. Fear, cold and tight pressed through her skin and gripped her.

Why couldn't she give her life for a mark on Marmie's grave? Marmie deserved it. Why did the survival instinct have to be so strong? Reality laid itself bare in front of Talise.

She didn't want to die. Not yet.

She fell from the gate when she let go. Her body smarted against the gravel, but she didn't bother breaking her fall. She just fell into a heap and pulled her knees up to her chest.

Her body shook and shivered with each sob. She didn't know crying could hurt so much. Her muscles jumbled and her bones shattered, but it only acted as fuel for her tears. The arms in her muscles strained as she clutched her knees closer to her chest. They couldn't come any closer, but that didn't stop her from pulling.

She clung to them like she clung to the past. To Marmie. But the past was gone, and she had to accept that. She had to let go, or her future would crumble.

That was the truth, no matter how much she hated it.

Steeling herself against the storm inside, Talise pulled herself off the ground. She brushed away the gravel that had stuck to her. When she rolled her shoulders back, Wendy smiled.

"I know you can beat him," Wendy said as she wiped the tears off her cheeks.

"I can't." Talise's voice no longer shook with fear. Indecision had plagued her before, but now she was filled with certainty. "Not unless I change my demonstration."

"Again? But the competition is in three days. Can't you adjust your demonstration?"

Talise threw the bags over her shoulder as she began walking toward the academy living quarters. "No. You were right. I need something dangerous to catch the emperor's attention. But the fire ribbons aren't dangerous enough. I have to do something no one has ever attempted. Something no one could forget."

♕

Chapter Thirteen

While recovering from her fever, Talise threw herself into research. After three days, her body had healed but she was getting nowhere with her demonstration. The stacks of books surrounding her were so high, she could barely see past the library table.

Flipping through the pages of her current book, she let out a groan. "There has to be someone who's shaped ice before."

Wendy sat across the table, pursing her lips together. Talise didn't have to guess the thoughts running through her friend's mind since she'd already spoken them aloud several times. *Ice is too dangerous*, Wendy had said. *It's impossible. You'll regret it.*

It didn't matter how many times Wendy protested, Talise knew what she had to do. She slammed the book shut and added it to the stack on her right.

"Here's something," Wendy said, though she seemed to regret having to let those words out of her mouth. "It's from Master Shaper Luca. The one who discovered internal shaping."

The passage was only a few paragraphs, but it gave Talise the courage to hope. It came from Master Shaper Luca's personal journal. He had lived many years ago and worked for Emperor Flarius's grandfather.

Water shaping comes from the eyes. Everyone knows this as easily as they know earth shaping comes from the feet and fire shaping comes from the heart. Lately, I have experimented with shaping elements inside of the body. It seems they all appear in different places while inside. Air travels through the muscles and bones. Fire seems to travel through the veins. Water, which I had guessed would travel through the veins, actually seems to travel just under the surface of the skin.

I discovered something else that deserves to be taught to all shapers everywhere. A warning no one should forget. After a fair bit of fire shaping, my insides were too hot for comfort. I thought I might cool myself by doing internal water shaping, and then freezing the water. I gave myself frostbite, and one of my fingers will have to be removed. Luckily, it's only the pinky.

I'd heard ice shaping was dangerous, but I thought because I was cooling a part of my body that was already hot, it would be fine. I was wrong. I can irrevocably say, only a fool should ever attempt ice shaping.

"Are you sure you can't adjust your fire ribbon demonstration?" Wendy asked while twirling her typical bit of hair. Her face was all pinched up.

None of that mattered to Talise because she finally had an idea. Master Shaper Luca had attempted to cool the heat inside his body, and it still led to frostbite. She had the same thought when she practiced her fire ribbon demonstration. What if she used ice to cool the heat?

Sitting here now, she could see it was all wrong. It would never work because ice was so much colder than the normal body temperature of a human. No wonder Master Shaper Luca had gotten frostbite.

But she had another thought. A magical thought. What if she tried it the other way around?

What if she didn't use ice to cool the heat from a fire? What if she used fire to warm her body while she shaped ice?

That was the trick. She would have to use them both at the same time. That was the skill everyone else had always missed. Both she and Master Shaper Luca originally thought they could cool parts of the body that were only slightly higher than body temperature.

But what if she froze her skin and shaped a fire through her veins at the exact same time?

Simultaneously shaping two elements was difficult. For many shapers, it was impossible. But she wasn't just any shaper. Ten years ago, she had promised Marmie she would be the best shaper Kamdaria had ever known. Now it was time to make good on that promise.

"I need some water," Talise said. She knocked a stack of books over as she jumped from her seat. Not bothering to right them, she scurried to the back of the library where the containers of elements were kept. Just past the nearest bookshelf, she nearly toppled over Aaden.

His eyes went wide as he scrambled to grab a book off the shelf. He was suddenly pouring over the book with a little too much enthusiasm.

"Spying on me?" Talise asked.

He slapped the book shut, dropping all pretense that he cared about the words inside. "You'll never be able to do it. No one has ever shaped ice without regretting it."

She lifted her chin and stepped past him coolly. Of course it had never been done, but that wasn't going to stop her from trying. It was the only way she could beat him.

When she got to the back of the library, she took a bowl of water and a bowl of dirt. Before she attempted ice shaping, she needed to practice simultaneously shaping two elements. She'd start with earth and air since they were easiest for her. Maybe she'd make dirt rings and blow bursts of air through them.

Aaden was gone by the time she made her way back to the table. Why did he care so much about becoming Master Shaper anyway? He didn't need it like she did. Then again, he was from the Crown. This was probably the first time in his life he didn't immediately get the thing he wanted on a silver platter. Whatever his reason, he'd just have to live without the victory.

She bowed unconsciously to the portrait of Emperor Flarius as she passed it. His rich fire orange robes were made of silk, but he also wore a brown cloak of speckled fur. His clothes were different in some of his portraits, but the crown was always the same.

Gold with rubies embedded around the middle. Each of the tines grew up to equal height so the crown looked the same from every angle. That crown was almost as old as Kamdaria itself, and Emperor Flarius loved it.

It was only a portrait, but his eyes seemed to watch her as she walked back to the table. What would he think of her plan? If she succeeded, she'd easily become Master Shaper. But if she failed? He'd think her a fool.

Her heart pattered as she sat at the table. The thought of seeing the emperor in person always made her nervous. All she could do now was practice.

Claye had joined Wendy at the table. They both stopped talking the moment Talise appeared, giving her the impression they had been talking about her. Claye raised an eyebrow when Talise began shaping dirt rings. Both he and Wendy were surprised when Talise shaped bursts of air through the dirt. Wendy let out a breath of relief.

Talise sighed. "I'm just practicing simultaneous shaping so it will be easier when I start shaping ice."

"You're still going to do it?" Claye asked. He and Wendy shared a look that told her everything she needed to know about what they'd been saying behind her back.

She ignored them and kept shaping. It didn't take long to learn two things. One, simultaneous shaping was easier when she could focus one half of her body on one element and the other half of her body on the other element. And two, that method wouldn't work when she started shaping ice.

Hour after hour she practiced in the library. Wendy and Claye had long since left. Wendy begged her to take a break so she could come to dinner, but Talise refused. The muscles around her eyes were starting to tire from all the strain she put on them when she narrowed her eyes.

The more she practiced, the easier simultaneous shaping got. She would have liked another week to practice, or truthfully, another year, but two days was all she had.

The next day, she skipped her shaping lessons altogether and kept practicing in the library. There weren't any lessons left to learn anyway. At this point, everyone was just preparing for the competition. It was much easier to practice simultaneous shaping without the other students gaping at her.

Aaden hadn't returned to the library. Or maybe he had, but she'd been too busy to notice. She tried not to think of it too much because it made her as nervous as the thought of seeing Emperor Flarius.

By the end of that day, she had started simultaneously shaping fire and water. Nothing inside her body yet. Her latest exercise involved bouncing balls of water through the air while fire arrows would shoot straight through them. It would have been enough to beat any other student besides Aaden. Against him, it would still be a tie.

When the exercise became too easy, she shaped the water back into its container and let the fire die around her.

One more day.

She just had one more day to practice. The day after that would be the competition. She always intended to rest the day before the competition, but she knew now that wasn't an option. She hadn't even shaped ice yet, let alone decided what to make with it.

Even as she had that thought, the image of Emperor Flarius's portrait came to her mind. Aaden's idea to make fire sculptures of the cherry trees Emperor Flarius loved was brilliant. An idea like that might be worth copying.

She wouldn't make trees. Her ice shaping would never be as detailed as Aaden's, especially with only one day to practice. She needed to make something the emperor would recognize and love, but something that would be easier. Something flashy.

His crown.

The crown would be easy enough to replicate, but it would still be recognizable. It wouldn't be gold or have red rubies, but the emperor would still understand even if it was made of ice.

Sitting the library chair, Talise closed her eyes as she took in a deep breath. It was close to evening now and the other students were all busy getting ready for bed. She had nothing left to distract her mind. The time had come for her to shape ice.

Fear roiled through her. Her brow glistened even though her fever had healed.

This was it.

She took in another deep breath and sent a fire burning through her veins. The heat felt nice at first, but it grew unpleasant after only a few minutes. During those minutes, she figured out how to localize the heat in specific parts of her body. The fire always began in her heart, but once it was started, she could move it to only burn inside the veins of her arms and hands.

Now the true test came. She shaped the water out of the bowl, so it levitated over one palm. She started with a small amount of water, no bigger than a coin.

The fire burned harder inside her, and she took a steadying breath to calm it. Based on Master Shaper Luca's journal, she knew to note her heartbeat, her internal temperature, and her breathing. If any of these seemed off, she'd have to adjust her fire shaping to compensate.

Talise shaped the water into a square. Then she shaped it into a flower, and then a fish. She was stalling, but the shaping helped calm her nerves.

At last, she shaped the water into a simple ball. With her eyes narrowed to tiny slits, she internally shaped water around her fingers. The urge to hold her breath was strong, but she knew it would be best to keep breathing normally. She had to regulate her breath to know if frostbite or hypothermia were imminent.

Now.

She froze the water in her fingers and let the cold air rise so it could freeze the levitating water into ice. Again, she paid special attention to her vital life signs. Her heart kept beating at a steady tempo. Not too fast. Not too slow. Her breathing remained constant. The skin temperature in her hands was cold.

Feeling the fire in her veins, she sent it just a little closer to her hands. Too close and it would melt the ice in her fingers. Too far and she'd have frostbite.

She spent a few seconds getting it just right, but soon the truth became clear. This was going to work.

With less fear, she sent another wave of cold through her fingers, and the levitating ball of ice began to freeze. Ice crystals first formed at the bottom of the water ball, but soon they crept up the sides until the entire ball had frozen.

Someone gasped behind her.

She lost control of the ice shaping immediately, and the ball turned back to water. But it didn't matter because it had worked. One more day would be plenty of time to learn how to shape an ice crown. The emperor would never forget her demonstration, and neither would anyone else.

Talise smiled as she turned around to face the person who had gasped behind her. She smiled because she recognized him the instant she heard his gasp. It was such beautiful symmetry that he gasped, just like she had when she snuck in to see him shape fire cherry blossoms.

When her eyes met Aaden's, she saw true fear in them.

He said nothing.

They both knew what that ball of ice meant.

She was going to win.

Chapter Fourteen

Ice through the fingers; fire in the veins.

Talise closed her eyes as she pushed the mantra through her mind, willing it to become reality within her. Shaping the water was easy, but freezing it still came with the threat of hypothermia. With only the previous day to practice, ice shaping required her utmost concentration.

Talise stared at the porcelain bowl of water sitting on the desk in front of her. Mrs. Dew stood at the front of the classroom, fiddling with a stack of papers. Talise knew she was watching her from the corner of her eye. Everyone was.

The competition was an hour away, which meant it was too late for anyone to change their demonstration. Now she could practice in front of them with no fear.

Ice and Fire.

She could do this.

With a sharp intake of breath, she shaped the water until it levitated out of the bowl. Holding her palm upward, she moved her fingers through the air as if twisting an invisible ball.

The puddle of floating water slowly started spinning. Round and around until air appeared in the center and it resembled a spinning donut. Her fingers twisted faster and soon the water shape went from donut to a thin circle of water just big enough to fit on the crown of a head.

She continued spinning the water, taking several deep breaths to prepare herself for what came next. Biting her lip, she let her fingers freeze both literally and figuratively. As the water stopped spinning, tiny ice crystals appeared around the bottom edge, freezing the water.

Talise stood her fingers straight up, willing the water to grow tines and slowly froze the tines as they grew. As the ice crown took shape, her heart thumped in her chest, reminding her of the cold.

Momentarily ignoring the crown, she breathed a fire through her veins until her heart stopped its complaining. When both the crown and the heat were just right, she used her fingers to levitate the crown through the air until it landed on her head.

After exactly five seconds, she levitated the crown off her head and dropped it back into the bowl. She melted the ice as it moved through the air, so it was nothing more than a puddle of water by the time it hit the porcelain.

A victorious smile spread on her lips as she stared back at the water. She had this competition in the bag.

"Elements in their containers please," Mrs. Dew said. She clapped her hands together, pressing her lips into a thin line. "We leave for the palace in a few minutes. Remember, Emperor Flarius will only choose one of you as Master Shaper. Whoever is chosen will receive a permanent place at the palace with the other Master Shapers. But even more importantly, that person will receive great honor. A silver crescent moon will be stamped on the ID cards of the Master Shaper's children, grandchildren, and great-grandchildren."

In the seat to her left, she noticed Aaden mockingly opening and closing his hand while mouthing *blah blah blah*. He rolled his eyes and whispered to whoever would listen, "She says this like it's the first time we've heard it. As if this wasn't what we've been preparing for all our lives at the academy."

Talise pinned him with one of her most wicked glares, hoping he would squirm in his seat. The entire point of this competition was to win honor. If Aaden mocked his elder so openly, he had no business winning anything.

Unfortunately, her glare did nothing but make Aaden chuckle, and run a hand through his hair coolly. Despite his bravado, she noticed his hands shaking the tiniest bit. It made the corner of her lip cock up in a smile.

Seeing her confidence, Aaden scoffed. "You're still afraid I'll win. Maybe you can shape ice, but my fire sculptures are more detailed than anything the emperor has ever seen."

He'd developed a cocky attitude since he caught her ice shaping in the library. His fire sculptures were exquisite. She'd never argue that, but she didn't think he'd win now. Not even Emperor Flarius Ruemon himself could shape ice, and he was a talented shaper. Her ice crown would win everyone over.

Mrs. Dew announced the arrival of the boat that would take them across Ridgerock Lake right to the entrance of Ridgerock Palace. Talise hung back to take one last look at the classroom. She'd spent ten years on the academy grounds, and it seemed impossible it was finally time to say goodbye.

Her thoughts drifted to Marmie so suddenly, she almost grabbed the desk to steady herself. She had to shove away the thoughts of the funeral or else she'd turn into a sobbing mess. But she didn't push away all thoughts of Marmie.

As she stood there looking at her empty classroom, Talise made a promise. *I'll find your grave someday,* Talise thought. *And I'll leave the four most intricate marks any Master Shaper has ever left.*

CHAPTER FIFTEEN

A STUFFY, HUMID HEAT HUNG in the air, reminding her of the riverboat she had taken to get to academy testing. She had forgotten boats felt like that. Except this time, there were wooden chairs nailed to the deck, so she wouldn't have to stand the whole time. Wendy waved at her so they could sit together, but Claye took the seat just before Talise got there.

Wendy's cheeks turned pink as she bit her bottom lip. "I forgot I told Claye we could sit together."

Talise gave a simple smile and kept moving toward the back of the boat. Nothing could sour her mood now. Her nose wrinkled when she realized every seat on the boat had been taken.

All except one in the very back, right next to her least favorite person. Aaden didn't bother to acknowledge her existence as the boat began to slip away from the shore.

"It seems wasteful to take a boat when the palace is so close, don't you think?" Talise asked. Maybe she shouldn't dislike him so much, especially now when she was going to win.

He seemed to have the opposite thought. Deliberately ignoring her, he held his palms out in front of him and narrowed his eyes until flames appeared above his hands. The flames quickly formed into trees, and the branches grew out of the burning trunk just like real branches.

It took Talise far too much concentration to not be mesmerized as the flame trees grew in Aaden's palms. Soon, little blossoms popped out from the branches, perfectly mirroring the cherry blossoms that covered each of the trees surrounding the palace. They looked so much better up close.

Forgetting her anger, Talise leaned forward to get a closer look. Exquisite. This surpassed what she had seen before. He must have been practicing in secret like she had.

Without warning, a few branches grew out of control until one licked her face. "Hey," she said, putting a hand to her cheek. "You burned me."

The flame trees vanished, and Aaden turned to her with a sneer. "Then use your ice shaping to cool your skin." He turned away from her without a trace of guilt.

Her jaw flexed as she clenched her teeth together. She had already pushed ice through her fingers and against her cheek, but what if he'd been sitting by anybody else? He should have been more careful. And besides, they weren't supposed to practice on the boat anyway. Mrs. Dew had been telling them for weeks.

Just as Talise prepared to give him the lecture of the century, sharp footsteps brought her gaze to the aisle.

"Aaden," Mrs. Dew said with no small amount of contempt. "Were you shaping on the boat?"

"No," Aaden said, looking straight into Mrs. Dew's eyes.

Talise let out a huff. "You compete for honor, yet you lie to your elder like it's nothing? You don't deserve to win, no matter how detailed your fire sculptures are."

Aaden held his chin high wearing a face that declared *she* was lying, not him.

"Was he shaping, Talise?" Mrs. Dew asked her.

For a moment, her breath stilled. If he admitted to lying, he would be punished. But if he said nothing and she told the truth for him, his punishment would be much more severe. She stayed silent for a few breaths, giving him the chance to come clean. Still, he said nothing.

Clenching her jaw, she shot him with another glare. Today was too important to protect someone like Aaden. She needed to win the competition. Years spent living in the Storm had taught her how much one good mark could change a life. She *needed* to be chosen as Master Shaper.

"He was," Talise said with her eyes to the ground.

"Aaden," Mrs. Dew said through an exasperated breath. "I told you no one was allowed to practice on the boat, and you did it anyway?"

He said nothing as he stared back, never once breaking eye contact.

"Nothing?" Mrs. Dew said. "No explanation?" With a tiny shake of her head, she turned around. Over her shoulder she said, "Then, you are disqualified from the competition today."

"What?" Aaden said in a whisper. When Mrs. Dew kept walking, he stood up and shouted the same question. "What?"

With no response still, Aaden shouted, "You can't do that! I've been training all my life for this."

"Aaden Sato," Mrs. Dew said. "You will keep your thoughts to yourself until I decide what to do you with you." She clapped her hands, then waved toward the boat exit. "Everyone file out in an orderly fashion."

Talise's jaw had dropped, which she only noticed when she realized she'd been holding her breath. Aaden Sato? *Sato*? The name distracted her more than the events that had just transpired. Was he really going to be disqualified? Aaden deserved punishment, but this?

Every ounce of sympathy drained out of her when Aaden gripped her by the shoulder. "You," he said. He didn't speak another word, but he didn't have to. Another pair of flames burned out of him, this time not from his hands, but around his irises. As his eyes burned, they said one thing as they glared at her.

Revenge.

The fire in his eyes was meant to frighten her, but nothing terrified her more than his name. She gulped and jumped from her seat, eager to put as much distance between them as possible. They exited the boat, but not even the sight of Ridgerock Palace was enough to distract her.

The name Sato had been revered in the Crown for years. Aaden's family was more respected than almost anyone. Every member of his family had a silver crescent moon on their ID cards.

All except one.

Now Talise could only wonder, was Aaden honorable like his grandfather? A shiver crawled up her spine. Or would he be more like his father?

WIND CROWN

CHAPTER SIXTEEN

LIFE WAS NEVER AS SIMPLE as a game.

Emperor Flarius dropped his waterfall tablet onto the marble game board. Six of his tablets now sat on the one tile, all in enemy territory.

Sitting across from him, Commander Blaise Sato raised an eyebrow. After years of playing Forces of Kamdaria, Blaise was wise enough to refrain from commenting. Emperor Flarius didn't expect anything less from his advisor.

He took note of how tight he clenched his jaw, relaxing slightly in effort to keep his own face free of emotion.

Blaise would be suspicious of the move, but then, his job required him to be suspicious. Even still, Flarius hoped he would take the bait. When Blaise moved a tornado tablet to the edge of the game board, it became clear that he would *not* take the bait. Not yet at least.

Flarius held his disappointment inside as he moved an insignificant blank tablet to an empty tile.

Blaise eyed the board with the same calculation he gave to all his problems. Too much. Always too much analysis and never enough action. This was why Flarius had chosen him to be an imperial advisor. He was a balance to the emperor's methods.

"Your mind is weighing heavy on you today," Flarius said with a nudge. Perhaps he could win the game by getting into his commander's head.

A twitch appeared at the edge of Blaise's mouth, but Flarius suspected his words had not been the cause. The commander cleared his throat in that almost silent way he always did before bringing up a difficult subject. Blaise had been his principal imperial advisor for nearly twenty years now. His quirks were as familiar as the weight of the crown sitting on the emperor's head.

Blaise moved a blank tablet to the left side of the board. Now he had a line of them standing like a flank against the emperor's tablets. "The competition is tomorrow," he said without elaboration.

Of course, Emperor Flarius didn't need any elaboration. He knew exactly what Blaise was thinking. In truth, he had known even before he asked. "You are thinking of your grandson, Aaden."

Blaise idly scratched the tablecloth with increasing speed as the seconds wore on. His eyes kept jumping from the game to his fingernail as he seemed to form words in his mind. He stayed silent through the emperor's next move and through his own next move as well.

At last he spoke. "General Gale said there were two shapers who deserved to win on pre-competition day. Both had extraordinary skill. He said the judges couldn't choose between the two of them."

"I read his report." The words came out flat as Flarius moved yet another tablet into Blaise's territory. The commander was old enough to be Flarius' father. That was another reason Flarius had chosen him to be his advisor. The man had wisdom only an elder could provide.

That wisdom had been a great strength to Flarius throughout his years as emperor. Blaise was calm, even-tempered, and wise. He truly helped Flarius be the best emperor he could be.

Of course, Blaise's steady service made it difficult to deny him when he made a request. And Flarius knew a request was coming. He weighed the options carefully, looked at it from every angle. Could such a request ever be granted?

Blaise eyed the game. Even as he squirmed and delivered soft, unspoken appeals, he moved his pieces skillfully. Quite unexpectedly, he jumped a fire tablet over three of the emperor's blank tablets, claiming them for his own.

Flarius blinked at the board. It wasn't often that he was taken by surprise.

Seeming to take advantage of his distraction, Commander Blaise cleared his throat. "I thought perhaps…" He cleared his throat a second time. "I thought maybe two Master Shapers could be chosen this year." He stared intently at the game board and then hastily added, "Considering the circumstances."

Flarius leaned back and stroked the short beard covering his chin. Blaise sat taller in his chair and braved a glance into the emperor's eyes.

"Perhaps," Flarius said. He paused so his next words would have the proper weight. "But both Master Shapers would need to have unquestionable honor."

As the emperor moved another blank tablet to the middle, Blaise spoke again with a defensive edge to his voice. "Aaden hasn't seen his father in eleven years. My wife and I raised him more than his parents ever did. When Aaden leaves the academy on pass, he visits us, not his father."

Flarius raised an eyebrow. "And yet, you raised your son—Aaden's father—as well, did you not? I think we can both agree his honor was highly questionable."

Blaise's eyes dropped until he stared into his lap. A line of sweat seemed to spontaneously appear along his hair line. "Of course,

Your Highness," he said in a low voice. "Please forgive me, Your Highness."

It pained Flarius to bring up the past like that, and not just because it pained his advisor. Any reminders of the heinous mistake Blaise's son made were generally not permitted at Ridgerock Palace. Flarius preferred to forget but never forgive.

Blaise gulped as he made his next move. A drop of sweat slid down his cheek, dropping off his goatee like a raindrop. Flarius could sense that his advisor was frightened. Afraid that he had asked too much. Afraid for his job.

Flarius let out a sigh. He didn't wish to be vindictive. Not anymore. All he wanted now was peace. He moved his fire tablet directly in front of Blaise's fire tablet, prompting the final fight.

Blaise seemed to shrug off his fear for a brief moment, considering the board. Now he could see why Flarius had sacrificed so many of his tablets to Blaise's territory. More than half of the area held stacks of the emperor's tablets. Blaise couldn't move a single piece without it being taken by one of Flarius' tablets.

Flarius had won.

Commander Blaise dipped his head in a bow, graciously accepting his defeat in the game. He held his breath, apparently anxious to hear the emperor's next words.

"I still might choose two Master Shapers," Flarius said.

Blaise had enough self-control to mask most of his surprise, but Flarius caught a hint of it. "As you said, the circumstances are such that choosing two Master Shapers makes sense."

Blaise's head bobbed up and down in an eager nod.

Flarius looked back at the board, still surprised that his technique had been so effective against his ever-analytical advisor.

Narrowing his eyes, the emperor said, "I will have to devise a scheme to test the honor of your grandson. If he is trustworthy, his skills could be very valuable to us."

Chapter Seventeen

TALISE STOOD AT THE BACK of the line as she and her classmates trailed through the palace halls. Aaden had long since rushed past to her to get to Mrs. Dew. Apparently, he thought he still had a chance at changing Mrs. Dew's mind about disqualifying him from the competition.

It didn't seem likely to Talise. When she thought back on the interaction in the boat, something strange stood out to her. Something about the way Mrs. Dew delivered the news to Aaden. It was almost as if she had been searching for a reason to disqualify him even before she knew he was shaping on the boat.

This sent a wave of guilt through Talise. Had Mrs. Dew done it for her? To ensure Talise's success by removing her only competition? She couldn't believe the honorable Mrs. Dew would do something so dastardly. But no matter how Talise tried to extinguish the impossible reasoning, she kept coming back to the same idea.

Mrs. Dew must have disqualified Aaden just so Talise could win.

The dark wooden columns leading to the throne room seemed overbearing as Talise slipped past them. Not even the intricate paintings on rice paper could distract her. Soon, they were in the throne room. The students were directed to sit cross-legged against one wall. Aaden was still arguing with Mrs. Dew when the demonstrations began. She maintained that he wouldn't be able to participate.

Guilt crawled through Talise's shoulders, settling into a knot at the base of her neck. It wasn't her fault Aaden broke the rules. She *did* accuse him of it, but she accused fairly. He deserved to be punished. It was his own fault for breaking the rules.

No matter how she tried to justify it, she was still partially responsible for the punishment he now bore.

Tearing her thoughts from Aaden, Talise turned to face the emperor. Another student, Ari, dropped a bundle of scarves and ribbons on the ground in front of the throne. With a timid smile, Ari used his wind shaping to lift the scarves in swirling dances around him. It wasn't the most original demonstration for a wind shaper, but the effect was nice.

After Ari, a few more students did their demonstrations. Wendy's was perfect. She released an arrow through a window, then shaped air behind it to increase its distance. The emperor's eyebrows nearly touched his hairline when he saw how far her arrow flew.

The emperor insisted Wendy go to the library with General Gale immediately so they could discuss shape training while the other students finished their demonstrations. Talise was glad for her friend, but she suddenly felt more alone than ever in the line of students.

Another student, Terra, plodded over to her spot in front of the emperor when it was her turn. One of the imperial guards handed her a small box of dirt. She arranged several clay bowls around the box before she began separating the different minerals from the soil. Muscovite in one bowl, olivine in another, feldspar in a third. While this skill was certainly practical, the demonstration wasn't as flashy as the others had been.

Terra finished with a glum expression, apparently realizing too late that she had missed out on the flash. When her bowls were cleared away, she came to join Talise at the end of the line.

"That was great," Talise whispered to her fellow student.

Terra's lips folded into a frown. "Don't patronize me. I know it looked stupid."

With a grin, Talise said, "At least it's over."

"True, and I was never going to win anyway. I can't wait to see your demonstration. It's sure to win."

Talise rubbed a hand up and down her arm as the first bite of anxiety stung her.

"Oh, don't make that face. Even the emperor can't shape ice. I know he can manipulate all the elements, and he's amazing at shaping fire, but ice is beyond even his abilities. He's sure to be impressed."

Talise bit her lip as she watched another student shaping a huge puddle of water into a fountain and then into a dragon. Shaping ice *would* be impressive. That was the entire reason she chose ice in the first place. But it came with risks. If she didn't get the temperature in her body just right, she could get hypothermia or frostbite. And if she warmed her body too much, even for a split second, her ice crown would fall apart.

Two fire shapers went next, one after the other. The first shaped a circular fire that cooked two fish to perfection. The second student did fire sculptures shaped like the palace, but hers lacked the detail and control Aaden's sculptures always showed.

Talise glanced back at him feeling another surge of sympathy. He glared at the fire sculptures as if they were personally responsible for destroying his entire family and everything he had ever loved.

Finally, it was her turn. Talise stood tall, remembering that her presentation of self was just as important as her presentation of shaping. She wore a light smile that spoke of confidence but not arrogance.

In front of the throne, she bowed deeply to the emperor until her nose brushed the ground. When she stood, he wore an expression that was difficult to decipher. His lips twitched at the corner of his mouth, almost as if they wanted to smile. But maybe only because he was laughing at her on the inside. His brows were knit close together, giving his eyes a hardened stare.

He looked... disappointed? But how could he be disappointed when she hadn't even started yet?

A thrum of fear rippled through her muscles, but she did her best to ignore it. A guard brought her a bowl of water. Before he even placed the bowl on the ground, she had the water in the air.

Her heart was beating faster than usual, which was usually an indication that her body temperature was off. In this case, it was all thanks to nerves. She breathed in deeply as she spun the water into a thin circle.

If she couldn't rely on her heart to tell if her internal temperature was right, then this would be even more difficult than normal. A quick smile and an even faster spin of the water made it seem like she had everything under control. Or, she hoped it looked that way, at least.

When she stiffened her fingers and brought ice through them, she breathed a fire through the veins in her arm, careful to keep it far from her wrist.

Stretching her fingers through the air to form the crown, she made sure the tines growing up from the circle of water weren't just any tines. With narrowed eyes, she shaped the crown to look exactly like the crown now sitting atop Emperor Flarius' head. Tines of equal height all the way around. Symmetrical.

Three quarters of the way through its creation, the emperor recognized the crown. The crease between his eyebrows disappeared as his eyes widened. Talise wore another smile, but this one was genuine.

She felt a slice of cold through her forearm but tempered it with fire almost as quickly. When the ice crown was finished, she levitated it higher. It wouldn't land on her head as she had practiced back at the academy. She had to place it on the emperor's head so he could feel that it was truly ice.

As the crown flew toward the emperor, a smile curved onto his mouth.

She had impressed him. The crown was inches from his head now. Close enough that he could feel how cold it was. She'd leave it on his head for three seconds before bringing it back to the bowl.

Just as she lowered her creation onto his jet-black hair, the crown melted. With her fingers working to levitate ice, the change to water caused her to lose control. Just for a split second, but it was enough. Too much.

Water splashed all over the emperor, soaking his hair and shoulders. The crease reappeared between his eyebrows, even deeper than before.

Everyone in the room gasped. Though they were whispers, she still heard the comments from onlookers.

"How embarrassing."

"She'll never be chosen now."

"What a shame. She was so much better than the others."

Talise tightened her hand into a fist. *What happened?* She had control. Everything was going perfectly. She ran her thumb across the tips of her fingers. Just as she suspected, they were as cold as they should have been. Colder even. She hadn't done anything that would make the crown melt.

But if it wasn't her…

While the guards hurried to supply the emperor with unnecessary towels, Talise scanned the students along the wall until she found who she was looking for. Aaden held his palms out in front of him so they were directly facing the emperor. Even more incriminating, he wore a smirk and stared back at her with fire in his eyes.

He had done this. He sabotaged her demonstration by sending a wave of heat that must have melted her ice. She wanted to burn him and freeze him all at once, but a tiny part of her couldn't help be impressed by his skill. He must have sent the world's smallest and most direct heat wave in order to do what he did.

Still, no matter how skillful, what he did was wrong. She wasn't about to let him get away with it.

Just as Talise opened her mouth to accuse him, Mrs. Dew appeared in front of her, giving a short bow to the emperor. "Your Imperial Highness," she said. "I have one more student who is very skilled, but he was disqualified from participation because of an incident on the way here."

"Who?" Emperor Flarius asked. Even after shaping the water out of his hair, he looked regal and unperturbed.

Mrs. Dew pointed out Aaden who had somehow arranged his face to look submissive and innocent. It was a stupid act, but annoyingly convincing.

Talise wanted to scream.

The emperor snapped his fingers at one of the nearby guards. He pointed at Aaden and then at her. "Take these two to the antechamber while I make my decision. Everyone else will wait in the library with General Gale."

Talise barely had time to register the hand around her elbow before it began yanking her away. "Wait," Talise called out in desperation. It was bold to defy the emperor's orders, but she was desperate. "I can't leave yet. I have something to…"

Her voice trailed off as her eyes met with the emperor's. He didn't shape fire over his eyes like Aaden had on the boat, but rage burned through his facial features with even greater passion. In a steady voice, he said, "You will leave my presence without another word."

She gulped as the arm at her elbow yanked her again. This time, she let herself be pulled away.

♛

CHAPTER EIGHTEEN

THE GUARD PULLED TALISE THROUGH a side door. They entered a small corridor that was empty but for a few servants. The corridor seemed to go on forever and was filled with unmarked doors.

One door, halfway down the corridor was painted fire orange with a silver moon painted on it. The imperial crest. With four heavily armed guards standing in front of the door, Talise knew the door was important. It must have led to the emperor's personal quarters.

She wished Wendy wasn't in the library. Even one friendly face would have been nice to see right now. The guard shoving her down the corridor didn't seem eager to be gentle.

In front of her, Aaden glared at the guard who pushed him down the corridor.

A few moments after passing the orange door, the guard pushed Talise into a small room. The walls and floor were made of stone. The door she had just come through was made of heavy wood, but there was another door on the other side of the room.

The other door was made of metal. Several locks held it in place. Metal bars went across a small window at the top of the door. She didn't have to guess where that door led. The bars made it obvious. It led to the dungeons.

"Wait," Talise said, before the guard could leave. "I didn't melt the crown. It wasn't my fault. You have to tell the emperor."

The guard brushed her hand away while a look of disgust fell over his face. "You dare address your elder with such fire in your tone?"

She shrank away from him, biting her bottom lip.

He continued. "What makes you think you can disrespect me like that? Aren't you from the Storm? You're nothing more than filth."

The wooden door slammed shut as he left the antechamber. A moment later, the lock inside it clicked shut. "Please," she said, slamming a fist against the thick wood. "Somebody has to listen."

"Disrespecting your elders now, are you?" Aaden said. He leaned against the stone wall with one shoulder, still wearing his ridiculous smirk. "Welcome to the dark side."

"How could you?" she said, grabbing his shoulders and slamming them against the wall. "Do you have any idea what you've done?"

He used one finger to push her away. "What *I* did?" he asked, raising an eyebrow. "What about what *you* did?"

She growled at him in response.

Folding his arms over his chest, he leaned toward her until his face came dangerously close to hers. "I deserved a chance to win just as much as you did. I needed this." Without warning, he turned away from her and punched the wall so hard, the stone seemed to crack on the inside. "I really needed this."

"So did I," she said. But it seemed weak compared to his argument. His whole body was alive with passion. It came out as rage, but there was something deeper to it she could just barely discern. His whole body rocked as if he had just lost the only thing that had ever really mattered.

They stared at each other for a few seconds as understanding seemed to ignite between them. Both of them had lives so much deeper than the other person knew. They'd gone to the academy together for a few months, but they'd never really known each other in the least. In this one moment, their souls seemed to communicate to each other how important this competition was.

"Why?" Talise asked. Maybe it was because he was so exhausted, but he opened his mouth on her command.

"My father made a huge mistake when I was only five years old. I have a black X on my ID card because of him. After today, I'll be sent to the Storm. Becoming Master Shaper meant my children, grandchildren, and great-grandchildren would get silver crescent moons on their ID cards. Silver moons. For three generations! But now?" He shook his head. "Now my future children will have a fate even worse than me. They'll have to be raised in the Storm all because of my father's mistake."

His head hung. He stared at the ground while the muscles in his face slackened. She'd never seen him look so… defeated.

Of course, she knew his story before he admitted to it. His father's mistake would live in infamy for generations. But she had the decency to let him believe she was ignorant of the specifics.

"I'm sorry I said I hate you."

His eyes flicked up to hers while confusion painted his features.

She shifted her eyes downward and began picking at a loose thread in her school uniform. "You helped me find out the funeral was…" Her throat swelled with emotion as she pictured Marmie's gravestone, completely bare. Swallowing hard wasn't enough to erase the image, but it did make it easier to speak. "You helped me find out the funeral was today, and then I said I hate you when it wasn't even your fault. I'm sorry."

A thick silence hung in the air long enough to twist her nerves. When she looked up, Aaden stared at her with his lips parted and his eyes boring into her. Confusion still painted his features but not like before. He seemed to understand her words perfectly, but what he didn't understand was *how* she could have said them. Had he never heard an apology before?

When the intensity of his gaze didn't relax, she turned her attention back to the loose thread. "I was going to run away from the academy after I found out, but I realized how much I'd be giving up." When she lifted her eyes, she matched his gaze with something even more intense. "I can't go back to where I used to live. I *can't*."

He stared at her for a few seconds but then finally looked away, the spell broken. "Are you really from the Storm? I know the guard said that, but I thought people in the Storm couldn't shape."

She rubbed her hand over her arm, faster and faster, as if that would make the words seem less horrifying. "They have the biological ability to shape all four elements, just like anyone. But you're right. Most of them can't do it."

He leaned closer to her, his face softening with each of her words. "Is it really as bad as they say it is?" he whispered.

"Worse."

He gulped, and the last inkling of bravado slipped away. His usual arrogance was replaced by an expression of such genuine concern, it almost made her feel guilty.

Turning away from him, she said, "Most people in the Storm are malnourished. It makes their bodies weak and incapable of shaping. Not to mention they'd have no time to perfect the skills even if they had them. They're too busy worrying about survival."

"Then how did you get to the academy? How are you so good at shaping?"

"It's a long story," she said with a sigh.

He stood still, waiting for more of an answer. When she didn't give one, he said, "Just tell me. We could be here all day; it doesn't matter if it takes a long time."

Raising one eyebrow, she asked, "Are you going to tell me the huge mistake your father made?"

He laughed. "Uh, no."

"Then don't expect to hear my story either."

"Fair enough," he said with a nod.

It wasn't fair at all though. She knew everything about him, and he knew almost nothing about her. That didn't make her any more willing to share.

He glanced at her, but then he quickly looked away. Then he did it again a second time while the tips of his ears turned red. "I'm sorry about your crown," he said. Then he reached out to her and brushed his thumb over her forearm.

Her body jolted as she instinctively pulled away. "Your skin is hot."

"Yeah." He ran his fingers through his hair with a lopsided smile. "Fire does that." His spine straightened as he looked her in the eye. "It didn't burn you, did it?"

She shook her head quickly from side to side, since she had apparently lost the ability to form words. Her skin bristled where he had touched her. On the inside, sparks went through her unlike any kind of fire she had felt before. This flame had nothing to do with elements and everything to do with touch. *His* touch. She tried to shake the thought away as he tucked his hands into his pockets.

"Aaden."

His eyes lifted at the sound of her voice. A trance seemed to come over him as he stared back at her. He seemed less interested in her eyes and more interested in her lips where his name had escaped.

"Tell them what you did," she said. "Tell them you melted my crown, and then I'll be able to leave the Storm and live at the palace."

The trance lifted as Aaden took a step back. "No," he said. He turned away from her and said it more forcefully. "No, I'm sorry, but I can't do that. I have to defend myself to the emperor. If I defend you, you'll become Master Shaper, and I'll be sent to the Storm. I know it's bad for you, but if I help you, I'll resign myself and my future family to that same fate. I can't do that. I won't. I have to fight for myself."

Her body steeled as another fire surged through her, but this one felt more like rage. She clenched both her hands into fists and immediately started pacing the floor. Of course he wouldn't help. *Of course* he wouldn't. She'd been stupid to think he ever would.

Now they would have to wait here until the emperor decided to deal with them. She just hoped when he did get there, he would be willing to listen. The longer she thought about that, the more ridiculous it seemed. Aaden wouldn't change and neither would the emperor.

In fact, maybe he didn't intend to meet with them at all. Maybe he just planned to send one of his guards to deal with them.

She paced the floor until her feet ached. There had to be a way out of this. The emperor needed good shapers. That was the whole reason for the competition in the first place. And she and Aaden were better shapers than any of the other students in their class.

All they really needed was another chance to prove themselves. Just one little chance to show the emperor what they were capable of. But if the emperor never saw them again, they'd never have that chance.

A spark of an idea took hold inside her. She bit her lip as the idea grew. It would require skilled shaping with no mistakes. That she could handle. But it also required one other thing she really wished she could eliminate. No matter how she played through the scenarios in her head, she still needed the one thing she didn't want to use. Aaden.

But it was just once. Once she could handle.

Letting out a huff, she resigned herself to the inevitable. Crossing her arms over her chest, she said, "I have an idea, but in order to do it, we have to work together."

♕

Chapter Nineteen

Talise tried to hold her head high as Aaden looked her over from head to toe. His nose seemed to be caught mid-wrinkle, as if he was trying to decide whether or not to trust her.

She rolled her eyes. "We don't have time for this. Are you in or not?"

"What's your plan?" he asked, still reluctant to commit.

He agreed to everything once he heard the plan, but he made sure to scowl as they worked. "Are you sure this is a good idea?" he asked. "They locked us in here. Don't you think we'll get in trouble for breaking out?"

"Seriously?" she said as she used her shaping to pull water from the air. She added it to the puddle levitating above her palm. "You care about breaking the rules now? If you were so worried about rules, you shouldn't have practiced shaping on the boat ride here."

His jaw flexed as he gave her a sideways glance. "No need to rub that in." He narrowed his eyes at the air as he also pulled water from it. Since fire was his primary element, he had a harder time with the process than Talise.

It took several more minutes, but eventually they had a big enough water puddle. When Talise nodded, Aaden got on his knees in front of the door and lit a fire above his palms. It took some time, but soon he had lit the bottom of the wooden door on fire.

She stood over him carefully, strategically dousing the wood with water so the smoke wouldn't get out of control. When the smoke was eliminated, Aaden would re-ignite the door.

At first, the wood turned to blackened-but-perfectly-strong wood. After more fire and more water, it began to weaken. Eventually, some of it turned to ash. It turned out, the puddle of water they'd shaped from the air wasn't big enough and they both had to stop and pull more water from the air before they could proceed.

Aaden continued lighting the door on fire, and finally, *finally*, they had an opening big enough for them to crawl through. He went first and helped her to her feet after she had gone through.

Her skin prickled with heat where his hand had touched her. She wished she could remove the feeling and all memory of it from her body. But another part of her wished it would never go away.

She clenched her jaw at that thought. Aaden was a competitor and nothing more. He proved that when he melted her crown.

As they drew closer to the guarded door of the emperor's quarters, Talise began pulling more water from the air. She needed a big enough puddle that would make a loud sound when she turned it to ice and smashed it against the stone wall. The distraction had to be big enough so all four guards would come running to investigate.

It seemed strange that shaping ice felt so natural now, when she had only been doing it for a mere two days. But each time she did it, it got a little easier.

While she worked, Aaden stared at the fist sized piece of wood he had taken from the door. He blew embers into the wood but kept them low, so it didn't smoke too much.

Finally, Talise nodded to Aaden and he blew on the wood until it glowed from the embers inside. On cue, they threw their objects down the corridor, far from where they stood. Talise slammed the ball of ice against the wall as hard as she could. Aaden threw a fireball at the piece of wood while it flew in order to increase the smoke level.

Just as they intended, the ice smashed against the wall at exactly the moment the smoke started billowing. The effect made it sound and smell like an explosive rather than a piece of ice and a piece of wood.

They both hugged the walls as the four guards came crashing down the corridor toward the sound. The guards didn't notice Talise and Aaden, which gave them the chance to sneak up to the fire orange door without any interference.

"Wait," Aaden whispered as they reached the door. "Are we just going to walk in?"

Talise's patience had ended long before this moment. She glared at him. "It's a little late to get cold feet."

Aaden tapped his teeth together, wearing fear in his eyes. "Yeah, but we're just going to waltz into the emperor's bedroom and expect him to listen to us?"

"It doesn't lead to his bedroom; it leads to his quarters. Offices."

"How do you know that?"

Talise grabbed the door handle. "Are you coming or not?"

He nodded and didn't say another word as she pushed open the door.

Talise and Aaden pushed through the fire orange door and entered a sitting room with a desk and a few cushy chairs. To the right of the chairs, a long hallway led to several more doors.

"Don't you think it's a little weird the door wasn't locked?" Aaden asked as he shut the door behind him.

Considering his question, she locked the door and then nodded. "If we lock it, they won't know we got in."

Aaden rolled his shoulders back and closed his eyes. He moved his head side to side to stretch his neck. All his fear seemed to have been forgotten as he stretched and moved. After a moment, he opened his eyes and cracked his knuckles. "We should practice. How long do you think we have before the emperor gets here?"

She shrugged. "I have no idea, but you're right. We do need to practice. We have to make this bigger and better than anything the emperor has ever seen, or he'll never listen to us."

Without a word, they both raised their hands and started shaping. As they had previously decided, they both grew trees out of their palms with little cherry blossoms growing out of the branches. Aaden's trees were fire and Talise's were ice.

When they had both grown their trees, they moved their palms closer together and let the trees sit directly beside each other. The flames licked at the ice, forcing Talise to push even more cold through her fingers than usual. She had to compensate it with a thick fire inside her veins.

With a deep breath, they began the next stage. This would be the most difficult shaping either of them had ever attempted. Aaden let a one flame branch move through the ice tree until it seemed that the flame was coming off the ice trunk, not the fire trunk.

Then, Talise moved one ice branch, careful to keep the ice tree intact while also levitating the one ice branch until it looked like it was coming out of the flame trunk. When she had moved it into position, both she and Aaden let out a breath of relief. But this was just the beginning.

Beads of sweat lined Talise's brow as she added more heat to compensate for the added freezing temperature in her hands. She and Aaden took turns moving their branches from one tree to the next. Each one became more difficult as her need to compensate for the heat was constantly counteracted by the need to keep her body a reasonable temperature.

When they each only had one branch left to move, she was vaguely aware of a noise coming from nearby. The cause of it remained a mystery since her senses were too focused on shaping.

At last, they had moved all their branches, so the ice trunk had only flame branches growing out of it and the flame trunk wore ice branches.

She and Aaden both heaved a sigh, but their relief was short lived. From the doorway, a familiar voice said, "How did you manage—"

Both Talise and Aaden dropped their hands in alarm. Water splashed around their ankles as they turned to face Emperor Flarius. He *did* seem impressed by their shaping, but more than that he seemed angry. Too angry.

Talise fell to her knees in a bow and Aaden wasn't far behind.

Dropping his head into his palm, the emperor said, "What are you doing here?"

"We had to show you our abilities." Aaden had found his voice much faster than Talise. She was still busy watching that crease between the emperor's eyebrows grow deeper by the second.

"What did you think would happen?" the emperor asked with a frown. "Did you think you'd sneak into my private quarters—the most secure part of the palace—and then I'd suddenly be interested in your shaping?" He snapped his fingers, and two guards appeared at his side.

"You deserve black *X*s for you and your generations to come for what you've done. Maybe a life in the dungeon as well." He squeezed the bridge of his nose and let out a sigh. "One of you has to be punished for this, and one of you has to become my next Master Shaper because the rest of your class was pathetic compared to you two."

Talise gulped and felt the color drain from her face. The emperor eyed them both for a moment, and time seemed to stand still.

Finally, he pointed to Aaden. "Lock him up. And use the fire gloves, so he can't escape again."

That meant Talise had won Master Shaper after all. Except.

Aaden would be punished and thrown in the dungeon. His father's mistake was heinous, and Aaden *did* share that same blood. Maybe he didn't deserve a second chance. But… maybe he did.

A lump hardened in Talise's throat as the guards put him in chains. They dropped orange gloves over his hands while a sense of finality washed over her.

She stared, but swallow after swallow did nothing to help. He had to fight for himself, and she had to fight for herself. That's what they had decided. They would only work together to show the emperor their abilities, but whatever happened, they didn't owe the other person anything.

But she never imagined this.

As the guards forced Aaden to his feet, a strangled cry left her lips. "No. Please, Your Highness. Breaking out of the room was my idea. Aaden didn't want to do it, but I convinced him." With a sniff, she forced the final words out of her mouth. "If you're going to punish somebody, punish me. Not him."

She glanced up to see the emperor staring at her with a contemplative look. But it was nothing to the look Aaden wore. His jaw had dropped. He stared at her like he had never really seen her before.

"Fine," Emperor Flarius said, his voice steady. "Then you will be punished and sent to the dungeon instead. Aaden will be my newest Master Shaper."

The emperor snapped his fingers, and the guards moved so fast, she barely had time to blink before shackles were clapped over her wrists. They fitted blue gloves over her hands and started pushing her through the door before three seconds had passed.

"Wait," Aaden said, blinking furiously. The moment the guards removed his shackles, he ran both hands through his hair. The blinking never stopped as he looked side to side. His words failed him.

The emperor stood patiently for only a moment. Then, he snapped at his guards, and they started pulling Talise out the door.

"No, stop!" Aaden shouted. "I…" He gulped and pulled his hands into fists. "I melted her crown. In the throne room, it was my fault you got wet. I wanted revenge because I got disqualified from the competition. But this was my fault. All of it."

"I see," the emperor said.

The thumping inside Talise's chest was nothing to the way her muscles had frozen. The dungeon. The emperor had planned to throw her into the dungeon.

He stared at the pair of them while the hardness in his face drifted away. "It seems you both possess honor, which is the greatest trait of all. Since you are also two of the greatest shapers I've even seen, I think no one will complain if I choose two Master Shapers this year."

Talise narrowed her eyes as the guards removed the shackles from her wrists. Her brain worked double speed, trying to make sense of everything that had just happened. "This was a test?" she asked. "You threatened to send one of us to the dungeon as a test?"

"Are you questioning my methods?" the emperor asked with one eyebrow raised.

"Of course not, highness." A part of her wondered if this test had been designed more for Aaden than for her. Perhaps Mrs. Dew had been in on it too.

Emperor Flarius waved to one of his guards. "Take them back to the antechamber, but this time leave the door unlocked." He looked at Talise and Aaden now. "You will have to help fix the door, but that should be punishment enough. Someone will be by soon to bring you back to the throne room when I make the announcement."

With a snap of his fingers, the guards led them out of the room before they could say another word. Once they were back in the antechamber, Talise paced around the room trying to forget the way Aaden had looked at her when she offered to be punished in his place.

The emperor thought Aaden had honor. Did that mean she could trust him too? Her feet shuffled as she traveled from wall to wall. "I can't believe this. I never expected us both to become Master Shapers. Now—"

She stopped mid-step when Aaden suddenly appeared in front of her. His eyes were soft and his breath warm. "Talise," he said, reaching out until his fingers wrapped over her hand.

Everything inside her seemed to freeze all at once, but in a delightfully tingled way.

Aaden gulped before he spoke again. He kept his eyes away from her face, staring at their hands instead. "Thank you for…"

He squeezed her hand, and the heat seeped through her skin so fast, she worried it would burn her insides. She had never appreciated heat more.

"I'll never forget what you did for me today," he said. Finally, he looked into her eyes, and a thousand sparks seemed to ignite within her. She had a feeling neither of them would forget. Not ever.

Chapter Twenty

A PALACE GUARD'S SILK TUNIC made a pleasant swishing sound as she led Talise and Aaden to the throne room. The rest of their academy class was gone, or so they'd been told. Talise never even got to say goodbye to Wendy.

But maybe she'd see Wendy again soon anyway. Wendy had impressed the emperor with her demonstration. She wasn't chosen as Master Shaper, but the emperor employed many shapers in his palace. Unless something went terribly wrong, hopefully Wendy would be working at the palace soon.

As she passed through the doorway into the throne room, the rice paper paintings seemed more vivid than they had before. Gorgeous landscapes adorned the paper, making the room feel more alive.

Dusty blue mountains were tipped with carefully painted black lines. Green trees and their thin brown trunks littered the base of the mountains. A tiny likeness of Ridgerock Palace sat in a deep corner of the farthest mountain. The palace's red clay tiles stood out beautifully against the blues and greens.

Breathtaking.

Her eyes couldn't be forced from the paintings until the emperor began speaking from his throne. "Welcome," he said, "to my two newest Master Shapers."

He addressed her and Aaden, yet he didn't seem to be speaking to them at all. After a quick glance around the room, she realized they were far from alone.

The edges of the room were filled with a variety of people. She recognized a few of the emperor's advisors, including Commander Blaise Sato, Aaden's grandfather. But apparently the emperor had invited his entire court to this announcement as well.

Women with yards of silk and red-painted lips dotted the crowd. Men in yellow guard uniforms stood stiff with hands in fists at their side. Children with mischievous eyes kept poking each other and giggling. Even men and women wearing the brown tunics that marked them as servants filled the room.

People of all ages and shapes and sizes stood around the throne room. They seemed intent on listening to the emperor, but not because of interest. Instead, they seemed bound by honor to hear each of his words with perfect clarity.

"I have done something highly irregular this year as many of you can see," he continued. "I have chosen two Master Shapers instead of one."

Talise expected a reaction from the crowd but noticed none. Maybe the people were afraid of looking as though they questioned the emperor's judgment.

But as she looked deeper into the eyes of the crowd, she sensed another emotion that may have stayed their reactions. They all seemed to be fighting a frown. The edges of their eyes drooped downward.

Was it sadness? Grief?

It looked the way she still felt about Marmie, except that didn't make any sense. Why would they be sad? Not just a few people, but everyone. Including the servants.

Maybe it wasn't grief. What did she know? These people were strangers to her. Maybe this was how they always looked.

"The reason I chose two Master Shapers is simple. Their shaping far surpasses anything I've seen in years. Show them. Do the trees of ice and fire."

The command came so suddenly, Talise had no time to react. Her hands shot out in front of her as she tried to suck in a burst of fear. If she was going to be a Master Shaper, she'd have to get used to performing in front of others.

Aaden's hands came close to hers and soon they were busy moving branches one by one from their own tree to the other's.

"That will do," the emperor said before they were halfway through. A flash of irritation appeared in his eye, and he seemed to look right at Talise when it appeared.

She wanted to stuff her hands into her pockets and step into the shadows of the room. It wasn't her fault it took so long to move ice branches.

Emperor Flarius sat straighter on his throne. His golden crown glinted in the light of the room. "However, their titles as Master Shapers are only probationary. Since it is irregular to have two Master Shapers in one year, I have decided to put these two students through a set of trials that are meant to test their skill and honor. They will not be competing against each other in these trials. They will earn points and each of them can win or lose based on their points. I sincerely hope to have two official Master Shapers after the trials, but only time will tell."

A few murmurs drifted through the air as the crowd nodded and showed the first hint of interest. It didn't seem so exciting to Talise. She had already spent ten years training for this moment. She didn't need any more tests.

Without warning, the emperor snapped his fingers. "You are all dismissed."

A collective bow went through the room, and then the crowd began to disappear faster than should have been possible. Their heads stayed bent as they left.

"You two," the emperor said pointing to Talise and Aaden. "Come closer."

Talise's body reacted without thought. She stepped toward Emperor Flarius and bowed once her feet were settled. Aaden did the same, and he looked remarkably subdued while doing it.

"Are you both familiar with the terrorist group that calls themselves Kessoku?" the emperor asked.

Talise's throat went dry and a slice of horror cut through her. She never expected the emperor to bring up *them*. Of all things.

She tried to nod, but her spine shivered at the same time and it turned out looking more like a jerk of the head. *Pull yourself together*, she thought.

When she tried to straighten herself, she noticed Aaden's face had lost its color. His throat bulged as he swallowed. In the quietest voice she'd ever heard him utter, Aaden said, "Yes, Your Highness. Thirteen years ago, they murdered the entire royal family including your oldest son and your first and only grandchild. Everyone except you."

"Yes." Emperor Flarius shifted further back in his chair. Perhaps he wasn't expecting such a detailed reminder. His voice seemed lower when he spoke again. "During your trials, you will train as though Kessoku is the enemy you are fighting. It will prepare you for future incidents."

Aaden lowered his eyebrows, leaning forward the slightest bit. "But I thought Kessoku was gone. I thought they were all executed thirteen years ago."

A wrinkle appeared at the edge of the emperor's nose for the smallest moment. His spine curled forward as if a great weight had suddenly been dropped on his shoulders. The regal attitude he always exuded melted away. He looked to the side. "A few of them got away."

The emperor's spine suddenly straightened, and he held his chin a litter higher. "They have spent the last thirteen years gathering new members and attempting to assassinate me. But I assure you, their attempts are pathetic. They're little more than a nuisance. However, they are a nuisance we would like to eradicate in the near future."

"When do we meet the other Master Shapers?" Talise asked.

A twitch appeared at the emperor's eye as he gave the smallest glance to Talise. Apparently, she could say nothing without irritating him.

"You will meet them after you've passed the trials."

She cocked her head to the side. "Aren't they going to help us train?"

"They are not at the palace at the moment. They are busy on an assignment in the Gate."

"All of them?"

It seemed like an innocent enough question, but the emperor only responded with a look of frustration. "No more questions. Your first trial is tomorrow morning. It would be most useful for you to study theory and strategy. You may use the library and you may study together if you like. The servants will show you to your living quarters and any other rooms you require. If you need anything, just ask."

He dismissed them both with a wave of his hand. Aaden didn't wait for more instructions. He headed straight for the nearest exit.

Talise stood still as she watched him go. When she was sure he couldn't hear, she took a few steps closer to the emperor. He didn't comment on her tenacity.

With the greatest reverence she could manage, she dipped her head in a bow. "Your Highness," she said.

He stared back without a word; his face careful to not betray any emotion.

She bit her lip, ever feeling the child in his presence. "Do you know who he is, highness? Aaden?"

The emperor pursed his lips. "You mean do I know his last name?"

Her lip burned as she clenched it between her teeth. "I thought it was a good decision at first. I thought he deserved to win because of his skill. But then…" She wrapped a hand around her elbow and pulled it tight against her body. "He only showed honor when you forced it from him. Before that, he sabotaged my demonstration. I don't know if he should be trusted."

"You dare question my judgment?" His voice was so soft, she had to lean forward to hear it. They both had taken to whispering, eager to keep their conversation from the inquisitive ears of nearby servants. Though the emperor's words were almost silent, the way he sneered down at her made her stomach squirm.

Talise gulped. "You know what his father did."

The emperor waved his hand through the air, his voice slightly louder than before. "His father got carried away trying to impress strangers and unwittingly gave away palace secrets."

"Secrets that led to the death of your family."

The emperor clenched his fingers around his knee. "I don't need a reminder."

She was walking on very thin ice now. At any moment, the emperor could revoke her probationary title as Master Shaper and send her to the dungeons. He certainly seemed angry enough to do it.

Fighting her fear, she said, "Aaden's ID card bears a black X. How can you trust him so easily?"

The emperor glanced to the side before he leaned closer toward her. When he spoke again, his voice was softer than a whisper. "I don't trust him yet. But he will stay at the palace while I determine how much honor he holds. Until then, I will remember not who his father is, but who his grandfather is." He gestured toward Commander Blaise, still standing in the corner of the room.

That was his answer. It should have been enough for her. She should have let it alone. But even as she tried to will her feet to walk away, a question ate away at her insides. It writhed and niggled and forced her to ask what she knew she should not.

"Then why mark ID cards at all?"

A flash of rage appeared in the emperor's eyes.

But she'd already started now. All she could do was finish. "Why punish Aaden for his father's crime while his father, the guilty one, goes unpunished? His father still lives in the Crown. He still has a silver crescent moon on his ID card. Why punish anyone for something he did not do?"

"Leave my presence." The emperor's voice sounded feral. The hairs on her arm stood on end while the emperor's gaze spoke volumes more than his words. "You will not question me again, especially not in my throne room."

After the shortest bow of her life, she scuttled out of the room. This time, he meant it. She had used up all the special privilege she earned from being the best shaper he had ever seen. If she wasn't careful from here on out, he would deliver punishment.

No matter how her insides writhed with unanswered thoughts, she'd just have to keep her questions to herself.

Chapter Twenty-One

THE EMPEROR HAD SAID TO study theory and strategy. Talise hadn't gone to her living quarters until late in the morning. Even then, she brought a few books with her.

Now that morning had come, she fully regretted the disrespect she had given to a proper night's rest. Her eyelids felt like sandpaper each time she blinked. It felt so good to keep them closed. And resting her head on the wall of the library felt even better. Maybe if she just rested for a moment…

"Hey."

Her head shot up at the sound of Aaden's voice. He let out a quiet chuckle that set her on fire. She'd have to get used to this. After their joint breakout the day before, he seemed to think they were the closest friends.

He'd spent half the time in the library yesterday giving away his best shaping secrets. She had to give away a few of her own, or else he might realize how suspicious she was of him. But that was the only reason she gave anything away.

The warmth of his eyes certainly had nothing to do with it.

Mostly nothing.

She shook her head again, trying to dispel the errant thoughts.

Luckily, a guard pushed open the library doors wearing a fierce look that stopped Aaden from opening his mouth again. The emperor appeared behind the guard and Talise gladly ducked her head in a bow. The longer she could avoid eye contact with the emperor, the better.

"Prepare the tables," the emperor said in a booming voice.

Talise held her bow a little longer than necessary. When she stood up straight, it seemed the emperor was just as intent on avoiding eye contact as she was.

It took another moment for her to realize what the guard was doing to the tables. Or, more accurately, setting *on* the tables. It was a white marble game board with black lines etched into the surface to make sixty-four square spaces. Eight by eight.

The slate tablets he produced next were carved more intricately than anything she'd ever seen in the Storm, but they bore the same symbols. Two waterfall tablets, two tornado tablets, two tree tablets, two fire tablets, and eight blank tablets. One black set and one white.

Forces of Kamdaria.

The game was a favorite pastime of all Kamdarians whether played in the Crown with artisan-carved slate tablets or in the Storm with wooden tablets that had the symbols crudely scratched on with a nail. Everyone loved Forces of Kamdaria, though most of the time, everyone just called it Forces.

For the first time all morning, Talise smiled.

"Forces?" Aaden asked in shock. "This is our first trial? It's just a game. It doesn't even require shaping."

The emperor narrowed his eyes before he stuck his nose in the air. "Forces of Kamdaria is of the utmost importance. It requires skillful strategy that will help even the worst shapers. If you can win this game, you can win a war."

Aaden's eyes looked ready to jump into an argument, but his lips remained pressed together. Maybe he wasn't really angry. Maybe he was just afraid. He had spent so much effort improving his shaping, perhaps he never took the time to play Forces.

Luckily, Talise hadn't made the same mistake.

She and Aaden each took a seat at a different table. The emperor considered them both for a moment before taking his place across from Talise.

He stared off at nothing in particular as he said, "I will play each of you. If you win, you gain three points in the trials. If you lose, but you play well, you gain two points. If you lose and you play satisfactorily, you gain one point. If you lose and you play dismally, you gain zero points. I sincerely hope you each gain at least two points, or your place in the trials will be in question."

Aaden audibly gulped beside Talise, but she ignored it. Biting her bottom lip, she began placing the tablets on the marble game board. Unlike some games, there was no specified placement for the tablets. Instead, placement was just as vital a component as her moves would be.

It helped to know how the opponent played before beginning a game. Though the emperor wasn't the most predictable person, so perhaps that advantage wasn't worth much anyway.

She placed her tablets without taking a single moment to think about it. Four symbol tablets on the first row with a blank tablet in between each. Then the same pattern on the second row with the symbol tablets offset from the ones on the first row. This arrangement had helped her win plenty of matches. Now wasn't a time for questioning her previous methods. Now was a time for action.

The emperor raised an eyebrow, surprised by how quickly she placed her tablets, and maybe even a little bit impressed.

She was off to good start.

When Emperor Flarius placed his last tablet, he gestured toward Talise to begin. Since she had finished placing her tablets first, she also got to take the first turn. Yet another reason it was beneficial for her to act first.

Her first move was a bold one. She placed a fire tablet in the middle of the marble game board. Fire tablets couldn't be jumped over and stolen by an opponent, just like objects couldn't jump over a real fire without getting burned. But a waterfall tablet could be placed on top of a fire tablet and then another tablet could jump over and steal both of them.

This made fire tablets powerful, but also vulnerable as long as waterfall tablets were still on the board.

Talise didn't care. She had a feeling the emperor would go straight for the kill.

Just as she suspected, the emperor placed a waterfall tablet on top of her fire tablet. Now for the next step.

It took four moves and a bit of baiting, but the emperor fell for each of her tricks. Just when he thought he was about to steal her fire tablet, she double-jumped over his waterfall tablets, stealing them both. Now her fire tablets were invincible.

"That was a cheap way to begin the game," the emperor said wearing a snarl. Maybe he was only grumpy about losing both of his waterfall tablets, but Talise wondered if his frustration had more to do with her than anything.

She ignored his censure and prepared for the next move. As the game progressed, it became obvious that the emperor had many more years of practice than she had. His moves were clean. Precise. He took control of the board like it was nothing more than a stroll through the gardens.

Talise's only chance to win came by doing things so unique that the emperor had to blink at the game board when she moved. He called it cheap, but she called it smart. Each time he offered advice in his haughty voice, she ignored it and moved the tablets in ways he had likely never seen before.

Her methods were messy. Chaotic. But they were also effective.

Soon enough, she prompted the final fight and let him chase after her immortal fire tablet only to steal all his blank tablets and win the game.

It took the emperor a few moments to realize he'd lost.

At first, she thought he might smile. It was a strange time to smile, given that he had just lost. But maybe she had finally done something to make him proud.

The moment that absurd thought entered her mind, the emperor's almost-smile vanished, and a vacant expression replaced it. "You didn't win through strategy or skill. You won through underhanded trickery. I sincerely doubt you could replicate the result you got today."

Her stomach sank with each word. What was so wrong with trickery anyway? The point was to win, wasn't it? If she won by doing the unexpected, then she merely won by playing to her strengths and knowing her opponent.

She wasn't about to say it out loud, but she *could* win against the emperor again. She was sure of it.

He looked away as he rose from his chair. With his eyes far from Talise he said, "You will receive three points since you won, but I hope you realize how much of your win came from sheer luck."

Her heart sank again. Even if she did manage to beat the emperor in another game someday, he'd probably still be disappointed in her.

Aaden smoothed his thin goatee starting under his nose and then down to his chin. He had remained silent during Talise's game. Now that the emperor sat down across from him, his hands seemed to be shaking. She noticed a light line of sweat under his shiny black hair that made his dark skin glisten.

She wanted to shake him and tell him to show confidence before the emperor. He could lose the game before he even started by showing too much fear.

But rather than be disappointed, the emperor looked rather amused by Aaden's expression. He finished placing his tablets long before Aaden did, which was honestly ridiculous.

Aaden could have spent Talise's entire game deciding how to place his tablets. Apparently, he'd been thinking of nothing at all. His shaking fingers kept moving the tablets from one tile to the next, not willing to commit to any one placement. When he finally finished, his frown said he still wasn't happy with the result.

Too bad for him because Emperor Flarius moved his first tablet and Aaden had to play.

He lost.

It didn't take long. The emperor didn't go easy on Aaden even when it was obvious that Aaden didn't know Forces very well. Instead, the emperor played as if he expected to win in ten moves or less.

In the end, it took thirteen.

Aaden's face had taken on a green tinge as he pulled at his shirt collar.

For some reason, this made the emperor laugh. He patted Aaden on the shoulder. "Don't fret, my boy. Almost everyone loses when they play against me."

The emperor's sudden joviality made Talise more than a little angry. She tightened her fingers into fists and held them under the table where no one could see. How could the emperor be so kind to Aaden when he had played so much worse than her?

"You will receive one point. You do have some skill in strategy, but not enough to gain two points."

At these words, the emperor left his seat and stood before them both with an imposing expression. "Tomorrow, your lessons will begin. Meet in the training hall immediately after breakfast. Now that I have a better idea of your skill level, I know just where to start with your training."

He swept out of the room with all the grace of a rusty wheelbarrow. Just before leaving the room, he said, "Don't be late."

Chapter Twenty-Two

TRAINING HALL DIDN'T SEEM LIKE big enough words to describe the vast space Talise now stood in. The size alone was enough to still her breath. It could have held two, maybe three, of the old training building back at the academy.

The size wasn't even the most impressive part. The hall contained obstacle courses, weapons, blindfolds, and tools she had never seen before.

Then there were the bowls. Bowls full of elements, shelves full of bowls, and walls filled from end to end with shelves.

So many bowls.

She placed a finger on the nearest contraption, running her finger along the strange metal design. Several guards and servants set up even more contraptions in the four rooms along the back of the training hall.

She recognized General Gale in the midst of servants running in and out of one of the four rooms. The same moment she saw him was the same moment she recognized Wendy.

Her friend stood a few steps behind General Gale with eyes wide as she took in the training hall. When she saw Talise, her face brightened, and she ran toward her.

"You're here!" Wendy said, nearly bouncing out of her shoes in delight.

Talise took her friend's hands in a quick squeeze. "Yes!" Talise looked over her shoulder. In a quieter voice she said, "But Aaden is here too."

Wendy waved a hand through the air. "Oh, I already know all about that. General Gale explained about the trials. The first one was yesterday, right? How did you do?"

Talise wished they were in a more private place. If they had been, she would have told Wendy all about Aaden's father and how she wasn't sure if Aaden could be trusted. But with more palace workers entering the training hall, she decided to save that conversation for another time.

Instead, Talise grinned. "I got three points. Out of three."

"I knew it," Wendy said. "I bet the emperor was wildly impressed."

Talise's bottom lip ended up between her teeth as she looked away. "Uh, not really. But Aaden only got one point, so at least I'm doing better than that." Forcing herself to look back, Talise said, "But what about you? Are you officially a palace worker?"

Wendy tapped the silver pin on her tunic with a triumphant smile. "I finished the paperwork last night. I wrote a letter to my mother and father, and General Gale said the palace servants could get it delivered in one day. One! Oh, and Claye is here too."

When Talise glanced through the room, Wendy laughed. "No, not in this room. I just mean he's working at the palace. He's in the gardens right now. Apparently, they're testing him in a few different jobs to see where he does best."

Her search of the room hadn't helped her find Claye, but it did remind Talise of another question she had. "How's your brother? He still works at the palace, doesn't he?"

"I haven't seen Cyrus yet. General Gale said he would find out where he's assigned, and I should see him soon." Wendy snapped to attention when General Gale beckoned her toward him. She gave a quick wave to Talise and was soon off with General Gale.

Wendy hadn't seen her brother yet, and Talise still hadn't seen any of the Master Shapers. Since the Master Shapers were on an assignment in the Gate, the middle ring of Kamdaria, it was probably unrelated. Before she could consider it anymore, her thoughts were immediately interrupted by another voice.

"That was your friend?" Aaden asked.

Apparently, this mixture of fear and excitement was doomed to spark inside her every time he made an appearance. Talise nodded. "Wendy. She started academy training in the Gate but came to the elite academy here in the Crown once she started the second stage of training. We've been friends ever since."

"For five years?" Aaden asked, sliding his thumb across the tips of his fingers.

As Talise nodded, a strange look came over his eyes. Though they didn't change colors, his eyes seemed to lose their warmth. A shadow clouded over them as a darkness spread over the rest of his features. Somehow, his eyes looked older and heavier than they should have in a person who was only eighteen.

Could he be thinking of an old friend? A lost friend? Or was he thinking of something else entirely? His father?

The emperor appeared before Talise could consider this any further. He wore practical clothing today. Nothing like the silks and furs she was used to seeing on him. In fact, his brown canvas clothing looked nearly the same as the tunic and pants that she wore.

She shifted on her feet, trying to turn inward. Out of sight. Invisible. She didn't like the idea of looking like the emperor, even if it was just because of their clothes.

The emperor looked over the two of them with a more affectionate expression that he'd shown in the past two days. "Before we begin," he said. "Do you have any questions for me?"

Both she and Aaden uncomfortably shook their heads, but the emperor pressed. "Come now, you've been in the palace for two days. I'm sure you must have some questions."

Aaden seemed to be eager to gain the emperor's approval because he merely shook his head and flashed a winning smile.

Talise inched her hand upward, biting her bottom lip as she did. She raised one small finger to get the emperor's attention. When he noticed, he flinched. Or maybe that was her imagination.

He gestured with a hand for her to go on.

Even after clearing her throat, her voice sounded so much smaller than she meant it to sound. "I was wondering when we'll get to meet the other Master Shapers."

This time she definitely didn't imagine the grimace on the emperor's face. He turned away to examine a nearby weapon. "I already told you. You'll meet the other Master Shapers when you have finished the trials. The second trial takes place in a month."

The emperor didn't hide his disdain as he glanced back at her. He nodded once as if to say, *That is the end of that.*

"I have a question," Aaden said.

She didn't know if he was purposefully trying to bring the emperor's attention away from her, but he did, and she was grateful.

Aaden walked toward a table with weapons spread across it. The emperor followed after him. "Was this sword forged by Artisan Graund?" Aaden asked.

Now the emperor smiled. Nothing about Talise ever seemed to pique his interest. No, only when Aaden pointed out an interesting detail did the emperor manage to convey an emotion other than disappointment.

With a growing smile, the emperor said, "Yes, that's right. Very impressive. Artisan Graund's expertise is well known, but not many can pick it out."

The emperor waved them to the middle of the training room as he continued speaking. "Now that you are Master Shapers, you no longer have a primary element. Now you must become equally skilled at all four of them. We will begin with air since it is the easiest element."

Emperor Flarius planted his feet on the ground and waited for Talise and Aaden to do the same. When they were ready, the emperor levitated a clod of dirt from one of the nearby bowls. He explained that he would throw small dirt clods toward them and they would have to use air shaping to burst the clods until they were dust.

Even though Talise felt confident about her air shaping, a part of her still wanted to grumble. It probably didn't matter how good she was. The emperor would most likely fawn over Aaden and shoot disappointed glares her way.

To her surprise, the emperor sent dirt clods toward them at the same time, which didn't give her room to worry about how Aaden was faring. Instead, she focused on the exercise, pausing only to tuck a stray hair behind her hair every now and again. Since her black hair fell just below her chin, she wouldn't be able to pull it back. But maybe tomorrow, she pin the front pieces of it back at least.

When her arms began to ache from so much shaping, the emperor finally declared that they would move on to the next exercise. She glanced at the ground.

As she suspected, the dirt on the ground surrounding Aaden had tiny dirt clods. None of his dust was as fine as hers. Still, she always assumed Aaden had trained so much with fire in order to win Master Shaper that he wouldn't know the other elements as well. That assumption had been proven wrong.

Aaden did know wind shaping, and he performed better than she would have guessed.

Also, as she expected, the emperor did fawn over Aaden, and Aaden seemed to enjoy every bit of it. Talise gritted her teeth, more determined than ever. No matter what they did next, she'd train with more ferocity until the emperor had to notice her.

ONE WEEK LATER, training hadn't changed much.

"No, no, no Talise. You must grasp the sword, but don't strangle it. And try using your fire to heat the blade. It makes the hits more lethal."

The emperor always spoke to her like a child. She gripped the hilt of her training sword again and didn't bother to understand the difference between grasp and strangle. A flood of heat left her fingers and burned through the sword, turning the blade red hot.

Her fingers flinched when the hilt also began to heat up. It took more concentration than she cared to admit to cool the hilt. It was so easy for her fire shaping to get out of control when she was angry. And she was angry most of the time these days.

The emperor looked down his nose at her. In the condescending voice he reserved just for her, he said, "Try again. And this time, at least *attempt* to stay light on your feet. The lumbering around is embarrassing for all of us."

She held the sword in front of her and barreled toward the wooden dummy at the end of the room. The heat of the blade created a burn mark on the wood when it landed. Unfortunately, the burn mark landed on the dummy's arm, much too far from the heart where she was supposed to be aiming.

A blush warmed her cheeks and neck as she clomped back.

The emperor didn't bother to make eye contact with her as she returned. He was too busy giving detailed pointers to Aaden about the perfect twist to deliver on impact to provide the most internal damage.

They'd finally found an area where Aaden's skill surpassed Talise's, and the emperor couldn't get enough of it. He seemed content to spend the entire day fawning over Aaden. Though strangely, Aaden didn't seem to enjoy the attention today as much as he usually did.

"Remember, the twist is just a small flick of the wrist. Your stance and delivery are perfect. If you can add the twist, you'll have extra killing power."

Aaden nodded but his eyes had wandered over to Talise. In one small glance, he conveyed a look of sympathy. Her face flushed as she turned away. She didn't want his pity. Didn't need his pity. What she needed was to improve so she could stop disappointing the emperor so much.

That's just what she planned to tell Aaden when they met in the library that evening for their nightly studying.

CHAPTER TWENTY-THREE

TALISE GROWLED AS SHE SMACKED a wooden rod against the floor. Aaden had the decency not to laugh.

The emperor wouldn't let them take any weapons from the training room, but Aaden had somehow found the rod. He insisted the weight and balance were close enough to that of a sword that they could use it to practice.

"It's because of your grip," Aaden said gently. "You want to hold it like you would a baby. Not too tight or you'll hurt it, but not too loose or you'll drop it."

"How many babies have you held in your life?" she asked with a scoff.

The facial hair under his nose fluttered as he let out a nervous chuckle. "Not that many, I'll admit, but the analogy is still helpful."

She let out a snort as she backed up to the wall. Her eyes narrowed as she concentrated on the small black dot Aaden had drawn at the other end of the library. It really was embarrassing how terrible she was at fighting. In elemental training she excelled. When she and Aaden played Forces, she always beat him, even when she was trying to let him win. But swords?

Her movements were always too gentle or too sharp or too weak. Never good enough.

"Go," Aaden said.

On his command, she barreled toward the black dot, and this time she felt it when her grip was too tight. Enough to strangle a full-grown man, let alone a baby. Okay, so maybe Aaden's analogy *was* somewhat helpful.

She missed the mark by an entire hand's length this time. Before she could throw the rod to the ground and stomp on it, Aaden was at her side.

"Hold it again, like you did just now."

She always wanted to argue with everything he said, just because he made it too fun. But she also wanted to get this right, so she complied without question.

While gripping the rod, she could feel her muscles straining like silk fabric right before it ripped in half.

He stepped closer until she could feel her shoulder brushing across his chest.

"Can you try to loosen your grip?" The breath from his words landed on her neck, sending a shiver down her spine.

Could he hear how fast her heart was pounding? She hoped not.

"Like this?" The rod nearly slipped from her fingers, but she didn't drop it. That had to be an improvement, didn't it?

Trying to ignore the tingling under her skin, she focused on her grip. She knew it was too loose, but when she tried to tighten it, the muscle strain returned.

Before she could loosen her grip again, Aaden wrapped his hand over hers. A flood of heat streamed through her skin just like it did every time they touched.

Where had all the air gone? Someone couldn't just forget how to breathe, could they?

"It's right here," he said, touching the knuckle at the bottom of her thumb. "This is where you're straining too hard.

Of course she could feel it now that he pointed it out. But she was having a devilish time relaxing anything now that his chest was pressed firmly against the back of her shoulder.

Suddenly she was questioning her loyalty to the emperor, to Kamdaria, to everything. Aaden's father had inadvertently given away secrets that led to the deaths of the royal family. His actions nearly destroyed Kamdaria.

Despite what the emperor thought, Talise was certain Aaden wasn't as innocent as he seemed. At the very least, he lacked restraint, which was especially obvious given how his thumb kept tracing circles over her knuckle.

Unfortunately, her own restraint had a difficult time convincing herself that she needed to pull away. The warmth in his hand was pleasant and it helped to relax her grip. Somehow, she was holding the rod in a whole new way. Firm but not tight.

"Yes," Aaden said. "Do you feel how much better that is?"

She nodded in reply, afraid that if she opened her mouth, she'd say something she'd regret. Something silly like how the warmth in Aaden's hands matched the warmth in his eyes.

She felt a breath even closer to her neck than before and she sensed a moment of hesitation in Aaden. His hand was ready to move away, ready for her to try again with her new grip, yet he didn't move.

"What are you two doing over there? Dancing lessons?"

Talise whirled around to face Wendy as she entered the library, simultaneously grateful and irritated by her appearance. The rod nearly clattered to the ground as she lost her grip. Tightening her fingers around it, she said, "Sword lessons."

"Aren't swords supposed to be sharp?" Wendy asked as she gave a sideways glance at Aaden.

His face didn't reveal any emotion, but Talise knew from how he flexed his jaw that he was purely irritated at Wendy's sudden appearance.

Talise pushed past him and joined Wendy at one of the tables. She dropped the wooden rod on top. "The emperor won't let us take the weapons out of the training room, but Aaden says this is a good enough substitute for practice."

Aaden lowered himself into the chair next to Talise without a word. He didn't seem to notice the suspicious glance Wendy threw at him.

"You *are* here," Claye said, his black hair disheveled as he came through the doorway.

Wendy nodded. "They were over there in the corner dancing."

"We were *not* dancing," Talise said, trying not to notice how Claye's eyebrow cocked upward. They'd been friends for years, but his teasing still irritated her more than it should have.

"Did you learn anything?" Aaden asked Claye. The words came out in a rush, sounding a little too forced. It was always like this when others were around. Aaden's words felt like a pebble dropping into a still pond. Unnatural and causing a ripple that always took a moment or two to settle.

"Yeah," Clay finally said. "We've been planting hedge bushes all over the palace garden."

Talise leaned forward, eager for every word. She and Aaden had been trying to guess what their second trial would be. It helped that Wendy and Claye saw a lot more of the palace than they did.

"One of the head gardeners complained that the hedge maze was ruining the aesthetic of the gardens," Claye said.

"A maze." Talise sat up straighter while a flood of ideas danced through her mind.

Claye sat back in his chair lacing his fingers behind his head. "Maybe. But maybe the gardener just meant it as a metaphor."

Wendy pulled a hidden pastry from her bag. "Just think of all the possibilities. There could be obstacles around every corner. Things you have to use your shaping to get past, things you have to run past."

"Beasts." Again, everyone stilled for a moment as if they had all forgotten Aaden was there until he spoke.

As usual, Talise was the first to come back to herself. "I don't think the emperor would use something as dangerous as beasts for something that's only a trial."

"He might." Aaden held a challenge in his stare. It was times like this that she thought he enjoyed their arguing as much as she did.

She really hoped no one could see the rush of heat that had just risen in her cheeks. This had to stop. As they sat there discussing the possibility of a maze, Talise made a decision.

She couldn't be alone with Aaden. Every time he looked at her, it made her insides jumble. No matter how she scolded herself for trusting him, she found herself wanting to spill her deepest secrets whenever they were together.

It was probably some ruse. He was probably trying to get in her head, so she'd do poorly in the next trial. Even though they weren't competing against each other, she was pretty sure he still remembered that she had three points and he had one.

No matter how much she wanted to trust him, she couldn't. No more late-night study sessions in the library. At least not without Wendy or Claye around. Otherwise, there was no telling what secrets she might let out.

ANOTHER TWO WEEKS passed and now the second trial was only a week away. After so much speculation, the growing maze in the garden was all the proof they needed.

Their training sessions seemed to get longer with each passing day. Talise ran through a field as fast as her legs would carry her. Her eyes glanced side to side, desperate to pick out a target. She spotted one in the corner of her vision and noticed its color almost a hair too late.

Blue.

Fire flooded her veins as she shaped a ball of water out of a nearby pond, turned it to ice, and then threw it at the target all in one fluid motion.

Her legs carried her forward as she searched out the next target. Red. And nearly hidden behind a bush.

She shaped a burst of wind at it so hard, it almost knocked the target to the ground.

Nearing the end of the training course, she didn't expect to see another target, but an orange one practically jumped out at her a few steps from the finish line.

She shaped a messy fire ball and hit the target just as she stepped over the line.

Aaden was grinning wildly, impressed by her speed and skill. He had done well too. Over the last four weeks, his shaping had improved, his strategy had improved, even his conversational skills had improved.

It made her all the more determined to have other people around when they were together.

"Next time," the emperor said through his teeth as he glared down at her. "Don't forget to shield your eyes when you do a fire ball that big."

Aaden balked at the emperor's words. "Did you see how fast she was going? She didn't even need to shield her eyes. That was amazing!" It could have been her imagination, but Aaden seemed to show the barest hint of irritation when his eyes flicked toward the emperor.

The emperor spared him a single glance before he snapped his fingers and began walking back to the palace. "I'm leaving tonight for an assignment in the Gate."

"With the Master Shapers?" Talise asked.

The emperor continued as if he hadn't heard her, even though she was pretty sure he had. "You must spend the next week training together. I will see you again in exactly one week. The morning of the second trial."

♕

CHAPTER TWENTY-FOUR

IT HAD BEEN A MIRACLE, but Talise managed to keep a guard or two close by any time she and Aaden had to train together. In the evening, she relied on Wendy.

Soon enough, the day of the second trial arrived. Lush green hedges towered overhead in the palace garden. Their branches were so tight and the leaves so dense, it was almost impossible to pull them apart. A wisteria-covered arch marked the entrance to the maze and immediately to its left, a tiger lily arch marked its exit.

The only other clue she had to the inside of the maze was the sound of a trickling stream.

She did her best to avoid eye contact with the emperor as he made a show of preparing them for the trial. He hadn't answered any of her questions about where he had been or what he had been doing in his week-long absence.

The best thing she could do now was focus on the maze.

"Points will be awarded based on time it takes to complete the maze," the emperor said. "Just like last time, the highest possible number of points is three and the lowest possible is zero. You may begin."

Talise felt his stare on her back as she entered the maze. The hedges grew far enough apart that there was just enough room for her and Aaden to walk side by side.

She didn't look at him as they traipsed down the path. Instead, she kept her eyes sharply on the point ahead where the path diverged. She could go right, or she could go left. At the end of the path, she gave a quick glance to Aaden.

His eyes shone, almost begging her to stay with him. The maze would probably be easier if they went through it together. She shoved the thought away and returned his glance with a glare.

Without a word, he understood. They would not be traveling together.

He nodded once and lumbered off to the left with his hands raised, ready to shape. She turned her back on him and turned to the right.

The light trickling of the stream sounded closer with each step she took. Before she could imagine what obstacle might lie ahead, she turned a corner and walked right off a cliffside.

Her heart nearly leapt outside her chest as she arched her back to grab the rock where her feet had just been. Unable to reach the rock in time, she reached for a root growing out of the cliffside.

The muscles in her fingers strained as she gripped the root with all her might. Her heart pounded, and a tiny part of her wished that Aaden was there. He could have pulled her to safety.

Then again, if he had been there, maybe he would have fallen off the cliff and she would have tumbled off behind him, and then they would both be in peril.

Better to be alone.

With her thoughts firmly away from Aaden, she stuck her toe into the cliffside, searching for a foothold. It wasn't until then that she realized the trickling stream was flowing just below her feet.

Glancing down, her heart stopped for a moment. The sight caused her a moment of fear, but now that the moment had passed, her brain started working. She wasn't as far from the ground as she realized. If she did fall, it probably wouldn't cause more than a few rough bruises. But that wasn't what caught her attention.

The trickling stream underfoot gave her an idea. If she could shape the water under her like a staircase, she could freeze it, and then climb up to the path. Now that the idea took hold, it seemed so obvious. Surely, the emperor must have designed this obstacle with her ice shaping in mind.

The fire in her veins felt like a warm hug after the icy fear had gone through her. When it came time to shape the water staircase into ice, she held off as long as possible, savoring the warmth inside.

Soon enough, she climbed up the ice steps and put her feet firmly on the path. As she melted the ice, the sound of the stream distracted her once again.

An old memory came to the front of her mind. It was so old, the edges of it crinkled and blurred as she tried to recall the details.

She had been sitting on the edge of a stream with her knees up to her chin. Her arms were wrapped around her legs so tight, the muscles in them burned. The faint sounds of people screaming at each other was just close enough that the stream couldn't drown it out. The smell of chrysanthemums filled the air. She remembered the salty taste in her mouth as tears snuck in through the corners of her mouth.

She had been so young at the time it was hard to believe her memory even went back that far.

She hadn't been by the stream for long before Marmie found her. Her hair was thick back then, with no trace of gray. Or maybe Talise's memory was playing tricks on her. Marmie had said nothing as she sat down by Talise.

Marmie had stuck her fingers in the stream and flicked the water at Talise, trying to get her to play. But Talise only buried her face in her knees with a loud sniff.

This was where the memory lost its crinkled edges. The details sharpened and Talise could close her eyes, and it was like she was there.

Marmie gently rubbed her back. "It will be all right, love. When people are scared, they often act like they are angry. But everything will be okay. You'll see."

That's when the screaming had gotten louder. Marmie said nothing then. She just squeezed Talise's shoulders, making her feel much more important than the child she was.

That had always been the hardest thing for Talise to bear. The screaming. But Marmie had been right about the fear. She saw it every day while she lived in the Storm. People were always angry and picking fights, but only because their bellies were so empty.

Talise shook her head bringing her back to the present moment. After brushing away a tear, she was even more glad Aaden had gone the other way. She didn't need him thinking the maze had made her cry. It wasn't the maze at all. It was Marmie and the emptiness in her heart that was so much heavier than an empty stomach.

With a swallow, Talise marched forward. This time she moved at a slower pace so she wouldn't go careening off any more cliffs.

Her skin prickled with anticipation as she followed the maze. There didn't seem to be any paths until the very end. Even then, it wasn't much of an opening. But that wouldn't stop her. Maybe that was part of the trial.

She pushed through the tiny opening and continued. The next three obstacles were nothing more than dead ends. On her fourth dead end, she let out a huff.

She tried prying the branches apart in one of the hedges to get a look on the other side of it.

No luck.

Then she had a devious thought. One she knew the emperor would not approve of. He would call it a trick. Dirty.

But she'd been in the maze long enough, and she really, really wanted to beat Aaden this time. With her hand hovering under the bottom of a hedge, she shaped a fire into her palm.

The fire licked at the leaves and branches, but it barely even smoked, and certainly never burned. It took several more tries before she gave up completely.

She kicked the hedge for good measure before she stormed off. The emperor must have had some of the palace workers shape extra water into the branches and leaves so they couldn't be burned.

It irritated her that the emperor had already guessed she would try something like that. The only consolation was that Aaden would probably try it too. And he would also fail.

Talise went all the way back to the trickling stream before she looked up at the sky. Using the sun's position, she followed a path that she hoped would get her out of the maze. This time, she met much more exciting obstacles than just dead ends.

On one path, there was a gaping hole with a pile of dirt nearby. At first, she tried filling the hole, but there wasn't enough dirt. After abandoning that idea, she shaped the dirt into a bridge and walked over it.

Another obstacle required her to shape wind to move vines of wisteria out of the path, and through another, she had to burn a hole through an ice wall.

The best part of that ice wall was the fact that it had absolutely no holes melted into it before she got there. That meant Aaden hadn't found it yet. Her spirits lifted even higher when she rounded the nearest corner and saw the sun's light streaming in through the maze's exit.

With a victorious smile, she walked out of the maze. She tried not to be too proud of herself. The emperor would probably goad her for the prideful expression. She managed to set her face into something more neutral, but that didn't stop her from being excited.

She had now beaten Aaden in two of the trials. And she thought the maze trial had gone reasonably well. It hadn't taken her *that* long to find the exit.

Once the heat from the sun shone down on her hair, the excitement she felt barreled down to the bottom of her stomach.

Aaden was waving his hands through the air, in the midst of some story and the emperor was hanging onto every word. The emperor let out a breezy laugh before either of them noticed Talise on the path.

Aaden saw her first. He stopped midsentence and his face dropped. Something lingered there. She wanted to call it anticipation, but deep down she knew it looked more like pity.

His face was nothing compared to the emperor's. Emperor Flarius glanced at the nearby clock tower and clucked his tongue. His lip curled in disgust.

She had a feeling she did not want to hear what he was about to say.

CHAPTER TWENTY-FIVE

TALISE'S MUSCLES WENT RIGID AS the emperor prepared to speak. His mouth curved downward while his nostrils flared with each breath. Apparently *reasonably well* was the farthest thing from how she had done in the maze.

For a moment, she wasn't sure whether the emperor would yell at her or storm off before she could speak. Once he sucked in a breath, she knew exactly what was coming. She braced herself for the yelling.

"That was embarrassingly poor." He hadn't raised his voice, but the disappointment dripped off his words like acid.

Her feet begged her to take a step back, to re-enter the maze, to run away, anything. Somehow, she convinced them to stay.

The emperor slammed a fist against his palm, and this time, he did raise his voice. "You excelled in the strategy trial, but you have absolutely no common sense. None! Kamdaria needs shapers who can do more than pretty demonstrations and tricks in a board game."

"It's not her fault," Aaden said. From the way he took a step back, it seemed like he had spoken louder than even he expected.

"Of course it's her fault," the emperor said, never breaking eye contact with Talise while he punctuated each of his words with perfect precision. "She had as much opportunity to find the shortcut as you did. It was right by the entrance. If you were able to find it so quickly, she shouldn't have been far behind."

The words hit Talise in the chest sinking down like rocks. A shortcut right by the entrance? In a flash, she understood the trial. It was all a trick. A ruse. The huge hedges. The simple obstacles. It was all designed to look like a difficult trial, but the true test was in common sense.

Right at the beginning, there were two places to go. Left or right. When she chose right and nearly fell off a cliff, she should have gone back to the beginning and gone left instead. The way Aaden went. If she had done that, she would have found the shortcut almost as quickly as he had.

But she hadn't done that. Instead, she found a tiny path that was never meant to be used.

Aaden stood in front of the emperor now with his hands almost in fists at his side. "We decided to separate at the beginning of the maze. I went toward the shortcut, so she had to go the other way. It's not her fault it took her so long. She was just trying to give me space."

The emperor spared a small glance at Aaden before he pushed past him to sneer down at Talise, raising his head to its full height. "Then you shouldn't have separated. You could have passed the trial with flying colors, but now I don't know if you deserve any points at all."

Aaden's fingers clenched into fists, but he stayed rooted to his spot. At least he did until the emperor spoke again.

"Despicable," the emperor said so forcefully that a spray of spittle shot out of his mouth. Somehow, Talise resisted the urge to wipe the speck that landed on her forehead.

Aaden's fists grew tighter. He stepped in front of Talise, blocking her from the emperor's view. "Stop lecturing her," he said through clenched teeth.

"Aaden." Talise touched his arm, which prompted him to face her. "Stop," she said.

He kept his eyes firmly locked on hers until the emperor spoke again. "She knows she performed dismally. She deserves these words."

Aaden let out a huff and for a moment, Talise was certain she could see a ring of fire in Aaden's eyes. "She did great. She always does great. She didn't find the shortcut, but she still got through the maze. It didn't take her that long. Judging by the marks on her hands, she had to fight through some of the obstacles, so she probably didn't just do okay. She probably did amazing."

Talise was looking at her hands before she could stop herself. They were covered in red welts from when she had held onto that root for dear life. How had Aaden even noticed that?

"Kamdaria needs better than this!" the emperor shouted. He was glaring at Talise after sidestepping Aaden so he could meet her eye.

Aaden immediately stood in the way again, this time raising his fists ever so slightly from his sides. "It's not like she's going to be leading an entire army on her own any time soon. We'll have the other Master Shapers to help us with whatever we do. You have to stop being so hard on her."

The emperor stopped shifting in attempt to meet Talise's eye, and his whole body went rigid. Talise wanted to tell Aaden to run, but she knew that would only make things worse. He never should have gotten involved in this. He should have stopped when she told him to stop. She didn't need him defending her like this. It would only lower whatever status he had with the emperor.

Emperor Flarius leaned in so close to Aaden that Aaden arched back uncomfortably. In a low, punctuated voice, he said, "I. Am. The emperor."

Aaden gulped.

The emperor drew his eyebrows together. "I would think long and hard before you question my training methods again."

Though the words couldn't have been spoken in a more threatening voice, Aaden's jaw flexed for several seconds. Clearly, he was still considering whether he should defend Talise.

She wished she could speak to him without the emperor hearing. She didn't need him to defend her. She really didn't. Doing that would only make him lose grace in the emperor's eyes.

The two of them stood for a few more moments in a heated staring contest. In the end, Aaden broke. Just like he should have much earlier. He didn't apologize, but Aaden did bow his head low enough that his shoulders bent too.

The emperor seemed appeased by this. For now.

He stood to his full height again, while Aaden continued to bow. Apparently, it was now beneath Emperor Flarius to make eye contact with Talise. Instead, he spoke into the wind.

"Your next trial will be in another month. You will train with me…" Now he turned to Talise and pinned her with a stare that felt sharper than a knife. "Unless I decide it isn't worth my time to work with someone as incompetent as you."

Talise felt her soul crush to dust as he turned and marched away.

He couldn't stop training her. He *couldn't*. He couldn't give up on her now.

CHAPTER TWENTY-SIX

TALISE EYED THE FORCES BOARD carefully. Wendy sat across from her, but Aaden sat to her side. Talise was only a few moves away from winning, and then it would be Aaden's turn to play the winner. For the fifth time in a row, she wondered if there was a way to let Wendy win.

If Talise won and no one else was here to keep Wendy busy during Talise's game with Aaden, then Wendy might leave. And then Talise would be alone with Aaden. The game board did not have any sympathy for Talise's predicament.

She couldn't throw the game without Aaden knowing. The huff she wanted to let out obediently stayed in her mouth as she jumped her fire tablet over one of Wendy's blank tablets.

Wendy let out a groan. "How did I not see that? I should have seen that!"

Aaden's shoulders twitched with the chuckle she knew he was holding in. *He* saw it. He had used almost the exact same move on Talise the night before when he finally won his first Forces game against her. The emperor would have been proud.

Wendy triumphantly placed a waterfall tablet on top of Talise's fire tablet.

Exactly as Talise expected.

It almost hurt as Talise double-jumped to earn two more of Wendy's blank tablets.

Wendy's mouth dropped, and then she began grumbling to herself. Before she could make a move, Claye entered the library wearing dirt smudges on his face and arms.

Talise let out an inaudible breath of relief. Now Wendy would stay even after their game ended. What took him so long?

"I decided," Claye said as he fell into the chair next to Wendy, "that gardening is murder."

Wendy let out a twinkling laugh as she moved her next tablet. Her investment in the game seemed to vanish. "And what *dreadful* task did they have you working on today?"

Claye let out a loud sigh and buried his head in his arms.

For the briefest moment, Aaden made eye contact with Talise. One of his eyebrows cocked up and back down so fast, Talise would have missed it back at the academy. But she knew him better now. Those micro-expressions were becoming more familiar than she cared to admit.

"We had to plant about a thousand vegetable seeds."

Wendy tried to stifle her giggle. "Oh, you poor thing. Make you plant seeds? How could they?"

Claye's head shot up. "No, you don't understand. They made us do it *by hand*. We couldn't use shaping at all. They said knowing how to do it without shaping will make us better when we do it *with* shaping. I think they just wanted us to suffer."

Wendy giggled while Talise prompted the final fight in their game of Forces. Wendy hardly even glanced at the board while Talise took the rest of her blank tablets.

Claye made a great show of massaging the tips of his fingers. "The only thing this planting accomplished is a guarantee that I won't break any laws in the entirety of my life."

"Why?" Talise asked, giving him a sideways glance.

Claye raised his eyebrows as if telling her the answer was obvious. "Because then I'd have to go to the Storm and always plant seeds by hand. No crime is worth that."

Wendy was laughing again. And wiping the smudges off Claye's arm with the cloth she had used to wrap her now-eaten pastry.

"Did you have to plant seeds by hand?" Aaden's voice surprised them all, but Talise especially didn't expect him to be looking at her with such intensity. Did her heart really have to stop *every* time he looked at her? This was getting a bit ridiculous.

"Why would Talise have to plant seeds by hand?" Claye asked with a laugh. "She's a Master Shaper. I doubt either of you will ever have to work in the garden."

Aaden's eyes left hers, and suddenly she could breathe again.

"I meant when she lived in the Storm."

Something inside of Claye shifted at the sound of these words. It must have just been surprise, but his eyes widened a little more than necessary. For a moment he looked older. Wiser.

But the moment was gone in half a breath and his normal expression returned. "I didn't know you were from the Storm."

"I did," Wendy said, giving up on a particularly large dirt smudge.

In a flash, the other expression on Claye's face returned. It seemed strange until Talise finally recognized the way his lip curled. He was jealous.

It made some sense she supposed. Claye came to the elite academy at the same time as Wendy, and the three of them had all been friends ever since. But surely, he must have known she wasn't as close to him as she was with Wendy.

He tucked his shoulders back as he glanced at Wendy. With an attempt at indifference he asked, "Why did you know that and not me?"

Those words earned him a light smack from Wendy. "Stop getting all huffy. Did you like to broadcast that you were from the Gate when you first got to the elite academy? Of course not. We were all embarrassed to be from the Gate instead of the Crown. How do you think Talise felt when she was from the Storm?"

Claye frowned as Wendy began cleaning the dirt smudges on his face, but he didn't say anything else.

With a swallow, Talise cleared the Forces board for her game with Aaden. Wendy stood up to let Aaden take her place, but instead of sitting down, she linked her arm around Claye's. "Come on," she said. "This cloth isn't helping at all. Let's go into the kitchen to get you cleaned up."

Claye complied without a word of argument, which normally would have been impressive. Instead, it left a hollow feeling at the bottom of Talise's stomach that was quickly filling up with fear.

Now she and Aaden would be alone.

Talise kept her eyes on the board while she placed her tablets. She didn't even look up when the door closed behind Wendy and Claye. Best not to take any chances with eye contact.

They made their first few moves in silence. After the fifth move, Aaden cleared his throat. "So, *did* you have to plant seeds by hand?"

"I don't want to talk about it." Talise's throat was suddenly dry. She felt Aaden's eyes on her, but luckily, he didn't press the conversation.

Another few moves passed in silence. She probably should have felt grateful. Instead, she felt awful for cutting off the conversation so soon. But Aaden didn't need an explanation. Why should she have to give all her secrets away?

Aaden cleared his throat again as he moved his fire tablet. Even with her eyes on the board, she could see him slide his tongue over his lips. He was thinking, trying to get the words just right. She hated herself for knowing that.

He placed his fire tablet, and before she could make her move, he said, "My father…" He swallowed.

It didn't matter how determined she'd been to avoid eye contact earlier. Now her eyes lifted straight to his. She tried not to notice the brim of tears settling at the bottom of his eyelids.

"My father got a little too friendly one night and told a stranger all about the palace guards. He gave away secrets like how often the guards changed and what weaknesses in security it exploited. He never intended to give so much away. He was only bragging to a stranger. He never wanted anyone to get hurt."

Here, Aaden rolled his hand into a fist and curled his other hand over it. He held both hands under his chin while his eyes wandered off to a back corner of the room, staring but not seeing.

"The stranger was a member of Kessoku. They used my father's secrets to infiltrate the palace and murder the royal family."

Talise's heart pounded so hard that the pulse shook through her entire body. Beat after beat ringing in her eardrums, pulsing in her toes. Even holding her breath couldn't calm the merciless drumming.

Words came to her lips, but they all fell away before she could speak them. Those words wouldn't do. Still, the pounding in her heart thumped.

Finally, she said, "I know."

The blurry look in Aaden's eyes disappeared as he shifted to focus on her.

A wave of shame burned through her skin. She wrung her fingers in her lap, hoping he wouldn't notice how she chewed on her bottom lip. With her eyes averted, she whispered, "The servants talk about you when they think I'm not listening."

Every feature on Aaden's face hardened. He nodded once, and she could see how much effort he used to pretend he didn't care. But as surely as he hated his past, she could see that he was hurt. That servants, people who should have been below him, whispered and gossiped about him in such an unkind way was awful.

His throat swelled as he swallowed. He moved a blank tablet on the Forces board and went back to staring off in the distance.

Talise allowed her mind to be filled with strategy for the game. She imagined tablets in different positions and guessed moves

Aaden would make in response to hers. It helped to have something to think about because she couldn't imagine what else to say.

A few moves later, Aaden broke the silence. "I've been angry for so long. Even when I realized I might escape the Storm by becoming Master Shaper, I still wanted revenge against my father. He ruined my life. I know he regretted it, but he never regretted it enough. And I was scared to go to the Storm. All I could think about were the faces of my future children—weak and starving. That image gave me all the motivation I needed to become worthy of being Master Shaper."

He set his next tablet down with so much force, she thought the slate might chip.

His lip curled. "But I think what disgusted me the most was the truth that my *father* did this to me. I was motivated to become Master Shaper in order to protect my future children, people I haven't even met yet. My father didn't even love his only child enough to keep himself from making a disastrous mistake that would send me to the Storm."

It should have been easy to keep tears out of her eyes. She knew the story, had already guessed Aaden's part in it. But his words cut into her, knifing away at all her defenses. If it hadn't been for years of practicing restraint, she probably would have reached out and taken his hand. Who knew what problems that might have caused?

When he looked back into her eyes, it melted a hole straight through her heart. His eyes were heavy, but they held purpose. And they were warm. So warm. Dark brown like tree bark but with flecks of orange and gold, especially around the middle. His eyebrows hovered over them in a sweet and open way. Too open.

"I know the past hurts." His velvet-soft voice floated through the air, touching her to the core. "I *know* it hurts. But trying to ignore it will only make things worse."

She wrapped both arms around her stomach, pulling them tight as she stared at the ground. She had heard his unspoken words. "I can't talk about it yet," she said, trying not to think of Marmie's gray hair and kind eyes. "The memories are too painful."

He looked at her carefully before he nodded and glanced back at the game. This disarmed her more than anything. He had opened up to her so much, admitted to things he maybe had not admitted to anyone else. And now he was perfectly happy to continue the game and not push her any further.

Her gut twisted and knotted when she confronted the truth. He had opened himself up to her, but he hadn't done it for himself. He hadn't done it to get things off his chest or to share the burden with someone else. He had done it merely so she felt more comfortable sharing difficult things about her own past.

It was the selflessness that did her in. If he'd shown even an inkling of scheming or desire, she could have easily kept her mouth shut.

But here he sat with such genuine care that the words began speaking themselves.

"It's just that I'm still grieving."

Aaden had the decency to keep his eyes on the Forces board.

"Marmie died and I couldn't be at her funeral. They don't keep grave records in the Storm. I don't even know where she was buried, and since I wasn't at the funeral, I don't know if I'll ever be able to find her grave."

The Forces board was forgotten now. She could see how Aaden's jaw almost dropped and how he had caught it at the last second. Now that the words had started, they continued to flow. "And that's not even the worst part. Marmie's grave is bare. Without me to make a mark on her grave, she has nothing. I couldn't be at her funeral, and now her grave will stand in shame, not a single mark to honor her life."

Sorrow lined the edges of Aaden's eyes, not replacing the warmth, but enhancing it. "Don't you have any other family in the Storm? Anyone else who could mark her grave?"

Talise pulled her arms in closer as she shook her head. She knew Aaden had other questions. She could see them in his eyes. *What happened to the rest of your family? Did they die too? Or were you forced to live in the Storm because of something Marmie's parents did? And if so, how long were you there?*

But Aaden didn't ask any of those questions. He just stared, letting his eyes do all the speaking.

She gulped and looked away. "And now we have to do these stupid trials to prove we're worthy to be Master Shapers. To prove we're honorable." She winced. "Well, I'm not."

She got to her feet, and in her haste, she jumbled the tablets on the Forces board, ruining their game. She didn't care. "I was the last of Marmie's family, and I didn't even leave a mark on her grave. How can I claim to have honor now?"

Aaden didn't call after her as she fled from the room. He didn't follow her either, which she appreciated especially with a fresh sheet of tears falling down her cheeks.

This was exactly the reason she couldn't be alone with Aaden. It had been everything she suspected but worse. She couldn't allow herself to be alone with him again, or he would peel away her layers one by one until he held every one of her secrets.

She'd just have to work harder to avoid him. Perhaps it was time to tell Wendy, so she wouldn't leave them alone again.

♛

Chapter Twenty-Seven

TALISE LEVITATED A SMALL BALL of water over her palm, turned it to ice, and slammed it against the wall. Then, she melted the ice shards and levitated them back to her palm only to start all over again. She worried the wall in her living quarters might show wear if she kept this up for too long, but it calmed her more than pacing the floor did.

The stained mahogany walls were painted with a glossy layer that had protected them so far. Fire sparked in her veins as she slammed yet another ice ball at the wall. The ice shards flew away harder than they had so far. One of them bumped the rice paper screen she used for dressing. Two more shards landed on the butter-yellow silk of her bed covers.

Not wanting to get water on the silk, she retrieved the ice shards by hand, then she set about gathering all the other ice shards from around the room.

Her living quarters were simple, though probably bigger than most of the palace workers. She had a sitting area with a breakfast table, a desk, and a few bookshelves. Her bathroom was bigger than her entire room had been back at the academy. It had a large tub, a decorative sink with gilded gold edges, and a mahogany vanity stained cherry red. The vanity held all sorts of combs, pins, and every other impractical hair thing she could imagine. It didn't get much use during her training since her hair was short enough to stay out of the way. Occasionally she pinned the front parts of her hair back, but that was it.

The paints, lipsticks, and other cosmetics had also sat unused since she got here. After life in the Storm, she had no idea what to do with any of it and thought it best to not touch the stuff. No need to embarrass herself.

Her bedroom was simple. A large bed sat low to the ground with a different colored silk bed covering gracing it every day. A wardrobe held her training clothes, plus a few gowns that she had definitely tried on even though she had no occasion in sight to wear them.

But the best room of all was her personal training room. As she gathered the last of the ice shards, she melted them back into water and shaped another water ball above her palm. Pushing through the doorway into her training room always relaxed her.

She dropped the water ball into a bowl that sat on one of the many shelves full of elements. There was also an entire bookshelf of shaping theory books. A small table in the middle of the room with two chairs was the perfect place for playing Forces.

A few training tools she had collected were gathered in the corner, right next to the boots she had unceremoniously thrown there earlier that day.

The crowning glory of the room was on the west side. A large window with a balcony faced the garden. Green vines with wisteria and roses twisted around the banister of the balcony. A cherry tree grew to one side, which gave her privacy from the other balconies. Standing out there with her hands on the iron beam and the wind blowing on her face, she could pretend nothing in the world besides that garden even existed.

The garden's trickling stream ran close enough to the window that the sound of it was always close by.

As Talise dropped the water ball into an empty bowl, the urge to go out onto the balcony overtook her. She was only able to ignore it because night had fallen, and she didn't care for the chill the evening air would give her.

Instead, she stomped across the room and grabbed the rod she used to practice her sword fighting. It took one run across the room at the target to realize that was a bad idea. She missed her target by even more than normal.

Letting out a huff of frustration, she threw the rod at the ground.

This wasn't working.

She'd been avoiding Aaden, but now her evenings were boring her to tears. No more Forces, no more sword practice in the library. Wendy and Claye were around sometimes, but they always had other things to do.

She glared at the rod. What she needed to do was find out what the next trial would be. The emperor had been training them on so many different things lately, she couldn't even begin to guess what he was preparing them for.

A specific moment from the day's training came back to her all at once. She and Aaden had been running through an obstacle course and had to spear through targets with a sword. Obviously, Aaden had been perfect. Her? Not so much.

The emperor growled at her like he always did. He had said, "What good is your shaping if you can't even defend yourself in a fight?"

Aaden had immediately come to her defense. "Maybe she'll just use shaping instead of a sword if she ever has to defend herself. There are a hundred ways she could weaponize shaping, and she could probably do it better than anyone."

Talise let out another huff as she kicked the rod across the room. This was happening more every day. The emperor would criticize her, Aaden would come to her defense, a little angrier each time. She kept telling Aaden to stop.

She knew he would never understand, but she really didn't need him defending her like that. But apparently, he didn't like to be told what to do because he kept on defending her as if his life depended on it.

Talise stomped across the room just so she could chuck the rod another time. Nothing was going the way she had imagined. She was technically a Master Shaper, but she still had to do these stupid trials. She hadn't been to any parties or strategy meetings like the other Master Shapers usually did. All she did was train all day every day. She hadn't even met a single Master Shaper yet.

The truth of her fear came to her as she dug her feet into the wooden floor. What if she failed the next trial? She had done so badly in the maze trial, the fear of failing the next one was starting to get to her.

There was nothing she could do except keep training and keep trying to guess what the next trial would be.

Unless…

A wild idea entered her mind and she knew it was crazy, but somehow, she didn't care anymore. Setting her jaw, she shoved her feet into her boots before stealing a thick dressing gown from the wardrobe.

And then she was off.

THE GUARDS OUTSIDE her door barely raised an eyebrow as she strolled out of the room. She had never wandered out so late at night, but she didn't care what they thought. And maybe they were too professional to think anything.

She noticed one of the guards held a dagger instead of a sword. She remembered Wendy saying her brother carried a dagger instead of a sword. And suddenly, she realized how strange it was that she still hadn't met Wendy's brother.

Ignoring that thought, she traipsed down to the throne room, and then down the hall that she knew led to the emperor's personal quarters. He had an entire building that was supposed to be his home. The emperor's mansion. It had rooms and kitchens and gardens.

Those rooms had once been filled with his wife and his children. He had seven children, four sons and three daughters. His two oldest sons were both married and had lived in the emperor's mansion with their wives. The oldest son had even had a baby. A boy. That baby was supposed to be third in line for the throne.

Until Kessoku had come and killed them all. In her mind, she imagined the shrieking cries of an infant. Ones that pierced the night until, suddenly, they stopped altogether.

Talise pushed away the thought and pounded on the door to the emperor's quarters. She had a feeling he never stepped foot in the emperor's mansion these days. He probably spent most of his time in these palace quarters, even though they were only meant to be used occasionally.

The emperor didn't say a word when he opened the door and saw her standing there. He merely waved her into the room where she and Aaden had previously broken in to do their ice and fire trees.

Once the door was shut, Talise asked, "What is the next trial? I need to know so I can be prepared."

She probably should have eased into the conversation. But now she had started, and it was too late to stop. She gave a quick bow to the emperor as an afterthought and hoped he wouldn't be too annoyed she had only just thought of it.

His stare pierced through her, the same as it always did. She felt so small and insignificant in front of the great Emperor Flarius of Kamdaria. When he spoke, his words filled up the room. Not loud, but regal. Commanding.

"The trial will be an obstacle course similar to what you did today. Sword skill will be greatly important."

She blinked at him. She wanted to pinch herself to make sure this wasn't some dream. She settled for sending a wave of fire through her veins. It warmed her so fast it stung.

Not a dream.

Gratitude sat on her lips for giving her the information, but a more pressing thought suddenly burst out before she could convey her thanks. "Sword skill? This trial favors Aaden."

The emperor nodded, his face even and emotionless. "Yes. Maybe you should ask him for help."

The last time she practiced swords with Aaden came to her mind. All she could remember was his words on her neck and her strong desire to close any distance that separated them.

That was not something she would let happen again. No more training with Aaden, no matter how much she needed his help. She couldn't trust him; she was sure of it.

The emperor eyed her curiously which made her gut twist. Perhaps now was a good time to change the subject. "How many points did I get in the maze trial? You never told me."

"Zero." Again, the emperor surprised her by answering immediately.

Her stomach sank. Even Aaden had gotten one point in the Forces trial. Now he had four points and she had three. And the next trial would favor him.

"How many points do I need to maintain my title as Master Shaper?"

"As many as I deem necessary."

Talise almost rolled her eyes at his response. So much for getting a straight answer.

The emperor turned away from her and went to the desk in the corner of the room. He began shuffling the papers with his back to her. How did he always manage to make her feel so unimportant?

Her thoughts wandered back to Aaden. Maybe she could convince Wendy to get sword lessons from Aaden too. If they were both there, it wouldn't be so dangerous. She tried to clear her throat and stand a little taller. "Do you expect Aaden to perform better than me in the next trial?"

The emperor looked back at her with one eyebrow raised.

Yes.

The answer was there on his face as obvious as if he had said it out loud. Talise scowled.

To her surprise, the emperor turned around and reached for the short beard on his chin. He looked to the side of the room with a thoughtful expression. "I think you may have been right about Aaden. Perhaps he is not as honorable as he should be."

She wanted to roll her eyes and tell the emperor she was obviously right about him. But the memory of Aaden coming to her defense that day stopped her. She lowered her eyes to the ground, remembering how he stood in front of the emperor with eyes blazing. "He was only trying to help me."

"Indeed," the emperor said, pinching the beard between his fingers. "He seems to have taken quite an interest in you."

A rush of emotions flooded through her, and she was only certain of a few of them. Inexplicably, she was drawn yet again to the defense of Aaden. With her jaw clenched and her eyes on the ground, she said, "Maybe if you stopped criticizing everything I do while praising everything he does, then it wouldn't be an issue."

"Maybe," the emperor said, and she could hear the smirk in his voice. When she looked up to meet his eyes, she saw a scheming in them she hadn't noticed before.

With the smallest hint of a chuckle, the emperor said, "Or maybe I know exactly what I'm doing."

CHAPTER TWENTY-EIGHT

THE SWORD CLUTCHED IN TALISE'S hand had more sweat than shine on it. She'd been so busy worrying about her stupid grip that she forgot to tone down her fire shaping. Now the sword was red hot, and she was losing her perfect grip because of all the sweat.

A target seemed to jump out from behind a bush and Talise barreled toward it with a growl. The burn mark from Aaden's sword already sat perfectly in the middle of the bull's eye, which made her growl even louder.

Yep, she was definitely going to lose this trial.

Her sword clanged against the wooden target. The wood sizzled from the heat of her sword, not on the bull's eye, but closer than she expected. Despite her frustration, she was actually doing okay.

She probably would have done better if she'd taken the emperor's advice to train with Aaden, but of course she hadn't. Even being in the same room with him now was making her stupid stomach fill with butterflies. She wasn't about to take any chances with one-on-one training.

Another target came into view. She ran at it with as much wrath as if it was an actual member of Kessoku. This time, she made it even closer to the bull's eye.

A triumphant smile played on her lips as she headed forward. She pushed through a clump of bushes and into a small clearing. Just beyond the clearing, she could just make out her next target. Beside the target, Aaden was cutting away branches.

Her feet froze in place as she realized what he was doing. He was making the target more visible. He was making the trial easier. Just for her.

Maybe she should have been grateful, but instead she felt foolish. She thought she had been doing so well in this trial. To find out Aaden had been cheating for her all along, just made her grumpy.

A branch cracked beneath her foot, and Aaden glanced back with a start. His eyes went wide when he saw her, but he didn't attempt to speak. He just lifted his sword and ran forward as if he hadn't just been caught cheating for her.

With a fresh wave of embarrassment encompassing her, Talise barreled toward the target. Her grip was too tight. She could recognize it easily now thanks to the advice Aaden had given her in the library.

That thought only made her angrier.

When she struck the target, it was farther from the bull's eye than any of her other hits had been. When the wood sizzled from the heat of her blade, she suddenly realized her hand was close to burning.

Letting out a huff, she dropped her sword to the ground and wiped her sweaty palms on her pants. That didn't help much. Instead, she shaped the sweat out of her hands and formed it into a small ball over her palm.

Just to get the heat out of her body, she shaped the ball into ice. She spun the ice ball in circles letting the chill flow through her fingers and up her arm. When she had cooled off sufficiently, she slapped the ice ball as hard as she could.

The ice ball hit the target right in the bull's eye, even better than Aaden's sword mark. She clenched her jaw at the sight.

This was a stupid trial. If they were being tested on shaping, she could easily pass. But no, the emperor had to make the trial favor Aaden and his stupid sword skills.

She plucked the sword off the ground and started running. She'd have to go faster than before to make up for all the time she lost by ice shaping.

Her next target was hidden behind more branches than the others had been, but she had a feeling Aaden still cleared some of them away. A fresh trickle of sweat glistened on her brow as she ran at the target.

Better than before, but still not on the bull's eye. She resisted the urge to kick the target to the ground.

Letting out a grunt, she ran on.

The entire obstacle course took her almost an hour to finish. In the end, she came in right behind Aaden. Either she had been running faster than she realized, or Aaden had slowed down to purposefully let her catch up.

Somehow, this made her even angrier.

The emperor waved them over to an empty bench while his guards were sent to gather the targets. Their swords had been branded so the emperor could easily see which marks had been made by which sword.

"You did amazing," Aaden said once the emperor's back was turned.

Talise frowned. "Don't patronize me. You didn't even see any of my targets. You have no idea if I made it close to the bull's eye or not."

Aaden tilted his head, his expression softening. "No, but I saw your stance. And your grip. They were amazing. You've improved so much."

Talise jutted out her bottom lip in a pout, but her insides were busy having all sorts of emotions she had definitely *not* approved. Why did it have to feel so good to have Aaden's praise? Why couldn't she just hate him? Everything would be much easier if she could just hate him.

"Thanks." She didn't smile as she said it, but Aaden seemed to sense the smile in there somewhere.

Luckily, they were both too out of breath for any more conversation. When the guards finally retrieved all the targets for the emperor, Talise was too busy kneading her muscles to notice what Aaden was doing.

After a few minutes of studying the targets, the emperor called them both forward.

Talise's stomach already started sinking before Emperor Flarius spoke. The rubies embedded in his crown glinted in the sunlight, yet nothing about it was beautiful. Instead, it felt like the jewels were laughing. Mocking her for having such poor sword skills. For believing she could do this.

The emperor looked down his nose at her, and her stomach suddenly felt hollow. "Aaden will receive three points in this trial." He turned to face the young man, but even Aaden seemed disappointed by these words.

The emperor shifted the sword in his belt. A wide smile adorned his face, making him look almost fatherly as he spoke to Aaden. "You performed well. Each of your target's was within range of the bull's eye. You finished a little slower than I anticipated, but still within range of what I expect from my soldiers. Very well done."

Aaden's head bowed, but Talise could feel him looking at her. When he raised his head, he seemed to be bracing himself for the emperor's next words.

She wanted to kick him in the shins for it. He had no right worrying for her. She could do that plenty all on her own.

The fatherly smile on the emperor's face vanished when he glanced her way. His mouth tightened, and his eyes narrowed, giving him an expression just short of a scowl. "Talise, you earned two points today."

Aaden let out a breath of relief that made it sound like he'd been holding his breath for hours. Her fingers curled into a fist at the sound.

She didn't trust him. Couldn't. And she was sick of his measured glances warming her heart.

The emperor's jaw flexed. It seemed as though he had about three hundred and seventy-nine more things to say. Not surprisingly, he exhibited far more restraint than Aaden ever had. He glanced at Talise once more. "I expect you to keep practicing your sword skill. You still have ample room for improvement."

The emperor held his head high as he swept out of the garden. A festering anger was bubbling inside her, but the moment the emperor disappeared, it popped. She chucked her sword at the ground, then kicked it for good measure.

"Would it *kill* him to pay me a compliment for once? Would he *die* if he admitted how much I've improved?"

"At least you have five points now," Aaden said unhelpfully. "That's only two fewer than me."

Talise rounded on him with the kind of glare that could make a candle melt without any fire.

Aaden lowered his head in a nonverbal apology. He glanced up at the last second, but she decided to ignore it.

She pounded her fists against a nearby tree trunk. "I'm trying so hard." Her hands dropped to her sides as her forehead met the bark of the trunk. Her voice let out a tremor when she spoke again, and she screamed at herself internally for being so vulnerable. "Why can't he see that?"

Aaden was right behind her with his hand on her arm. The warmth in his fingers seeped into her skin, his warmth always a welcome distraction.

"I see it," he whispered.

Every cell in her body urged her to turn around and face him. To give in. But, how could she? He practiced shaping on the boat when it was against the rules. He lied to Mrs. Dew about it. He sabotaged Talise's demonstration. He even threw fire balls at her back at the academy when she peeked in on him practicing.

Over and over again he showed a propensity for being less than honorable. Just like his father.

And now she was just supposed to trust him? Just because he'd never forget how she was willing to go to the dungeon in his place? She hadn't sacrificed anything for him, not really.

But somehow, she was supposed to believe he was changed? That he was suddenly unflinchingly loyal to her because of that one moment?

Maybe he liked her, but that wasn't enough to guarantee his honor. She needed more proof. More time.

"Talise."

Her name rolled out of his mouth as if he'd been holding onto it for several days. As if he'd considered it, treasured it, and now he was just trying it out, seeing how it felt out in the open.

It felt amazing.

She hated herself for feeling like that, but she did. She wanted to hear him say it again. And then she wanted to cry on his shoulder and tell him just how insecure she felt. She wanted to give him everything, but she knew it would be a mistake.

Shaking her arm out of his grasp, she turned around and put her back against the tree trunk. "I don't want to talk about it." She stared at the ground, but out the corner of her eye, she could still see him.

His face stayed still, watching her with those brown eyes that could melt ice. After a few moments, his jaw flexed. "Too bad."

Her eyes flicked to his. "What do you mean *too bad?*" He was too close. Far too close. Her shoulder blades dug into the tree as she tried to back up. But with the tree there, she had nowhere to go. And now he was leaning in closer.

"I mean," he said, folding his arms over his chest. "The emperor treats you like filth and I'm sick of it. Which means you must be even more sick of it. So, talk about it."

She gulped and pressed her heels into the tree, trying to pull away from Aaden. Scowling, she said, "What else is there to talk about? You summed everything up perfectly. I'm terrible, the emperor knows it, and being here makes me feel like an incompetent child."

A flash of a smile appeared on Aaden's face for the briefest moment. "Incompetent? You can shape ice. No shaper in the history of Kamdaria has ever done that successfully. And you weren't even a Master Shaper when you learned to do it. I think *prodigy* is a better word for what you are."

The corner of her mouth tugged up. She quickly glanced at the ground and bit her bottom lip to keep the smile from getting out of control. With each breath, her heart sent waves of warmth into her bloodstream. But no amount of heat was going to change the real issue. With her eyes on the ground, she said, "I may be a skilled shaper, but I'm still not good enough for the emperor."

Aaden dipped his head down, so their foreheads were nearly touching. "The emperor wants us to be skilled in all areas. Not just shaping but strategy and weapons too. You already have strategy and shaping down, but you do need some improvement with weapons."

Her lip felt raw in her mouth because of how much she chewed it.

In a lower voice, Aaden said, "Luckily, there's an easy solution to that."

"What is it?" She looked into his eyes as she asked and immediately regretted it. He was even closer than before; she could practically feel him through her tunic.

He propped his forearm on the tree above her, closing the distance even more. As he stared into her eyes it seemed like their heartbeats were syncing. "Let me help you."

Those brown eyes had her magnetized. Her chest seemed to plummet with each heavy breath she let out. He was too close. She tried to look away, anywhere but into those eyes. But when she pulled away from his stare, her eyes landed on the worst place of all.

His lips.

He saw it. He saw how she glanced at his mouth, and she could feel how it brought him closer.

In a panic, she pressed her palms against his chest and shoved.

"No!" Digging her palms into her eyes, she finally stepped away from the tree, giving her the space she needed to breathe. To think.

She took a deep breath and looked him squarely in the eye. "I don't need your help. I can do this on my own."

She expected to see more sadness in his features, but they merely showed frustration. He glared at her with a clenched jaw. "Don't be so stubborn. I'm good with a sword, and you need help."

Talise took another step away from him, clenching her own jaw tight. "Not from you, I don't."

Aaden made a great show of rolling his eyes. "And who else is going to teach you sword skill?"

"Don't you get it?" Talise said with a huff. She felt words coming on that she knew she'd regret, but every emotion in her body ignited with fire. Nothing could stop her now. "These trials are for *you*. It's not about training or sword skill. It's about testing your *honor*. Maybe I need to improve my sword skill, but you have a past no one has forgotten. Especially not the emperor."

She whipped around and started running away, but it didn't stop her from seeing Aaden's mouth hanging open. And it didn't stop her from knowing her words had pierced him straight through the heart.

♔

CHAPTER TWENTY-NINE

STOMPING THROUGH THE GARDENS, TALISE unconsciously followed the stream that ran under her balcony window. By the time she reached the pond at the end of the stream, the sun had started setting. She wanted to scream when she saw that another person was already there, but her body relaxed when she saw it was just Wendy.

Wendy jumped at the appearance of her friend, but the surprise on her face quickly turned to apprehension. She put on a honey-sweet smile. "How did the trial go?"

Talise slumped against a tree with an exaggerated frown. "I got two points."

A short breath of relief escaped Wendy. All the apprehension in her face was quickly replaced with a smile. "I knew you could do it!"

Talise slumped down further. "I actually did pretty great, especially considering how much I've improved. But did the emperor acknowledge that? No, of course not. His exact words were, 'You still have ample room for improvement.'"

Wendy blinked as she chewed on her lip. Talise could see the dilemma inside her friend. It wasn't right to question the emperor, or to talk bad about him. As a brand-new palace worker, Wendy didn't want to cross that line. Not to mention Wendy actually had honor. That probably was the biggest thing holding her back from saying the things in her head.

Instead of speaking, Wendy grabbed both of Talise's wrists and pulled her away from the tree. "I know what your problem is. It's because you're using a sword when you're clearly a dagger person."

A smile tugged at the corners of Talise's lips. "Yes, that must be it. I'll just quickly learn how to use a dagger, and then all my problems will be solved."

With a mischievous smile, Wendy bent down and produced two daggers that had been hidden under a piece of canvas on the ground. "I was hoping you'd say that."

She pushed the handle of one dagger toward Talise while she took the other.

Wendy flashed another honey-sweet smile. It was a completely normal look for her but looked supremely out of place with the shining dagger now gripped in her hand. Her gentle voice was at odds with the words coming out of her mouth, which made it even more amusing to listen.

"First," Wendy said in the same voice she'd use to coax a kitten out of a tree, "is stance. Relax your body, stand up straight, and put your right foot slightly forward."

Talise did as she was told, still fighting down a giggle.

Wendy narrowed her eyes, trying to look serious, but it only made her look sweeter than ever. "Second, we need a target. I've been using that tree over there."

The fact that the tree Wendy indicated already had several cuts in it just made the entire thing even better. Not only did Wendy have two daggers hidden under a piece of canvas, but she had already been throwing them before Talise got there.

"Finally, grip the dagger with your thumb over your fingers and throw. You don't need to throw it as hard as you can."

Wendy released her dagger. It did a half spin before the point lodged itself deep into the tree trunk. A wide grin spread across her cheeks, and her eyes glinted like a child seeing a rainbow for the first time. "Your turn," she said.

The stance was easy. Aaden had already helped Talise get that right during their sword practice. But the grip for the dagger felt different just because the weight was so different. When Talise released the dagger, she was certain it would fall nowhere near its mark.

To her surprise, the dagger landed in the tree trunk. Not anywhere near Wendy's dagger, but still. *In* the tree trunk.

"See," Wendy said with a grin. "You're a dagger person."

They practiced for a few more minutes, and Wendy taught her a few fancy spins. By the time the sun had long disappeared beneath the horizon, Talise's biggest weakness became obvious.

Aim.

It was her same problem with swords. It was so easy to aim when she was shaping, but with weapons, nothing felt the same.

Wendy tapped her chin as she stared at the two daggers they had just thrown into the tree trunk for the hundredth time. She narrowed her eyes at Talise's dagger which was much lower than it was supposed to be.

"You know," Wendy said. "I have an air shaping trick that might improve your aim."

Talise's heart nearly jumped out of her chest at those words. "What is it?"

Pulling her dagger from the tree trunk, Wendy shaped a circle of wind over her palm. When the wind was moving fast enough that Talise could see it moving, Wendy levitated the circle away from her palm and in front of the tree trunk.

Wendy took a few steps back away from the tree. With her eyes on the circle, she said, "You learn at an early age to sense the space around you. When babies learn to use a spoon, they often hit themselves in the cheek and miss their mouth entirely. But over time, they learn exactly where their mouth is. A few months later, they can put the spoon in their mouth without even thinking about it because they learned where their mouth fits in the space around them."

Talise gave a careful glance at Wendy and then to the wind circle she was still shaping in front of the tree. Why did weapon analogies always have something to do with babies?

"Also," Wendy said, perhaps sensing her confusion, "When we shape elements, they become an extension of ourselves. Therefore, shaping gives us an even better sense of the space around us."

Now Wendy pulled her arm back and thrust the dagger at the tree. It landed in the dead center of the wind circle.

"So, the wind circle is like a target," Talise said.

Wendy screwed up her mouth into a knot. "Not exactly. You aren't trying to throw the dagger at it. You're trying to use the wind so you can feel *where* to throw. Like this. If you close your eyes, you can still touch the palm of your hand. Even without looking. The wind circle is like that. It helps you have a better sense in space where your dagger needs to land."

Talise nodded. "So, it's not a target. It's something special for the dagger, like a crown. It's a crown of wind for the dagger to wear."

Wendy let out a giggle. "Exactly. Now you try."

When Talise threw her dagger this time, it landed on the edge of her wind crown. Not perfect like Wendy's throw, but much better than her last throw.

"Excellent," Wendy said with a grin. She then tilted her head to the side like a small puppy might do. She pulled her mouth into a small knot that gave her a look of innocence. And then she threw her own dagger, letting it spin twice before it stuck in the tree trunk so deep, it made the hilt shake.

Talise let out a laugh at the sight. "Who taught you how to do this anyway?"

The smile on Wendy's face vanished for a moment. "My brother."

As they walked to the tree to retrieve their daggers, Talise looked at Wendy with a sideways glance. "And that makes you… sad?"

Wendy's head popped up and the smile immediately returned. She gripped her dagger, seeming to take more effort than usual to pull it out. "Of course not. I just miss him, that's all. General Gale told me he's in the Gate on an assignment. That's why he isn't at the palace. I've written him several times, and I finally got a letter from him. But it doesn't have any of his usual flair."

The circles under Wendy's eyes were easier to spot now that the sun had gone down. The darkness made them stand out. There was hardly even a pout on Wendy's face, but Talise knew her friend well enough that a tight expression like this meant things were not well.

"What is his usual flair?"

Wendy shrugged. Her lips parted for a moment like she wasn't sure what to say. She shook her head with a huff and then pulled a letter from her pocket. "He didn't even write it." Disappointment hung in her voice, even though she tried to hide it.

Talise took the worn letter and held it in the light of the moon so she could read.

Wendy,

My hand is injured right now so I'm dictating this letter to another soldier who is writing it for me. I'm sorry I haven't written you back yet, but we are very busy.

I cannot stress enough how important this assignment is to Kamdaria. I know you don't like me being away, but this is the way it must be. Tell Mother and Father I love them and know that I am working hard. Please don't send any more letters until I write you back again.

Cyrus

When Talise finished the letter, she looked up to find Wendy rubbing her thumb over the hilt of her dagger. "He didn't even write *All my love*. He always writes that. I know he was dictating to another soldier, so he probably felt embarrassed, but I'm his sister. He teases me endlessly and frightens me just so I'll jump, but he's never been cruel." Her bottom lip started trembling, but she pulled her lips tight to stop it.

Talise hooked her arm around Wendy's. "Maybe he's trying to protect you."

Wendy's eyes glistened as she turned to face Talise.

Talise nodded. "Maybe he asked you not to write because he's afraid someone will find out. Or…" Talise tilted her voice so it took on a teasing edge. "Maybe he's trying to keep the other soldier from finding out about you because he doesn't want the other soldier falling in love with you. Maybe he's just being a protective older brother."

This earned a giggle from Wendy. She rubbed the hilt again. "He *did* tell me a few months ago that one of the palace soldiers was asking about me."

A cool breeze whipped around them causing goosebumps on Talise's skin. She shaped a burst of fire through her veins and began rubbing her arms. "Maybe we should go inside."

Wendy nodded with a short glance back at the moon. "It is pretty late, and I do have to wake up early tomorrow to help set something up for your last trial."

"And no," Wendy said with a smug grin as she turned away, "I am sworn to secrecy. I can't tell you anything about it."

"Please?" Talise asked, giving the sweetest expression she could muster.

Wendy shook her head quickly. "No. I promised General Gale I wouldn't breathe a word. You'll just have to wait until the next trial."

The walk back to the palace consisted of Wendy trying to get Talise to talk about Aaden. Talise used every bit of her restraint and kept her mouth shut. The more Wendy prodded, the guiltier Talise felt about her last words to him.

You have a past no one has forgotten.

How could she say such a thing? It was true, of course, but Aaden already knew that. He didn't need a reminder.

Talise said goodbye to Wendy and trudged back to her own room while a weight pressed down on her. She rounded a corner to use a hall she didn't usually use, and suddenly came face to face with the door to Aaden's living quarters.

She cursed herself for even knowing where it was. Staring at the door, she considered knocking. But for what?

Even as she asked herself the question, the answer became clear. Because she *did* need him.

Maybe she didn't trust him. Maybe she didn't want to get closer to him, but she did need him. The emperor had made sure of it.

Her hand formed a fist to knock. Just before her knuckles hit the wooden door, she flattened her hand and pressed her palm against the wood instead.

She closed her eyes and rested her forehead against the door breathing in the scent of the wood.

Cedar.

Identifying the wood was only a distraction and she knew it. She was trying to avoid the apology she had to give because she had no idea how to say what she needed to say. It would be so much easier to just let Aaden hate her.

She closed her eyes and she could see the emperor in her mind. He told her this would happen. He specifically told her to get help from Aaden before the trial, and she had willfully ignored him.

She didn't want to trust him, but she knew Aaden was her only chance to win the trials.

But how could she ever apologize?

She looked up at the door, at her hand pressed against it, and then she let her arm fall to her side.

Tomorrow.

She'd do it tomorrow for sure. After a good night's rest, she'd know just what to say. Somehow, she'd find a way to get Aaden to work with her.

♔

Chapter Thirty

Black curtained Talise's vision as her mind lifted out of a deep sleep. Someone was shaking her shoulder, but maybe that was just the remnant of a dream.

"Wake up!"

Talise shot up at the sound of the voice. Her senses were on high alert, scoping out the room for danger. The maroon silk from her bed covers enveloped her lower body while her eyes scanned the room. Her room.

Then why the yelling?

And what was Commander Blaise doing in her room?

He stood tall with perfectly combed hair that had streaks of gray through the black. His shoulders were rolled back with military precision. He wore a goatee just like Aaden's except the commander's was much thicker.

Now that her eyes were on him, his voice seemed more professional than hurried.

"Your final trial begins now."

She blinked at him, still trying to make sense of everything. The light from the moon shone through her window telling her morning was still hours away. How long had it been since she and Wendy had left the gardens?

"Get dressed and meet me in the library. You'll receive more instructions there."

He disappeared before she could ask any questions, and a part of her wondered if he did it on purpose. Had Wendy known she would get woken up in the middle of the night for the final trial? Is that why she had suggested they go to bed? Or had Talise been the one to suggest it? She couldn't remember now.

Dragging a simple tunic over her head, Talise made a mental note to go to bed earlier tonight. She tried to rub the sleep out of her eyes as she moped around looking for her boots. Just as she finished lacing them, a long yawn opened her mouth wide.

Her fingers were too tired to pin the front pieces of her hair back, so she opted to let her rumbled black hair fall in its natural bob. At the last second, she decided to tuck Wendy's dagger into a belt hidden under her tunic.

Walking to the library felt like wading through a rushing river.

She was going to fail this trial if she didn't wake herself up more. She slapped herself in the face twice before the stinging in her cheek convinced her that had been a monumentally bad decision.

She was still trying to rub the sleep out of her eyes when she made it to the library. Aaden sat on top of a table with his ankles casually propped up on a nearby chair. He didn't look at her when she came in, but she saw how his arms crossed even tighter over his chest when she got closer.

A nerve inside her flinched. That was right. She still hadn't apologized.

Commander Blaise entered the room and gave a single disapproving glance at his grandson's stance. Aaden jumped off the table and quickly stood at attention. Talise's eyebrow quirked up the slightest bit. Aaden had never shown such instant respect. Not even to the emperor.

Commander Blaise didn't seem to notice since he was busy looking over his shoulder. A palace guard wearing fire orange approached him and they spoke in anxious whispers. The silver hem of the guard's tunic told her he was a high-ranking guard. Someone important.

She didn't think their final trial was important enough for a high-ranking member of the palace guard to be involved. And now she started to wonder why the emperor wasn't here. He had been at all the other trials.

"Your trial begins now," Commander Blaise said suddenly. "A small group of palace guards are in the palace pretending to be members of Kessoku. You must capture them and take them to the antechamber that leads to the dungeons. You may use any force necessary to accomplish this goal." The commander gave a significant look to both of them at these words.

Then, he gestured behind him at four guards with yellow-hemmed tunics. These guards were some of the lowest ranking in the palace.

"These four guards are at your disposal. Use them however you need in order to accomplish your goal. The emperor will meet with you after the trial is finished."

Commander Blaise turned on his heel and took a few steps before he froze in place. He glanced back at them and lifted a finger to his mouth as if thinking. Without making eye contact, he pointed at nothing in particular.

"You must also determine what purpose Kessoku has for being here. Their goal is likely to kill the emperor, but if they have any other motive, you need to find out. The guards posing as Kessoku have been instructed to never break out of their role until the emperor announces the trial is finished."

With a short nod, he turned to leave again.

"How do we know which guards are pretending to be Kessoku?" Talise asked just as the commander walked through the library doorway.

A hint of irritation flashed in his eyes. Spitting the words out in a rush, he said, "Members of Kessoku wear a patch on their tunic just above the heart. It looks like three rings interconnected."

He didn't wait for any more questions.

Talise was left with the weight of her unspoken apology. She glanced at Aaden, but his hands were back to being crossed over his chest. He tilted his head away from her as if looking at her might turn him into stone.

With the apology on the tip of her tongue, Aaden marched out of the library, his nose in the air. She swallowed the huff threatening to spill out of her mouth. He wasn't going to make this easy.

She probably deserved it, but that didn't make it any easier to endure. Stomping after him, she tried to catch up. The four guards followed right on her heels. Each one took meticulous steps, and their lips were pressed into thin lines.

Not that she expected it, but apparently, she wouldn't get any sympathy from them. Internally, she growled. Why did the last trial have to be today? Before sunrise? Why couldn't she have apologized *before* it started?

Once outside the library, Aaden glanced down the hall to the servant's quarters. He cupped his hand over his ear, which prompted Talise to mimic the action. Before deciding with absolute certainty that she couldn't hear anything, Aaden was already turning down the other end of the hallway to get to the ballroom.

Luckily, Aaden couldn't see when she rolled her eyes. *Yes, surely the members of Kessoku would be busy looking for the emperor in the ballroom.* She shook her head. They'd have better luck searching in the strategy room or the emperor's personal quarters.

Before she could voice her latest thought, a loud clatter sounded through the room. Aaden glanced back at her with wide eyes, momentarily forgetting to ignore her.

"I think it came from the throne room," Talise said under her breath.

Aaden barely nodded before tearing down the hallway toward the throne room. She followed right on his heels and nearly knocked him over when he stopped with a start. She tried to lean around him to look inside, but he threw his arm out in front of her stomach and pushed her back.

Once again swallowing her huff, she whispered, "How many are there?"

He pushed her back even more as he peeked around the door frame. "Five." He shook his head and leaned further around the doorway. Suddenly, he pulled his head back. "No, there are only four. One of the guard's has a tunic that billowed and I—" He shook his head and turned away from her. "It doesn't matter. There are four of them."

The muscles in his neck tensed as he glanced back in the throne room. Was he embarrassed? That would be a first. Her thumbnail found the edge of her tunic and she began scratching it. Maybe now was just as good a time as any for that apology.

She took a deep breath, but Aaden seemed determined to keep her from saying anything.

He shaped a fire ball over his palm, then shot it into the room. After a few shouts, two of the guards wearing the Kessoku emblem appeared in the hallway. Without thinking, Talise charged at them.

Their eyes went wide when they saw Talise, Aaden, and the four guards in the hallway. The Kessoku men both shaped a wave of wind which knocked Talise and Aaden off their feet along with the guards with the yellow-hemmed tunics.

As they were getting back up, Aaden jabbed a thumb at the two Kessoku men running down the hall. "Take some guards and get those two Kessoku. I'll take care of the other two."

Splitting up probably wasn't the best idea. That's how she had lost her last two trials. But with the Kessoku men already running past the council room, she didn't have much of a choice.

In a desperate attempt to stop them, she shaped a wall of fire just in front of them, halting them in their tracks. Rather than turn back toward her, they shoved open the door to the training room.

Talise grinned as she followed after them. With an entire wall filled with bowls of elements, the training room had more than enough tools to help her stop these two men on her own. She wouldn't even need the two guards on her heels.

She started shaping the water out of the bowls before she even reached the doorway. By the time she entered the training room, she had two large puddles of water hovering in front of each hand.

Bending her body at the waist, she ran into the room with her head low. Both the Kessoku men sent fire balls toward her. Since they aimed where her head should have been, they both missed. This gave her enough time to throw the puddles of water at their feet.

She froze the water around their ankles just as they were mid-stride.

Wearing a triumphant smile, she strode toward them. "That was easier than I expected."

After their momentary shock, the Kessoku men sprang into action. One of them tried to use water shaping to melt the ice. The other used fire balls. It was obvious that air was the primary for both of them, but the fire balls still did the trick.

As Talise prepared to tackle one of the Kessoku men, he threw another burst of air that knocked her down. By the time she got to her feet, they were both free of the ice and running for the door.

She frowned. Apparently, they weren't going to make this easy on her.

She shaped a burst of wind to slam the door shut in their faces. She could freeze their feet in ice again, but they'd just use fire balls to melt it and be back to where they were now. What she needed was a distraction.

They threw another wall of wind in her direction, but this time she was ready for it. Just as she ducked, she shaped the dirt from an entire shelf of bowls out into the open space between them. When the dirt was spread out evenly in the air, she shaped a small cycle of air through the dirt, making a mini dirt tornado.

After she added more dirt to the tornado, the Kessoku men threw their hands in front of their faces, trying to see through the cloud of dirt.

As she stepped closer, she motioned to the guards, showing them where to walk. With one hand shaping the air, she shaped a large puddle of water at their feet and froze it again. One of her palace guards wrapped a set of chains around the wrists of a Kessoku man. The other Kessoku man was still slightly out of reach.

He bent down and burst fire ball after fire ball into the ice puddle. When his feet were free, he stepped forward, but Talise stood in his way. "Going somewhere?" she asked with a smirk.

His jaw flexed, and he turned on his heel.

But just behind him, her other palace guard stood with chains ready to clasp over his wrists. The Kessoku man's shoulders twitched as if about to run, so she shaped a wall of fire around his sides and back, making sure the only place he could run was right into her guard.

Soon, both Kessoku men were in chains, and Talise was whipping the hair out of her face as she pushed open the door to the antechamber.

Aaden was already there with the other two Kessoku men in chains.

Her stomach sank at the sight of his smug expression, but at least his hair looked uncharacteristically windswept. His tunic was even burned on the side. It hadn't been easy for him either.

When they shut the door on the four Kessoku men, Talise asked, "What do we do now?"

Aaden shrugged, looking down the hall instead of at her.

Talise screwed her mouth into a knot. "I guess we should go wait in the throne room."

Aaden didn't seem to have an opinion on this, so she decided to take action. Pointing to his two palace guards, she said, "You two stay here and guard the antechamber." Pointing at her two guards, she said, "You two come with us to the throne room."

They waited in the throne room for a few minutes. Talise cleared her throat, once again thinking now was as good a time as any to apologize, when the sound of metal hitting stone wafted in from the hall.

Chains.

Neither of them said a word as they ran down the hallway toward the antechamber. They saw long before they reached the room that the door stood wide open. The Kessoku men were nowhere in sight. Aaden's two guards lay on the stone doing way too good a job pretending to be passed out.

Her stomach sank down all the way to her toes.

Of course the final trial wouldn't be this easy.

Chapter Thirty-One

TALISE REACHED FOR HER ELBOW as she looked at the empty chains on the ground. Before she could curse herself for thinking the trial was over, Aaden began pounding his fist into his palm.

"There were five of them. I knew there were five of them! How could I be so stupid?" He stomped down the hall with every muscle in his body rigid.

"Aaden." Her voice shook as she said it. Her palace guards could hear every word. Too close for comfort, but she couldn't help that now. She had put this off long enough.

When Aaden whipped around, he had fire in his eyes. "What?" he said through a clenched jaw.

She let out a breath, and her shoulders dropped. "I'm sorry." She reached again for her elbow, pulling it close. "I'm sorry I said all those things yesterday. I didn't mean it."

The vein in his jaw pulsed as he clenched his jaw tighter. "You didn't mean it?" He let out a vicious chuckle. "So, you *don't* think the emperor is using these trials to test my honor?"

Her chin dropped as a wave of shame trickled down from her shoulders and into her gut. "I do think that, but…" She glanced up, forcing herself to look him in the eye. "I think he's testing me too. I just haven't figured out what he wants from me yet."

He didn't say anything, but the ice in his demeanor began to melt, even if it was just a fraction.

Talise bit into her lip, wishing the guards weren't standing so close. "And anyway, I still shouldn't have said those things. You already knew them and for me to point them out like that…" Her voice froze. Nothing would be sufficient for the apology he deserved. No words would be strong enough. With a glance into his eyes, she simply said, "I'm sorry."

He stared back at her with a gaze that could have pierced armor.

She reached for the ends of her hair as she looked away. "I don't think we should split up again. The only chance I have of passing this trial is with you." In a resigned voice, she finished, "I need your help."

Aaden stared at her for a long time. Talise could practically feel the guards behind her, twitching with their weapons. Still, Aaden stared.

Finally, he said, "I heard one of the Kessoku say something about the library. I bet that's where they are now."

She felt her face lift at these words. They were the beginnings of an olive branch. An offering.

When he turned, he tilted his head, beckoning her forward. "Maybe we can set up an ambush. You go into the library first and make them think you're alone. Try to catch them with your shaping. Then, when they're busy trying to catch you, I'll come in with the guards and tackle them."

"Using me as bait. Nice." The sarcastic edge to her voice was unavoidable.

Aaden turned back long enough to give her a sideways glance. Something about his expression made her stomach jump. Perhaps it was the way the corner of his mouth turned up with an amused grin. "I'd never suggest it if I thought you couldn't handle yourself."

It was good that he turned back around after those words. If he could see how fiercely she was blushing, she'd probably have to skewer herself. But with his back turned, she didn't mind the heat spreading through her cheeks and neck. With Aaden around, warmth never seemed far behind.

They stopped at the training hall to gather bowls filled with elements. The water spilled as they walked, but she could shape it back into the bowls once they set them down. Once they reached the library, they arranged the bowls close to the door.

She and Aaden peeked in the library from the doorway and whispered to each other in the quietest whispers they could manage. After some quiet planning, now it was time to act. Aaden nodded to her.

Talise allowed his confidence to give her courage. A small thought at the back of her mind suggested that maybe he was trying to trick her. Maybe he was trying to make her fail again by facing the Kessoku men alone.

But she quickly brushed that thought away. She didn't trust Aaden, not completely, but maybe that didn't matter. She trusted him enough to follow through on his part of the plan.

With a final calming breath, she charged into the library. As she expected, fire balls were thrown toward her immediately. She used water from a nearby bowl to put out the fire balls before they reached her.

While shaping another tornado, she scanned the room. As they had hoped, all five of the Kessoku men stood in the room. Three of them had their eyes on her, already busy shaping weapons to use against her. The other two men seemed intent on wreaking as much havoc as possible.

They tore books from the bookshelves and knocked over tables. She wondered if the emperor had instructed them to be so dramatic, or if he'd make them regret it later.

Commander Blaise's earlier words rang in her ears. *Use any force necessary.* Yes, this was just a trial, but if she really had to face Kessoku someday, it would be good to practice as if this were real.

The tornado in front of her spun with increased velocity until the Kessoku men's hair and clothes whipped around them. She knocked them off their feet. Out the corner of her eye, she noticed one of the Kessoku men racing toward the door to the library. She shaped a wall of fire blocking his way, which caused him to stumble backward.

Maybe she was showing off her shaping a little bit, but next she made icicles out of the water puddle and sent them flying like daggers. The Kessoku men all waved their hands through the air with startled cries.

It was hard to keep track of all five Kessoku men at once. She hoped Aaden would be coming soon because the five men had apparently realized the only way out of the room was to get rid of her.

Thinking the men would probably report back to the emperor on her shaping skills, she decided to shape earth next. Summoning the dirt from a nearby bowl, she sent clods at the Kessoku men each time a fist was raised. When their fists made contact with dirt instead of her, they seemed to get angrier each time.

And now she had lost track of one of the Kessoku men. Hopefully Aaden would be here soon.

With her eyes on a flying dirt clod, one of the Kessoku men grabbed her wrist and twisted her arm painfully behind her back. Without thinking, she jabbed her elbow into his stomach causing him to bend over with a gasp.

And then Aaden was there.

He shaped a wind blast that sent the Kessoku men to the floor. While they were still disoriented, Aaden and her two palace guards tackled the men to the ground and had them in chains.

But when she counted, there were only four.

Aaden seemed to notice at the same time as her. It took her less than a moment to react. She reached for the nearest Kessoku and bundled his collar in her fist. "Where is your comrade?" she demanded.

The four men looked back at her as stoic as ever. No emotion was betrayed in any feature. Talise wanted to huff, wanted to scream, but the trial wasn't over yet. If she could just do it right this time maybe she could win the emperor's approval for once.

If she wanted them to talk, she'd have to show them she meant business. She snatched Wendy's dagger from the belt under her tunic and held the tip against the neck of the nearest Kessoku man.

"If you don't answer, I'll kill you." She tried to put as much fury into her voice as if this were real. It sounded mostly believable, but it probably could have been better. She drove the dagger forward until the tip pressed against the man's skin, just shy of breaking it.

The Kessoku man gulped. She had to pull the dagger away a fraction so it wouldn't draw blood. With her mind so focused on the dagger, she almost didn't notice how the man's eyes flitted to a darkened corner of the room.

It would have escaped her notice except Aaden immediately took a step forward and stared at the exact same spot. Talise tried to remember what was on the other side of that wall.

"The treasury!" both she and Aaden shouted at once.

As they ran for the door, Aaden gave quick commands to the two palace guards. "Gag them so they can't scream out to the last Kessoku man. Keep them in chains and put wind gloves over their hands so they can't shape. Follow behind us and shout if anyone comes."

His final command turned out to be unnecessary. Talise had never seen the door to the treasury open, not even a crack. So, when she saw a garish jade vase propping it open, they knew the last Kessoku man was inside.

They peeked through the doorway and saw the man standing atop a delicately painted table with gilded gold edges. He used the height to reach a shelf where rows of gold bags sat. The man's pockets were stuffed full of gold, and now he was stuffing the gold bags down his tunic, letting his belt hold them in place.

Her tunic tightened around her neck before she realized Aaden was trying to pull her away from the door. She quickly moved back into the hallway and looked at him anxiously.

His words were so quiet, he mostly mouthed the words rather than whispered them. "I think the emperor wants this to end in a sword fight."

He gestured to the floor of the hallway where a lone sword lay. Now that she saw it, she remembered the Kessoku man had been wearing a sword as well.

She was more grateful than ever that she had decided to work with Aaden because his sword skill far surpassed her own. Unfortunately, he picked at his goatee with a look of… hesitation?

Aaden shook his head, keeping his eyes to the ground. "I can't do it like this. He has the higher ground. We have to immobilize him *before* he comes down, or we have to get him to come down. But he knows we're looking for him, and he knows he has the higher ground. I don't know what to do."

Talise pulled the dagger from her belt again, this time wearing a small smile. When she peeked around the doorway, she eyed the Kessoku man carefully.

"*What* are you doing?" Aaden pulled her away as he breathed the words into her ear. "I know my grandfather said to use any force necessary, but I don't think he wants you stabbing one of his guards."

She wriggled out of his grasp and shook her head with a condescending look. "Calm down. I'm not going to stab him. I have another idea."

"Does this idea require you to aim? Because if it does—"

She jabbed her elbow into his side maybe a little harder than he deserved. "Just trust me," she whispered as quietly as she could.

When she looked back into the room, the Kessoku man was now dropping royal jewelry over his head and arms. He was far too distracted to notice the small circle of wind that appeared on the edge of his clothing.

As she shaped the wind, Talise let her body feel the space around her. She allowed the wind crown to become an extension of her own body.

Using the stance and throw Wendy had taught her, Talise threw the dagger from her fingertips. Her breathing had been perfect as she prepared for the throw, but now she held her breath.

The dagger spun three times. As it drew nearer, her breath hitched. It was closer to the man's body than she thought it would be.

But then the dagger stuck in the man's tunic just under his armpit. Not in his body. It pinned him to the wooden shelf.

"Nice," Aaden said as he jumped into the treasury. The man reached for his sword, but with the dagger pinning his clothing down, he couldn't reach it in time. Aaden jumped onto the table and shoved the man up against the wall.

As soon as Talise pulled the dagger from the its place, Aaden swept his foot against the man's ankles causing him to fall on his hands and knees. Aaden retrieved a length of rope from his pocket and tied the man's arms behind his back.

She and Aaden shared a triumphant look, and she swore he almost winked at her. As Aaden led the man out of the room, a line of dust on the wall caught her attention. She ran a finger over the dust noting how straight the edge was. But why?

She traced over another line of dust a little farther down the wall. It was almost as if a picture had been hanging there, but now it was gone.

CHAPTER THIRTY-TWO

THE FACES OF THE KESSOKU men remained impossible to read as they were brought to the antechamber. The room was now empty. The two palace guards from earlier must have left for other duties. As Talise's guards shoved the Kessoku men into the antechamber, her gut began twisting at the thought of that dust line.

They had already removed the gold and jewels from off the man who had been in the treasury, but what if he had pretended to steal more than just gold? She couldn't shake the feeling that this trial wasn't over yet.

She became even more certain when the emperor didn't arrive to announce the end of the trial.

Straightening her spine, she pointed to her two guards. "Stand outside and shut the door. We aren't done with these men yet."

The shorter of the two guards clenched his jaw, but the taller one's lip trembled ever so slightly. Soon, the shorter guard was pushing the other through the door, giving him a look that dared him to step out of line.

"Of course," the shorter guard said as he pushed his friend out the door.

Once they were alone, Talise knelt down and clawed at the last Kessoku man's pant legs.

"Uh," Aaden said with confusion lining his words. "Care to share what you're doing?"

It gave her tremendous satisfaction to hear the barest hint of jealousy in Aaden's voice. "I'm trying to find— Ah ha!"

She pulled a fabric painting that had been tucked deep into the side of the Kessoku man's pants. The soft fabric unrolled easily and when she saw it, she gasped.

A painted tree filled the fabric. The rich green leaves went all the way to the edge. In the most intricate calligraphy she had ever seen, names were carefully painted overtop the tree, covering the leaves and branches. In the exact middle of the tree trunk, Emperor Flarius' name was painted just over Empress Isla's. And just below their names were the names of their children. Talise's thumb brushed under the seven names as she counted them.

"Is that the emperor's family tree?" Aaden asked.

Talise started and immediately rolled the painting up while her stomach did somersaults. "If anything happens to this, I think the emperor will personally murder us. We better not touch it."

Aaden nodded emphatically though maybe he was a little disappointed he hadn't gotten a closer look. Talise turned for the door but quickly turned back again.

She glanced at Aaden as she tapped the fabric roll against her leg. "Commander Blaise said we need to find out what they wanted. Maybe that's part of the trial. Why would they steal the family tree?"

Aaden shrugged. "I'm sure it's over. I bet one of the guards is getting the emperor now."

With the memory of her last two failures still fresh in her mind, Talise turned on the Kessoku men, glaring especially at the one who had been in the treasury.

She leaned in toward him and said in her fiercest voice, "Why did you steal the family tree? What did you want with it?"

Pure rage filled the man's eyes as he spit in her face. The water splattered all over the right side of her face, especially under her eye.

"Okay," Aaden said wrapping his arm around her shoulder. "We're done here."

She didn't resist as he pulled her away from the men and toward the door. She was too stunned to do anything besides use her shoulder to wipe the spit from her face.

Aaden looked over his shoulder as they walked. "Was that really necessary?" he asked through a clenched jaw.

Talise turned the doorknob slowly. The spit had been too much, but at least she had passed the trial. She was certain of it. It wouldn't have come to spitting otherwise. When the door cracked open, she heard the voices of her palace guards talking in the hallway.

"They deserve to know the truth."

Talise recognized the voice of the taller guard, the nervous one. She threw the door open and stared at the two guards who looked frightened at her sudden appearance. "Who?" she asked.

The shorter, more serious, guard peered at his companion through the side of his eye. "Don't say a word."

Chapter Thirty-Three

Talise stood gaping at her two palace guards who were in the middle of a staring contest with each other. What truth? What could they be talking about? The sinking feeling in the pit of her stomach told her that her triumph of passing the trial had been premature.

The nervous guard dragged his hand down the side of his face and whispered, "They're coming."

Talise's eyes narrowed. "Who?"

"Shut up!" The serious guard slammed his palm against the wall as he glared at the man. "Don't open your mouth again."

The nervous guard turned toward his companion. He held his hands out in front of his body and they shook as he spoke. "Kessoku is coming."

The serious guard shook his head side to side slowly. "I swear on the emperor, I'll run my sword through you if you keep talking."

Talise glanced at Aaden, who looked as confused as her. She squared her shoulders. "The emperor said Kessoku was nothing more than a nuisance."

The nervous guard let out chuckle. "A nuisance? Is that what he called them?"

Aaden took a step forward. "And he said they were in the Gate."

The guard's chuckle transformed into an unhinged laugh. "The Gate? Not all of them are in the Gate. Not those ones." He pointed to the door of the antechamber.

Talise felt her stomach dropping down down down. Images flashed in her mind. The stoic faces of the Kessoku men, their willingness to fight, how one of them had spit in her face.

"This wasn't really a trial? This was a real attack?" For the first time since she met him, Aaden's voice sounded small.

The serious guard shoved the nervous guard's shoulders against the wall. "The emperor will kill you himself if you say anything else."

The nervous guard turned to him with a look of resignation. "We're going to die anyway. Kessoku is coming."

A chill spread through Talise's arms, causing her to shiver despite the warmth in the hall. "But we captured all five of them this time. They can't escape."

"Not them," the nervous guard said as he slapped him palm against his forehead. "They were just a scout group. Kessoku is here with an army. I saw them at the base of the mountain. The army will be here by sunrise."

The serious guard shook the man's shoulders, but this time a hint of worry lingered in his own eyes. "Calm down. Commander Blaise is in the strategy room with the generals and high guard. We've been training for this. They just needed someone to take care of the scout group, so Commander Blaise could have time to prepare for the attack. And these two did it. We're going to be fine."

The nervous guard dropped to the ground and began rocking himself back and forth as he clutched his knees to his chest.

It hurt too much to watch after a while. Talise moved her gaze back to the antechamber door. They had caught them this time. She was sure of it. But suddenly the memory of their earlier failure brought goosebumps to her flesh.

"The other guards." Her words came out soft, but she pushed out the rest so they couldn't be mistaken. "The ones who got knocked out. Where are they?"

"They're dead," the nervous guard moaned as he clenched and unclenched his fists. "Palace servants came and took them away so you wouldn't get suspicious."

Talise just managed to hold in her gasp. She had spent all that time apologizing to Aaden and complaining about her earlier failures. And all that time, Kessoku, the real Kessoku, had been in the palace.

She didn't dare glance at Aaden. His face must have been as horrified as hers, and she couldn't bear the sight of it. After a gulp, she asked, "They have an army?"

The nervous guard slammed his forehead against his knees and began grabbing fistfuls of his hair as he let out groans.

To her surprise, the shorter guard began to speak. Apparently, he had realized it was too late to keep any secrets. "Kessoku came a few months ago during a party. They hadn't attacked in years, so none of us expected it. They…"

The words lingered on the tip of his tongue, but they caught, as if he couldn't bring himself to say the words.

Trying to find courage, she asked. "What happened?"

"It was a bloodbath." The nervous guard was now using his tunic to mop large splashes of tears off his cheeks.

The serious guard stood tall, but he looked away. "They killed the Master Shapers and half the guards. They took some of them as prisoners, but we haven't heard anything from them since that night. They're probably dead. Flint's entire squad was murdered in front of his eyes," he finished by pointing to the nervous guard on the ground. Suddenly, his distress made sense.

A hollow chuckle escaped Talise's mouth. "So, the assignment in the Gate that all the Master Shapers are busy with is…" Her gut twisted again, but this time with such force that bile ran up her throat. She clutched her stomach, trying to hold it in.

Wendy's brother. Wendy's brother was supposedly on the assignment in the Gate. Did that mean he was dead? Did Wendy know?

When Aaden's hand pressed into the small of her back, she immediately turned into him. No part of her could resist him now. Her body shook as he held her. Reality crashed down around her with dire pain.

The serious guard spoke again. "I'll take you to the strategy room. Since you know the truth now, Commander Blaise could use your help with the attack. The emperor is hidden for now, but he'll see you when this is over."

Talise took in a deep breath and stepped away from Aaden. Now she really had to pull it together. All her frustration with the trials melted away while a grounding fear took over.

The trials were over now. It was time for the real fight to begin.

PART THREE

DUST

CROWN

CHAPTER THIRTY-FOUR

THE EMPEROR'S MANSION HAD TO be defended with shaping.

Talise understood the plan when Commander Blaise explained it an hour ago. It all made sense on paper. A perfect strategy. She wasn't prepared for the way her heart pattered as she trudged across the palace gardens to the mansion.

One step forward. Then another. Now step again and remember to breathe.

She hadn't even looked at the emperor's mansion since arriving at the palace a few months ago. The lonely building stood on the opposite end of the garden from the palace. Its roof curved up at the ends just like all the buildings on the palace grounds. Unlike the palace's jade tiles, the emperor's mansion had charcoal tiles adorning the roof. For some reason, its presence seemed more terrifying than the army of Kessoku that would arrive soon.

She dug her fingernails into her palms, forcing herself to the present moment. *Not* an army.

Commander Blaise had explained it was just a *company* of soldiers. Two hundred fighters, and probably some of Kessoku's best, but not all of them. They knew Kessoku had at least a few thousand on their side.

A bitter taste entered her throat. Her muscles twitched as she remembered, yet again, how she had been lied to. Almost everyone in the palace had known Kessoku was out there, probably planning another attack. The emperor knew. Commander Blaise knew. General Gale. All the guards. The servants. Most of the court.

They all knew how dangerous Kessoku was, and not one single person had bothered to tell her or Aaden. Even Wendy had known. That cut Talise deeper than anything.

Wendy hadn't known everything, but she had picked up enough hints from General Gale that he swore her to secrecy.

Secrecy.

It didn't matter that the emperor had forbidden everyone from revealing information about the attack. No one could explain how Kessoku infiltrated the palace months ago, and all the Master Shapers and half the guards had been killed or taken prisoner. It didn't matter that the emperor threatened to execute anyone who let the truth slip.

What mattered was the emperor kept the secret from *her*. She and Aaden were the only two Master Shapers in all of Kamdaria. No wonder the emperor had chosen two Master Shapers. The palace had never needed them more desperately. And still, he didn't even trust them with the truth about their enemy.

That hurt.

The guards stopped short when they reached the chrysanthemum patch just outside the emperor's mansion. Nobody seemed to notice when Talise gasped at the sight of those flowers. Claye was still rubbing the sleep out of his eyes. Wendy whispered with the guards, probably going over the plan another time.

A warm set of fingers brushed against her elbow causing her to turn around. Without a word, Aaden stared into her eyes. He seemed to know instinctively how much anxiety was rushing through her.

Of course he did. Of course he was the only one who noticed her gasp. She tried to plaster a nervous smile on her face, but he seemed to know that was fake too.

He didn't say anything.

Neither did she.

They had both remained silent during the explanations and the planning. Perhaps he was just as frustrated as she was about being kept from the truth. It was all they could do to listen and nod and go along with the plan.

And they did have an important part in this plan.

"I see them." Wendy's whisper quivered through the air as she pointed. Following the finger, Talise saw ten heads pop over a ridge. One of the many advantages to the location of Ridgerock Palace was the fact that it had been built on a mountain. Already, Kessoku had used a great deal of energy just climbing the steep rock that led them to the palace grounds.

What type of weapons would they have? Perhaps it was a strange thought to have, but there it was anyway. They knew Kessoku's base was in the Gate, the middle ring of Kamdaria. That meant they didn't have access to the same resources or artisans as the elite had in the Crown. But, if any members of Kessoku had a silver crescent moon on their ID card, they could easily purchase excellent weaponry in the Crown, and have it delivered to the Gate.

At least none of the fighters would be from the Storm. A shiver shook through Talise's shoulders as she recalled her former home. Though weak and desperate, no one fought more fiercely than those who lived in the outer ring of Kamdaria. She had once seen a man keep fighting even after he had one arm sliced clean off. Even with weakened bodies and no shaping, no one could match the ferocity found in the Storm. Because in the Storm, people had nothing left to lose.

With a small glance at Aaden, they both raised their hands and started shaping.

As discussed, they began by shaping the water out of the stream that ran through the garden. They levitated the water through the air and sent it splashing down on Kessoku like a waterfall. When the water hit the men with its full force, they levitated it back up and sent it crashing down again. Over and over.

She didn't look closely enough to know if any Kessoku lost their grip and fell because of the water. A part of her didn't want to know.

Their shouts were unintelligible from so far away, but they *were* shouting. Each time the water crashed down on them, the shouting became more distressed.

Stage one of their plan was a success. As they had suspected, Kessoku never expected to be attacked with shaping. Since the other Master Shapers were dead, they must have assumed the palace soldiers would rely on swords and arrows.

The water didn't stop them for long. Luckily, their plan never expected it to.

She and Aaden glanced at each other again. He dropped his hands to prepare for the next stage. Fist-sized rocks began levitating off the ground as Aaden used earth shaping to drop them into a pile at their sides.

The moment he stopped shaping, she felt the absence of his power. He had shaped so much water and made it look effortless.

She continued levitating the water and making it crash down. She tried to lift as much as they had done together, but it was more difficult than she expected.

At least twenty Kessoku soldiers cleared the ridge now and moved past her waterfall. They ignored the emperor's mansion completely and marched toward the palace. Gritting her teeth together, Talise shaped a wall of water about ten feet in front of them. They laughed at the barrier and kept marching without missing a beat.

She felt the eyes of the palace soldiers on her, watching, waiting for her to make the next move. But she ignored them. No Kessoku had ever seen what she was about to do, and she planned to fully exploit the element of surprise.

As the Kessoku soldiers marched on, their expressions hardened. It wasn't until the first row of soldiers made contact with the wall of water that she began to act again.

Fire flooded through her veins as she froze her hand and arms all the way up to her elbows. She pushed her hands through the air to send a chill to the wall of water.

Just as the Kessoku soldiers began sticking their toes and hands through the water in a march, it crystalized into a wall of ice.

Even through the ice, she saw how every jaw of the Kessoku soldiers had dropped. When they tried to free their feet from the ice, it held firm.

Stage two. Success.

Talise gulped as more Kessoku climbed over the ridge. There were at least fifty of them now. Their momentary surprise at seeing ice shaping had already vanished. Using the hilts of their swords, plus a bit of fire shaping, they tore the ice wall down.

She shaped it back up again each time, but they were getting faster. She wouldn't be able to hold them with the ice wall forever.

Behind her, the others were getting into position. Two rows of guards stood in front of the mansion, holding a sword in one hand and a spear in the other. Wendy and Claye stood among them. Aaden took his place at her side.

Her heart rate increased as Kessoku broke down her wall again. The time drew near for the next stage of the plan. Even after years of training on focus and restraint, nothing could prepare her for this.

A real enemy marched a garden's length away. No matter how good her shaping, one wrong move could lead to death at their hands.

Gulping again, she raised her hands and gave a nod to Aaden.

Time to fight.

CHAPTER THIRTY-FIVE

THE ICE WALL HAD BEEN forgotten. Kessoku stomped over the ice fragments with the same determination they wore while climbing over the ridge. In the violet hue of sunrise, they stomped, looking ready to kill.

Guilt washed over Talise as they drew closer. The dilemma had roiled through her mind at least a dozen times already. She wasn't a killer. She didn't want their blood on her hands. She didn't want any blood on her hands.

But this was a war. One that Kessoku had started.

An urge to fight hardened inside her. The feeling was almost opposite to when she'd been safe in the strategy room with Commander Blaise making these plans. In her head, she didn't believe she could ever kill anyone.

But out here, it was different. Each member of Kessoku had murder in their eyes. It was obvious they meant to destroy any obstacle between them and the emperor without regard for life.

In this moment, she finally understood the words Commander Blaise had spoken an hour before. "Don't think of it as killing the enemy. Think of it as defending Kamdaria."

The distinction didn't seem significant in the strategy room. But with their weapons glinting in the sun, it made sense now.

It was her life or theirs. They were the ones who made the rules, but she still had to play by them. She wasn't about to die now.

Clenching her jaw, she levitated a handful of the rocks off the pile Aaden had made earlier. Once in the air, she shaped the rocks across the garden until they slammed against the faces of the Kessoku soldiers marching toward her.

Her first wave of rocks drew blood from at least five of them. One Kessoku soldier used the bottom of his tunic to wipe the sticky liquid dripping from his forehead. Another soldier spit out a broken tooth. Even after her attack, none of them showed the slightest sign of giving up.

Shaping more rocks from the pile, she began again. Aaden sent rocks toward them as she did, but then he added a new strategy. He shaped a small mound of earth in front of a soldier just as the soldier began to step forward. The solider immediately tripped over the earth mound. He took another soldier down as he tried to regain his balance.

Talise used Aaden's technique, and soon soldiers were tripping in every direction.

Anger twitched at the muscles around their mouths. They glared at the earth as if angry something so simple impeded their progress. Soon, the soldiers lifted their knees to their chests with each step, and the earth could trip them no more.

Talise shaped more rocks, sending them straight for their skulls. Though the rocks drew blood, they never hit hard enough to knock anyone out. Perhaps her shaping wasn't strong enough. Or perhaps she didn't have it in her to kill.

Despite that, Kessoku did get injured. The effects were more psychological, but that was a win. When Kessoku came to the palace months ago, they breached the palace without anyone realizing until it was too late.

Now they were met with painful resistance, and they hadn't even gotten past to the garden. Their boots stomped through the mud with clear determination, but Talise could see their steps were more measured than before. It gave her a wave of hope. Maybe they'd leave if they realized what they were up against.

She shaped a rock from the pile. Eyeing the soldiers who wore Kessoku's patch of three interlocking circles over their hearts, she chose the weakest looking one. Her rock arched over the garden before she slammed it into the soldier's stomach with as much force as possible. This time, she didn't hold back. Shaping all her strength into the rock made a much bigger impact than her other attacks had.

The Kessoku soldier dropped to her knees. She clutched her stomach with a grunt. A moment later, she fell onto her back passed out cold.

Talise allowed herself to accept the victory. She still couldn't bring herself to hit the soldiers in the head, but this was close enough. She had dropped the soldier, hadn't she?

Aaden seemed to like her idea. He began shaping rocks into the stomachs of more Kessoku soldiers. Soon, a line of them lay on the ground. The ones behind had to climb over their fellow soldiers before they could continue down the path.

"Stop it," one of the palace guards hissed in her ear.

She turned around with a start, surprised to see the guard so close. He must have come away from his spot by the emperor's mansion just to talk to her.

The guard had a thick, spidery scar on his chin and a silver hooped earring in one ear. His eyebrows furrowed. "If you don't have the stomach to kill them, then let someone else do it. Knocking them out does us no good."

Aaden nodded and went back to throwing his rocks at the Kessoku's heads and shoulders.

Talise gave a short nod to the guard with the spidery scar, but her stomach twisted as she turned back to the fight. The plan had been simple. Defend the emperor's mansion with shaping. Make Kessoku think this was the real fight.

And then fail.

That was the most important part. They had to give Kessoku an early victory, so their enemy would be overly confident when the real fight began. Then, when the palace army took over, Kessoku wouldn't know what hit them.

That part of the plan didn't allow for members of Kessoku to be knocked out or taken prisoner. All of them were supposed to be killed. Talise gulped and tried to distract her mind by shaping.

At least the killing part wasn't her responsibility.

A clump of rocks flew at her command, but it lacked the necessary force to truly injure anyone. Yes, the Kessoku soldiers had to die, but she didn't want to be the one to do it.

Her heart squeezed as she shaped more rocks from the pile. She tried to convince herself to hit harder, but the conviction for it was buried deep underneath the fresh grief of Marmie's death.

When she shaped another wave of rocks, they didn't reach their targets. Instead, a wave of air made them bounce to the ground. Finally, Kessoku had decided to use more shaping against them.

Before she could think of a counterattack, a Kessoku man on the edge of their ranks lifted his sword and let out a loud cry. The rest of Kessoku yelled with him as they began charging the emperor's mansion.

They didn't just march, they ran. Talise took a step back. The Kessoku had already closed half the distance between them. Her stomach lurched. It was time to enact the next part of their plan.

"Raise your spears!" Talise shouted.

Aaden grabbed her wrist and pulled her to safety behind the two rows of palace guards. She didn't bother pulling her hand out of his grip or telling him how unnecessary it had been. There was no time.

Once behind the palace guards, Aaden dropped her wrist and immediately raised his hands to shape. Talise joined him and together they shaped a wall of air that would push Kessoku away from them.

"We need more air!" Wendy shouted. She stood just in front of Talise with her spear pointed toward the Kessoku.

Talise shaped harder, letting the width of the air wall grow thicker. Next to her, Aaden shaped so hard, the muscles in his forehead twitched.

At last, Kessoku reached the air wall that separated them from the palace guards. Without any hesitation, they pressed forward through the air.

Talise shaped harder. She could feel Kessoku stepping through the wind as she and Aaden shaped it. It took effort for them just to move each foot forward. They had to shove against the wind, fighting through it with as much effort as it took to move a boulder.

Talise held her breath.

She couldn't help it. Their swords were so close, she was certain something would make it through the wall of wind.

A breath rattled through her as she gritted her teeth together. With a new resolve, she shaped even harder, knowing this would only make Kessoku push harder as well.

In front of her, Wendy pointed her spear forward. Her knuckles had turned white from the death grip she maintained.

Since their lives were on the line, now probably wasn't the best time to be angry at Wendy. Yet, a rush of resentment trickled up through Talise's toes anyway. Wendy had lied to her. Her *best friend* had lied to her. Considering the circumstances, Talise had no right to be upset about it. She knew that. But it was surprisingly difficult to let it go.

If she and Aaden had known Kessoku was coming, they might have been better prepared. They might have been able to do more than just pretend to defend the emperor's mansion with shaping.

Wendy raised one fist into the air, and Talise sucked in a breath. She glanced at Aaden. He had one eye on her and one on Wendy's fist.

Talise tried to ignore Aaden, which was also surprisingly difficult. She narrowed her eyes at Wendy's fist, waiting for the signal.

Kessoku pressed forward.

Closer.

Still Wendy's fist hung high in the air.

When Talise could make out the freckles on a Kessoku man's face, her breath hitched. They were too close. Her hands shook, which sent a vibration through her perfect wall of wind. Her eyes narrowed again. She *needed* to focus.

But they were right in front of her. A whole row of Kessoku marched into the wind, their swords raised. One wrong move and those swords would run through the palace guards. Once they were gone, they'd move on to the next row of guards.

Wendy's fist was still raised. Talise curled her toes and held her breath.

Waiting.

Finally, when the Kessoku were only a few steps from the guards' spears, Wendy's fist dropped. On cue, Talise and Aaden shaped away the wall of wind.

With the sudden absence of resistance from the wind, every member of Kessoku stumbled forward. They were unable to catch their balance until… they landed on the spears of the palace guards.

Talise grabbed Aaden's arm as she watched the life go out of a woman's eyes. She gulped.

This was real now.

"Charge!" a Kessoku man called from behind the others. Talise tripped over her feet as she tried to back away. There were too many of them. The wind trick had only killed a handful of Kessoku, and the rest barreled forward.

The death of their fellow men had barely given Kessoku any pause. They climbed over the fallen soldiers as if they were earth and rock, not people they knew. And now they moved toward Talise and the others looking eager to kill.

There was no chance in fighting anymore. Kessoku would win. Their swords and spears glinted in the morning sun.

"Run!" Aaden shouted.

He'd been pulling her along, but somehow, they had gotten separated in the chaos. Talise lunged over a nearby bush to avoid the point of a sword. She was back up a moment later, ignoring how her hands stung from the recent fall. Her feet found every branch and bush as she sprinted through the garden. With each step, she could practically feel Kessoku's swords straining to reach her neck.

She had to remind herself this was part of the plan too. They were *supposed* to retreat. They were supposed to make Kessoku think they had won an early victory. But it didn't feel like things were going according to plan. It felt like Kessoku was right on her heels, and she was about to die.

The world seemed like a fog of gray around her. The Kessoku were behind her, she knew that for sure, but the palace guards could have been anywhere. She was vaguely aware that Aaden's arm was tight in her grip, but she couldn't remember when she had caught back up to him. Her fingernails were probably digging into his skin, though he said nothing about it.

When Wendy tripped on a nearby rock, Talise gasped and fell to a halt. Fear gripped her as she helped Wendy to her feet. A dagger whistled past her ear.

Aaden was pulling her now. And she was pulling Wendy.

In that moment, her sense of direction evaporated completely. Were they still by the emperor's mansion? Had any of the palace guards been injured? And Claye.

Panic ripped through her insides, causing her to grip Aaden harder.

Where was Claye?

"Over here! Hurry!" Claye's whispered voice was a relief amidst the chaos. At the sound of it, Talise found her feet and began running with a renewed sense of direction.

She ducked through a dense bush and then shaped a clump of earth toward her pursuers. Aaden threw fire balls over his shoulder, which pushed back a few Kessoku.

They entered the hedge maze from their trials and lost the rest of Kessoku through there. When they exited the maze through a brand new opening, Talise rushed for the foxhole where they were meant to hide.

Her breath came in sharp pants as she scanned her new surroundings. How many of them had made it?

CHAPTER THIRTY-SIX

TALISE PRESSED HER PALM AGAINST the wet earth of the foxhole, hoping it would ground her. She tried to take steadying breaths, but with each inhale her lungs shuddered. *Relax*, she told herself. *We made it.*

She finally admitted to herself the real reason she was afraid to look around. *Had* they made it? All of them?

She let out a breath of relief when she saw Wendy, hand over her heart, sucking in air like it was her first time breathing.

Aaden stood nearby. His forearm was red where she had been gripping it, but at least her fingernails hadn't dug deep enough to draw blood. He glanced over the foxhole, out of breath but still on alert.

The palace guards were there too. Eleven of them. Was that all? She hadn't counted them before, but shouldn't there have been an even number? That thought was interrupted by an even more pressing one.

Where was Claye?

Gripping her stomach, she jerked her head side to side. No, Claye had to be there. He had just told them to hurry. He *had* to be there.

"We deserve a medal for this." The voice was low enough that Kessoku wouldn't hear, but it was Claye's.

Her head zipped toward him. He stood behind a few of the palace guards, almost out of view. He was bent at the waist, gripping his side like his guts would spill out if he let go. He sucked in a huge breath then let out an even bigger one. "I thought gardening was murder, but this?" He shook his head while a solemn resignation filled his eyes. "Look at this injury."

Her heart stopped. *What injury?* Claye was panting heavier than any of them. And the way he gripped his side…

But when Claye lifted his arm, he displayed his hand with a short scratch on the back. He'd probably gotten it from a tree branch.

Talise heaved a sigh of relief as she rested her forehead on the soil of the foxhole.

Wendy had her hand over her mouth, eyes as wide as lemons. She blinked several times before she moved again. When she did, she curled her hands into fists and began jabbing every inch of Claye with soft thuds. "You absolute *vermin*!" she whispered. "How could you scare me like that?" She pounded on his arms even as he tried to get away. "That was not funny!"

A breath of relief came out with the chuckle that escaped Talise's lips. Even if it was small, it felt good to laugh.

When Aaden glanced over the foxhole again, Talise decided to join him. "Can you see the palace from here?" she asked.

He jerked his head to the left, pointing toward the palace grounds with his chin. Following his line of sight, she peered between two bushes and finally saw Kessoku. They weren't far from the main palace, but a small group of them hung back.

The small group stood around the emperor's mansion doing something with their hands. A moment later, they let out war cries as the wooden walls of the mansion burst into flames. The sight of it made her stomach clench.

The mansion wouldn't be missed. No one used it now that Emperor Flarius refused to enter its walls. Commander Blaise had made sure the mansion was empty before Kessoku arrived.

Still, seeing it on fire made Talise think of all those years ago when Kessoku had attacked the first time. They had killed the emperor's family, only missing the emperor through a small miracle. The flames felt like a message. This time, they were back to finish the job.

She pulled her eyes away from the mansion and directed her attention back to the rest of Kessoku. No one would miss the mansion anyway, what did it matter if it burned? A tiny knot in her stomach reminded her of the sweet smell those chrysanthemums made. Maybe those would be missed.

The faces of the Kessoku were hard to see as they stormed through the gardens on their way to the main palace. The Kessoku had given up trying to find them. They seemed to think it would be easy to enter the palace.

When they had first been attacked with shaping, they almost seemed dejected. First the waterfall, then the ice wall, then the rocks slamming into their faces. The psychological warfare had been as effective as they intended.

But none of them seemed the least bit frightened now. Even after several of their men had died on the palace guards' spears, they looked as eager as ever. Confident.

Good. That was exactly what they hoped for. Make Kessoku think they had earned a great victory. Build them up just to crash them down.

Perhaps the victory would have tasted sweeter if there were something to watch. Talise narrowed her eyes at the Kessoku soldiers. Ignoring the shiver that threatened to pass through her, she said, "Shouldn't General Gale's men be shooting arrows by now?"

No one responded.

Talise glanced back at Wendy, but her friend only shrugged. Despite the lack of words, the crease between Wendy's eyebrows spoke volumes.

Had something gone wrong? Had Kessoku found a way into the palace after all? The emperor's mansion, that was nothing. Unimportant. But if Kessoku had already breached the palace, they were definitely in trouble. No matter how much the emperor criticized Talise, she knew he couldn't die. Kamdaria needed him.

Her gut twisted around and around. Everyone else seemed tense, but no one seemed nearly as anxious as her. Why wasn't anyone doing anything?

She pulled herself up out the foxhole to get a closer look through the branches of a hedge bush. The Kessoku weren't running toward the palace anymore. They were regrouping.

They still had an entire garden to march through before they reached the palace walls. Still, they were closer than they should have been, and Talise couldn't take it anymore.

She inched back down to the foxhole and faced the others. "We have to do something. No one from the palace is attacking. Kessoku is regrouping. They're going to start marching soon, and we can't let them get to the palace."

The twisting in her gut didn't ease when she noticed one of the guards rolling his eyes and another scoffing at her words.

She gritted her teeth. Maybe they didn't like her idea, but they were just guards. She bore the title of Master Shaper, which gave her authority. They'd have to learn to respect that. Lifting her chin, she said, "I need five guards to use dirt and leaves to disguise themselves. Those guards will distract Kessoku by slipping through the trees unnoticed until they attack on my command. They'll never see it coming. When those five guards have all been killed, the rest of us will start to attack from here."

The guard that had scoffed earlier shifted on his feet until he faced Talise. "Are you insane?"

The words cut through her, making her feel as incompetent as she had after the maze trial. After setting her jaw, she said, "It's a good strategy."

Now the guard laughed and slapped a nearby guard with a friendly pat. "Oh, of course, *strategy*. That's all that matters."

Talise dug her toe into the ground. Her shoulders tensed but she managed to keep them from bunching up. The image of the burning mansion came to her mind, along with the Kessoku who had been impaled by spears. "What could be more important than strategy at a time like this?"

The palace guard blinked in return. Maybe he expected her to know what was going on in his head, but she didn't. When he seemed to sense her confusion, the guard let out a huff. His fingers curled into a fist, which matched the vein pulsing in his forehead. His demeanor held so much rage, it almost frightened her.

"I think food could be more important. It's always a good time for food." Claye attempted a smile, but Wendy only shushed him.

The air around them turned thick as the soldiers glared at Talise. They were all as angry as the one who argued against her. Finally, the first guard gestured to the men behind him. "These are people, not Forces tablets. Your so-called *strategy* involves five people sacrificing their lives just to create a diversion." He took a step back and all the guards around him stood tall, sneering at Talise. "People. People are more important than strategy."

A lump hardened in Talise's throat. She let the words pierce through her and sting. She deserved it.

It didn't matter that she'd been trying to save everyone in the palace. The guard was right. Strategy on a Forces board would never be the same as strategy on a real battlefield. Because a battlefield used real people.

She had no time to let these thoughts sink in. Kessoku had just finished regrouping and were now ready to march again.

"Look." Aaden had come to her side. It seemed to be his favorite place now that the trials were over. He pointed up at the palace roof. The jade tiles looked the same as they always did, which she was about to point out.

But then she noticed movement in the tiny slits of windows just under the roof. Glinting in the morning sun, the tips of several arrows sat just under the jade roof tiles. Her breath relaxed. The shooters were there. Ready.

Her heart thumped in her chest as she waited. And waited.

♔

CHAPTER THIRTY-SEVEN

ONE HUNDRED SEVENTY-EIGHT KESSOKU soldiers marched toward the palace. Once Talise had counted them all, she finally realized what the palace army had been waiting for. The Kessoku were all there now. None of them was still climbing the ridge that led to the palace. Now they all stood in the palace garden, ready to be slaughtered.

Talise climbed out of the foxhole and crept closer to the march. She wasn't supposed to fight, but she couldn't bear sitting back and doing nothing. At the very least, she wanted to see everything as it happened.

Aaden and Wendy joined her but not Claye. The three of them crawled behind a large hedge bush where they could see everything without being in danger.

Kessoku marched forward and soon hit the natural barriers the garden provided. The large hedges forced Kessoku into a funnel shape, one that got smaller the closer they got to the palace.

Breathing became a forced task instead of something natural. Kessoku looked even stronger than before. They marched with an air of invincibility, probably because of their recent victory.

Why wasn't the palace army attacking?

Just as that thought entered her mind, the arrows began showering down. One fourth of the Kessoku soldiers fell in that first wave. They dropped to the ground while the others scrambled to climb over them. Another wave of arrows fell and even more Kessoku dropped.

Now that the arrows had started to fall, Kessoku figured out where they were coming from. They shot their own arrows toward the tiny windows just under the palace roof.

When cries of pain erupted from the windows, Talise knew some of the Kessoku arrows met their marks. Her insides writhed, filling her with the need to act.

Commander Blaise had made it painfully clear they weren't supposed to engage Kessoku in any way once they had left the emperor's mansion.

But she couldn't just stand here and watch. Not with the palace under attack. Lifting a hand, she began shaping dirt from the ground.

"What are you doing?" Aaden stared at her hands as he spoke.

She kept her eyes on the dirt and continued shaping. "I did this against those other Kessoku in the training room. I'm going to shape dirt and air together into a dirt cloud. Then Kessoku won't be able to see well enough to shoot arrows into the palace."

Without another word, Aaden began shaping his own clumps of dirt in the air.

Wendy squeezed Talise's shoulder and shook her head so hard her black hair skittered across her shoulders. Though her voice was timid, the words were clear. "You can't do that. If you cover Kessoku with a dirt cloud, the palace soldiers won't be able to see them either. They need to see Kessoku in order to aim."

Talise bit into her bottom lip as she nodded. Wendy was right. The dirt clouds would confuse Kessoku, but it would probably give them more of an advantage than anything. She needed something that would help the palace soldiers and hurt Kessoku.

Perhaps she could throw rocks at their hands so they couldn't fight. Or maybe she could try tripping them again.

When she dismissed those thoughts, she noticed Aaden staring at her. He focused on her face, but the wheels in his head seemed to be turning too. "What if we make the dust clouds cover their faces, but not their heads?"

A bubble of excitement filled Talise. She clapped her hands together and leaned toward him feeling an almost smile on her face. "Yes. We'll make the dust cloud cover them from the crown of their head and down. Then the palace soldiers will still be able to see the crowns of their heads, but Kessoku won't be able to see the palace."

Wendy opened her mouth to say something, but Talise and Aaden were already busy shaping the dust clouds. Instead of speaking, Wendy had apparently decided to help.

Wendy chewed her bottom lip as she shaped wind through a dirt clod. The dirt burst open to a cloud of dust, but it fell to the ground a moment later.

Talise could see her friend struggling to shape both air and earth at the same time. She almost offered to do the dust part so Wendy wouldn't have to fail. But Wendy seemed intent on shaping the two elements, no matter how hard it was.

That made it a little easier to forget the anger she still harbored for her friend. It was times like this Talise remembered Wendy hadn't made it to the elite academy because of her sweet smile. Wendy's skill didn't match Talise's or Aaden's, but her shaping was still far better than most Kamdarians.

When the three of them had produced a large enough dust cloud, they carefully shaped it into the crowd of Kessoku. The soldiers began swatting the air, trying to clear the dust away.

Talise stepped closer. The dust had to cover the Kessoku's eyes but not their heads. The balance had to be just right. Soon, the palace soldiers began picking off the Kessoku soldiers like they were the single cherry in a bucket of blueberries.

The arrows soared. Talise kept shaping.

Minutes passed. Then even more passed. Then even more.

It felt like hours since the fight had begun. Maybe it had been.

Wendy's breathing became shallow. Finally, she dropped her arms to massage her muscles. Watching it made Talise's muscles feel like fire. A growing fire.

With a bout of determination, Talise sent a fresh wave of dust through the Kessoku. The effort cost her. Her arms shook with the effort of keeping them in the air.

After a quick glance at the sky, it became clear a few hours had indeed passed. The sun had cleared the sunrise stage and was climbing in the sky. If it were a regular day, she and Aaden would have been training for several hours already. It all came back to her then.

She remembered how she had stayed up late the night before throwing daggers with Wendy. Then she had been woken up long before dawn to capture the Kessoku scout group with Aaden. Now it was several hours past dawn, and her arms and body could take the stress no more.

One glance at Aaden told her his body fought for strength the same way hers did.

She let her arms drop to her sides.

With her weakened muscles, there was nothing else to do. She had done everything she could. It was up to the palace soldiers now.

Aaden also let his arms drop. Within seconds, the dust cloud cleared. A hollow grief took hold of Talise's stomach. Kessoku soldiers were still there, fighting to reach the palace.

But so many more were dead.

The ground was littered with their bloody bodies. Muddy footprints covered many of the fallen soldiers' tunics. Limbs were twisted at strange angles. A wave of nausea shot through Talise.

She did this.

She hadn't shot the arrows that killed them, but her shaping had helped. And now they were dead.

Without thinking, she grabbed onto Wendy and Aaden. A lump lodged in her throat, making it hard to swallow. She didn't see the soldiers who were steps away from the palace walls. She only saw the wave of destruction before her.

There were only about thirty Kessoku soldiers left. They charged the palace, letting out loud war cries. They tried to ignore their fallen friends, but it was difficult to do so when they kept tripping over them.

Their final steps to the palace were made into a funnel with large hedges. Smoke billowed above the hedges, but they must have been shaped with extra water in the leaves because the hedges seemed unable to burn with fire shaping. The Kessoku were forced to charge the palace in the tight funnel. By the time they got there, they could stand in rows no wider than two by two.

All at once, the palace doors swung open, revealing a squad of palace soldiers with swords in their hands. They cut down the Kessoku before them without a trace of exhaustion. The palace soldiers had the clear advantage. These were obviously fresh soldiers who had been able to rest recently. They also had many soldiers to fight against the few Kessoku that could make it through the tight funnel. Behind the palace soldiers, even more soldiers stood on tables and shot arrows at the remaining Kessoku.

Talise's gut twisted at the destruction. The palace soldiers cut down one Kessoku after another. Though she was glad to see the palace soldiers winning, she was conflicted at witnessing so much death. Even if they were the enemy, these people must have had families. And those families would soon be grieving.

Without warning, Aaden jumped through the bush and closer to the palace. Before he could run off, Talise scrambled over to his side. "What are you doing?" she asked, even as he jogged toward the destruction.

He scanned the ground, staring closely at the dead men. "I'm checking for survivors. Some of them might have passed out from blood loss but aren't actually dead."

A reminder in her head told her Commander Blaise—not to mention the emperor—wouldn't approve of her getting so close to the battle. But she couldn't stand around waiting anymore.

Splitting up, she and Aaden took careful steps through the carnage. She placed her fingers on the necks of every fallen soldier to check for a pulse. Each time her fingers were met with cold stillness.

These were people littering the ground, but in her head, all she could see were rows and rows of unmarked graves. Then she started thinking of silly things. Would the palace return the bodies to their families? Would the Kessoku even ask to have the bodies returned? How were dead bodies transferred? How much would it smell?

"Over here!" Aaden's voice carried over the shouts and clinks of swords that still came from the palace doors. Talise scurried to his side.

He had found a still-breathing soldier, but this was one of their own men. A palace guard who had been with them at the emperor's mansion. The spidery scar on his chin looked as pale as the rest of his face. With a growing panic, Talise tore the man's shirt collar down to search for the injury that had knocked him out.

Aaden grabbed her hands with a gentleness she didn't expect. He pointed to the back of the man's head. A large gash had blood pouring from it, but just under the blood, she could make out a cracked skull.

Her hands flew to her mouth as she sucked in a gasp. This man was a living ghost. When he let out a groan, her heart nearly stopped. He blinked and reached for his head.

She didn't know much about healing, but seeing that wound, she didn't think it would help if the man touched it. Instead, she took the man's hand in hers and said, "Try to relax."

The man balked at the sight of her. He squirmed, pushing her away as his jaw worked up and down. Then, he moaned when his head seemed to proclaim its pain.

"It's okay," she said. "Don't move."

But her words only distressed him more. He opened his mouth but couldn't seem to find any words. He looked her straight in the eye and let out a groan that made her feel like she should have left him alone.

And then everything changed again. His eyes slid to the back of his head, so only the whites were visible. His muscles went rigid and then they started shaking. She grabbed his hand, trying desperately to stop whatever was happening.

The healers were skilled. They must have had a way to fix this. But the man only shook harder. She couldn't shake the feeling that this was the end. Why did she have to be here to see it? Heat roiled with sadness went slicing through her.

She turned to Aaden, desperate for help, but he looked as much at a loss as she felt. "Do something," she said while clutching the guard's hand.

Aaden only swallowed and looked away. "I don't know how."

Her heart pounded in her chest. She knew he couldn't know what to do. She didn't know either, but that didn't take away the bitterness of battle. They had found a survivor. And it had come to nothing.

The guard's throat gurgled as he tried to speak. He let out a cough which sent blood spattering everywhere. And then, everything stopped. His body relaxed, the shaking gone. His eyes fluttered closed.

In his final breath, he uttered one word. "Aria."

And then he was gone. The lump in Talise's throat grew so large she could barely breathe. Tears stung in her eyes before they fell in thick drops from her lashes. She wanted to scream. She wanted to reach for Aaden. She wanted to close her eyes and wake up from this nightmare.

Before she could act on any of those things, a movement from behind made her turn.

"Watch out!" Aaden shouted, but it was far too late.

A sword was crashing down, ready to strike her skull. Her body reacted before her mind had even processed the moment. She sent a blast of fire at her attacker's face. He cried out and took a step back. But then he swung his blade again.

The tip of it brushed across her shoulder. It pierced her skin, though the muscle seemed untouched. He swung again, and Aaden was there. Talise shaped a wave of wind to help, but then she tripped, and it did nothing.

Everything was a jumble of limbs and dust. She wanted to send another burst of fire, but she didn't want it to hit Aaden. She reached through the air, clawing at the arms that seemed eager to harm her.

Aaden cried out and then another voice came. The Kessoku solider. She was lying on the ground, her face pressed into the soil. A heavy boot sank into her back, crushing the spine. She tried to crane her neck back, but all she saw was the glint of a sword in the sunlight.

And then Aaden fell to the ground with a grunt. The sword came swooshing down over him, and everything seemed to move in slow motion.

Talise shoved the boot off her back and sent a burst of fire at the Kessoku soldier. His sword faltered at the sight of the flames but not enough.

The sword kept falling. Talise could see he intended to strike both her and Aaden in one blow. She prepared to shove her boots against his ankles, hoping to trip him and make his grip on the sword falter.

Before her feet could reach their target, an arrow sliced through the air, piercing the soldier in the heart. She screamed as his body, not just his sword, fell toward her. She barely had a moment to breathe before his body crushed hers to the ground.

The sense of suffocation overtook her, but it seemed completely insignificant when Aaden's strangled cry cut through the air. She barely had the strength to push the dead soldier off her.

When she did, she saw Aaden throwing the soldier's sword off his chest before he buried his face in his hands. She moved toward him, but he jerked away.

She probably would have given him space, except a drip of blood seeped out from between his fingers. This time, she didn't give him the chance to protest. She moved quickly, jerking his wrists away from his face before he had time to react.

A deep gash from his forehead to his jaw sliced through his dark skin and over one eye. The blood seemed secondary as she took hold of his cheeks, pulling his face toward her. The eye. Had the sword sliced through his eye?

He pulled away and covered his face again. But she had seen what she needed. His eye suffered no damage.

Without another word, Talise scanned the desecrated gardens for a spare piece of cloth, preferably one that wasn't too dirty. A suitable cloth came from a nearby body. She refused to look at it as she tore a piece of fabric away from the cold skin.

Aaden wouldn't let her press the cloth against the blood. He stole it from her hands and turned his shoulder to her. He held his face at an angle so she couldn't see the injury. It didn't make any sense why he wouldn't let her help. Unless.

Was he embarrassed?

By this? He had fought against the Kessoku, even fought to protect her, and he was embarrassed about an injury from it?

But she didn't have time to consider that. In a heartbeat, she realized how quiet everything had gotten in the air around them. When she turned to look back at the palace, one lone Kessoku soldier stood staring at the palace.

The palace doors had been shut in her face and she stood all alone. She took one glance around the battlefield and the message was clear.

One survivor had been allowed. One survivor who could go back and tell Kessoku about the slaughter of the entire company. One survivor to make sure Kessoku never came back.

And then the woman was running. She jumped over bodies and clutched her sword. The veins in her face pulsed as she moved, desperate to get as far from the carnage as she could. When she disappeared over the ridge, Talise finally dared to move.

She pulled Aaden to his feet but let him keep his face hidden. As they tumbled back to the palace, his breath got heavier. Talise noticed the others also heading for the palace doors. Wendy, Claye, and the other palace guards.

When they got closer, the doors burst open, and Commander Blaise himself rushed out through them. He pushed his way through the tiny crowd and it suddenly hit her. He was heading for them.

Her gut twisted in horror. While gripping Aaden's elbow, Talise felt the muscles in his arm contract. She held onto him for dear life, fearing the commander's words.

He started speaking even before he reached them. "I expressly ordered that you two would not engage Kessoku after the mansion. What were you thinking?"

He had reached them now. Her knees knocked together as she swallowed. Commander Blaise reached for the cloth over Aaden's face, which Aaden gave up with no argument.

The commander's shoulders twitched at the sight of the blood. His face was a hardened slab of grit and determination. But that didn't stop a hint of horror shining through his eyes. He swallowed once and forced Aaden's cheek to the side so he could see it better.

"That will leave a scar." He spoke with precision, each word cutting through them both.

Aaden's eyes dropped further and further to the ground the longer the commander stared at him.

"I'm sorry, Grandfather," Aaden said in a tight voice.

Commander Blaise huffed, apparently unable to accept the apology.

"And *you*." The commander let out an exasperated sigh as he turned to Talise. He looked straight into her eyes, not allowing her to look away for even a moment. His exasperation turned to a hardened glare. He jabbed his pointer finger toward her chest. "You should have known better."

Talise's arms had frozen in place. A slice of terror cut through whatever resolve she had left. She blinked back at him, unable to think of a single retort.

He covered his eyes, shaking his head. Fear lined his words as he spoke. "What am I supposed to tell the emperor?"

She gulped again and gripped Aaden harder. It was only then that she remembered she was holding onto his arm. She swallowed and swallowed, trying to blink away her tears.

Commander Blaise spared her one more glance before he turned his back on them both. "Go up to the library. I'll send a healer once the more serious injuries are dealt with."

Talise didn't let go of Aaden as they shuffled through the garden. Every time she swallowed all she could imagine was the emperor. What would he say about her decision to go back onto the battlefield? He might never forgive her.

CHAPTER THIRTY-EIGHT

TALISE SNATCHED THE CLOTH FROM Aaden's hand and threw it across the library before he could snatch it back. "You're being a baby," she said with exasperation. "Just let me look at it."

He folded his arms across his chest and turned away with an angry huff.

"Just." She wrapped her fingers around his chin and pushed his face toward her.

His skin warmed at her touch. She wondered if the heat had been on purpose or if he involuntarily warmed his veins just because she was around. Either way, she didn't have time to worry about it.

He didn't pull his chin out of her grip. For the briefest moment, he looked into her eyes. By the time she glanced back, he had looked away. And let out another huff.

She rolled her eyes at the reaction. "Would you calm down? One of the palace soldiers had his arm cut off. This is nothing."

He didn't respond. She had a feeling she had finally gotten to him, at least a little.

Now that she could examine the injury, it didn't look too bad. It was deep enough to scar, but it didn't go down to the bone. As long as the wound got cleaned, it shouldn't have any lasting damage.

"Hold still. I'm going to clean it."

Aaden's shoulders shifted. He tensed under her touch, but he seemed to finally accept the inevitable.

She shaped the water out of a nearby bowl. The bowl was still there from when she had brought it to the library early that morning. Back when a Kessoku scout group ravaged the palace and she thought it was nothing more than a trial.

She shook her head at her own naivety. With the water levitating in the air, Talise felt inside it for any trace of earth. A few minerals wouldn't be a problem, but to clean a wound, she needed clean water.

After concentrating for a few moments, she felt through the water and shaped the dirt and other contaminants out of it. For drinking, she would have left more of the minerals, but for cleaning, she removed them.

The wet patter of crumbs landed on the library table.

With the water clean, she shaped it over the slash in Aaden's face. It wasn't until the water rushed over his wound that she realized the water was getting in his eye. Maybe she should have found some salt to dissolve into the water so it wouldn't sting. But the salt would have made the wound dirty, so it was probably best she hadn't.

Her fingers moved in soft strokes through the air as she shaped the water in a steady flow over the wound. The dried blood at the edges of the wound came away freely. But deeper in the wound, it was harder to tell how clean it was.

Talise cupped her fingers under Aaden's chin and leaned closer to get a better angle. She'd propped herself atop one of the library tables so it would be easier to reach his face. Letting the water sink deeper into the wound, she leaned even closer still.

With her face close enough now, she could see how one of his eyes had more orange than the other. The left eye, the one with a gash running over it, had tiny spots of orange spiraling out from the pupils. The orange looked soft against the brown of his irises, almost like tiny chrysanthemums growing out of fresh summer soil.

She found her thumb stroking his cheek and immediately tipped his head up so he wouldn't recognize the motion for what it was.

When she was certain the wound was clean, she began shaping the water away from his face and into a ball above her palm. Two competing voices argued inside her head, one telling her to back away and run, the other telling her to move even closer.

Ignoring them both, she kept the water levitating while she visually inspected the wound. The healers would be able to do more than her, but the sooner the wound was clean, the better. She wondered how long it would take before it faded to a scar.

A heated finger traced over her bare shoulder, sending a shiver through her body. She had forgotten all about her own wound from the Kessoku soldier. And she hadn't realized it cut so much of her sleeve away.

"It doesn't hurt," Talise said as she dropped her hand away from Aaden's face. She shaped another ball of water out of a bowl. After removing the contaminants, she shaped the fresh water over her own wound, forcing Aaden to move his fingers off her skin.

The wound was nothing. Hardly a scratch when compared to the gash Aaden wore. Considering they had been attacked by a fairly angry soldier, it had been lucky to get away so clean.

She took extra time cleaning her wound because she had a feeling Aaden was itching to touch her skin again once the water was out of the way.

To prevent that from happening, Talise immediately hopped off the table as soon as she shaped the water away from her wound. Dropping the water back into the bowl, she carried the bowl to another table closer to the entrance of the library.

Whether he realized she was trying to get away from him or not, Aaden didn't move toward her. He fell into one of the library chairs and dropped his head in his hands. Dejected.

But why? Why should this injury mean so much to him?

After setting the bowl on the table, Talise was drawn back to the place she had been trying to avoid. When she sat down next to

Aaden, he turned his face away from her so she couldn't see the wound.

"What is it?" she said, folding her arms over her chest. "Why are you so embarrassed?"

He scoffed in response. "Oh, of *course* I'm going to explain. Because you're so good about sharing things with me and all."

She flicked him in the arm which earned her a sharp gaze before Aaden remembered to turn his face away from her. "Are you afraid it's going to affect your shaping?" she asked.

"No."

"Are you worried the emperor won't like you with a scar?"

Aaden shifted one eyebrow upward as if the suggestion were a joke. It mostly was.

Talise tapped her chin with mock thoughtfulness. "Is it because you can see the wound out the corner of your eye, and you're worried it's going to distract you?"

"No." Aaden was shaking his head while wearing a frown.

But another thought entered her head. Her fingers were wrapped around his wrist before she even realized she'd moved them. "Did it affect your eyesight?"

This time his voice came out softer. "No." He stared at her fingers. "Stop asking me."

She pulled her hand away—maybe a little faster than necessary—and stuck it on her hip. "I won't stop asking until you tell me, so you might as well get it over with."

He let out a grunt that was probably supposed to sound a lot more irritated than it did. He hadn't quite removed the hint of pleasure in it. But then his shoulders dropped, and he looked away again. A heavy frown tugged the corners of his lips down. "It's stupid. Vanity. I know I shouldn't care, but…" He shook his head and buried his face once more.

When she pulled his hands away from his face, she did it gently. Not touching more than necessary, but not getting it over with quickly either. Once his hands weren't covering his eyes, she quirked an eyebrow up, begging him to tell more.

Finally, he let out a sigh of resignation. "My name, Aaden, comes from my great-grandfather. Apparently, he was known for being handsome. All the ladies pined after him. Most eligible bachelor in all the land, that sort of thing. When I was born, everyone said I was such a beautiful baby, so they named me after him."

He shook his head once more as he flexed his jaw. "I know it's stupid. I shouldn't care how handsome I am compared to the person I was named after. I just…" His shoulders slumped. "Now this scar will always remind me of how unfitting my name is."

He pressed his fingers into his elbow, staring at a knot in the wood of the table. His fingers kneaded over his elbow, back and forth while the muscles in his face seemed to droop.

Vanity? Maybe that would have been stupid, but this was different. He mourned something deeper than his words had said. Something a name represented. He mourned the connection he had to that great-grandfather. And now he felt like that connection was severed.

Or maybe he mourned his parents. It hadn't escaped her notice how he carefully omitted any mention of them when he told his little story. For the first time, she wondered what relationship he had with his father, if any.

"I'm sorry." It was all she could think to say. Almost as an afterthought, she said, "Names can have power. I understand feeling a loss because of one."

His eyes flicked to hers and the kneading over his elbow stopped. "Are you named after …," his voice dropped, almost to a whisper, "Marmie?"

She shook her head, begging the tears to get back where they belonged. After a gulp, she said. "No, no one in my family is named Talise. It's just a name my parents liked. It's my middle name that has the loss."

It took her three heartbeats to work up the courage to say it. Three heartbeats full of terror. But she swallowed the fear, hoping she could smooth everything over without any suspicion. "Isla."

Aaden's eyebrows bounced upward as he leaned back in his chair. "The empress? You were named after her?"

Her nod was so tiny she worried he wouldn't see it. But of course he had.

She swallowed again and let her words out in a rush. "It was a popular name when I was born. Lots of children were named after her."

Aaden nodded in agreement. "Yeah, especially in the Crown. At least three different girls in my neighborhood were named Isla. Four if you include the princess."

Talise glanced at him, but she didn't dare speak. Afraid that any word would betray her.

He must have taken her silence for confusion. "The youngest princess," he said. "Her name was Isla too."

She nodded quickly. "Yes, I know that. I was just thinking, I'd forgotten you grew up so close to the palace. Did you ever meet the princess?"

He let out a long laugh and it surprised her how much she enjoyed seeing his smile. "No, I wasn't allowed to visit the palace when I was younger. I was too rowdy."

She let out a chuckle but found her eyes tracing the lines his smile made in his cheeks. When he glanced back at her, the warmth in his eyes seemed to penetrate her skin. She narrowed her eyes and leaned forward as if that was her plan all along.

"You don't need to worry anyway. It doesn't look bad." She made sure he could tell she was looking at the gash across his eye.

"Oh really?" he said wearing a smirk. "Are you calling me handsome?" He leaned forward, and her heart thundered in her chest.

Before either of them could react, the door to the library burst open. The emperor swept into the room, his silk tunic billowing behind him. His voice was gruff and low as he looked over his two Master Shapers. "Have the healers seen you yet?"

Talise was just lifting her head from a bow when she shifted to shake her head no.

The emperor looked them over again, his eyes lingering on Aaden's face a little longer than hers. He looked away only to stare at a wall. "I've been informed that a guard told you about the attack from Kessoku that occurred a few months ago."

The emperor lifted his head, not deigning to look down on them. "Now that you are aware, we will dismiss with the trials and have you train our newest recruits instead."

Talise blinked twice before the words sank in. The trials were over? Just like that? Apparently, they would both be staying.

The emperor nodded once, which wasn't strange. The strangest thing was the absence of certain words. Wasn't he going to criticize them for going back out among Kessoku after they had been told not to?

Perhaps he didn't know.

Since the emperor never missed an opportunity to criticize her, that must have been the only solution. But it gave Talise a bit of pause. Why would Commander Blaise withhold information from the emperor?

She shook the thought away. The emperor trusted the commander more than anyone. If the commander hadn't told him yet, maybe it was just because he hadn't had the time.

Emperor Flarius looked them over once more. "You will meet in the training hall tomorrow morning. I will be there to teach you how to train the soldiers."

Talise nodded, afraid to say anything that would turn his wrath toward her. Tomorrow she would begin leading the soldiers just like she was meant to do as Master Shaper. Finally, her years of training would allow her the position she'd been working for.

Now she could only wonder, would she succeed or fail?

CHAPTER THIRTY-NINE

THREE WEEKS HAD PASSED SINCE the latest attack on the palace. Talise and Aaden had finally taken their place as true Master Shapers, but it didn't feel like it at all. They'd been given the task of shape training the palace soldiers with yellow-hemmed tunics. These were the newest soldiers.

A handful of higher soldiers were also added to their classes. Those few with red, green, blue, or orange hems were soldiers who had achieved higher ranks based on their combat skills, but ones who still needed practice with the basics of combat shaping. Wendy worked with General Gale to teach advanced shape training to the higher ranked soldiers.

Each day, Talise and Aaden met the many groups of yellow-hemmed soldiers in the training hall, eager and willing to teach.

And each day, they were met with disappointment.

Talise fought to stay positive. She strived to only grumble when she was back in her living quarters. At the academy, she had been surrounded by such talented shapers she had forgotten most Kamdarians only received five years of shape training.

These new recruits seemed to struggle more than any of the students she had known. The ones with the red, green, blue, and orange hems were even worse. They were cocky since they were higher ranked, but their shaping skills were dismal. Things that were so simple to her, took great effort from them. Their sword, spear, and arrow skills were all impressive, but their shaping needed work.

A lot of it.

Talise stood at the head of the training hall wearing a blue training tunic and pants. The white belt tied around her waist had small silver swirls embroidered into it. That morning, she had thought dressing in blue might make her seem more relatable. It might help the soldiers see her as a shaper whose primary was water, rather than a Master Shaper and the only shaper in history to conquer ice shaping.

The idea had been ridiculous. She realized it only a few minutes into the morning. The soldiers stumbled over their training the same as they always did. Even simple things like throwing a fire ball took more effort than it should have.

"Like this," Talise said, straining to force a smile. Her left foot was positioned slightly behind her right. The stance was the same as dagger throwing, so it shouldn't have been hard. Even the yellow-hemmed soldiers were decent at dagger throwing.

She held her palm flat in front of her chest, shaping a fire ball in front of it. When she pushed her hand forward, the fire ball soared until it landed squarely in the center of the bull's eye where she aimed.

She turned back to the soldiers with what she hoped was an encouraging smile. "Go on," she said, hopefully not as strained as she felt. "Try again."

The squad of soldiers turned to face their targets and did the move just as she had done. Except none of them did it like her at all. One soldier stood with her feet right next to each other. She lost her balance when she punched the fire ball forward.

One soldier pushed his palm forward slowly, as if pushing a curtain aside. His fire ball lazily fell to the ground only a few steps in front of him. He sucked in a breath as he quickly stomped on it to put the fire out.

The other soldiers did no better. The one closest to her hadn't even produced a flame. He scratched his head as he turned to Talise. "Where does fire shaping come from again? The veins?"

"The heart," she replied with a sigh. "Not the veins, the heart."

She held in a second sigh and glanced over at Aaden. He was shaking his head at the soldiers looking as frustrated as she felt. They'd been working with different squads all morning. She was certain this one had been the worst.

Making a quick decision, she snapped her fingers at the soldiers. They dropped their hands to their sides and stood at attention. She decided to ignore how much slower they moved than they usually did for the emperor or Commander Blaise.

"We're going to finish a little early today. Go on down to the kitchens and see if dinner is ready."

She expected them to be excited. Maybe be grateful for her generosity. Instead, they nodded with hardly any expression and left the room. She wanted to whack them upside the head and force gratitude from their lips. Though, she suspected that wouldn't be an effective way to earn their trust.

Aaden was still shaking his head as he walked down the room to look at the targets. "Pathetic," he muttered under his breath. "Fire balls should be easy."

Talise let out an exasperated sigh as she grabbed the nearest target to put it away. "I didn't think it would be this hard. Shouldn't palace soldiers be capable of basic shaping before they get recruited?"

Aaden shrugged. "They accept anyone into the palace army. That's the big pull, you know. They'll take anyone who's willing and then feed them and give them a place to live. A lot of the soldiers are probably only here because they couldn't find a job anywhere else."

The muscles in her arms shivered as she grabbed the next target. She thought it best not to mention that not *everyone* was accepted into the palace army. Not people from the Storm. And those people needed the food and shelter more than anyone.

She rubbed a thumb over the hem of her tunic, staring absently into the training hall. "I thought we would have more help. I thought the other Master Shapers would be here. I thought we'd have more resources to help us. Instead, it feels like we've been given nothing, and we're expected to turn the army into shaping prodigies."

"Maybe you're putting too much pressure on yourself," Aaden said, grabbing the last target. "No one ever said we have to get them shaping at a certain level."

Talise gritted her teeth. "The emperor implied it. You know he did. He expects us to have them shooting perfect fire balls by Fire Festival. Which is utterly ridiculous. He expects too much and then refuses to give us the resources we need to deliver."

"It is unwise to speak ill of your emperor at any time."

Talise froze as Emperor Flarius's voice filled the training hall.

"But especially when you are in a large room where anyone can hear."

Talise gulped before she turned around to bow deeply to her sovereign. Aaden's head dropped almost as low as hers.

The emperor sneered at them both. She raised her head slowly, afraid of the punishment awaiting her.

"You blame others, when the fault is your own."

His words weren't so terrible, but like always, they cut her to her core. The emperor had a way of finding the truths she tried to ignore.

"We are so sorry, Your Imperial Highness." Aaden bowed again, his words more submissive than usual.

More than anything else, Aaden's reaction was the biggest indicator that they were really in trouble this time. She should have known better than to speak against in the emperor in such an open room. Her mounting frustration was no excuse.

The emperor ignored Aaden completely as he stepped toward Talise. "You have shaping skills, but you know nothing about being a leader."

She gulped and took a step back, unconsciously trying to put as much distance between herself and the emperor as possible.

"You complain about the soldier's lack of progress, but you are the real problem. *You* are the only reason these lessons are failing."

Her bottom lip trembled as she fought to regain control of her emotions. She kept her head high. "I'm doing the best I can."

The emperor scoffed in response. "Then maybe you aren't worthy of the authority you think you deserve. A true leader doesn't complain about the incompetence of soldiers. A true leader looks within to solve problems."

His words only hurt because they were true. She pinched the bridge of her nose as she looked away. "I'm trying, but nobody taught me how to teach. I only know how to shape. I don't understand what I'm doing wrong."

"You have none of the natural leadership you need. None of it!"

Those words hurt more than they should have. All she could think about were the people she knew who *did* have natural leadership skills. Marmie was the top of the list. Marmie always found ways to inspire confidence, but she never used cruel words like the emperor did.

The emperor was highly respected too. There was an element of fear there, but it wasn't just that. He took care of Kamdaria, and the people knew it.

The emperor frowned. He stood a step toward her, towering above. "You must do better than this. Their lack of progress isn't acceptable. Do you understand?"

A wave of tears stung in her eyes. She wanted to scream and sob all at once.

Aaden came closer. "Do you have any tips?" His voice was submissive again, but now that Talise knew it so well, she could hear the edge in it.

The emperor ignored him and stepped even closer. He pinched her chin between his thumb and forefinger, forcing her face up to meet his eyes. "Do you understand?" he asked again.

Her bottom lip trembled no matter how hard she clenched her jaw. She tried to stop the tears, but they fell before she could do anything about it. Her heart ached inside. All she wanted was to be back in the Storm. She wanted to sit on the dirt floor of the crumbling mud hut and huddle in front of the tiny fire. Their bellies had been empty, but there wasn't as much pressure.

There wasn't as much pain.

Talise tried to take in a breath, but it came in a staccato, shuddering with her silent sobs. "I'm trying," she said through a sniff.

Emperor Flarius had no sympathy for her tears. His face was unflinching. Demanding. He wouldn't accept anything less than perfection. "Try harder."

She tried to pull her chin away, tried to escape his grasp, but he pinched tighter still. His eyes bore into her, making her feel not just like an incompetent child, but like a burden. A mistake.

Her lip trembled while a fresh set of tears left her eyes. She kept trying to stop, but each attempt was only met with more tears.

The emperor opened his mouth to speak again, but Aaden stepped near enough to catch his eye. He held his arms at his sides, both hands in tight fists, one gripping a short training rod. Through clenched teeth he said, "Stop it."

The emperor eyed Aaden carefully. His face showed no intention of stopping, but he did let his hand fall away from Talise's chin. The moment the emperor's hand left her face, Aaden took a step closer, forcing his shoulder between her and the emperor.

Raising an eyebrow, the emperor said, "It isn't your place to question my methods." He turned to Talise again, having to crane his neck to see past Aaden. "I expect—"

"I said, *stop it*." Aaden took another step to the side, fully blocking Talise from the emperor's view. He used one hand to push her back behind him. While she feared how his actions would get him in trouble, she couldn't bring herself to stop him. She needed a break from the emperor's eyes. If only for a moment.

Stuck behind Aaden, she couldn't see the emperor's face, but it was easy to imagine the haughty expression that went along with his words. "You do *not* tell me what to do. I am the emperor."

"I don't care," Aaden said, his voice even and unforgiving.

Talise managed to silence the gasp that tried to escape. It didn't matter now if she wanted a break from the emperor. If Aaden continued like this, he would be thrown into the dungeon, she was sure of it.

She grasped his arm and forced him to face her. "Don't do this," she said in a whisper. "Just leave. I can handle it."

He gave her a careful look. One of his hands still gripped the short training rod, but the other relaxed. She knew he was about to reach for her.

"I will train my Master Shapers in any way I see fit." The emperor's voice rang through the training room. Loud and not allowing any argument in return.

Aaden whipped around, the muscles in his neck tensing. "You leave her alone."

She tightened her grip on his arm. "Stop, Aaden. I don't need you to do this."

He looked into her eyes then. She understood the dilemma going on in his head. She knew he didn't understand why she refused his protection. But it didn't matter if he understood. She just needed him to listen.

She stared back, pleading with her eyes. Not explaining but begging him to let it go. The longer he stared, the more he seemed to understand. She wouldn't let him do this for her. And for some reason, he seemed hurt by that.

The emperor balled his hands into fists and held them in front of his chest. The movement brought both her and Aaden's attention to him. Probably just as he intended. He gave a measured glance to Aaden. Even without words, the look spoke volumes.

It was a threat. Not just a threat, but a promise. Finally, the emperor said, "If you try to stop me again, I will strip away your title of Master Shaper and send you to the Storm where you belong."

This at least gave Aaden pause. He sucked in a shallow breath, but his fear was soon outweighed. By what, Talise didn't know, but it felt like something noble. He glanced back at her, and she could see it in his eyes. He was willing to fight for her, no matter the cost.

Drawing her eyebrows together, she gave her head the tiniest shake, willing him to stop fighting. Again, she begged using nothing more than her expression.

He stared back, begging in his own way. Showing her that he wanted to help.

But she wouldn't let him.

His face fell, and he let out a huff. "Fine." He threw the training rod to the ground with a clatter. He gave one last glance to Talise and the emperor before turning his back on both of them. "But I'm not going to stand here and watch."

As he marched out of the room, she waited for the emperor to condemn him. To punish him for leaving without being dismissed. But he never did. The emperor merely stared at the back of Aaden's head before it disappeared through the doorway.

As usual, his face was a blank slate, impossible to read. He turned back to her. The muscles in his face stayed frozen in place as he spoke. "Fire Festival is coming. There will be a masquerade ball here at the palace the evening of Fire Festival. If you haven't proven your ability to lead before then, I'll send you back to the Storm."

Her nose wrinkled at his words. Every vein inside her was on fire, burning through her fear. "You wouldn't," she said, daring to let a hint of the anger escape.

He shrugged. "A Master Shaper must be able to lead." With a small glance in her eyes, he said, "Intimidation is effective, but it's not the only method."

With that, he turned on his heel and marched away. Gritting her teeth together, she slammed her fist into her palm. When that did nothing to improve her mood, she shaped a fire ball only to slam it against the wall. After the fire ball, she sent a wave of air to crash into a nearby shelf.

The wind hit the shelf with a great shudder, sending several bowls through the air only to shatter into pieces when they hit the ground. She let out a scream.

No matter what, she would not use intimidation. It didn't matter how effective it was, she had no desire to be anything like the emperor.

And now she had to prepare for Fire Festival. She had been so wrapped up in the competition and then the trials, she hadn't realized how close the mid-summer holiday was.

The weeks leading up to Fire Festival usually involved all sorts of ancient traditions that were supposed to be fun. Now, she guessed those weeks would only be stressful.

She let out a breath, trying to calm her racing heart. At least with the masquerade ball, she'd have one good thing. Now she had a chance to use one of the many gowns tucked in the wardrobe in her living quarters.

♔

CHAPTER FORTY

TALISE SHOVED ANOTHER GOWN BACK into her wardrobe. The silky red orange dress was beyond beautiful. A huge ball gown skirt with a thick bodice that would hide any imperfections in the stomach area. The long sleeves made the dress look more regal than anything. The smooth velvet fabric was perfect.

As gorgeous as it was, the long sleeves and velvet were impractical for Fire Festival. She needed something that would allow her to breathe on a hot summer evening.

She ran her fingers over an ivory gown with delicate blue flowers, but she wouldn't allow herself to look at it closely. It didn't matter how beautiful it was, she couldn't wear a blue gown to Fire Festival.

Just then, a timid knock came at the door to her living quarters. After shutting the wardrobe, she skipped through her bedroom and into the sitting room. When she opened the door, a wave of disappointment washed over her at the sight of Wendy. But she wasn't sure why. She hadn't been expecting anyone else, so why should she care that Wendy was there?

Wendy chewed on her bottom lip as she kept her head tilted down. Looking up through her eyelashes she said, "Can I come in?"

The guilt inside Talise came on strong, but she did nothing to temper the feeling. It had been three weeks since Kessoku's attack, and Talise had only seen Wendy once since then. That conversation hadn't lasted long.

Wendy's throat contracted as she swallowed.

Talise pressed her lips into a thin line. "I'm busy with—"

"I know you're avoiding me." Her voice was soft and sweet, but a real pain danced through it.

Talise's stomach clenched in a knot. Now she was the one who swallowed. "No, I've just been busy. I haven't had time for…" Her voice trailed off. It didn't matter what excuses she had been feeding herself over the last three weeks. She *was* mad at Wendy. But she also missed her. Ever since coming to the palace, they had seen each other less and less. And Talise needed her best friend back.

All at once, Wendy's eyes filled with tears. She must have been working hard to hold them back because they slid down her cheeks in steady streams. "I'm sorry I didn't tell you about Kessoku. I know you hate me for it. I didn't know very much. And General Gale said the emperor would execute me if I said anything." When a hiccup escaped her mouth, she clasped her hands over it and closed her eyes.

All the anger Talise had been harboring shattered with wave of sympathy. "Oh, stop that," she said, pulling Wendy into the room.

Once the door was closed, Talise let out a sigh. "I know they threatened to hurt you if you said anything. And I know I shouldn't have been mad."

Wendy gave a knowing frown. "I would have been mad too. I thought of all the people they would tell it would be the Master Shapers."

Talise nodded, grateful someone else shared her exasperation.

With a sniff, Wendy carefully tucked a piece of her long, black hair behind her ear. "But I guess since the other Master Shapers were killed, maybe they didn't want you to worry you'd be next."

This didn't seem likely to Talise. They probably just didn't want the rest of Kamdaria finding out how close Kessoku got *again* to murdering the emperor. But she wasn't about to dwell on that. She'd already spent enough energy being angry over the last few weeks.

Talise found a handkerchief inside her desk and handed it to Wendy. "How much did you know?" she asked.

Wendy blew her nose for a long time before answering. The resulting sound seemed louder than a crashing avalanche. Far too loud to have come from her timid friend. When she finished blowing, Wendy whimpered and dabbed at the corners of her eyes. In a flash, it seemed impossible the horrendous noise had ever occurred. That thought made Talise want to snicker.

Clutching the handkerchief close to heart, Wendy dropped her lips into a frown. "It all started with the letter from my brother. It didn't sound like it came from him. I kept asking questions and one of the soldiers finally admitted it didn't come from Cyrus at all."

"Then who wrote it?"

"One of the palace soldiers," Wendy said through her teeth. "After I found out, I went straight to General Gale and demanded answers. He didn't tell me everything. He just said Cyrus might still be alive, but they didn't know for sure. And he also told me Kessoku was more dangerous than everyone thought. That's it. That's all I knew. I had no idea they were going to attack the palace."

Talise began pacing the floor. "Why didn't they tell you Cyrus was missing? If they didn't tell you or your parents, that means none of the other families know either. How can they justify keeping secrets like that?"

But Wendy wasn't listening to her. She had found the door to Talise's bedroom and her mouth hung open, her eyes transfixed on something inside the room. "Your rooms are so much bigger than mine. And they're so fancy."

A cold thread of guilt tripped over the knot in Talise's stomach. She managed a little shrug. "I think it's because I'm a Master Shaper."

"I should have trained harder," Wendy said tracing the carving that adorned Talise's doorframe. "I had no idea Master Shapers had it so good."

This brought a chuckle to Talise's lips. And it gave her an idea. "Do you have a gown for Fire Festival? There's going to be a masquerade ball."

Wendy's eyes lit up. "A ball?" But then she twirled a bit of her hair over a finger. "I've made a little money since working here, but I don't know if—"

Talise cut her off by grabbing her wrist and yanking her into the bedroom. She threw open the wardrobe and let the gowns burst out.

A twinkle appeared in Wendy's eyes as she reached for the delicate fabrics.

"Do you think one of these will work?" Talise asked. "You can borrow one."

Wendy laughed as she pulled out a burgundy gown with gold beads decorating the bodice. The color was dark, but the chiffon fabric was light and airy, making it perfect for a summer evening.

Wendy's mouth seemed to have stopped working. Her jaw dropped further as she held the dress up to her body. The gold beads had been sewed into intricate patterns and lines. In the center of the bodice, swirls of gold beads funneled down to the waistline, creating an abstract tornado shape. Perfect for a shaper whose primary was air.

Talise pulled her friend across the room so she could admire the dress in front of the mirror. When Wendy saw herself with the dress, she twirled around as if unable to stop herself.

"Try it on," Talise said, grinning. "See how it fits."

Soon they were both in gowns. They giggled over paper fans as they pretended to flirt with invisible suitors. When they tired of that, Talise dragged Wendy into the bathroom and forced her to use the cosmetics.

Wendy didn't wear cosmetics regularly, but she certainly had more experience than Talise. After an embarrassing amount of time,

Talise finally produced a perfect line of black paint above her eyelashes. It ended in a sharp point at the corner of her eye.

When she attempted a similar line over the other eye, it resulted in a sloppy mess and Talise gave up with a snort.

"Are you going to wear this one, then?" Wendy asked, touching the black sleeve of Talise's jewel encrusted gown.

Talise shrugged in response. "I guess. I liked the tangerine one too, but it's a little bright for my taste."

Wendy tapped her chin thoughtfully before she ran into the bedroom to dig into the wardrobe. "Oh Talise," she said, emitting a soft gasp. "What about this one? It's perfect."

The ivory dress came out of the wardrobe and the light glinted off the shiny blue embroidery thread. No matter how Talise had tried to ignore it earlier, she couldn't help gazing at it now.

The ivory silk started at the top with delicate cap sleeves and ended with a thick ball gown bottom. A layer of white tulle covered the ivory silk. In the tulle, blue flowers had been embroidered. The flowers were thick around the waist of the dress then became sparse around the hem and neckline.

Breathtaking.

If only the emperor weren't so obsessed with fire shaping. She let out a sigh that carried all the way from the bathroom door where she stood to the wardrobe where Wendy held the dress. "I can't wear blue to Fire Festival. The emperor would never forgive me for broadcasting myself as having a preference for water shaping. The flowers are gorgeous though."

"Flowers?" Wendy asked, tilting her head to the side. "No, look at them carefully. They aren't flowers at all."

With curiosity moving her, Talise stepped across the room. After only a few steps, she realized why Wendy was so excited. They *weren't* flowers. Instead, small blue flames burst out around tiny dots. They looked like flowers from a distance, but up close, the flame shape was obvious. The dress was covered in blue *fire*.

Talise's mouth dropped in awe. She didn't protest when Wendy held the dress up to her shoulders and forced her in front of the mirror.

With a honey sweet smile, Wendy clapped her hands together. "It's like this dress was made for you. Everyone knows you're the first ice shaper in Kamdaria, so it's fitting for you to wear blue. But the flames…" her voice lingered off while they both admired the exquisite embroidery.

Not even the emperor himself could find fault with this dress. Orange was traditionally the color associated with fire, but blue flames did exist. Wendy was right. The dress was perfect.

Staring at the ivory silk made it easy to ignore her deeper problems. But the more she tried to ignore them, the more quickly they came to the forefront of her mind. Talise started to put the dress away, unable to focus on it anymore.

Noticing the change in her demeanor, Wendy asked, "What's wrong?"

Talise bit her bottom lip, trying to decide how much to share. Finally, she said, "I'm trying to teach the soldiers fire shaping, but apparently they don't even know basic combat shaping. I don't know what to do."

Wendy scratched her ear and looked away. She didn't say anything for a while. When she did, she finally said, "I know a few books in the library that might help."

It was easy to let the smile shine through her face. She'd spent three weeks being angry at Wendy for lying to her. And all this time she could have had help with her greatest trouble if only she'd asked.

"Let me change out of this dress and I'll show you," Wendy said.

Talise nodded and let hope blossom through her. With Wendy's help, maybe she had a chance of figuring this out.

Chapter Forty-One

CONVERSATION CAME EASILY AS TALISE and Wendy entered the library. Wendy had told her the titles of a few books, but they hadn't found them yet. When they turned the corner to check another shelf, Talise almost ran into a pair of young men.

Her interest piqued when she saw Aaden standing not alone, but with Claye. Her neck flushed with heat when she saw Aaden, just like it always did, but the heat vanished almost as quickly. Her stomach dropped.

Aaden tried to hide his face, but he seemed to realize it was already too late. He was right about that.

Talise gripped her stomach, unable to form words. Instead, Wendy formed them for her. "What happened to your face?"

Aaden's jaw flexed, which made the purple bruise on his chin bulge. He had another, darker bruise gracing the eye that had a gash running over it.

Two bruises. Both fresh.

A sinking feeling at the pit of her stomach told Talise who had given them to him. Her mind immediately went back to the last time she'd seen Aaden. He had disrespected the emperor and then stormed off without being dismissed.

He had been trying to protect her, which made him seem more honorable in her eyes. The emperor clearly had seen it the opposite way.

A wave of nausea churned in her stomach, forcing her to clutch it again. She wanted to hear what happened. But Aaden only stared at Wendy, unable to answer her question, and suddenly Talise understood. He didn't want anyone else to know what had happened. She could understand that. If everyone knew the emperor had hit him, or made one of his guards do it, they would think less of Aaden.

When Aaden remained silent, Claye chimed in. He shrugged and said, "Yeah, he won't tell me either. Are you wearing eyeliner?" He finished by taking one step too close into Talise's personal space.

Heat burned through her cheeks as she remembered the perfect line over her right eye accompanied by the sloppy line over her left. "Oh yeah," she said attempting a chuckle. "We were practicing for the ball."

Claye quirked one eyebrow up. "I thought it was a masquerade ball. No one would be able to see your eyes anyway."

Unable to respond, Talise merely blinked back at him. Why hadn't *she* thought of that?

Wendy glanced at Aaden once more, but apparently gave up on learning more about his bruises. Instead, she leaned over Claye's arm to look at the book in his hand.

"Why are you reading about the emperor's genealogy?" she asked.

"That is an excellent question," Claye said with a smile. "Come see what we're working on."

Wendy followed Claye, which gave Talise a brief moment to be alone with Aaden. Unfortunately, he seemed unwilling to let her use it. Instead, he gestured toward Claye and Wendy. "You should see this too."

When they made it to the table where Claye and Aaden had been earlier, Wendy peered over the books. "You said one of the Kessoku soldiers stole the emperor's family tree from the treasury?"

Claye nodded. "Yes, and we're trying to figure out why. The public records only mention the emperor's five youngest children by first name. That's standard until they become adults. But some of the empress's family isn't well known either. There must be additional information on the family tree that isn't in the public records."

Talise sat down in the chair next to Claye, trying not to notice how Aaden scooted his chair closer to hers.

Claye lowered his voice to a whisper, careful to let his words have the highest possible impact. "We think Kessoku is looking for an heir. If they can't kill the emperor, at least they can make sure he has no one to pass the throne to, right?"

When Wendy let out a faint gasp, Claye smirked with satisfaction. He glanced at Talise to see her reaction.

She raised one eyebrow, careful to let him see her skepticism. "Is there any evidence of an heir?"

Claye opened his mouth excitedly, but a moment later his face fell. "No. Sadly, there is not. But…" He raised one finger, that excitement crawling back again. "Look what we found."

He pointed to one of the open books on the table. "These are accounts from people who attended the funeral after the royal family was murdered. Look at this one."

The empress looked as beautiful as ever lying in her grave box. The little children from the Crown left chrysanthemums beside her, knowing it was her favorite flower. The empress's sister suffered a far worse fate. Her face was mangled beyond recognition. I could hardly look at it for fear of being sick.

The details brought the funeral to life in Talise's eye. It took great effort to see past them and try to discover what had made Claye so excited. When she couldn't figure it out, she looked up at him with another skeptical frown.

"What's so interesting about this?"

Claye jabbed the paragraph with his finger. "The empress's sister! Mangled beyond recognition? Doesn't that seem suspicious to you?"

Talise shrugged, unwilling to play along with his excitement. The emperor had seven children, two daughters-in-law, and a grandson who had all been killed in the attack. The empress, the empress's sister, and their parents were also killed. None of it seemed like information that needed to be resurfaced.

Wendy's face screwed up into a knot. "Didn't Kessoku use boulders in their attack? I thought a lot of the victims were mangled beyond recognition."

Claye let out a huff before falling back into his seat. "She was the only member of the family who was mangled like that. It does seem suspicious."

Talise leaned closer to look, scanning the rest of the account before flipping through a few more pages. Absently, she said, "What would Kessoku want with the emperor's sister-in-law anyway? The empress was only royal by marriage. Her sister wouldn't be an heir even if she were alive."

"That's what *I* said," Aaden said in a low voice.

Claye threw his hands into the air. "Well, I don't know. Maybe Kessoku doesn't want an heir. Maybe they're trying to get the empress's sister on their side. That could be a powerful symbol, you know. If they turned someone who was so close to the emperor."

"But why look now?" Talise asked. "It's been twelve years since the attack."

He jutted out his bottom lip by way of response.

Always quick to dispel contention, Wendy reached for his hand and gave a sweet smile. "Aren't you excited about the masquerade ball for Fire Festival? You could dance with that pretty soldier you're always talking about."

Claye showed a hint of smile after that, his anger subsiding for a moment. He rolled his shoulders back with an air of confidence. "I *have* wooed many women with my dancing skills. She'd probably fall for me if I got her to dance."

"But I thought…" Aaden's voice stopped abruptly as he glanced from Claye to Wendy and then back again. When they only stared back in response, he pointed between them. "I thought you two were…" He blinked, willing one of them to finish his sentence. When no one did, he finally said, "You know, in love or something."

Talise couldn't help her eyebrows from flying up to her forehead. Wendy let out a snort, which Claye pretended to be offended by. A moment later, he was laughing. He wrapped his arms around both Talise and Wendy and pulled them in close. "Sadly. These two know way too many embarrassing things about me to ever see me romantically."

Aaden blinked again. Not so subtly, his eyes drifted away from Claye's face and over to the arm that was now wrapped tight around Talise's shoulder. "Oh," he said, a bit anticlimactically.

"I just had an idea," Talise said, jumping out of her chair. "Do you remember how Mrs. Dew made us hold those hot rocks close to our heart? It was back when you two first came to the elite academy. She made us hold them so we could feel the heat in our hearts. It helped us shape fire better because we could feel that it came from the heart. I think it might work for the soldiers too."

Aaden followed after her when she left the library. She was grateful the other two didn't. He must have forgotten about the bruises on his face, but she hadn't. Once they were alone, she would get him to talk.

Chapter Forty-Two

Talise waited until they were far down the hall before she attempted conversation. She even glanced over her shoulder to make sure there were no prying ears she hadn't noticed.

Aaden seemed mildly interested when she looked over her shoulder, but then he seemed to realize her true intention all at once. His jaw flexed and he began to walk faster.

When she touched his arm, his steps faltered. "What happened?"

He wouldn't look at her. He shifted his arm out of her grip and turned his head the other way. "Does it matter what size the rocks are? Can they be pebbles from the garden or do we need to find bigger ones?"

"Aaden." She stepped in front of him, forcing him to a stop. She held her bottom lip between her teeth for a moment, desperate to keep it from trembling. "What did he do to you?"

That was her only real question. She already knew exactly what happened and why. But were there more injuries she couldn't see? How bad were they?

He shifted away again, making eye contact impossible. But then his shoulder twitched as he looked back for one small moment.

"You have to tell me." Her voice was higher than she meant it to be.

He folded his arms over his chest, turning away again. Every sign made it clear he would not discuss the incident. Desperation took over. She did the only thing she could think of.

She reached for his arm. Letting her fingers slide over his warm skin, she let them land over his hand. And finally, she wrapped her fingers over his, squeezing just enough that he couldn't ignore it.

His gaze fell to her hand much quicker than she expected. He abandoned all hope of ignoring her and turned to face her instead. Using his thumb, he held her fingers into place over his hand. When he looked at her, a sadness lingered in his eyes that she had never seen before. "Why do you let him talk to you like that?"

Her shoulders dropped. Her heartbeat slowed to a thundering pulse. "*Let* him? I can't control what he says to me."

Aaden looked away. He unfolded his arms just enough to pull her fingers closer to his chest. Each of his breaths sounded heavier than the last. "Yes, but you worry so much about his words."

A weight seemed to drop on her chest, making it difficult to breathe. She chewed her bottom lip, afraid to speak. The truth was too painful to speak, but it was also too painful to ignore. "Everything he says is true."

Aaden looked up, exasperation in his eyes. "Yes, that. *That* is exactly what I'm talking about. You take his words too hard. Why do you care so much? Why is his approval so important to you?"

"He's the emperor." Her words came out with a sense of finality. It should have been impossible to argue with her logic.

He didn't even try. His arms unfolded from in front of his chest, but he managed to keep a tender grip on her hand. He looked deeper into her eyes which sent a trill through the furthest edges of her body. Without a word, his argument was clear.

Some people's opinions were more important than others.

Still communicating in silence, he was making a pretty strong argument for his opinion being the only one she should care about.

She had a feeling his argument would include some more nonverbal communication soon. Particularly one that involved lips.

Most of her wanted to give in without any thought to the consequences. Yet, another part of her worried what his attitude meant. If he didn't think the emperor's opinion was important, what did that say about his honor? Was he only being loyal to the emperor because it kept him out of the Storm?

If he didn't actually respect the emperor's authority, then how was he any different from Kessoku? He wasn't actively trying to murder the emperor. That did make him significantly different from Kessoku, right? But was the difference significant enough?

Another moment of looking into his eyes and she wouldn't have cared anymore. But before he could lean in, the jovial laughter of nearby soldiers interrupted the silence. The soldiers were just around the corner and soon their words became crystal clear.

"It's their own fault for expecting us to make fire balls after a few weeks of training," said a female voice. "The other Master Shapers always started their training with air."

Talise gave a nervous glance to Aaden while she backed up closer to the wall. It didn't warm her heart to know the soldiers were talking about them behind their backs, but it probably would have been even less pleasant for the soldiers to run into the pair of them while they were doing it.

Following her lead, Aaden pushed open the door to the training hall. They both slipped inside moments before the soldiers appeared around the corner.

"Who do they think they are anyway?" A gruff voice said, in contrast to the earlier one. "She's just a girl from the Storm and he's the son of a traitor. They come in here thinking they're better than us because they're Master Shapers, but they're both nothing more than vermin."

"You said it," agreed the female soldier.

Talise held her breath as the soldiers passed by the training hall door. Her heart raced as their steps echoed down the hallway.

The soldiers didn't trust her. They looked down on her. She had to accept that now.

All this time she thought the title of Master Shaper was all she needed to lead. In one short conversation, these soldiers had proved her wrong.

The emperor's words from the day before rang in her ears. *A true leader doesn't complain about the incompetence of soldiers. A true leader looks within to solve problems.*

If she kept complaining about her soldiers' inability to shape, she'd never get anywhere.

When they were far past the training hall door, she turned to Aaden with a start. Pointing toward the hallway, she said, "That is why I care about the emperor's words. Like I said before, everything he says is true."

CHAPTER FORTY-THREE

THE LIBRARY WAS ALWAYS A vast source of knowledge, but for the first time in her life, Talise wasn't sure what to look for. The polished wood shelves towered high above her. Rolling ladders were attached to the end of each long row so the highest shelves would be reachable.

She loved the musty smell of the old books. Sometimes she would lean in close just to breathe in the smell. And the spines were always so lovely. Leather and cloth with such designs on the cover, as beautiful and intricate as pieces of art.

She traced a finger over a friendly green spine. The title had seemed silly at first, but she kept coming back to it. Glancing over her shoulder, she checked to see if Aaden was nearby. He wasn't.

They were supposed to be looking for books that would help them be better teachers. She had already spent the last two days poring over books on teaching theory. The strategies were helpful, but they tended to focus on concrete concepts like management and curriculum design.

What she needed was much more abstract. Loyalty, respect. Not for the first time that day, her thoughts drifted back to Marmie.

Even in her earliest memories, Talise recognized how Marmie could gain the respect of anyone around her.

Marmie had been firm when she needed to be, but she had never treated Talise the way the emperor did. What was it about Marmie that made her so endearing to everyone she met?

Talise traced her finger over the title again. *Eternal Friendships.* A part of her still felt silly about it. What did friendship have to do with leadership? But another part of her felt like it might be the answer she needed.

When she attempted to abandon the competition back at the academy, Wendy had packed food for her. She implored her to stay, but she never forced her to.

It wasn't a title or intimidation that made Wendy react the way she did. In that case, friendship was all she needed.

Glancing over her shoulder for a second time, Talise pulled the book off the shelf. Enough of the going back and forth. She needed answers, and she needed them now. Fire Festival was only two weeks away. She didn't have time to waste.

The first few pages held words that should have seemed obvious.

More than anything, a friendship blossoms when both parties are genuinely invested in the other's lives. If an eternal friendship is what you desire, begin by asking about the person's life. But that is only the first step. Next, it is imperative that both parties then support each other and help each other succeed in their desired goals.

She wanted to roll her eyes at the words. She wanted to scoff and laugh and write the book off as useless. Except she couldn't. As obvious as the words were, she couldn't help but realize she had never once made any attempt to get to know her soldiers.

Their hopes and desires were mysteries to her. She knew nothing of their families, their homes. When she passed by them in the halls, they were like moving statues. Nothing more than decorations or tools.

A knot twisted through her stomach as she continued to read. How had she lived seventeen years and never realized how incredibly self-involved she was? She knew the servants and soldiers had their own lives and troubles. So, why had she never thought to care about them?

This was a problem. A problem that bit into her. She had been so self-absorbed, so desperate to win the competition, that she'd barely been able to see outside of her own life.

Her stomach wrenched. If she'd grown up the rest of her life in the Storm, this wouldn't have happened. Marmie would have taught her to be kind to people, to be invested in their lives.

She gritted her teeth and rolled her shoulders back. *No.* Hating herself for past mistakes would fix nothing. She had done wrong to ignore her soldiers and expect their respect when she'd done nothing to earn it. But she didn't have to continue doing wrong.

Balancing the open book on her hands, she read as she walked back to the table. She scanned the words with voracious interest, trying to soak them all in. She found herself reading certain passages several times, trying to commit them to memory. At one point, she nearly underlined a particular passage for its utter truth.

True friendship is about building each other up, not using the other for gain.

She wanted to pull out her hair for being so stupid. This whole time she saw the soldiers as nothing more than tools, weapons. Of course they hated her. They had every right to.

She had already gotten a quarter of the way through the book before Aaden joined her at the table. He carried another theory of teaching book, but his fingers pinched the book at the corner, as if the book wasn't worth the effort of holding it properly.

"Looks like you were more successful than me. Should I read that one too?"

She bit her bottom lip, ignoring his question altogether. Instead, she asked one of her own. "Have you talked with any of the soldiers?

More than to give them orders, I mean. Do you know any of their names? Any of their dreams?"

The very thought made Aaden chuckle. "I'm not very good with people. I'm sure you've noticed."

"Sit down by me," she said, and as always, he looked more than happy to comply. "We need to read this together.

— ◆ —

"I WISH THERE weren't so many of them all together."

Talise eyed the group of four soldiers from around the corner. "I know," she said, lengthening out the syllables so her exasperation was clear. She tucked the green book under her elbow as she swallowed.

"Come on, we've already read the whole book twice. We have to do this now."

Aaden nodded, setting his face with determination. Even as he struggled to focus, the terror in his eyes was clear.

She might have laughed at him if her own expression hadn't been an exact mirror of his. They both took a deep breath before they waltzed around the corner toward the soldiers.

The soldiers grimaced at the sight of them. Two of the soldiers turned their backs on them. Had she been such a terrible leader that even looking at her was such a task now?

She shoved the thought away, not giving it residence in her mind. The past was behind her. All she could do was move forward the right way.

"Hello." Aaden's greeting sounded as formal as a soldier giving a report to his commander. He cleared his throat, which somehow made his actions even more awkward. "I see you like to talk to each other."

One of the soldiers who had turned her back on them turned around now just to give a most confused face to the pair of them.

276

The air around Talise stilled as she grasped for any words that could smooth this over. What would Marmie do? What would Wendy do?

Smile. Talise attempted a smile as sweet as Wendy's. Based on the sour looks the soldiers gave her, it hadn't been successful. She gave that up with a sigh. At this point, there was nothing to do but be honest.

"We want to get to know you better. We realize we've spent all this time trying to teach you, and we don't even know your names." She shrugged, grateful the words were coming more easily the longer she spoke. "We thought it might be easier to teach you if we spent more time getting to know you."

Now a smile came but this one wasn't as forced as the other. It wasn't as big or sweet as before, but it was genuine.

The soldiers seemed to be able to tell the difference.

One of them laughed at her. He was making fun, though not in an unkind way. "You realized we're actual people, have you?"

A blush warmed her cheeks, but there was no use denying the truth now. "Sorry it took so long. What are your names?"

After they all introduced themselves, the questions started to flow more naturally. The soldiers started taking on more detail around her. No longer were they moving props milling around the palace like mindless lumps.

Now they had life. One of them was excellent at Forces and had even beaten the emperor in a game once. Another of them liked to bake bread. His parents owned a bakery in the Gate. He joined the army because his wife needed extra medical care, and it was easier to get in the Crown.

One soldier had just joined the army a few months earlier when she turned eighteen. She had dreams of guarding the palace by day and talking long walks in the garden at night.

Even their faces seemed clearer now that she took the time to look at them. One had a crooked tooth and bright eyes. One wore a uniform that looked even more crisp than Aaden's. One had a long scar on his neck, and the story of how she'd gotten it promised to be a good one.

Even Aaden warmed up the more they talked. His words were stilted at first, just like when he first started talking to Wendy and Claye. But the more they talked, the easier they fell into conversation.

The whole thing only lasted a few minutes. The soldiers had to leave to meet with General Gale. But once they left, Talise could tell her face was beaming.

Chapter Forty-Four

THE TRAINING HALL DIDN'T SEEM so ominous these days. Talise's heart didn't feel like crushing every time she walked through the doors. Now, almost every time she entered, she encountered a friendly face. She had started greeting the soldiers by name.

Many of them still didn't trust her. Gossip about her and Aaden's goal to get to know the soldiers had spread through the palace like wildfire. Some of them responded enthusiastically, excited to get to know the Master Shapers better.

Others still thought she and Aaden had no place being Master Shapers at all. Talise rested against the wall as their new class entered the room. It was Aaden's turn to head the lesson.

As the soldiers filed in, her expression grew darker. This was a squad they continually had trouble with. Every single one of the soldiers was firmly in the "don't trust the Master Shapers" camp. They had not only laughed at Talise and Aaden's attempts to befriend them, they also actively fought against their efforts.

So much for a good lesson.

To her dismay, the emperor entered the training room wearing an expression just short of a scowl. Aaden fidgeted at the sight of him. His jaw flexed, which made the bruise on his chin bulge. The bruise was almost faded now, but the memory had surely made an imprint.

Aaden bowed low, his voice the picture of respect. "What a great honor it is to have you here, Your Highness."

The emperor nodded at these words, momentarily appeased by Aaden's submission.

"I am here to check your progress. Fire Festival is approaching. I hope the soldiers will be ready to do a demonstration during the masquerade ball. The guests are expecting to see them shoot fire balls."

Talise's heart jumped into her throat. The emperor had implied they had until the festival to improve their leadership skills, but he had never mentioned a demonstration.

Letting her eyes travel the length of the room, the soldiers seemed just as surprised as her. Two looked frightened, one looked apprehensive, one looked annoyed. But the last soldier frightened her more than the others. The last soldier almost smiled beneath her haughty expression. She gave the tiniest glance to Talise, seeming intent on letting the mischief in her eyes shine through.

Great.

Sweat seeped through the skin of Talise's palms. The last thing she needed right now was trouble. The emperor seemed more eager every day to find fault with her methods. If she couldn't demonstrate some kind of progress during this lesson. No, best not to consider that.

Aaden nodded to the emperor. Though he maintained an air of calm, the pulsing vein at his throat told a different story. He was swallowing way too often. The trembling in his fingers wasn't obvious until he gestured toward the nearest soldier. Luckily, it was a small enough movement that no one would notice besides her.

"Gather the targets and place them along the back wall."

Talise admired how Aaden could speak in the face of fear without so much as a tremor in his voice. Their eyes met for a moment. Though they didn't speak, she hoped he would feel the encouragement in her glance.

Nearby, the soldier Aaden had spoken to glared at his request. His mouth shriveled up, and he made no attempt to hide his contempt from the emperor. Heavy footfalls sounded through the room as the soldier grudgingly complied with Aaden's order.

How would he like to be smacked upside the head? That might cure him of this unnecessary disdain. It would also probably undo all the work she had done to befriend the soldiers, but at the moment, she cared less and less.

A tiny quiver hung in Aaden's voice when he addressed the room again. His throat contracted like he was preparing to clear his throat, but he must have resisted the urge. "Before doing fire balls, try shaping a small fire over your palm. Just like we practiced a few days ago."

The soldier at the back of the room made a point of rolling her eyes. When that didn't illicit the reaction she wanted, she scoffed loudly.

One of the emperor's eyebrows cocked up slightly. His eyes drew away from the soldier and over to Aaden, perhaps awaiting his reaction.

Aaden wiped his palms on the side of his pants. He cleared his throat in two awkward coughs, apparently unable to resist the temptation a second time.

Smacking the soldiers upside the head seemed like a more viable option the longer Talise stood there. Aaden seemed to think the best option was to give a stern glare at the female soldier before he gestured at the soldiers to begin.

Most of them still struggled to shape a simple fire, even without throwing it. Were they doing it on purpose? Most students could shape all four elements when they finished the first five years of academy training. And yet these soldiers seemed to struggle with the simplest of tasks.

The female soldier at the back was the most concerning. She wore a blue-hemmed tunic, which meant she was a higher ranked guard. She'd already been trained by the other Master Shapers, yet still needed basic shape training. Why was shaping so difficult for her?

The emperor tapped his foot impatiently. As always, he was unhappy with their progress. He gave a pointed stare to both Talise and Aaden. Aaden responded by addressing the class again. He nearly growled as he told them to now throw fire balls at the targets.

His sudden intensity took the entire class off guard. A soldier in the front wore pinched lips as he turned toward the target. Another soldier had a shiver pass through his shoulders before he let out an audible gulp.

Guilt immediately lined Aaden's features, especially when he turned to Talise with an apologetic gleam in his eye. They'd both been trying to avoid this. They had decided to befriend the soldiers and gain their trust that way. Intimidation wasn't supposed to be the solution.

But when the soldiers aimed for the targets this time, all of them performed better than they ever had before.

The only one who neglected to produce a fire ball was, unsurprisingly, the female soldier in the back. Her haughty smirk was gone now. It had been replaced by a crease between her eyebrows that deepened as she began chewing her bottom lip.

She looked over her shoulder twice before holding her palm out in front of her. After staring at it for a moment, she began whispering and looking over her shoulder again, as if begging her hand to produce the fire needed.

Talise and Aaden shared another glance. His shoulders drooped as he stuffed his hands into his pockets. The guilt in his eyes was ever present, though the twitch in his lips made it clear he wasn't sure what to say.

"I'll talk to her," Talise whispered so the emperor wouldn't hear.

Aaden's chest heaved with a silent sigh as he bounced his head a little too enthusiastically in a nod.

When the soldier noticed Talise coming her way, she dropped her hand and pasted the haughty expression back onto her face.

"This is a stupid exercise." She spit out each of her words like they tasted bitter in her mouth.

She's just scared she's going to get in trouble, she thought. *Remember what Marmie said. When people are scared, it often comes out as anger.* If she could be patient and gain the soldier's trust, she could be the leader she needed to be.

"Feel it in your heart first," Talise said, attempting a gentle smile.

The soldier responded by glaring through the side of her eye. "You're lucky to have a heart at all. No one should survive life in the *Storm*. They deserve to die."

The way her lip curled up when she said *Storm* sent ice prickling through Talise's veins. Her lips froze in place as she tried to formulate any sort of response that wasn't filled with wrath. People said awful things when they were scared or desperate. She knew that from living in the outer ring. But for someone to suggest that everyone in the Storm deserved to die?

Breathe in. Breathe out. Don't say something you'll regret. Talise pinched the side of her leg, forcing her focus on the pain and not on the anger.

The soldier's mouth twisted into a smile. Not only had she noticed the rush of anger Talise was battling, the soldier seemed to be enjoying it. In a scathing whisper, she added, "I hope your family members are all dead."

Talise took a breath so sharp, it sucked in her cheeks. Her fingers curled into fists without her permission.

And just like that, the emperor's silver and ivory tunic appeared at her side. How long had he been watching her? How much would he punish her if words like this went unchecked? This was about more than anger. It was about more than friendship or leadership too. If the emperor continued to disapprove her methods, he would do something about it. This was about survival now.

When Talise jabbed a finger under the soldier's collarbone, it seemed to be acting of its own accord. "You'll produce a fire ball and hit the target by the end of the lesson." Her voice was low and dangerous like a burning ember fighting to burst back into flames. "If you don't, you will suffer the consequences."

The soldier scoffed. Her head jerked to the side when the emperor shifted, and the barest hint of fear flickered through her eyes. The fear only lasted a moment. "What consequences? Are you going to make me sit in the corner?" The sing-song lilt of the soldier's voice begged a reaction.

Feeling the emperor's eyes on her, Talise jabbed the soldier again. "How does a night in the dungeon sound?" She spit the words out, surprised at how much wrath they held.

The soldier blinked. Then blinked again. "You can't...you..." The soldier stammered over her words as she glanced from the emperor back to Talise. Seeming to make a decision, the soldier lifted her chin. "You don't have the authority to do that."

This time, Talise turned her own mouth into a twisted smile. "Don't be so sure about that."

The soldier's eyes flitted back to the emperor's. When he remained silent, the soldier's throat contracted with a swallow. She looked at Talise once more, but soon her eyes fell, not exactly in a respectful way, but close enough.

"I'll do my best," she said, head pointed down. It wasn't until the soldier turned that a spark of guilt lit inside Talise.

The way the soldier's fingers shook as she glared at her palm. The way she glanced over her shoulder and kept chewing on her bottom lip.

That was because of Talise.

Talise pinched her leg again, eager to take back her threat. Perhaps it was better to walk away. Maybe it was better to let her thoughts clear before she faced the soldier again. When she took her first step backward, the emperor jerked his head side to side, refusing to let her leave. He pointed his chin toward the soldier, apparently urging her to watch.

But Talise didn't want to watch. That spark of guilt inside had already blossomed into a field of weeds that punctured through her insides. She'd been so eager to avoid threats. Anything to be different from the emperor. In the end, she had bowed to the pressure and acted just like him.

She was suddenly overcome with the desire to seek out Aaden. What would he think? Would he be impressed that she had frightened the soldier? Or would he be disappointed that she had been so cruel? For some reason, his opinion seemed to matter a lot more than the emperor's.

Just when the guilt exploded like the feathery seeds on a weed, the soldier produced a fire over her palm. The soldier let out a small shriek of delight before she clapped her other hand over her mouth.

After glancing back once more, the soldier focused her attention on the target. She reeled her arm back and punched it forward, which sent the fire ball arching through the air.

Talise expected another shriek delight when the fire ball hit the target. Instead, the soldier let out a breath of relief that made her shoulders sag. For a brief moment, she turned to the emperor, seeming to seek his approval.

He did not acknowledge the glance, instead he kept his eyes on Talise. As soon as the soldier turned her back on the emperor, he gave a simple nod to Talise.

He said nothing more as he left the room. The interaction left Talise at odds with herself. For possibly the first time ever, the emperor had not criticized her. Yet, the guilt crawling through her veins made the victory feel false.

Maybe she imagined it, but when she trudged back to the front of the room, the entire squad of soldiers seemed to hold their breaths as she passed. One of them definitely bowed to her.

It hadn't been her favorite method, but it had been effective. Maybe it was time to stop worrying so much. Maybe it was time to just accept the victory and do whatever it took to be a leader.

♛

CHAPTER FORTY-FIVE

THE REMAINING DAYS LEADING TO Fire Festival went by in a blur. Soon it arrived and Talise was still trying not to think about the demonstration the emperor expected that evening.

Immediately after lunch, she prepared to head down to the streets for the Fire Festival parade. When she pulled a fiery orange tunic over her trousers, she made sure to hide a dagger-clad belt underneath it. She'd been going around with the dagger a lot these days. After the attack on the palace, she just felt better having it close.

The streets were crowded by the time she left the palace. For some reason, she didn't want to think about how this was the first time in too long since she had been on a public road. She'd gotten a special pass, signed by Commander Blaise, that allowed her outside the palace grounds. But city soldiers wouldn't ask for passes today. They had too many other things to do during the parade.

She ran her thumb along the bottom hem of her orange tunic as she pushed through the crowds. The smell of hot candy made her mouth taste sweet. She eyed one of the popular confections. A hollow glass ball sat on a wooden stick. The design was reminiscent of something glass blown over a fire, a perfect treat for Fire Festival.

The translucent candy had an orange hue. Just by the smell, she knew it had an extra large dose of cinnamon to make it taste like fire.

Her eyes lingered on the treat for another moment before she forced herself to look away. The streets were bathed in orange banners and streamers. Almost everyone in the milling crowd wore orange as well, from vibrant tangerine to understated copper. Everyone was eager to show their love of fire during Fire Festival, for fire brought the heat that melted the mountain snow. And the snow provided water for all of Kamdaria throughout the rest of the year.

Two old women nearly trampled over Talise as they held their heads close together sharing juicy gossip. A man called out the name Isla from across the street. His waving arms suggested he sought Talise's attention, which made her stomach flop. But it turned out, he was seeking his daughter, who was walking a few steps behind Talise.

Another smell lifted through the air. In a small market stall, a woman used fire shaping to roast a duck while her son turned the spit. A thick marmalade sauce coated the duck with orange peel shavings inside the sticky sauce. The woman's husband shaved the peels of oranges, tangerines, and mandarins into a bowl for another batch of sauce.

Licking her lips was inevitable. But when the small family offered to sell her some already cooked duck, Talise had to politely decline. She'd eaten breakfast in the palace and would have a grand dinner at the masquerade ball that evening. She didn't need anything in between. Besides, she didn't tend to carry around extra coins.

She marched down the street again, eyes narrowing to stay focused. Wendy and Claye came down hours ago to secure a good spot for the parade. Aaden offered to go down with her, but she told him she had one last thing to finish before she could go.

In truth, she didn't want him to get the wrong idea. He'd been getting bolder lately. He hadn't tried to kiss her yet, but everyone in the palace seemed to know exactly how much he wanted to. The latest palace gossip was all about whether she felt the same way. It probably would have been easier to tell if she knew herself.

Talise glanced over her shoulder to count the number of flags she'd passed. Wendy had said they would try to get a spot no more than seven flags past the palace gates. Since Talise had just passed her eleventh flag, she was beginning to think she should go back and look closer.

A sea of children appeared from nowhere, all screaming with delight as they charged for a nearby candy stall. They forced Talise forward with no time to check her surroundings. A moment later, someone tugged on her elbow freeing her from the mob.

Before she could rip her arm from the mysterious grasp, Aaden's voice lilted in from behind her. "We're back this way."

Talise's other hand flew up as she nervously tucked a strand of hair behind her ear. "I couldn't stop. The children, they…" For some reason, her stomach decided to start fluttering, making it difficult to form words.

The smile in Aaden's eyes didn't help at all. "I saw."

With his hand still on her elbow, he led her through the street. Even once Wendy and Claye came into view, he seemed to think it necessary to keep his hand over her elbow.

Wendy freed her from his grasp when she forced Talise onto a red and white quilt that had been spread onto the ground.

"We got this for you," Wendy said with bright red cheeks. She pushed a pastry topped with orange icing into Talise's hands. "Oh, and this!" Wendy retrieved a small bowl filled with diced cantaloupe, papaya, and mango.

Before Talise could pop one of the mango pieces into her mouth, Wendy bent at the waist and began digging around the quilt. Cloth napkins and empty tin cups went flying as she searched. "Claye, where are the meat skewers? You know, the ones with carrots and venison and that nice honey glaze?"

Claye didn't look up from the game of Forces he was playing with a stranger. He did chuckle slightly when he said, "You ate them all."

Wendy's cheeks turned even brighter red as her spine shot up straight. After biting her bottom lip, she let out a sigh. "Oh well, at least you have the pastry and fruit. I know I should have saved more for you, but…" She threw her hands into the air and spoke to the sky as if in prayer. "The food here is so good!"

Talise chuckled as she popped a second mango chunk into her mouth. "This is plenty, Wendy. Thank you."

Aaden folded his hands into his lap, somehow managing to look serious and ready for battle even though he sat cross-legged on a quilt. He stared across the street at a market stall that seemed to sell the exact meat skewers Wendy had mentioned earlier.

Even with his attention so diverted, his knee brushed against Talise's, which made her think he wasn't quite as distracted as he seemed. At least not by the market stall.

Claye dropped one of his Forces tablets onto the game board with a click. He grinned at his move and then turned to the others. "Talise, you have to tell me how you learned to shape all four elements before academy testing. My cousin is coming to the ball tonight. He has a daughter whose testing is coming up, and he's begging me for tips."

The stranger sitting across the Forces board from Claye looked up with mild interest but clearly not enough to say anything. He went back to the board right away.

Meanwhile, Talise's insides froze. She had difficulty chewing the pastry that had been soft only a moment ago. After some effort, she managed to choke out, "How did you know about that?"

Claye shrugged, his eyes on the board. "Everybody knows that."

The response didn't tell her anything because, as far as she knew, *nobody* knew about that. The only people in the room during her academy testing were her, Marmie, and the two guards.

Maybe the two guards had told other people, but what were the odds of Claye hearing about it from them and somehow connecting the event with her?

Wendy stopped brushing crumbs off the quilt and looked up with huge eyes. "*I* didn't know that." Her eyes opened even wider. "You could shape all four elements before academy testing? I couldn't even shape two."

"You didn't know that?" Claye rubbed the back of his neck as he glanced at Wendy. A nervous chuckle escaped him before he moved another tablet.

Talise pinned him with a questioning stare. He gulped and shifted in his seat, which only made her stare harder.

Her heart thrummed while a tingle of fear spread through her fingertips.

Claye leaned forward, suddenly over interested in the Forces board. He waved a distracted hand toward her. "Aaden told me about it. I thought everyone knew."

Talise whipped around to face Aaden, but his muscles seemed frozen in place as he looked at the market stall across the street. He seemed intent on pretending he hadn't even heard the conversation.

She wasn't fooled by his act. Her hands shook as she folded them tight. She blamed the bead of sweat dripping by her ear on the heat of the day, though deep down she knew that had nothing to do with it. "How did *you* know that?"

Her heart pulsed as she waited for his answer. Each beat felt like the sound of a gong reverberated through her veins.

Aaden finally turned, wearing an annoyingly convincing air of indifference. "I looked up your record from academy testing. They keep the testing records for every single student in the palace library."

"Why?" Talise took great care to keep her voice measured. And why was that information public anyway?

Aaden responded with a shrug. "It seems like a logical place to me. I guess they could keep the records in the treasury, but they aren't valuable. I mean, information is valuable, but not like jewels. And anyway, information is usually kept in a library."

Momentarily stunned by his masterful avoidance of her question, she blinked. Her elbow shot out to nudge him, which turned out more playful than she meant it. "I meant why did you look up my record?"

When her chest stilled in anticipation, she forced herself to suck in a breath. She wanted to let it out slowly, but that might make the others wonder why she cared so much. Instead, she did her best to breathe like normal. *In and out. Nice and slow.*

But really, *why* would Aaden look up her testing record? She'd been so slow to trust him because of his father's actions, so sure he couldn't be trusted. Had she been right about him all along?

He paused for a fraction, letting his eyes glance down the road before he spoke again. It wasn't enough to raise suspicion from anyone else, but now she knew him so well, she imagined he took the extra moment to formulate a lie.

"I wanted to know how someone from the Storm could shape. I thought maybe the guards who tested you left some notes or something."

Everything inside her felt like a thick-trunked tree just moments before an axe forced it to the ground. Her bones were cracking, her muscles were cracking. Her feelings. They were being ripped to tiny shreds that would scatter in the slightest wind. Torn and tattered, never to be repaired.

Her mind filled with all the moments they'd shared. Of how he'd helped her, of how she'd opened up to him. Of how he'd touched her. A shiver ran up her spine.

She wanted to take it all back now.

Could the others feel how the air around her shifted? Could they see how her body twitched, trying to get away from him without moving?

Aaden seemed to know. He *always* seemed to know. And she could see how his own face changed. The difference was subtle. The skin around his eyes softened. His chin tilted downward the tiniest bit. His shoulders rolled toward her.

He gazed into her eyes, but she knew he wasn't just looking. He was begging. He wanted her to know he had no nefarious purpose for looking up her testing record.

No matter how his eyes warmed her from the inside out, how could she believe that? What reason could he possibly have for looking up her testing record? And how, in all of Kamdaria, could it be innocent?

Claye seemed to think that was the perfect moment to change the subject entirely. While picking his teeth, he said, "Wendy told me the soldiers you've been training have to do a demonstration during the masquerade ball tonight."

The stranger sitting across from him didn't react to this statement. He probably worked in the palace too. Perhaps he worked with Claye in the gardens.

Talise forced her breaths to be even and slow. If she let herself worry too much, the others would notice eventually. She needed to tuck this information away and deal with it later. For now, she'd try to pretend it had never happened.

As Claye moved one of his blank tablets across the board, he pouted. "Why don't you ever tell me anything? You tell Wendy everything."

Talise took in another breath before she forced a friendly smirk on her face. With as much nonchalance as she could muster, she said, "Did you want to spend hours helping me pick out a mask and practice doing my hair for the ball? Because that's when I told Wendy."

Wendy giggled at the wrinkled face of disgust Claye made.

To Talise's surprise, the stranger spoke next. He raised one eyebrow. "Are you really doing a demonstration? My friend is a palace soldier, and she said only half of them can throw fire balls that actually hit the target."

More fear, cold and heavy, stabbed Talise in the gut. Her breath tried to shudder, but she controlled it at the last moment. She glanced at Aaden, who was inexplicably even closer than before. The same guilt laced his features that she felt in her own. At least in this they still shared common ground.

"Well *I* heard," Claye said, forcing all eyes on him, "that you two drastically changed your training tactics about a week ago. You went from trying to befriend the soldiers to barking off orders and doling out threats."

"We had to," Talise argued. But it sounded even weaker out loud than it did in her head. Could she ever get these emotions under control?

For the briefest moment, Wendy's lip curled. She hid the expression immediately and started scratching her nose. Perhaps she was trying to hide that her moment of disgust had ever appeared.

Talise folded her arms tighter around her chest, as if that could keep her calm. "The emperor expects a demonstration tonight, and intimidation was the only method that got us results. We're trying to protect them."

Wendy's head whipped around so fast it made her hair fly. "Trying to protect them? Or trying to protect yourselves?"

The moment the words left her, Wendy clapped a hand over her mouth, as if shocked they had escaped. Her eyebrows lowered apologetically. They dived down even deeper when Aaden glared at her.

"You don't know what it's like for her. You have no right to judge."

Talise touched his hand, which sucked the wrath out of his eyes in a single breath. When he turned to face her, Wendy seemed to be forgotten entirely.

Talise shook her head, staring at the ground. "No, Aaden. She's right. We should have tried harder to gain their trust. We should have done more to show we care about them."

When he spoke again, his words were just for her. They rang out soft and kind but no less piercing than they could be. "Then what are supposed to do? The demonstration is tonight, and they're not ready."

If an arrow had been shot in her heart it would have been less painful than this. A dozen different options fought for attention, but her mind kept coming back to one moment. One of the emperor's threats jangled through her, cutting away everything else.

I'll send you back to the Storm.

Her jaw clenched at the thought. She had won the competition, completed the trials. She succeeded in the battle against Kessoku, been officially named Master Shaper, and *still* he threatened to send her away.

If she couldn't prove her leadership skills, he'd never let her stay in the palace.

Gritting her teeth together, she said, "As soon as the parade is over, we'll gather the soldiers in the training hall. We'll practice through the entire masquerade ball if we have to. We'll find a way to make the demonstration succeed."

Wendy and Claye shared a skeptical glance before Claye went back to his Forces game. Wendy went back to fussing with the quilt. Only Aaden seemed to think her words had any truth to them. He nodded with a stoic face. Then, he squeezed her hand, which startled her because she had forgotten she was still touching him.

By the time the parade began, they were all laughing and talking like the conversation had never taken place. But as dancers glided through the streets with their fabric flames and orange streaked hair, Talise could only think of the demonstration.

And how she had to succeed.

Chapter Forty-Six

SOLDIERS LINED THE WALLS OF the training hall, each wearing a unique version of a grimace. None of them had been happy about extra training. Over half of them verbally protested when Talise suggested they might have to train through the masquerade ball, not just before it.

The grumbling only increased in volume the longer they trained. And now the room was getting hot from all the fire balls.

Aaden fanned himself as he glared at the targets. Once the soldiers were told they couldn't go to the ball until they could hit the targets every time, their skills had greatly improved.

But it still wasn't good enough.

Talise lifted the hair away from her neck as she approached a nearby soldier. "You're so close." She attempted a smile, which felt ridiculous after trying to intimidate the same soldier the day before, but Wendy's earlier words rang in her ears.

She wouldn't turn to intimidation again no matter what. "Remember the fire ball is an extension of yourself. It's not the same as throwing a ball. It might help to pretend the fire ball is actually your arm and it can stretch all the way to the target."

The soldier huffed in response. He looked to the side, giving a longing glance at another soldier in the line. Talise started when she recognized the female soldier who had forced her to use intimidation in the first place.

The female soldier's hair was tied up in a messy braid. The heat from the room had turned her cheeks red.

The soldier in front of Talise seemed to think it was the most beautiful thing he had ever seen.

"Were you hoping to dance with her tonight?" Talise asked in a low voice.

The soldier jerked his face back toward the target but failed to keep his face free of emotion. He pushed a hand through his long hair and tried to laugh. "Tempest wouldn't want to dance with me. She's a blue guard, and I'm a yellow."

For some reason, this made Talise pause. She knew all about the different colors hemmed to the bottom of the guards' uniforms. The hierarchy was simple. Yellow was the lowest guard and silver was the highest, with red, green, blue, and orange in between.

But that hadn't surprised her. It had been the mention of the female soldier's name that made her stop. She'd made such an effort to learn names, but it hadn't occurred to her to learn the name of the soldier who defied her in front of the emperor.

But here was a person who clearly admired her. Tempest had a life. Tempest had friends and dreams. She had people who wanted to dance with her but who might be too afraid to ask.

It wouldn't do Talise any good to only befriend the soldiers who were kind to her. She couldn't only care for the ones who already respected her. She had to care for them all.

In that moment, something inside her changed. When she glanced down the training hall, she didn't see an obstacle. She didn't see people who stood in the way of her goals. For the first time, she saw people she needed to protect.

As their leader, this should have been her ultimate goal all along. Even gaining their trust wasn't as important.

If she wanted the best for them and clearly acted in their best interests, the trust would come.

Just as she tried to wrap her head around this new idea, the emperor waltzed into the room. Her insides flinched at the sight of him, but she willed herself to bow anyway.

"Guests have already started to arrive for the masquerade ball," the emperor said.

A collective groan of disappointment rippled out from the soldiers.

One sharp look from the emperor set the soldiers straight. He touched the edge of his crown, adjusting it slightly. The gesture seemed unfamiliar, but it was probably just because he wore a different crown tonight than he usually wore.

This one was polished silver with decorative tines that had small cutouts underneath them. He only wore this one on special occasions. The way he touched the crown again with an annoyed frown told Talise why. It required too much adjusting.

After getting the crown just where he wanted it, the emperor stood straight and looked past Talise at the room. "I would like a preview of the demonstration I'll see tonight."

Aaden had appeared at Talise's side. His eyebrows rose, and she could tell his insides roiled with fear.

Her own insides sat still, as if waiting in anticipation. Her newest revelation had happened so recently, she hadn't had time to consider how it would affect her actions. But now was her chance.

She had finally realized the approach she should have taken all along. She didn't need to try to gain the soldiers' trust, she had to show them she would protect them.

A loose thread at the hem of her orange tunic provided the perfect distraction while she cleared her throat to speak. Even as she opened her mouth, she still had no idea what to say. How could she protect her soldiers? How could she demonstrate that she had their best interests at heart?

Her mind quickly passed over those questions and on to the next. What did they want?

Immediately, everything inside her changed again. Her breath halted as she stared at the room. The answer became clear even though it tore her apart.

At her side, Aaden seemed to think she had lost her tongue. When he opened his mouth to address the soldiers, she stopped him.

She cleared her throat once more, then she turned. Not to face the soldiers, but the emperor instead. "There will be no demonstration."

She expected Emperor Flarius to ridicule her, but he looked too shocked to react.

Before he could move, she went on. She let her voice ring loud and clear through the room. She wanted every soldier to hear. "My soldiers have worked hard and made great improvements. Three-fourths of them can now hit the targets with their fire balls. The rest are not far behind."

The emperor shook his head, the shock wearing off as he pinched his mouth into a knot. He glowered at her while a crease appeared between his eyes. "Did you say—"

"They have worked hard, and they deserve to enjoy the masquerade ball." It was bold of her to interrupt him. It was more than bold. It may have been suicidal.

His face continued to contort. It wasn't difficult to imagine the vicious words that threatened to spill from his lips. It was probably best to not give him the chance.

Talise turned to look out at the training hall. Her spine had never felt straighter. She feared the emperor's punishment, but something greater had taken hold of her now. It wasn't just about her anymore. She had soldiers to take care of.

"Soldiers," she said in a voice that surprised even herself. "Thank you for working so hard. We will continue your training in the morning. You are all dismissed." She couldn't help but smile when she saw how their faces lit up. With a rush of joy, she added, "Enjoy the ball."

Aaden stood by her side, but he added nothing to her words. His breathing had gotten shallow. Two different times, his eyes flicked to the emperor but he forced them back so he could stare ahead.

Talise didn't move. She smiled at her soldiers as they cleared out of the room. Tempest gave her the strangest look as she passed. Talise met it with a nod that she hoped conveyed the feeling she wanted.

She was on their side now. Even Tempest's.

Tempest nodded back. It seemed like understanding passed through her eyes before she left the room.

When the soldiers were gone, Talise didn't dare turn around to face the emperor. She could feel him standing in the same place he'd been the entire time, but she couldn't sense any of his other movements.

When he finally spoke, his voice was gruff. Deadly. "We will discuss this later."

His boots clomped as he marched out of the room. Her heart tightened with each of his steps. He hadn't punished her yet, but she knew it was only a delay, not a reprieve.

Punishment would come. Her heart fluttered as she imagined the possibilities. When she turned to Aaden, he said nothing. But he didn't have to either. His pursed lips and lowered eyebrows told her everything she needed to know.

He didn't approve.

♕

CHAPTER FORTY-SEVEN

TALISE'S FEET BARELY TOUCHED THE floor as Wendy yanked her down the hall. Wendy had just put the finishing touches on Talise's hair less than a minute ago. Her short hair fell to its normal length just under her chin. But Wendy had gathered up the front pieces and pinned them with decorative combs and pearls in a look far too close to a tiara for Talise's taste.

But there hadn't been any time to argue about it.

"Hurry!" Wendy had a death grip on Talise's wrist as she flew down the hallway. "The First Melt is about to begin. If we miss it, Claye will never forgive us." Wendy brushed a hand over her gold-beaded bodice and put a hand to her mask to make sure it was still in place.

Moments later, they arrived just outside the ballroom. The sound of harps announced the beginning of the First Melt. Talise smoothed her own ivory dress as they walked through the doorway.

The embroidered blue flames on her tulle dress shimmered in the brightly lit ballroom. Tight in her hand, she held the silver and blue ombre mask Wendy had helped her pick out. With no time to put it on, she'd decided to secure it once they arrived in the ballroom. Her gown swished as Wendy helped them edge around the room until they could see better.

Through the crowd, Talise caught small glimpses of the First Melt. It was just a short play that recounted how Kamdar, the first emperor of Kamdaria, took a team of fire shapers to the top of the highest mountain. They melted the snow so it would trickle down the mountain and provide water to Kamdaria for the rest of the year. Even in the heat of summer, the highest mountain was a treacherous place. The First Melt recounted the epic tale of how Kamdar and his shapers fought wind, ice, and wild animals just so Kamdaria could have the water it needed.

In the Storm, children usually performed the play. They wore ill-fitting homemade costumes and dirt smudges on their noses. Since no one in the Storm could shape, no one could move earth to act as the mountain. Wooden crates or overturned boats were used in their place. To add wind, a child who wore red weaved through the other children waving his arms wildly, usually while fighting a fit of giggles.

The First Melt at the palace had none of the same endearing characteristics. The play was serious with professional actors and extravagant costumes. The shapers who moved earth and wind were palace trained and performed their tasks with perfection.

When Wendy finally stopped, Talise gave a quick glance to the side to see where they had landed. The buffet tables stood only a few paces away. The smell of cinnamon baked apples and orange marmalade marinated chicken wafted in through her nose.

And Aaden was there.

He had been watching the First Melt, but once they stopped at his side, he glanced their way. His lips parted and his eyes went bug-eyed. His gaze brought a flutter through Talise's gut, but then he wouldn't stop staring.

He stared and stared while the tiniest smile appeared on his lips.

It was enough to make her squirm. "What is it?" she demanded. When his gaze lingered, she lightly slapped his upper arm with her cerulean paper fan.

"Her dress is stunning, isn't it?" Wendy said through a sigh.

"Not just her dress." One corner of Aaden's mouth turned up to a half grin that did all sorts of things to Talise's insides. The heat rising from her neck into her cheeks was probably turning into the brightest blush of all time.

She slapped him again, which brought a chuckle to his lips.

"Ooh look!" Wendy bounced on her toes as she pointed toward the middle of the ballroom. "Here comes Claye's part."

Aaden finally tore his gaze away from Talise, which would have been helpful except he also chose that moment to come to her side. Her insides bounced around as he took the mask from her hand and secured it in place on her head. Once finished, he stood close enough that their shoulders were touching.

Her breath caught in her throat. She had to spend an inordinate amount of time reminding herself he couldn't be trusted.

Still, no matter how she wanted to avoid him, she had a feeling he wouldn't let her be more than an arm's length away the entire evening. She'd have to find a way to get these emotions under control.

It didn't help that he wore a gorgeous gray suit made with such fine silk that it had a silvery sheen in just the right light. Under his high-collared suit jacket, a high-collared vermillion shirt peeked out with perfect frog closures holding it shut. The vermillion leaned toward orange just enough to be perfect for Fire Festival. But it also had enough red to make it stand out in the crowd. His mask was also vermillion with small gray accents.

And he must have trimmed his goatee recently because it looked neater, thicker, and, Kamdaria help her, more rugged than she'd ever seen it.

Yes, it would be hard to avoid him tonight.

When she finally managed to force her mind off Aaden, she focused on Claye. He wore a green mask to denote earth shaping was his primary. Even through the mask, Talise could see his eyes narrowed as he stared at the mountain of dirt in the middle of the ballroom.

Just as the actor portraying Kamdar reached the top of the mountain, Claye shaped the dirt under the actor's feet so it slipped away. The actor clutched his chest and cried out in mock fear. The dirt eventually stopped and held the actor in place halfway down the mountain.

Claye glanced over at Talise and the others before he waggled his eyebrows up and down with a triumphant smile. He had performed the dirt slipping trick perfectly. The rest of the First Melt had several shaping tricks thrown in. But Talise found herself pining for the version she had seen in the Storm.

When it ended, the crowd roared with applause while the actors took humble bows. And then the music began.

Not daring to give Aaden a chance to ask her to dance, Talise headed straight for the buffet tables and filled a plate high with the delectable food. Just as she suspected, Aaden was no more than a step behind her the entire time.

She ate until the seams in her dress were about to burst. And even then, she kept poking at the food on her plate, pretending she'd take another bite soon. This charade wouldn't last much longer. Wendy and Claye had long since finished their own food. They were busy dancing and laughing and enjoying every minute of the ball.

Aaden had delivered his empty plate to a waiter and stood patiently by Talise's side while she picked at her food. She needed another distraction immediately or he'd ask her to dance, and she might not be strong enough to refuse.

A nearby guest provided the perfect distraction. The guest wore a simple orange gown with a scoop neck and a feathery skirt. The girl tapped her toe just a fraction too fast to go in time with the music.

Her sequined mask hung funny on her nose like the tie had come loose, but she was too distracted to notice. The way she kept scratching a particular spot just under her chin proved she wasn't standing there waiting for a dance. She was nervous.

Even through the awkward hang of her mask, Talise could see how the girl blinked faster than normal. Every few seconds, her eyes would bounce from Emperor Flarius to General Gale and finally to Commander Blaise. All three of them were surrounded by a swarm of adoring guests who didn't look eager to leave.

Aaden cleared his throat. Before he could speak, Talise shoved her plate into his hands. "Give this to a waiter for me, will you?"

Rather than wait for his response, she walked over to the girl in orange. Even when Talise was at her side, her eyes kept shifting around the room from the emperor, the general, and then to the commander.

Apparently, Talise would have to do more than stand there to get the girl's attention. "Excuse me," she said in a polite voice.

The girl jumped and her mask slid off her face as the tie came completely undone. At once, Talise recognized her.

"Tempest?"

The soldier who had openly defied her only a week before stood blinking as she tried to catch her mask out of the air.

"Oh, Talise," she said when the mask was pinned securely between her fingers. "You startled me." Her lips pursed as her head gave a tiny shake. "I mean *Master Shaper* Talise."

"Are you all right?" Talise thought about patting the soldier on the arm the way Wendy probably would have done. But Tempest didn't seem like the kind of person who appreciated that sort of thing. Instead, Talise settled her face into an expression she hoped would convey the concern she felt. The mask covering her face probably didn't help.

Tempest did another quick head shake and started chewing on her bottom lip. Her focus had gone back to the head of the room.

Aaden appeared at Talise's side a moment later. The plate had apparently been delivered to a waiter.

"I'm fine," Tempest said when Talise didn't move. She managed a tight smile. "I'm just hoping someone will ask me to dance."

Talise raised one eyebrow and folded her arms in front of her chest. When Tempest's face fell, Talise knew her skepticism had been detected.

Her realization from earlier came back to her. If she wanted to be a true leader, she had to protect her soldiers.

She could walk away. She could pretend nothing was wrong and the soldier only wanted to dance. But the way Tempest kept looking around the room at the most influential men told Talise something bigger was happening.

This time, she did touch Tempest on the arm. In a gentle but firm voice, she said, "Is there anything we can do to help?"

For a moment, a huff of anger escaped Tempest. She tightened her fist around the sequined mask and started to shake her head. But then, she turned and looked at Talise with all new eyes.

It may have been her imagination, but Tempest seemed to remember how Talise had defied the emperor so the soldiers could enjoy the ball. If possible, Tempest probably still would have gone to the emperor or Commander Blaise first. But with no other options, she seemed to trust Talise enough to talk. "Can you find a way to talk to the emperor alone? I've been trying, but with so many people around it's impossible. But you two are Master Shapers. He might listen to you."

"Why do you need to talk to him?" Aaden's voice carried skepticism. Maybe even a hint of impatience.

Tempest must have been desperate. She stared at the two of them for a long moment before she leaned in with her head low. She glanced over her shoulder before lowering her voice to a whisper. "There are spies here tonight." She swallowed and leaned in closer. "Kessoku spies," she said significantly.

Kessoku? They weren't supposed to ever come back. Over two hundred of them had been killed when they tried to attack the palace. How had they been brave enough to try again? How had they gotten inside?

The question was answered in Talise's mind almost as soon as she asked it. Fire Festival. With so many people and so many festivities, it was impossible to keep track of everything. The members of Kessoku could have stolen an invitation from any number of people.

Talise opened her mouth, but Tempest didn't seem eager to allow an interruption.

She glanced over her shoulder again while fear flashed through her eyes. "I heard them talking in the hallway by the kitchens. As far as I know, they didn't hear or see me. I saw their masks, but I don't know why they're here. I just know they're looking for something. Or maybe some*one*."

Aaden's hand tightened around Talise's wrist in a firm grasp. He pulled her closer as he said, "You shouldn't have waited to tell anyone. Point them out immediately and we'll take care of them."

"No!" Tempest abandoned the whisper she'd been so careful to use earlier. She brought her hands to her mouth. Terror lined her brow with each jerk of her head. "They said if anyone discovers them, they'll attack the soldiers first. They don't care if they get caught and thrown into the dungeons. They're going to kill as many of us as they can before that happens."

"Then what do you expect us to do?" Aaden asked, pulling Talise even closer still.

Tempest started blinking furiously. She stuffed a fingernail into her mouth and began gnawing on it. Her shoulders shook as she glanced toward the emperor again.

By now, Aaden had his arm wrapped around Talise's waist. He held her tight with no indication of loosening his grip. Any other time she might have fought it. But right now, she was too busy thinking.

Her thumb traced over one of the fire flowers on her gown while she scanned the room. "The emperor will be too hard to get to. But we should be able to get Commander Blaise alone. We'll just tell him we have official Master Shaper business to discuss. He'll get the hint, don't you think?"

She intended to turn toward Aaden when she asked, but when she felt his chin brushing the top of her head, she thought better of it. "We just have to get across the ballroom without raising suspicion."

"Perfect." The first hint of agreement came through Aaden's voice. "We can dance over to him."

Talise's mouth wound into a tight knot. Before Aaden could steal her away, she gestured toward Wendy and Claye and begged Tempest to tell them everything including what the masks of the Kessoku spies looked like.

Only a moment later, Aaden swept her out to the middle of the ballroom. Apparently not even a pack of Kessoku spies could keep her from dancing tonight. She didn't dare protest for fear of raising suspicion.

But Aaden probably knew she wasn't a fan of this plan. He always knew.

He wasted no time in settling his hand as low on her back as possible. Soon his lips were at her ear, his breath kissing her skin.

He had something to say, and judging by how quickly he got into position, he had been waiting all night to say it.

Chapter Forty-Eight

MUSIC FILLED THE BALLROOM. AN orange and purple clad musician plucked a steady melody on a koto string. Another musician in a rust colored suit beat a grounding rhythm on a taiko drum while the final musician in a marigold gown rang twinkling bells at spread out intervals.

The laughter and conversation of the room were drowned out by the lovely sound.

Yet, nothing could distract Talise from the heat of Aaden's skin against hers. Cheek to cheek, his lips practically touching her ear. Her heart felt like bursting from equal parts bliss and terror. It was all she could do to keep her feet dancing in time with the music.

When he finally spoke, it was obvious she'd been right. He had been waiting all night to say these words.

"You shouldn't have cancelled the demonstration."

She tried to pull away with a frustrated huff, but apparently, he wasn't done yet.

"You shouldn't have gone against the emperor like that. Especially not in front of the soldiers."

For a brief moment, she managed to pull away. "He wanted me to prove my leadership ability, didn't he? Maybe he should have been more careful what he asked for."

To her surprise, Aaden didn't offer a retort. He only tightened the grip of each of his hands. Neither the hand at her back nor the one around her fingers felt tight. They just felt warm and strong. Comforting.

"Why do you care anyway?" she asked. "It was obviously my idea. He won't punish you."

Aaden swallowed as he gazed into her eyes. Beneath his mask, she could see his scar from the Kessoku's sword. It had just finished scabbing. Now it stretched bright pink from his forehead to his chin. She almost laughed when she remembered how embarrassed he'd been about the injury. He'd worried it would make him less handsome.

Looking at him now, she could only conclude it did the opposite. The scar made him look strong and mysterious. It gave a glimpse of the pain Aaden had born throughout his life.

And since she knew the origin of the scar, it only deepened how attractive it made him. For he had earned that scar by protecting her. It was a symbol of the lengths he'd take to keep her safe.

Aaden didn't break his gaze. "You have no idea how the emperor will react." His grip tightened again. "I'm worried about you."

"Well, stop it." She would have stomped her foot if they hadn't been dancing.

"No."

She was the one to finally break the gaze. Inexplicably, she found herself resting her head on his shoulder. It was supposed to keep her from staring into his dangerous eyes. Instead, the increased physical contact only made her heart leap and twirl before it threatened to explode.

With him close, it was easy to assume he was telling the truth. She could see it in his eyes that he wanted what was best for her. At least it *seemed* like she could see it. He'd gotten that scar protecting her, and he stood up against the emperor for her, and he was always willing to help her when she needed it.

But then *why* had he looked up the record of her academy test?

Just when she was ready to throw caution to the wind and give in to him, he had to go and do that.

He leaned down, and his cheek met hers again. His breath warmed her ear. Her neck. It became difficult to dance. To breathe.

"Whatever he does, I'll help you. If he tries to lock you in the dungeons, I'll break you out."

"Aaden."

His voice grew more insistent. "If he strips your title and sends you back to the Storm, I'll come with you."

"Aaden." She straightened her elbow to force more space between them. "Don't worry about the emperor. I can handle him. We have more important things to worry about right now." She tipped her head toward Tempest, who was now whispering to Wendy and Claye on the other side of the ballroom.

He didn't seem eager to drop the conversation, but the song ended, and everyone stopped dancing. Talise pulled herself out of his arms. Since she didn't want to draw any unnecessary attention—and she assumed Aaden would protest their separation—she wrapped a hand over his bicep and allowed him to escort her toward Commander Blaise.

The commander's perfectly stoic face showed a trace of movement when the two of them approached. It was a fleeting expression, but for a moment, his eyes flicked to where Talise held Aaden's arm. She swore a smile tugged at the commander's lips for the slightest moment.

He still had a crowd surrounding him, but they dispersed quickly when Aaden asked for a private moment of his time. Talise wished they could take the conversation to another room, but that would certainly raise suspicion. The farthest corner would have to do. At least a few of the emperor's personal guards stood nearby.

— ◆ —

"DON'T DO ANYTHING."

Commander Blaise's response stunned Talise into silence. She blinked twice and still couldn't imagine what to say. Looking at Aaden, it seemed words had failed him too.

"Maybe you didn't understand," Talise said giving her head a tiny shake.

"I understood perfectly." The commander held his back straight with one arm behind it in a fist. But the other hand he had casually placed over the decorative hilt of his sword.

"Kessoku is here looking for something." Aaden had explained this already, but when he said it this time, he put special significance on their name.

"Then we won't let them find it."

Talise swallowed. "What if they won't leave without it?"

The commander looked straight ahead. "Then we will wait until after the guests have left."

Aaden shifted on his feet before he answered. "If they get suspicious, Kessoku will attack the soldiers."

A vein on Commander Blaise's forehead pulsed. "It is their job to defend the palace. If they die, they will do it with honor."

Talise could feel Aaden's muscle go rigid under her hand. Her mouth had gone dry. This sounded like a horrible plan. "There has to be something we can do," Talise said through a croak.

At this, the commander's attention moved away from the ballroom. He glanced at her for the briefest moment before he looked to the side at one of the emperor's personal guards. "Perhaps," he said slowly, as if forming the thoughts as he went.

311

"You should go to the treasury." He closed his mouth for a moment but then added. "To make sure it's secure."

Talise nodded and hoped her eyes didn't betray any mischief. If they went to the treasury, she and Aaden could create a new plan that didn't involve so much waiting. They could probably bring Wendy and Claye with them. More people working together would mean a higher chance of success.

Hopefully Aaden would agree they needed a new plan. Considering how he had yet to agree with his grandfather, she guessed he already felt the same as she did.

"I'll send a royal guard with you," Commander Blaise said.

The nearest guard immediately turned toward them, which suggested he had heard the entire conversation, even though he had acted like he didn't.

A tingle of anxiety ran through her. This could complicate her idea to make a new plan. She tried to give a defiant glare. "We're Master Shapers. We don't need a guard to babysit us."

The commander didn't acknowledge her words. He pointed toward her and Aaden and nodded once at the guard. And then he disappeared back to into the crowd where privacy was impossible.

Talise scowled at the guard. When she turned to Aaden, his eyes were alight with ideas. That made her grin. Soon they'd come up with another way to stop Kessoku. They just had to get Wendy and Claye and get to the treasury. With any luck, they could convince the guard to keep watch outside the door.

Chapter Forty-Nine

Talise stared at the blank wall in front of her while a weight dropped in her stomach.

"So, this is the treasury, huh?" Claye seemed to hold a laugh under his words. "It's a lot bigger than I expected."

"Oh hush, Claye." The sound of Wendy's fan hitting silk rang through the air. "What is it, Talise? What's wrong?"

Aaden was silent at her side. Then again, what was there to say?

Talise reached for the empty wall and traced her finger over a line of dust. "It's gone," she said in a whisper.

"What is? A crown or necklace or..." Wendy appeared at Talise's side, watching her trace the empty wall. Her eyebrows rose. "The emperor's family tree?"

Talise's veins throbbed. Her heart hammered as if trying to force its way out of her chest. How had Kessoku already succeeded? How had they gotten into the treasury without anyone knowing?

Or maybe someone did know. Maybe Kessoku had a palace worker on their side.

The thought made Talise's stomach churn.

Aaden glared at the wall, his hands stiffening into fists. "Then why are they still here? If they have the family tree, why don't they leave?"

"It's obvious, isn't it?" Claye perched himself on top of a table with gilded gold edges. "They're looking for an heir."

Talise jerked her head toward him. "There is no heir," she spat. All the emotions of the day were bubbling just under her skin and little by little she could feel herself falling apart at the seams.

"Well," Claye said giving a significant look to all of them.

Wendy jumped toward him, her eyes widening. "Did you find something?"

Claye grinned as he ran his fingers through his hair. He was enjoying this attention a little too much considering the safety of the empire was at stake. "I found something in the funeral accounts from after the Kessoku attack. You know how I've been studying them with Aaden? Apparently Princess Isla, the emperor's youngest child, was playing with a friend when the attack happened. They both died, but the body of the other little girl was never found."

Talise just managed to stop herself from hissing through her teeth. Clenching her jaw, she said, "How is that significant in any way? If the girl was a friend of the princess, then she had no royal blood."

Claye leaned forward, his eyebrows cocking upward. "Apparently, the friend looked a lot like Princess Isla. It's possible the girl was buried in her place and somehow the princess is still alive."

Talise scoffed loudly as she rolled her eyes. "While you're busy thinking up wild conspiracy theories, I'm going to come up with a plan."

Her gown swished as she began pacing the room. Every few seconds, she'd glance back at the empty space on the wall. They *had* to do something now. They couldn't let Kessoku leave the palace with the family tree.

Claye wrinkled his nose at Talise before he threw his hands into the air. "Fine, maybe there is no princess. Maybe they're here for Aaden."

Aaden had been stroking his goatee, apparently deep in thought. But at these words, he glanced up with mild interest. "Why would they want me?"

With a shrug, Claye said, "To recruit you. They killed all the other Master Shapers. Having you on their side would be a big blow to the emperor. Plus, we all know what your father did. They probably think you'd join them in a heartbeat."

The scar over Aaden's eye seemed to pulse as his eyebrows lowered in a glare. His voice was low, daring anyone to disagree. "My father doesn't work for Kessoku. He was only boasting. He was idiotic, but not treasonous."

"I'm just saying …" Claye shook his head, apparently frustrated everyone had missed his point. "Kessoku probably assumes you're bitter about what happened."

Aaden jumped to Claye's side in one step. Even with Claye perched on the table, Aaden still seemed the taller one. He jabbed Claye in the chest with one finger. "My father destroyed my life the day he gave away those secrets. My great-great-grandfather was a Master Shaper, which means I should have automatically gotten a silver crescent moon on my ID card. But then my father made one mistake and my entire life was ruined."

His voice had started to crack. Each sentence came out shakier than the one before, but still he didn't stop. "He never even apologized to me. When my grandparents took me away, insisting they would raise me, my father didn't even put up a fight. So, forgive me, but I think I've earned the bitterness in my heart."

The others seemed affected by the shimmering in Aaden's eyes. Talise was not.

All the distrust she harbored for him came to a point. Ice curled through her veins as the room stilled. She let out a short laugh, hoping it sounded as cruel and cutting as she meant it. Her hands had formed fists and she could feel the blood rushing in and out of her fingers. Her skin felt hot, but her heart was ice.

"Every. Single. Person inside the emperor's mansion died that day." She took in a steadying breath, grateful the words sounded even crisper out loud than they had in her mind. "They're dead because of your father's actions. You spend so much time mourning how he ruined your life, but have you ever—even for one small moment—thought to feel a shred of guilt? Have you ever thought to mourn the *loss* of their lives instead of the destruction of your own?"

Her chest was falling in heavy panting breaths. The weight of her words filled in the room. She was glad for how she had spit the words out. Aaden deserved to feel ashamed.

It wasn't until this moment that she finally understood why it had been so difficult to trust him, but this was it. This was the heart of the issue. How could he dare to complain about his own life when so many were dead because of someone who shared his blood?

"You seem excessively passionate about the deaths of the royal family considering you never met them." Claye's voice cut through the air, and in a single moment, she could feel herself cracking from the inside out.

They knew.

Her breaths got shallow. Her heart seemed to stop.

They *knew*.

The royal family wasn't just the royal family. They were *her* family.

She could see it in each of their faces as understanding passed through them. Claye first. He knew before he spoke. His words and her reaction were only meant to provide confirmation.

Aaden was next. At first, he had been hurt. Truly ashamed after Talise's accusation but also offended that she could speak against him so openly. But then his eyebrows flicked up and his mouth dropped. Horror painted his features as the revelation hit him.

Wendy was last. She clapped a hand over her mouth as she let out a gasp. Then she stared at Talise as if trying to peel away the layers of their friendship, wondering how she could have missed something so huge. And then perhaps wondering how much more she didn't know.

Talise took a step back, grasping for the wall. Her legs had turned to the delicate hard candy children licked during the Fire Festival parade. And the candy had reached the point where its integrity failed. When it fell off the stick, and the children would pop it into their mouths, crunching it to dust before swallowing.

Breathe.

Twelve years of hiding. Two in the Storm and then ten in the academy. All those years she trained to ensure she'd become Master Shaper. It was the only way she could return without anyone batting an eye. Without raising suspicion. Twelve years of keeping her secret.

And it was all gone in a single breath.

Her legs still felt weak. She expected them to give out at any moment, but surprisingly, that wasn't the only thing she felt. Something inside her chest cracked under the pressure, but when it broke, she felt a wave of sweet relief.

Finally, she could share her secret. Finally, she had friends who could bear the burden with her. Years of loneliness and fear had wound her heart into a tight knot, but now it loosened.

For the first time in ten years, she felt like herself because she was finally surrounded by others who knew what that meant.

The relief was tangible, but it came at a cost. Because now that her secret was out, it meant any one of them could share it too.

She loved these people. Each of them had touched her heart in a different way. But as she looked at them, she couldn't help the fear that raced through her mind over and over, as steady as a drum. The question bit into her insides. No matter how she wanted to trust them, they now had a greater capacity to hurt her.

She couldn't help but wonder, *Which one of these three will betray me?*

Chapter Fifty

THE SOUND OF SHATTERING GLASS and urgent screams came through the closed door of the treasury. Talise jumped at the noise. Even through the door, she could hear the guard outside drawing his sword.

"Kessoku," Wendy said breathlessly. "They must be attacking in the ballroom."

Talise didn't have the luxury to consider how her revealed secret would affect the rest of her life. All she could do now was hope her friends wouldn't betray her. She'd consider everything more carefully later.

Her feet sprang to the door. "We have to help them."

"No!" Both Aaden and Wendy shouted at the same time. He was too far away to reach her, but Aaden held his hand out as if trying to hold her back.

"You have to stay here," Wendy said.

"Where it's *safe*." Aaden gave her a pointed stare. "Actually, we should get another guard outside the door."

"Or a dozen of them," Wendy offered.

Aaden nodded emphatically.

Talise glared at them both. "I'm not going to stand around while my soldiers are being killed." She threw the door open before either of them could protest.

"It's not like anyone else knows," Claye said from behind her. "What's the harm in her going?"

Wendy and Aaden were grumbling. Talise couldn't see what was happening behind her, but judging by the rustling of silk, she had a feeling Wendy was punching Claye in the arm.

Aaden caught up to her as she barreled down the hallway. "This is a bad idea," he said.

"If I put my life above that of my soldiers', what kind of a leader does that make me?"

"A living one." There was no humor in Aaden's response.

It didn't matter. He protested, but so far, he hadn't tried to stop her. He did the same thing he always did, which was to stand by her side. All those months of distrust and the truth had been there all along, demonstrated every day in each of his actions.

He was on her side.

She still had no idea why he had looked up her testing records, but maybe he had told the truth about that. Maybe he just wanted to understand how someone from the Storm could shape. Well, now he knew. She wasn't really from the Storm at all. She could shape four elements at academy testing because she'd been palace trained from birth.

No matter what his true intention, he was a part of her now. Not just in her life but in her heart.

The doors to the ballroom had guests spilling out, running for their lives. Talise had to elbow her way through the crowd just to gain entrance. By the time she pushed past them, she only had a split second to take in the scene of the ballroom.

Eleven of her soldiers in their masquerade clothes stood in a tight knot. A ring of fire burned around them like a rope. In a straight line in front of the soldiers, five men wielded swords. In a flash, they charged forward with their swords ready to pierce bone.

Time stood still as instinct took over. From the corner of her eye, Talise could see two large tubs from the First Melt sitting forgotten at the edge of the room. One of the tubs held the dirt that had represented the mountain. The other held water.

She levitated it into the air. There was no time to wonder if she could carry all the water on her own. No time to wonder if her plan would work.

She blasted the water at Kessoku. It formed a wall in front of them, which she froze to catch their swords inches before they met their targets. A few of the men fell when they collided with the ice wall. All of them stared at it in awe.

"Don't you touch my soldiers." She ripped off her heeled shoes and tossed them to the side. The water had splashed the fire rope before it turned to ice, which set her soldiers free.

The Kessoku's momentary shock had worn off. Apparently, they didn't think swords were necessary to attack. While their swords hung in the ice wall, two of the Kessoku spies blasted fire balls in her direction.

Using air, she blew them off course as she now marched toward them with bare feet. One member of Kessoku ripped off his masquerade mask, which prompted Talise to do the same. The added visibility would be imperative now.

With her eyes free of the mask, she noticed Aaden—also bare faced—charging at Kessoku with a sword in hand. She wondered where he had gotten the sword until she recognized the decorative hilt Commander Blaise had been stroking earlier.

The rest of the guards and soldiers were closing in on the spies now. These Kessoku had no chance for escape. That didn't seem to deter them in the slightest. They went back to their original goal of causing as much death and destruction before they got captured.

Waves of fire spread out through the room. Walls of wind knocked people and buffet tables to the ground. The dirt from the First Melt was being flung straight into soldiers' mouths, forcing them to stop and cough it out.

Talise was momentarily distracted from her goal of catching them. Her sole focus was on protecting the others in the room. When the members of Kessoku had spread out through the room, she melted the ice wall and started shooting the water at any fire Kessoku tried to start.

Everything was happening so fast, the passage of time seemed to have suspended.

But whenever her water met a fire ball, part of the water evaporated. Talise didn't know how much time had passed, but at one point, she ran out of water.

When they kept shooting fire balls, she began shaping the punch that had spilled onto the floor near the overturned buffet tables. The sugar hung in the air when the fire balls evaporated the punch, making the room feel humid and sticky.

Aaden had his back to hers. He sliced his sword near anyone who attempted to harm her. With his other hand, he shaped fire balls, tornados of wind, and anything else to keep Kessoku away. He was trying to stop them too.

They all were.

But Kessoku fought with the ferocity of men who knew they had to fight or die. Talise slid dirt over the ground in a slithering snake. When it reached a Kessoku man, she entwined the earth snake around his ankle and yanked him to the ground.

She held him in place with the earth snake and then sent another one to entwine around his hands. Aaden was shouting behind her. Other members of Kessoku were near, but she couldn't think about them now.

Her only thought was on the man fighting against her earth snake. Two palace guards were headed toward him with chains clattering in their arms. She just had to hold the man a little longer.

The Kessoku man fought against her snakes, which sent a rip through her insides as if she had pulled a muscle.

They reached him at last and forced orange gloves over his hands before they slapped the chains around his wrists.

She let out a breath of relief as she turned to assess the rest of the room. Aaden had a Kessoku spy trapped under his sword. That meant there were only three Kessoku left. At that moment, she realized Aaden was shouting at her to duck. The command reached her at the same moment as she saw two arrows made of fire shooting straight toward her heart.

Her hands raised to do something, but she already knew it was too late. Suddenly, a great whooshing nearly caused her to lose her balance. But it hadn't been a wall of wind coming at her. Instead, it felt like the air was being pulled away.

When the fire arrows vanished from the lack of oxygen, Talise understood why. She had just enough time to give a grateful nod at Wendy before she turned her attention back to the fight.

Wendy's air shaping had given her another idea. Talise sent a tornado into the drapes that hung from the ceiling to the floor. Soon they were coming loose from their hangings. When the last curtain ring popped free, Talise sent air through the drape that sent it swooping through the air. It almost looked like her earth snake except much larger.

Shaping air, she wrapped the curtain around the remaining three members of Kessoku, holding them tightly in place.

Everyone else in the room let out a collective breath. It wasn't until that moment that she got a good look around the room.

Her soldiers had formed a circle around her. They seemed to be protecting her just as much as she had been protecting them. One soldier had drops of blood sliding down his cheek, but he looked okay. Tempest's feathery skirt had been sliced off from the knee down. Her legs were burned and blistered, but she was still walking.

One soldier had a dagger stuck in his shoulder, but he ignored it as he glared at each Kessoku spy in turn.

They were okay.

They'd all been injured and beaten in the fight, but her soldiers were okay. Her friends were okay. She was okay.

It seemed like a good moment to collapse and let out a fit of hysterical laughter. Anything to release some of the tension inside. She settled on grasping onto Aaden's arm. Her eyes ran over his body, checking that she hadn't missed any of his injuries.

From across the room, the emperor was just visible behind a wall of his royal guards. It was clear from the way he looked at her now that he'd been watching her carefully during the fight. From behind the guards, he did something she never expected.

He nodded to her solemnly, almost like a bow.

When she had defied him earlier and cancelled the demonstration, he showed nothing but pure rage. But now, everything had changed. He had seen how she fought for the soldiers. He had seen how she gained their respect.

His nod was more than just a simple gesture. It meant one thing.

She had earned her place as a leader.

"Are you okay?" Aaden was pulling the hair away from her neck, checking the spot where a dirt clod had slammed into her earlier.

"I'm fine. Stop fussing." She pushed him away as she moved through the ranks of the injured soldiers. Almost all the ones who had been attacked were her soldiers. Not just any soldiers, but the ones whose uniforms had a yellow hem. The ones she and Aaden had spent the last few months training. Even in their masquerade clothes, the attack had centered on them.

This was too perfect to be a coincidence.

The last traces of doubt left her mind. Kessoku had someone on the inside. How else could they have targeted those specific soldiers in a crowd of hundreds of guests?

Two soldiers whispered to each other from behind her. "The people know about Kessoku now. Even if we hide what happened to the Master Shapers, the people still know."

The second soldier whispered back. "That's the emperor's problem. He'll think of a way to regain the people's trust."

Talise glanced at Aaden, who had also heard the words. For a moment, she allowed herself to consider the fallout this attack would cause. But the moment ended, and she brushed those thoughts aside. There was work to be done.

A group of healers had entered the ballroom. Their hands were filled with medical supplies. As one of the least injured people in the room, Talise jogged toward the healers. She let them tuck supplies into her arms and nodded through their instructions on how to treat the lesser injuries.

The next several minutes were spent mopping up blood and shaping cold water over burns. Ointments and herbs were applied where needed. She took a moment to check on Wendy and Claye, eager to confirm they hadn't been too badly injured.

Wendy did have a few small scratches on the back of her hand. Claye had twisted his ankle early on in the fight, which left him relatively unscathed otherwise.

Once she was certain she had done all she could, she wandered over to Aaden, her feet seemingly acting without her control. So many questions lingered in his eyes.

Her heart tugged, knowing that now she could finally answer them.

Before she could disappear with him, a member of the royal guard approached her with a tiny bow. "Master Shaper Talise," she said, holding out a long roll of paper. "Emperor Flarius believes his family tree should not be returned to the treasury. He would like you to deliver it to his personal quarters off the throne room."

Talise responded with a bow of her own as she took the roll. The paper felt warm under her fingers.

Aaden didn't ask to accompany her. He just fell into step beside her as if that was where he belonged. And truthfully, she liked it that way.

CHAPTER FIFTY-ONE

Talise and Aaden didn't talk much on their way to the emperor's quarters. Soldiers, palace workers, and lingering guests filled the hall. When they reached the fire orange door with the royal crest, Talise stuck her fingernail under a notch in the wall.

It took a moment to find the switch, but soon the lock clicked open. A hidden lock meant the door didn't need a key. It just needed someone who knew where the lock was hidden.

Aaden stared at the notch for a moment while the ghost of a memory passed through his eyes. He never had asked how she had gotten the door open when they'd snuck in to practice their ice and fire trees. Luckily, he'd been too distracted by the threat of getting caught.

Once inside the room, he took care to close the door tight while she placed the family tree on the wooden desk in the corner. She spread it open and traced a finger over the name on the tree that Kessoku was so desperate to find.

Talise Isla Ember Ruemon. Only her closest family members had ever known Isla wasn't originally her given name.

"Does the emperor know?" Aaden's first question came out the moment the door was secure.

She turned toward him and leaned against the desk. This first question was easy to answer, but it would bring a host of others. And some things she didn't know how to explain.

The words felt too tight in her throat. All she could manage was a nod.

Aaden's lip curled. "And still he treats you like… like filth?"

Her eyes averted. She rested a hand on the desk for support. Already the questions were heading in an uncomfortable direction. "He's trying to protect me. In his own way."

Aaden's jaw worked up and down while a dozen different responses seemed to dance on the tip of his tongue. In the end, he said nothing. He just shook his head and glared at the ground. "Does anyone else know?"

Talise bit into her bottom lip. She searched her dress for a piece of loose thread to fiddle with, but none appeared. Just as well. She couldn't avoid the truth now it was out. "Your grandfather knows." Her throat was tight, making it difficult to get the words out. "And a few of the royal guards. They've known since the beginning."

The brown in Aaden's eyes glowed as he blinked. He mouthed *my grandfather* while the shock seemed to settle on his insides. He shook his head again as if that would help everything make sense.

Her lip was getting raw under the weight of her teeth, but she couldn't bring herself to stop chewing. She wanted to answer his questions, but that didn't make it any easier. She hadn't faced these truths in a long time.

"Why does he treat you like that? The emperor." He returned to his earlier question apparently unable to move past it. He stared into her eyes, seeming to search for an answer that would make everything right.

Unfortunately, she didn't have one.

She shrugged, trying to move some of the weight off her heart. "He forced me to improve my sword skill because he wanted me to be able to protect myself… like the rest of my family couldn't."

Aaden curled his hand into a fist, once again mumbling silently as he glared at the emperor's desk. "And when he questioned your leadership?"

This question stung more than the others. The pain of it was still too fresh to ignore. Tears began swimming in her eyes. "He…" She swallowed. "He wants to make sure I'm ready to lead when the time comes."

One of Aaden's eyebrows raised as he folded his arms over his chest. "That's all?"

She let out a huff and squeezed the tears back inside. "Okay, and because he doesn't think I'm good enough. But it's more than that too."

Aaden peeled his arms apart as he leaned forward.

Talise reached for a piece of her hair, desperate for something to keep her fingers busy. Wrapping it around one finger, she said, "He's mad that I'm in this position in the first place. I was seventh born. I was his baby. He used to braid my hair and bring me ribbons. He taught me to play Forces. I was supposed to live a life of luxury with no need to understand the pain of grief and war. And now?"

"You're heir to the throne."

She ducked her head. Her hands fell and she kept folding and unfolding them in front of herself. "He blames himself, and he takes it out on me because he doesn't have my mother here to tell him when he's gone too far."

"Your mother?" Aaden's eyes narrowed as he said the words. She could see the way his muscles twitched as he tried to work out all the facts. He had known about Marmie for so long, it seemed as though it hadn't occurred to him until this moment that Marmie wasn't actually her mother at all.

His mouth hung open while his eyes narrowed more. She could practically see him putting the puzzle pieces together in his mind until finally he blinked. His eyes shot to hers. "Shyna, the empress's sister. Claye said she was mangled beyond recognition, that maybe it wasn't really her body that had been buried."

Talise nodded, unable to answer the question he suggested.

"Shyna was…" He paused, searching her eyes. When she didn't answer, he finally supplied the end of the sentence. "Marmie?"

Again, she could only respond with a nod.

Aaden shook his head, his eyes now wandering around the room. "She probably went by the name Shyna even in the Storm. It's such a common name, no one would suspect she was the empress's sister. Although, I'm guessing she went by a different last name than Malksur."

"Mori." Talise shared the last name she had claimed for most of her life, one that Aaden had never heard. "Also a common name. Especially in the Storm."

At these words, Aaden froze. His face fell and the energy around him seem to burst. Suddenly, he was in front of her, grasping her shoulders. "He sent you to the Storm. The *Storm*."

"It was the safest place." The words tasted bitter in her mouth. "No one would ever think to look for me there."

Aaden squeezed her shoulders while his eyebrows knitted together. "You could have died."

She looked away. Her stomach squirmed with the same discomfort as it always did when she thought about the Storm too much. "I don't think he understands how bad it is there."

They both stood in silence for a few minutes. The air shifted while these new truths fell into place. They both needed a moment to consider how everything had changed.

"Talise."

He was still gripping her shoulders. He seemed to notice it at the same time she did, and his hands fell away in an instant. He gulped. He reached for one of the frog closures on his vermillion shirt and she wondered at how their roles had switched.

Now he was the one whose fingers needed something to fiddle with. He sucked in air, but when she thought he was going to speak, he let out a breath instead. When he finally spoke, his voice was almost a whisper. "Because of my father, your family is dead." He buried his head in his hands. "I'm so sorry."

"It wasn't your fault." It surprised her how quickly the words came. But not just the speed, her sincerity surprised her too. She had questioned the laws of Kamdaria before. Several times. Especially after living in the Storm. She questioned the separation of the rings and how punishments were bestowed onto children. And yet, deep down, a part of her had still believed in them.

These had been the laws of Kamdaria for centuries. They'd been put in place by the great Kamdar himself. Even as she questioned the laws, there had always been a part of her that assumed they were just. She always thought there must have been something she didn't understand because she was too young or naïve. Something the adults understood that would make the laws make sense.

Deep down, she had always believed if two people shared blood, then they also shared disposition. If a person committed a certain crime, then his child must also be capable of the same crime. It was why she feared Aaden so much.

But now it didn't matter what she had believed in the past. Aaden stood in front of her, burying his face in shame while his fingers dug into his hair. The normally combed strands now fell at odd angles since he kept tugging at them.

She pulled his hands away from his face. "It wasn't your fault, Aaden."

The agony in his eyes seemed to lift briefly at the mention of his name. His eyes were red as he looked at her. He closed the little distance that remained between them. Reaching up for her face, he seemed to take on a new purpose.

"I couldn't do anything to help you then, but I vow to you—"

She tried to stop him by shaking her head.

With a gentle tug, he held her head in place. His eyes conveyed even more determination than before. Stroking his thumb across her cheek, he said, "I vow I will do everything in my power to protect you now."

She didn't want him to think a promise like that was necessary. She had already forgiven him moments before. But the way he spoke those words with such conviction, did something to her that could never be undone.

He must have seen it in her eyes because the next thing she knew, he leaned down, and his lips met hers.

Heat seeped through her skin, sending shocks that enlivened every part of her body. The warmth she expected. She leaned into it, allowing herself the thrill she had denied for so long. But it was soft too.

His lips were the softest things she had ever felt, which didn't make any sense because the kisses were not gentle.

It wasn't enough. She wanted more. Needed more.

She pulled herself away from the desk, launching herself deeper in his arms. As close as they could be. Apparently, that still wasn't enough.

Aaden's hand trailed across her jaw, reaching under her ear and around her neck just so he could pull her closer still.

Before she could fully enjoy the moment, two pairs of hands gripped her arms and yanked her away. She blinked and three more pairs of arms struggled to rip Aaden away.

Her first wild thought was the emperor had seen them kissing and ordered his guards to pry them apart. But after her second blink, she recognized the faces of the men beating Aaden to the ground.

Kessoku.

The same five spies she had just caught back in the ballroom.

Aaden screamed out her name as she raised her hands to attack. The men clamped her arms to her side.

A cold, slithery voice slipped into her ear. "Hello, Princess," it said.

Something heavy hit her on the back of the head and then black curtained her vision while the world fell away.

PART FOUR

FLAME CROWN

Chapter Fifty-Two

Another escape would be fun.

Talise eyed her cave-like prison cell imagining the look on her guard's face when she stole his key. Again.

Even as she pictured it, the nearby guard peered between the iron bars that locked her in. The veins in his hand pulsed as he gripped the hilt of his sword. His eyes narrowed to slits.

He seemed to know she was considering an escape. Or maybe he was naturally suspicious. In either case, she needed to throw him off.

Her fingers twitched at her sides, fighting her natural impulses. She wanted to blast a fire ball toward him, one that whizzed near enough that he could feel the heat on his cheek as it passed. She wanted to mock him for standing to the right of her cell which gave her the perfect vantage point to see the dungeon corridor and anyone who descended the staircase at its end. She wanted to point out his laughably incorrect sword stance.

But all those things would show him how powerful she really was. Though it pained her to act submissive, it also gave her freedom. When she first arrived, the spies who had kidnapped her told the others how she battled during the masquerade ball. It only took her a few days of acting weak and pathetic before the other Kessoku came to assume the spies' stories were nothing more than grossly exaggerated tales.

And right now, she needed every advantage she could get. After two weeks in a prison cell, she still had no idea what Kessoku wanted with her.

So, her actions reflected their ever-lowering opinion of her. With a whimper, she set her back against the wall. Her shoulders shivered while she brought her knees her chest and pouted. Then sniveled.

Just as she hoped, the guard rolled his eyes and turned his back on her. Now, thoughts were her only company.

Should she escape again?

If she did, it would be her second attempt. In the first attempt, she didn't expect to get far. But it did help her determine how long it took for guards to respond and how many would react. She'd also gotten a decent view of the staircase leading out of the dungeon as well as some of the rooms upstairs.

That knowledge would be invaluable for when she truly escaped. Now she had to determine if she already knew enough for the true escape, or if she needed a second fake escape to gain more knowledge of the building first?

Her knees ached the longer she hugged them to her chest. The prison cell had no bed or furniture of any kind. It merely had a pot in the corner for when nature called. Perhaps a bed would have been asking too much, but it would have been nice to be able to stand up straight in her cell.

The cave-like room had been cut from a mountain and its ceiling was slightly too short for her. When the ache in her knees became unbearable, she stretched herself out on the stone floor.

Only one spot in the cave was big enough for her to stretch out fully. She had to tuck her feet into a small indent in the stone wall, and her hair had to brush right up against the iron bars, but she fit. Barely.

At least the cave had one spot that fit her. The other prisoners brought to Kessoku's dungeons probably hadn't been able to stretch out at all.

Not that they'd been given much chance.

In the two weeks she'd spent inside the prison, six other prisoners had been carried down to the dungeons with her.

All six had been killed within hours of their arrival. After they relinquished the information Kessoku sought, they were no longer considered useful. Their executions followed immediately after.

Body odor had never been her favorite scent, but at least it masked the lingering stench of death seeping into the stone walls and floor of the dungeon.

Outside the iron bars, the Kessoku guard turned to face her again. His fingers stroked the hilt of his sword while his knees bounced. A look of eager anticipation danced in his eyes. Maybe he'd sensed how her mind whirled.

Before he could guess at her thoughts, she let out a desperate sigh and threw her head into the crook of her elbows. Her shoulders bounced up to her ears as she let out a wild sob. "I can't take this anymore. You must release me."

His hand fell away from the hilt of his sword. Shaking his head, he turned away. After only a few moments of stillness, he began tapping his toe.

The muscles in her shoulders pulled taut as she curled her body back to a sitting position. Little flutters went through her veins with each breath.

This was it.

Observation had been her only pastime for two weeks, and through it she had learned much. This particular guard always tapped his toe a few minutes before the changing of the guard.

In a split second, she made her decision. Another practice escape attempt was necessary. She knew one side of the prison corridor but not the other. Without more information, she couldn't plan a proper escape.

The shackles around her wrists turned hot while the thumping in her chest accelerated. It felt as though her heart wanted to leap from her chest and hide in that small indent of the cave where she tucked her feet at night.

Forcing another sob from her lips, she glanced toward the stairwell to the left of her cell.

Her heart quickened again, but she didn't dare fake another sob. The last one already sounded a little too hysterical.

Blink. She'd been reminding herself of the simplest things lately. *Blink or your eyes will water, and you won't see when the guard comes down the stairs.*

With a gulp, she sent another wave of fire through her wrists. The fire warmed her shackles until they glowed with heat. Without intervention, blisters would soon break out on her wrists.

Perfect.

Her shoulder scraped against the stone floor as she dragged herself toward the iron bars. "Please," she said in a pathetic sob. "I can't take another minute. Why don't you just kill me like you did the others?"

This earned her a sideways glance from the guard. She imagined the cosmetics from her eyes streaking down her cheeks along with the tears that now fell. It was nothing more than imagination, of course. After two weeks in the dungeon, the cosmetics leftover from the masquerade ball had long since faded away.

The only thing adorning her face now was a thick layer of dirt courtesy of her threadbare clothes. Still, the dirt gave something for her tears to streak through, which was sure to capture the guard's attention.

"Get back from the bars," he said through his teeth. After her last escape attempt, all the guards got jumpy when she came too close.

"I'm dying!" The chains clattered as she shook her wrists through the air. "If you want to kill me, can't you just do it quickly?"

It was a bold question, one she wouldn't have asked a week ago. But two whole weeks had passed since her capture, and they'd done nothing with her. No questions, no threats. They weren't even trying to starve her.

Even torture would have been less disconcerting than sitting in a cell day after day.

But then again, maybe that *was* the torture.

The guard pinched his nose as she neared. His curled lip reminded her she'd had nothing resembling a bath in the past two weeks.

"I said get back," he said with a snarl.

She pulled her face into a frown, but it was only half-pretend now. Apparently, he wouldn't answer her question. Not that she expected him to.

This time, he raised his hands. Sparks of flame shot from his palms in angry bursts.

He reached through the iron bars and gathered her collar in a tight fist. With sparks still bursting from his hand, he held it up to her cheek. Burning embers skipped across her skin.

The corner of his nose twitched. "My orders are to keep you alive. I don't have to keep you pretty."

An ache lanced through her throat, making it difficult to swallow. She'd nicknamed this guard "Angry" and this moment reminded her why. He liked threatening her. The singed material around her ankles proved he wasn't afraid to follow through.

Just as a flame burst from his palm, another guard finally appeared at the foot of the stairs.

Talise's wrists turned to ice a split second before she slammed her shackles against the iron bars. After heating them for so long, the sudden change in temperature, combined with the hit against iron, caused the shackles to split in half.

The guard by the stairs bolted toward her. Before he reached the cell, she'd already used air shaping to levitate the prison keys from his pocket.

His eyes widened at the sight of his keys drifting through the air. His trembling chin made his nickname—Scaredy—seem that much more appropriate.

"H-h-hey!" He had finally found his voice. "She's doing it again." His hand swatted the air as he tried to catch the keys.

They flew out of his reach not a second too soon.

Scaredy turned to the staircase and shouted even louder than before. "She's trying to escape!"

His shouts didn't cause her any anxiety. Due to her last escape attempt, she already knew what response time to expect.

However, the threatening guard—Angry—became a bigger problem with each second. He had lost his grip on her when she broke her shackles. Now, his fingers clawed at her through the bars. In one swipe, he managed to scrape off a chunk of skin from under her chin.

With one hand still shaping the keys toward her, she used the other hand to send a blast of flames at Angry's face. He ducked and caught her collar in his fist. When she finally reached for the prison keys, the shaping in her other hand stretched out in the space around her, searching for anything useful. A moment later, she shaped a clump of dirt off the cave floor.

The dirt clod slammed into Angry's neck in just the right pressure point. Even after practicing it in her head for a few days, she only half expected it to work.

To her near disbelief, Angry sank to his knees. His eyes rolled back in his head before he lost all consciousness.

Thank Kamdaria for the emperor's insistence that she learn each technique with absolute precision. Perhaps the trials had been beneficial after all.

Now it was Scaredy's turn. He dropped even faster than Angry.

She didn't dare kill either of them. Even though they kept her alive so far, if she killed any guards, they'd probably kill her in return. And there were too many of them for her to fight on her own. Her best chance was to run.

The lock on her cell door clicked open a moment later. Talise wrapped the key tight in her palm and rushed down the corridor to the doorway on the right side of the dungeon.

Now to see how far she could get.

CHAPTER FIFTY-THREE

THE DUNGEON CORRIDOR BENT INTO a curve, which perfectly obscured Talise from view once she rounded it.

Her eyes darted left and right while her feet propelled her forward. The narrow corridor could fit no more than two people running side by side. Still, two was one more than her.

More information bombarded her with each step. Splotches of dirt covered the gray walls. Creating a similar look would be impossible.

One of her escape ideas hinged on disguising herself with dirt and rocks to blend in with the walls. That idea was officially out. Even if she somehow mastered the necessary artistry of disguise, the corridor didn't have enough room to avoid being trampled by oncoming guards.

Weapons clattered together as backup finally trampled down the staircase. The Kessoku barked orders at each other as they went. If she counted their voices correctly, a small squad of six or seven hustled after her. Just like last time.

Based on her timing, she still had half a minute before she'd be in their view. Her eyes drifted upward. Could something up there be useful?

To her surprise, a small alcove sat in the ceiling. She could probably fit inside it perfectly, which would have been a genius way to hide from the guards. If only she could think of a way up there.

But her time had run out.

The guards barreled forward, which meant she had to barrel forward too. Her feet winced with each step. Not for the first time, she cursed herself for removing her shoes during that fight at the masquerade ball. On the next footfall, the ball of her foot landed squarely on a sharp rock. Her knee flew up to her chest on instinct while she let out a sharp cry of pain.

They had taken away her gown when she first arrived in the dungeon and given her an itchy burlap tunic and pants to wear. They never made any attempt to supply her with footwear.

Hissing at her bare feet, she ran again. This corridor went on longer than she expected. Even with Kessoku close behind her, she'd had time to find numerous openings in the ceiling, though none of them seemed to lead anywhere in particular. They were more like vents.

But for what?

The answer became clear a moment later. A cloud of black smoke billowed out of a hole in the ground. The smoke slithered across the ceiling until it found the nearby vents.

A sudden giddiness took hold inside her when she looked at the hole again.

An opening.

She rushed toward it without a thought. Smoke meant fire. She knew that. This was probably some sort of chimney with burning flames at the bottom. Dangerous, but was it really that dangerous for her?

She could shape ice inside her body. Kessoku would never think to secure an opening that led to flames because who could possibly walk through fire and live?

As the only ice shaper in history, she might be the only one.

The guards shouted as she lowered herself down the opening. Her feet quickly found footholds, which brought her out of their grasp just in time.

The tip of a sword brushed across her fingertips as she lowered herself again. Her other foot found a foothold much faster than she expected. She eyed the chimney as she lowered herself down a third time.

Several smoothed-out indents adorned the inside of the chimney wall. They worked perfectly as foot and handholds, but why would they be inside a chimney? Perhaps the Kessoku had once used this tunnel as a ladder before it became a chimney.

Black smoke filled her lungs as she drew in a breath. If only she'd had time to wrap a piece of cloth over her nose and mouth. A hacking cough escaped her lips. That's when the jeers began.

"Enjoy being cooked alive," one guard shouted down at her.

"Hope you don't lose your grip from all the sweat." This earned a round of raucous laughter from the other guards.

The drips of sweat sliding down her chin *had* been worrying her. But they didn't need to know that.

For a moment, she brushed the fear aside and imagined what she'd see at the bottom. She hoped to find a tiny kitchen with a wizened old cook who wouldn't know what to do when a dirty girl emerged from the chimney. It was unlikely, but that didn't stop her from hoping.

Kessoku's whole base, at least from what she'd seen, had been cut from a mountain side. Since the highest mountains in Kamdaria were in the Crown, she guessed this base was also in the Crown.

Either the emperor had been wrong about Kessoku's base being in the Gate, or—more likely—this wasn't Kessoku's main base at all.

That thought both excited and terrified her. If this *was* Kessoku's main base, then all the prisoners they took months ago, including Wendy's brother, Cyrus, were surely dead. But if this was only one of many bases, Cyrus might still be alive. But it also meant Kessoku was an even bigger threat than they thought.

More jeers bounced off the walls of the chimney while she found another foothold. Her hacking coughs came out faster now. She had already shaped ice into her skin to help fend off some of the heat.

The jeering grew louder.

"See you soon, Princess. It won't be long before you realize there is no escape."

The words felt like lead on her shoulders. She wanted to ignore them, but the rising temperature made it impossible. Each time she lowered herself down the chimney, the heat seeped through her skin, melting away the ice in her skin. The smoke coated her throat and burned her eyes.

She tried using air to shape away the black smoke, but more would replace it almost immediately. Even with ice shaping, the temperature in her body surged to dangerous heights.

After lowering herself down to the next foothold, she understood why the heat swelled with such intensity.

Her dream of a small kitchen fire cooking a pot of stew was far from the reality before her. The flames licking the bottom edges of the chimney burned as high as a bonfire. Higher.

Below her was an incinerator.

It didn't matter. That's what she wanted to tell herself.

She was the first ice shaper in all of Kamdaria. That had to mean something.

She lowered herself again, and it felt like someone had poured hot water down her back. It took a moment to realize, the water came from her own sweat. Heat roared inside her. She couldn't tell what was heat and was ice. The sensations blended into one stabbing stream under her skin.

Her foot hovered over the next foothold. She sent another blast of ice through her, but it felt more like fire. Her head hung as the truth settled like a rock in her gut.

Even with ice shaping, she'd never survive a fire that big.

Not to mention her lungs constricted from all the smoke inside them. Tears blurred her vision also thanks to the stinging black smoke. This was over now.

From above, she could just made out the roaring laughter of the guards.

"Give up yet? We have a nice cell for you up here."

Their laughter turned riotous. They must have seen how her progress had halted. They must have known she'd be climbing back soon.

Her heart sank, taking up residence where her stomach should have been. Had she gotten enough information? She knew the layout of the dungeon perfectly now. She'd found a few hiding spots. She knew where *not* to hide. She knew how fast the guards would come and how many there would be. Was it enough? Did she know enough to actually escape next time?

Clutching the prison key in her palm, she began the slow ascent up the chimney.

It had to be enough. She'd survived twelve years since Kessoku first tried to kill her. She wasn't about to let them succeed now.

THE GUARD'S TAUNTING became gleeful as Talise neared the top of the chimney. She still held the prison key tight in her hand. They'd take it back soon enough. Before they did, she let the sweat gather in her palm until she had enough water to shape over the entire key.

Moving water over the key helped her memorize the shape of it. The corners and rivets and curves all became familiar as she shaped the water into ice and back to water again.

The water gently flowed over the key as she climbed. Freezing and unfreezing the water allowed her to engrain its shape into her memory. Her mind wandered over the dimensions of it as she committed its every curve to memory.

The guards would steal the key as soon as she reached the top. Since she had now attempted twice to escape, she wasn't likely to ever be near the key again. They'd take even greater precautions to keep it out of her reach.

But if she could memorize its shape, she could make her own key with ice. As long as she got it cold enough, the ice key would work to unlock her cell.

The guards continued to laugh as she crawled out the chimney and onto the stone floor of the dungeon corridor. They didn't bother being gentle as they slapped a new pair of shackles onto her wrists.

She immediately fell back into her frightened princess routine. It wouldn't be as convincing with her recent escape, but that wouldn't stop her from trying.

Wiping a line through the soot on her arm, she let out a sob. "Can't I have some water to wash myself?"

Her shoulders shook with a shiver as she raised her arm up to her nose. No imagination was required to bring a look of disgust over her face. Even in the Storm, she had never smelled so bad.

The nearest guard held the chains between her shackles as he tore the key from her grip. "You think we'd give you water just so you could shape ice daggers or something at us? Think again, Princess."

Ice daggers.

Now *that* would have been fun. Sadly, they kept all water out of her reach, except just enough to keep her alive. As tempting as it had been to use that water for shaping, she needed it for drinking. She did have a fair amount of sweat still dripping down her skin. Perhaps that would give her the water she needed for the ice key.

To keep up her act, she scowled at the nearest guard and threw her nose in the air. "You all deserve to rot for how you're treating me. Why don't you just kill me?"

She hoped with half a dozen guards around, at least one of them would be stupid enough to answer. People tended to lose their heads in a crowd.

Luckily, one guard seemed delighted in her capture just enough to forget about holding his tongue. "There's someone you have to meet first, Princess. He has questions for you."

They all got some sort of sick pleasure from calling her *princess*. It roiled her insides every time. Regardless, she had gotten the answer she wanted. If someone had questions for her, then Kessoku wanted information. That was good. It put her in a position of power.

The loose-lipped guard had been jabbed by the four guards nearest to him. His feet shuffled forward as his ears turned bright red. He clamped his mouth shut and dropped his eyes to the ground.

When they arrived back at her prison cell, the threatening guard, Angry, stood. Apparently, he had regained consciousness. His jaw clenched as he beckoned Talise back inside her cell. "Welcome back, Princess." A smirk curled his lips up, and he made a sweeping mock bow. "I have a surprise for you."

Her shoulders shuddered as another guard locked the iron door, sealing her in once again.

Angry moved his hands in a small circle while he shaped a ring of fire between his palms. Soon, his flame took the shape of a crown.

The design was crude. Nothing like Aaden's magnificent cherry blossom trees. But it didn't matter. The implication was clear.

He had threatened to burn her earlier and hadn't been given the pleasure. He wouldn't be denied it a second time. His face screwed up as he levitated the crown toward her.

Though she had played the frightened princess since she arrived, her chin trembled with genuine fear. Her feet stumbled backward as her mind whirled.

Sweat. She still had plenty of sweat on her back and arms. Now it was time to use it.

Her hands fell to her sides as she shaped the water away from her body and into a water ball behind her back. She tried shaping water out of the air as well, but the dry heat of the dungeon wouldn't allow for it.

Moving her fingers as little as possible, she levitated the water ball up to her head. Once there, she shaped it into a thin layer that could rest just above her hair. She barely had a single moment to freeze the water before the flame crown landed on her hair.

The ice protected her, but she couldn't let the guards know that. With a firm hold on the ice shaping, Talise collapsed to her knees and let out a wail.

Her shoulders shook and her body shivered as the seconds crawled forward. Wincing and groaning were the only actions she could manage without losing a grip on her ice shaping. Still, it seemed to be working. One of the guards scratched his neck. Another looked away.

"Stop it!" Her screams reverberated through the dungeon walls, each more desperate than the last. The flames had melted through most of the ice now, so her performance really had to count. She clawed at her own face, letting her body shiver as her eyes rolled back in their sockets.

"Please," she said through a sob.

Scaredy, who had also regained consciousness, touched Angry on the arm. "That's enough, Flint. We need to keep her alive."

It surprised her that Angry would have a name as common as Flint. Even more surprising was the softness in Scaredy's eyes. He pretended to be unbothered by her pain, that he cared only for their orders to keep her alive. Yet, distress drifted through his eyes when he glanced through the iron bars of her cell. Perhaps her cries had reminded him of his humanity.

The moment Flint shaped the flame crown away, Talise threw herself to the stone floor in a fit of sobs. She bunched up her hair and let out unintelligible words that almost sounded like "hair" and "ruined" and "singed."

Luckily, the guards were too certain of their success to investigate. With any luck, they'd never notice that her hair was as thick and long as always, except for a few burnt strands. The ice she had used to protect her head had all turned to steam now, but at least it had protected her when she needed it.

She could rest easier now.

If someone was coming to see her, they weren't going to kill her. At least not yet.

That gave her just enough time to gather the water she needed for an ice key. In the meantime, she'd continue to observe their routines and learn as much as possible for her true escape.

No matter what, her third one would be successful. Hopefully she could get out before her mysterious visitor arrived.

CHAPTER FIFTY-FOUR

THE GUARDS WERE GETTING NERVOUS.

Talise had been in the dungeon for three weeks now, and the signs were easy to spot. Each changing of the guard came with tense whispers. Sometimes two would come down the stairs: one for watching her, the other for changing out the guard.

Despite her weak princess routine, they seemed to know she had plans brewing. And of course, they were right. She'd spent the last week gathering water for her escape. To her dismay, it took longer than she expected.

The dungeon air was dry, probably because of the nearby chimney. The dry heat made it difficult to shape water out of the air.

Her solution had been to keep small bits of water each time they gave her a drink. By taking a tiny bit each time, her stash had almost grown large enough for the ice key.

Since her visitor hadn't yet arrived, she took her time to make sure the water she had would be enough.

The guard in front of her cell started pacing. He did that a lot. So much, in fact, it had earned him the nickname Pacey. He kept throwing suspicious glances at her. It seemed like a good time to play the pathetic princess.

She pulled her knees up to her chest and let her head hang. Small whimpers escaped her next. When he still wouldn't stop staring, she went a step further. "I just want to go home," she said through a whimper.

Pacey rolled his eyes before turning away.

Once he turned, she rolled her eyes right back. Were they really convinced by her act so easily? Or maybe they didn't know her whole history. She had survived the Storm, after all. This was nothing in comparison.

With the guard's back to her, thinking became easier. She kept whimpering, but her mind wandered back to the night of the masquerade ball. When she first woke up in Kessoku's dungeon, she had thought Aaden would be there with her. But he wasn't. Without seeing or hearing anything about him in her three weeks there, she assumed the Kessoku spies had left him unconscious back at the palace.

While rocking herself back and forth on the stone floor, every other event from the night of her kidnapping played through her head. Just like it had a dozen other times.

One of her guards, Tempest, told them about Kessoku spies. Then, Commander Blaise told them to do nothing. Next, her friends found out her true identity while they were in the treasury. Then, they fought Kessoku in the ballroom.

Her heart always started beating faster when she remembered the rest of the night. Aaden's questions.

His kiss.

Everything played through her mind as she clung to the same question that had been with her since that night.

Who had betrayed her?

Kessoku *did* have someone working in the palace. She knew that for sure. The Kessoku spies had targeted her soldiers even when they wore masquerade clothes in a crowded ballroom. Plus, the spies had escaped after being taken to the dungeons. They couldn't have done it without help.

But did it have to be one of her friends?

Kessoku stole the family tree *before* she and her friends made it to the treasury. It had her name right on it.

Yes, it would have been a stretch for Kessoku to assume it was her by the name alone, but there were other clues. She was the right age. She was from the Storm but could shape anyway. She knew the palace better than she should have, though she didn't think anyone had noticed that.

They could have guessed it on their own. They could have figured it out.

Or, maybe one of the emperor's guards had let the secret out. The emperor had chosen his trusted guards based on loyalty. They all seemed eager to die a thousand deaths before they'd betray Kamdaria. So, it probably wasn't one of them either.

But maybe they had let the secret out unintentionally.

Maybe they said something in passing to a kitchen servant and the servant had repeated it to just the right person. Something that wouldn't have been incriminating on its own, but to someone who had other pieces of the puzzle…

Anyone could have given the secret away. Hundreds of people lived on the palace grounds. And it had been twelve years. Just because the secret got out, didn't mean it was one of her friends.

Talise hugged her knees tighter to her chest, surprised that her whimpering wasn't all pretend now.

Aaden.

That's who she really feared. Wendy and Claye she had known for years, but Aaden only a few months. And he always had an air of mystery about him. And why had he been so interested in her anyway? What did she have to offer? Did he only want her for information?

As soon as the thoughts came, they turned around again. It couldn't be Aaden. It *couldn't* be.

Yes, he would have had ample time during the fight in the ballroom to share her secret with the spies. And afterward when she had spent all that time dressing wounds and checking on her soldiers, he could have snuck off to help the Kessoku spies escape.

But what about his face when they'd kidnapped her?

She remembered clearly how her name came out of his mouth in a strangled cry. She remembered how he struggled against his own captors, desperate to get to her.

He never looked smug or relieved that Kessoku was there.

He looked surprised. Desperate.

Afraid.

He had tried to save her.

And what about the kiss?

It had occurred to her more than once that maybe the kiss was a ruse. Maybe he did it to distract her, so she wouldn't hear when Kessoku entered the room.

But it didn't feel like a ruse.

It felt passionate and raw. Nothing had felt more real in her entire life.

She had appealed to logic several times since getting captured. The simple truth was she couldn't know for sure if Aaden was involved with Kessoku. He *could* have betrayed her. He'd had time. He'd had opportunity. But there were just as many evidences he wasn't involved. Her brain couldn't tell her whether it was safe to trust him.

So, instead, she trusted her heart.

It wasn't Aaden. She didn't *know* it, but she could *feel* it.

The guard began pacing again. The torch flickered in its hanging on the wall. Being down in the dungeon with no light from the outside made it difficult to tell time. After her time there, she had picked up on several clues.

Twice a day, someone brought a new torch down and retrieved the old one. Morning and night, she had discovered. During the day, the guards looked more alert. At night, they looked more somber.

Plus, during the day, she could hear a smattering of voices coming from up the stairs. The voices were always loudest at mealtimes.

The noises were picking up now. Breakfast. Once everyone upstairs finished eating, they'd bring the leftovers down to her. Whoever guarded her got to eat off the plate first. Getting leftovers usually meant she received little more than burnt pieces of bread and tough meat. Sometimes small bits of bruised fruit sat on the plate.

None of it bothered her, though she always pretended to be disgusted by it. Of all the foolish things Kessoku did, feeding her was the stupidest of all. It kept her strength up. Ready for her true escape.

— ◆ —

TALISE CURLED HERSELF herself into a ball. Her cheek rested on the cool stone floor while heavy tears dripped from her eyes. It was dangerous to cry. Each tear brought her closer to dehydration. But it also gave her more water to collect for the ice key, so the risk was worth it.

Occasionally, she'd use one arm to pull her knees closer, just so she could wipe her tears on the burlap fabric of her pants. It would be easier to collect the water that way.

Her smell was getting out of control.

The guard stared her down as she trembled on the stone floor. She had nicknamed this guard Beady because of her small black eyes.

Beady never seemed as convinced by Talise's act as the other guards. Then again, she had every right to be suspicious since the entire thing was fake.

But, even if this guard knew to be cautious, it didn't make her smart enough to realize only one of Talise's arms was visible.

The other arm she had hidden behind her back while she continually shaped her little ball of water. With her fingers pressing through the air, she shaped the water into an exact replica of the prison key.

Once she had frozen it for a few moments, she would melt it and start the whole process over again. Each time, she imagined the key in her mind, tracing over each turn and edge. For the key to work, she had to get the shape exactly right.

Soft footsteps sounded down the corridor, coming from the staircase to the left. Beady immediately jumped to attention. She was at the bottom of the staircase in three steps.

Talise knew whose face to expect before it appeared. She had memorized the sound of all their footsteps during her imprisonment. The boy who brought her water had a round face with friendly eyes. He seemed more distressed by her capture than the others, but maybe her smell bothered him more than anything.

Beady frowned at the sight of the boy. Had she been expecting someone else? Her shoulders dropped as she gestured toward Talise. "Go on. Get it over with."

The boy wore the same brown burlap as Talise, which suggested he was also a prisoner in some way. But maybe not. His burlap wasn't as stiff as hers. It looked well-worn from lots of washing. He carried a wooden bucket with a wooden ladle.

The guards got water eight times a day and four times during the night. They allowed Talise half that amount. When her water came, the bucket was merely for show. Not even a ladle's worth of water sat in the bottom.

Talise froze her levitating ball of water and tucked the ice ball into her pocket. Smacking her lips, she crept toward the iron bars.

"Hey!" shouted Beady. "You know the rules. Stay more than an arm's length away from the bars."

Talise nodded as she stepped back. She wanted to roll her eyes. As if she'd be stupid enough to attack anyone from inside her cell. Something like that was sure to be a death sentence. Instead, she kept smacking her lips and eyed the wooden bucket greedily, trying to look as pathetic as ever.

When the boy stepped up to the bars, Talise curled her hands into fists and held them tight at her sides. Just like she was supposed to do.

Now, Beady shaped the remaining water out of the bucket and levitated it toward Talise. As always, Talise smacked her lips as she drank from the levitating ball of water. This caused great dribbles of water to slide down her chin.

Once the boy left and Beady turned away, Talise would collect the extra water and add it to the frozen ball in her pocket.

Soon, the boy left. She didn't have long to collect the water before another pair of footsteps sounded from the staircase. This pair of feet sounded different from her regular guards. Beady rushed to the foot of the stairs where a man wearing black stood.

"Is he here yet?" Beady whispered.

The sound of Beady's voice carried through the dungeon, but Talise had to strain to hear the response.

"He's just putting his horse in the stables," the man replied. "He'll be down in a minute."

Beady turned back to look at Talise with a nasty grin.

So, Talise's visitor had arrived. She had hoped for a few more days to prepare for her escape. Still, as long as she didn't give anything away to her visitor, she still had a little time.

Not wanting to appear like she'd heard anything, Talise sniffled and sat against the back wall of her cell with a frown. She tucked the ice ball into the small indent where she put her feet at night. Then, she rocked herself back and forth, trying to look weak and scared.

It didn't take long before heavy footsteps came tromping down the stairs. These were definitely unrecognizable from any of the feet she knew.

A tall man with broad shoulders appeared at the bottom of the stairs a few moments later. A gasp escaped Talise's lips before she could stop it.

"General," Beady said with a short bow.

He nodded in return and moved down the corridor. He carried a small red stool and puffed his chest out as he strode toward her. Over his heart, he wore Kessoku's symbol of three interlocking circles. Not just a member of Kessoku, but a high ranking one.

Talise's heart seemed to have forgotten how to beat. The man set his stool directly in front of her cell, and he dared to smile as he settled into the seat.

Of all the things she expected her visitor to look like, *this* was not what she imagined. Not this at all.

The man wore a goatee. It must have been a family tradition.

His brown eyes shined bright. Even in the torch light, she could make out small orange flecks around his irises. A few gray strands peppered his neatly combed hair. When he smiled, his lips curved into a look so familiar, it made her stomach churn with horror.

The resemblance was uncanny. While Aaden only looked vaguely like his grandfather, *this* man was practically his mirror image. The only difference was his advancement in age. Even with no introduction, Talise knew exactly whom she was staring at.

Lucian Sato.

Aaden's father.

Chapter Fifty-Five

Every limb in Talise's body had frozen. Her brain kept telling her to play stupid. To act weak. But her brain couldn't overpower the thumping organ in her chest.

The only movements she made now were the automatic ones. Breathing. Blinking.

Everything else had gone still.

"Talise," Lucian said with a nod. Her gut twisted, causing a shot of bile to dance up her throat. "You're much older than last time I saw you."

How dare he? Her stomach churned again. How dare he say her name so casually? And reference that he knew her as a child?

One part of her ached to clutch her stomach, anything to ease the churning inside it. Another part of her wanted to blast fire balls in his face regardless of the consequences. And the last part? It wanted to give up right there on the stone floor. It wanted her to collapse and never get back up again.

What had Aaden said to Claye during the masquerade ball? "My father was idiotic but not treasonous."

But here Lucian sat with three interlocking circles adorning his chest. Had Aaden known all along? Was he a part of the charade?

Lucian cleared his throat. "I'm sure I'm the last person you expected to see today—"

"I have no idea who you are." Talise cut him off, then tossed her head back with her best impression of boredom. Her brain had finally caught up to the moment. Apparently, she had decided to play a disinterested spoiled brat.

Lucian had no reaction to her act. He merely nodded. "Ah, forgive me. I have worked hard to keep my involvement with Kessoku a secret, for my family's sake. But I've been a member since the beginning. My name is Lucian Sato." His head tilted toward the bars as he raised his eyebrows. "I'm sure you know me now, don't you?"

Talise pressed her back into the stone wall behind her. Every trace of the disinterested brat fell away from her face. Feigned ignorance would be no help to her now. He knew who she was, and he knew she'd know the name *Sato*.

With her lips pressed into a tight line, she blinked back at him. She wouldn't give him the satisfaction of answering his question.

Silence was her only power now.

Lucian nodded. He understood her perfectly, and the nod seemed like his feeble attempt to gain back some control.

"Have you seen Emperor Kamdar's gravestone?" he asked.

The word *yes* very nearly popped out of Talise's mouth without her permission. The question took her off guard so completely, answering it almost seemed like the best option. She *had* seen Kamdar's gravestone before. Only once and it had been many years ago. The stone was so weathered, the markings in the gravestone were only barely visible.

Other than the faded markings, she couldn't remember anything significant about the gravestone. Had its location been secret? She didn't remember that, but then again, she had been four years old when she saw it.

What could Kessoku possibly want with it? Her confusion only led to fear. If she didn't know what information he sought, anything she said could give it away.

"Have you seen it?" Lucian asked again.

Her lips remained pressed shut. The disinterested brat didn't seem like such a stretch of the imagination now. What did she care about Kamdar's gravestone?

Lucian seemed intent to learn more, but she had more important things to consider. All the things she knew for sure. First, Kessoku had someone in the palace who worked for them. Second, Aaden's father was a member of Kessoku, which made Aaden the most likely spy. Third, Aaden wasn't the spy.

Maybe that last one she didn't know for sure, but it felt like the truth. She had seen Aaden's face when they all realized she was the princess. He had been just as surprised as the others. Maybe even more so.

And what about when he yelled at Claye for suggesting Kessoku might recruit him? Or any time he talked about his father? His father had ruined his life. He had shown genuine emotion. Genuine heartbreak.

He couldn't have known how deeply involved with Kessoku his father was. And he certainly couldn't be involved himself.

Maybe the whole thing was an act. Maybe Aaden had been lying from the moment he met her, but he didn't seem capable of that kind of deception.

When he was angry, she knew he was angry. When he wanted to kiss her, he made it clear in every part of his body language.

He *couldn't* have lied to her like that.

Which meant he had to have been as ignorant of his father's involvement as she was.

Lucian sighed. He seemed to understand all at once that she wouldn't answer any of his questions. "Do you know what Kessoku means?"

Again, his question took her off guard. As he spoke, Lucian traced his finger over each of the three interlocking circles on his tunic. "Kessoku means unity. Our mission is to destroy the division between the three rings of Kamdaria. We want all people to have equal opportunity, equal punishment. Equal livelihood."

Talise blinked.

Her enemy wanted the same things she did? Was that even possible?

Her mind whirled with a thousand possibilities. Maybe they could work together. Maybe they could fight the same cause. It was slightly inconvenient they wanted to kill her because otherwise…

In a flash, the truth came back to her like a crushing avalanche. They'd killed her entire family all those years ago. Not humanely.

And not just the royal family either. They'd murdered servants, guards, court members, Talise's friends. And what about their attack during the masquerade ball? They hadn't killed anyone that night, but not for lack of trying.

She felt her stare harden. It didn't matter what Kessoku wanted to achieve. She'd never approve of their methods.

"You see…," Lucian said, stroking his goatee.

Talise gulped, forcing her eyes away from his. The movement reminded her so much of Aaden. He always stroked his goatee when thinking. Lucian's eyes reminded her of Aaden too. Everything about it felt wrong.

Lucian continued. "What we fight for is a good thing. You lived in the Storm. I'm sure you've doubted the need for a division of classes."

She gritted her teeth. So, they did know about her living in the Storm. What else did they know?

For a moment, Lucian's eyes flicked toward the staircase. It was only then that Talise noticed Beady, her guard from earlier, disappear up the stairs.

Lucian's voice raised slightly, as if making sure Beady could still hear him though she headed up the stairs. "We have important work to do."

The intentional way he spoke brought Talise's attention forward. While her mind tried to work out what it could mean, Lucian stood. He wrapped a hand around one of the iron bars. His eyes turned tender.

"Please," he said in a brand-new voice. This one felt soft like worn leather. "I have a personal request."

Just like every new development during this interrogation, this one took her off-guard. Her eyes darted around her cell and back to Lucian. If his game was to confuse her, he played it well.

Yet, nothing about his eyes spoke of strategy. Like he said, it looked personal.

"I have devoted my life to Kessoku, which I don't regret, but it did require some sacrifices. I wanted to ask you about my son, Aaden. You've seen him? How is he?"

The words stabbed her in the gut. When she played them over in her mind, they stabbed her again in the heart.

How *is* he? Was he seriously asking after his son? The person whose life he had destroyed? And what about her own family? Considering his position, she couldn't believe the gall of him to ask such a request.

She had never been able to hate Lucian because his mistake had supposedly been an accident. He had tricked everyone with his act as a fool. Even the emperor never dreamed Lucian had been involved with Kessoku.

But now he stood here, and she finally knew the truth. For the first time in her life, she allowed the hate to flow through her freely.

Lucian didn't seem to notice how tight she had clenched her jaw. He didn't seem to hear the heavy puffs escaping her nostrils. The white-knuckled fists at her side? They seemed to be nothing to him. He was lost in his own world.

"I know he's a Master Shaper now." The pride in his eyes sparkled, which only gave her the strong desire to hurl fire balls at his face. "I can't get many reports about him, for his own safety. But I haven't seen him in many years. Is he tall like me? Or shorter like his grandfather? Does he still whistle when he's nervous? Does he stroke his goatee when he's thinking? Does he have one? I'm assuming he has one."

It took everything in her just to breathe. The questions came fast, and each one made her lose another ounce of control. She wanted to scream at him. Wanted to burn him. Knowing she'd probably be killed for either of those things, she managed to force her emotions down.

The best she could do was steer the conversation the way she wanted it to go. But she'd stick to the facts. The things Lucian already knew.

She parted her lips just enough to let words out. "Wasn't he supposed to live in the Storm? I thought he had a black *X* on his ID card. Because of you." She couldn't help adding that last part.

"I would have rescued him from the Storm." He said the words in a matter-of-fact tone, but a trace of guilt still lingered through them.

"That's…" *Impossible*. That's what she was about to say. Nobody could be rescued from the Storm. ID cards were checked at every gate between the rings. Special passes were required to travel between the rings. It had taken Marmie months to get the pass for Talise's academy testing.

Yet, he spoke with such certainty. Did he have a way to rescue people from the Storm? Had he done it before? She managed to ask, "How?"

But Lucian had moved on. Apparently, he didn't realize what he just admitted to. That was something she could use later, hopefully.

"It's better he's a Master Shaper. He can stay with his grandparents that way. What is he like? Tell me anything." Lucian stared through the bars with hope in his eyes.

Thoughts raced through her mind. She wanted to scream at him. *He has a scar across his left eye because of your soldiers!* More than anything, she wanted to scar his face with fire.

But the true power of her silence took hold. With her best imitation of Aaden, Talise smirked back at Lucian.

She could tell him many things about his son. All the things he wanted to hear and more. She knew him better than almost anyone.

With her smirk, she made sure Lucian understood how much she knew. And how much she wouldn't say.

The sparkle in his eyes darkened. His grip on the iron bar clenched. He had never seemed particularly kind, but all trace of friendliness vanished from his features. A cruel smile overtook his face. When he spoke again, his words were careful. Precise.

"It's a shame you're the princess. We thought you could be an ally when we first heard about you. A Master Shaper from the Storm? It seemed too good to be true."

He shrugged his shoulders as he settled back into his stool. His demeanor darkened with each word. "But Kamdaria is too ruined now. A simple change won't be a real change at all. For anything to get better we must completely overthrow the government. We must start over. There's no other way."

He glanced at her through narrowed eyes. "It's nothing personal, but we are going to kill you. You know that, don't you?"

He was trying to scare her. The way he curled his lips. The way he spoke the words with casual indifference. The way he made her feel like the tablet on a Forces board instead of a person. His life was nothing to her.

It *did* scare her.

Down to her core, the fear shook through her. But when it came time to react, she merely crossed her arms in front of her chest. With her earlier smirk still growing, she said, "Good luck."

She didn't know what possessed her to say such a thing. She'd probably regret it. A lot. And very soon. But as she sat back against the stone, she added with a touch of laughter, "You'll need it."

The cold, calculated look of Lucian's face fell away. Apparently, she had shocked him out of whatever game he thought he could play. He seemed to recognize mind tricks would get him nowhere. He seemed ready to try a direct approach.

He sat still on his stool. His voice cold, no emotion coloring it. "Have you seen Emperor Kamdar's gravestone?"

Silence had been her power, but this time, one word would give her even more. She looked him square in the eye and said, "Yes."

"Are there markings on it?" he asked.

Silence.

He narrowed his eyes. "Does the grave have a circle with four markings inside?"

Silence.

"It's the same as the symbol for Master Shapers. A circle divided into four sections. In the top section is a waterfall, the right section has a tornado, the bottom section has a tree, and the left section has a flame."

Silence.

He slammed a fist against the iron bars. "I know you know what I'm talking about. Is the Master Shaper symbol on his gravestone? Is it part of the stone or is it carved into a metal piece that's attached to the gravestone?"

The stream of questions came so fast, she couldn't help but react to the last one. One eye twitched. A memory had been triggered inside her. One so deep, she couldn't remember who had been there or what they'd been saying. All she remembered was the word *amulet*.

The memory frayed, slipping away. But then she snatched onto it again when she remembered Marmie had been there. The edges of her memory sharpened into focus. Marmie had been talking to a maid. They were trying to keep the amulet secret, but from who, Talise had never known.

"It's probably about this big," Lucian said, forming a circle with his thumb and pointer finger. "And the metal is probably thin like a pendant, but if it's attached to the gravestone, you wouldn't know that for sure."

That *sounded* like an amulet. Memories tugged at her from every corner. Had that been what Marmie wanted kept secret? Kamdar's amulet?

When Talise came back to the present moment, Lucian grinned at her. In a rumbling voice, he asked, "Where is the gravestone?"

She had given away too much. Even without speaking, she had revealed more than she intended. Now Lucian knew she had heard of the amulet. He also seemed to assume the amulet was a part of Kamdar's gravestone.

It wasn't. At least not as far as she remembered, but she wasn't about to correct his assumption. And even if the amulet wasn't on the gravestone, it could have been nearby.

He glared.

Her stomach roiled inside. How could she stop herself from divulging secrets when she didn't even speak a word? She decided to answer all his questions from now on. She just wouldn't answer them the way he wanted.

"Where?" he asked again.

A laugh danced from her lips. "If you're just going to kill me, why would I tell you anything?"

With the snap of his fingers, Talise's earlier guard appeared at the bottom of the stairs.

"Starve her," Lucian said. "Once she loses her shaping from malnourishment, she should be more cooperative. Relay my order to the kitchens."

The guard nodded and disappeared up the stairs.

Talise wanted to hold her breath but she forced a steady stream of air in and out of her mouth. Now they'd gotten smart. Malnourishment was a painful way to die. An effective form of torture. If she lost her shaping, she'd probably do anything for food.

Too bad for him. She wouldn't be there long enough for any of that to happen.

She'd escape tonight. Hopefully she had enough water now. She'd leave in between the second and third changing of the guard. When the guards were the most tired and the Kessoku's base was the quietest.

Lucian stared at her. The anger that flashed in his eyes only a moment earlier had faded away. Again, his face softened. "If you tell me about my son, I'll make sure you get a little bread each day. I just want to know, is he happy?"

Happy?

The words were like a punch to the gut. This man had killed her entire family. He had probably helped plan the recent attacks on the palace. He seemed to have no guilt for murdering as long as it fit his agenda.

But none of those crimes mattered to her now. What mattered was Aaden. This man had taken everything away from his son. He never even apologized. He did nothing when Aaden's grandparents took him away. Didn't try to protest.

He destroyed Aaden's life without a single glance back. And now he had the audacity to *care* what had happened to him?

Talise decided she would rather stab herself with an ice dagger than tell Lucian anything about his son.

She gritted her teeth together. Her words were fire. "Rot. In. Flames."

Chapter Fifty-Six

Beneath Talise's cheek, the stone floor shook enough to wake her from a fitful sleep. Her hand went straight for the ice ball.

Still safe in her pocket.

She shaped the water that had melted into the burlap and refroze it into the ice ball. And then she could breathe again.

A little more sleep would have been useful. She needed to be at her best for her escape attempt that night. But the shaking concerned her.

Letting out a long yawn, she turned to assess the dungeon.

Her latest guard wasn't even watching her. She stood at the foot of the stairs clutching a sword. Ready for battle.

In an instant, Talise leaned forward. This was new. Did it have anything to do with the shaking stone?

Two other guards whispered with the guard that was supposed to be watching her. They also carried swords.

Talise wanted to sit up. Wanted to lean closer. But she also didn't want her captors to think she noticed how tension thickened the air.

She settled on scooting closer to the bars of her cell while idly stretching and scratching various parts of her body.

Even though they spoke in whispers, she still picked out a few words of the guards' conversation. Most of the conversation made no sense, but one phrase stuck out to her. "General is safe, left earlier."

Talise's ears pricked with attention.

The female guard whipped around and snarled at Talise before more of their conversation could be heard. The guard looked ready to deliver a death blow.

This seemed the perfect moment to appear ignorant. And weak.

Talise gave out a long stretch before she curled back against the cave wall of her cell. After smacking her lips, she pouted, trying to look as pathetic as she could. "I'm so thirsty. Isn't it time for water yet?"

Now all three of the guards snarled.

"We're starving you, remember?" the female guard said with a snap.

Hugging her knees to her chest, Talise let out a whimper. "Even water?"

"Shut up!" the guard shouted in response. She turned to the other two guards who both stepped forward until they formed a tight huddle.

Their bodies shielded their whispers from reaching the prison cell. Little did they know, their antics only brought a wave of relief through Talise's body. If they were nervous, it could only mean good things for her.

The short phrase she overheard gave her all the knowledge she needed anyway. First, the general had left. Second, if they worried for his safety, then maybe the base was under attack.

Or perhaps it was a rescue. After three weeks in the dungeon, she'd long since given up hope that someone would come to rescue her. But she *was* the princess. The possibility wasn't too much of a stretch.

She hadn't planned to escape like this. She was supposed to leave at night when most of the Kessoku were asleep. But if they were fighting, that might be even better. Nothing like the distraction of a fight for her to hide behind.

The guards fidgeted as they spoke.

She hadn't been up the stairs since her first escape attempt. She'd been going over the layout of the base in her mind ever since then, but there were still so many areas she knew nothing about.

An escape would still be risky, but this was as prepared as she'd ever get, and she knew it. Now it was time to do it.

Slipping a hand into her pocket, she pulled out the ice ball and hid it behind her back. She decided to start moaning about how dry her mouth was. If she gave the guards something to watch, they were less likely to notice her shaping ice behind her back.

With one hand, she levitated the ice ball above her palm. With a flood of fire through her veins, she made the ball melt into water. The water flowed gently into the shape of the key. She'd practiced it so many times, it whisked into shape with barely any thought.

That was good, since her ridiculous moaning noises took most of her brain power.

One of the male guards lifted his head from the huddle just so he could roll his eyes at her. Nothing in his body language suggested he realized she had anything behind her back.

When his head lowered back into the huddle, she smiled. She'd played her part well as the scared, pathetic princess. Her burlap tunic hung stiff with dried sweat. Her hair had been matted. It still had the clumps of dirt she'd shoved into it the first day. Now it had even more dust that she'd added during her three weeks here.

Her face didn't have any cosmetics leftover from the masquerade ball, but she'd wiped enough dirt on it that it still looked frightening. Tear stains cut through the dirt on her cheeks. She couldn't see them, but she could feel the salty lines, and she was careful not to touch them.

Just as she hoped, she really did look pathetic.

Even her bare feet helped with the image, although she wished that part didn't have to be so authentic.

Time to break out. It would be slightly problematic because in all her planning, she counted on one guard being present. Not three.

Still, the opportunity was too good to pass up. Something was happening in the base, and that something would keep the Kessoku distracted.

With a silent breath, Talise began to freeze the key. The fire in her veins tempered the ice in her fingers, but this wasn't a normal freeze. The key had to be extra cold. Extra frozen. The colder the key, the more likely it would survive while turning the lock. She didn't have room for mistakes

With her ice shaping finished, her eyes swept across the dungeon corridor. How could she take out three guards instead of one? She usually had all four elements at her disposal. Since her last escape, the Kessoku had doused her cell and the surrounding corridor in flammable liquid. They hoped it would prevent her from using fire again. Since she wasn't an idiot, they hoped correctly.

They had also swept the dungeon corridor, so no extra dirt or stones lingered there. And even gathering enough water for the key had been a feat on its own. Which meant the only element available to her was air.

She'd have to get creative.

The dirt snake she made during the masquerade ball flashed through her mind. If she could make a snake from wind, maybe she could force the guards closer to her.

Shaping at that level of difficulty might be possible for her, but not immediately. It would take time and practice, neither of which she had now.

Another idea struck her that seemed too insane. She tried it anyway. At first, she was mostly curious about whether she could actually do it.

But then it started to work.

Pushing one hand in front of her, she reached out, feeling for the air that existed in the dungeon corridor. Then she reached upward, letting her sense of the air crawl up the stairs until she had reached the top of them.

Her sense ended at the top of the stairs. It probably wasn't possible to go much further than that in any circumstance, but maybe she'd practice again once she got out of prison.

Her next step took more effort. She grasped the air at the top of the stairs, then shaped it gently down the stairs. If the wind moved too quickly, the guards would know she used shaping to manipulate it. But if she did it slowly enough, hopefully they wouldn't realize what she had done.

Just as she hoped, the sounds from the top of the stairs suddenly seemed louder. Actually, they seemed closer, not louder exactly. It was like the sounds came from *on* the stairs instead of *up* the stairs.

Since the guards didn't realize she had shaped the noises closer, it probably sounded louder to them. Just like she wanted.

"What's going on?" one of them whispered in a voice loud enough to hear.

Soon, two of the guards disappeared up the stairs to investigate. Perfect.

Just one left.

The female guard, Beady, stepped closer to the prison cell. Distrust filled her eyes to the rim. But fear spiraled through them too. "Is this because of you?" she asked.

"Is what because of me? What's happening up there?" Talise tried to look innocent, but maybe a gleam of excitement snuck onto her face because Beady immediately scowled.

"I'm not telling you anything. I won't fall for your tricks like the others do."

Talise shrugged. "I wasn't planning to make you fall at all. This time, I thought I'd try a gag."

Beady jumped back, which only poised her even closer to the strip of fabric Talise levitated behind her head.

Using air shaping that even Wendy would be proud of, Talise wound the cloth around Beady's mouth.

Another strip of cloth soon wound itself around Beady's wrists. Since Talise moved the cloth with air, she couldn't pull it as tight as she wanted, but it was good enough for now.

The shackles clanked around as she stuck her ice key into the lock on the iron bars. Now it was time to find out if she really had enough water.

The key turned, but when the lock began to click, Talise could sense cracks forming in the center of the ice key. As quickly as she could, she melted only the very center of the key, then refroze it. Hopefully that would repair the cracks.

A wave of cold burst through her fingers. For a brief moment, crystals seemed to form under the skin. Terror swept through her.

Frostbite? She'd been ice shaping for months and had avoided frostbite completely. She'd gotten so used to ice shaping, had she gone too far this time?

Had she made it too cold?

She didn't dare send fire any closer to her fingers for fear of melting the ice key. But she did heat the skin under her wrists to get her shackles glowing hot. That would have to be enough for now.

The torch clattered to the floor after some impressive thrashing by Beady. This sent an alarm through Talise, but she couldn't remember why. The lock held her mind's entire focus. Her breath hitched as she turned the key.

The lock clicked open.

Freedom.

Talise immediately sent fire through her fingers, but the crystals still seemed to sit just under the skin of her fingertips. They didn't feel like crystals anymore anyway. They felt like needles.

One last blast of ice swept through her hands before she clanged her shackles against the iron bars. Just like her last escape, they cracked in half. She sent another wave of heat through her veins, eager to remove that frozen feeling from her fingertips. Nothing changed.

The heat around her didn't escape her notice, but she assumed it came from sending too much fire through her veins. But when she turned around, blazing flames burned through the corridor.

The torch. Beady had thrown the torch to the ground, and it had collided with the flammable liquid on the ground.

Everything around Talise burned. She had no water to douse the flames, and for the first time since she had learned it, she feared the consequences of shaping ice.

Just then, Beady's writhing form caught Talise's attention. The guard's wrists and mouth were still bound. The flames had nearly reached her.

Talise knew helping the guard would mean less time for her own escape. With a grunt, she rammed into the guard and forced her closer to the flames near the stairs. The guard's limbs flailed, but she wasn't strong enough to resist Talise's insistence. Or maybe the guard was simply too frightened to push back.

When the flames nearly licked the guard's face, Talise finally acted. She shaped her tiny ball of water into a spray of mist. This tempered the flames just enough so they wouldn't burn the guard. Beady made it safely through the flames to the staircase.

Talise stepped backward so the flames couldn't reach her. From the foot of the stairs, Beady eyed her carefully.

Talise had saved her life.

A flame roared between them. Now Beady was the one with a choice. Would she give Talise time to escape?

Even as the question entered her mind, Beady began to scramble up the stairs. Her eyes seemed intent on revenge rather than gratitude. No matter, Talise had a plan.

With any luck, the guards would put out the fire when they came down the stairs to catch her. That would help more than they knew.

Before she could think too much, she ran. Her feet slapped the stone corridor down the same path she took during her last escape attempt. With the flames roaring behind her, she easily ran faster than she had before. In almost no time at all, voices came from the staircase.

More guards would be down in the dungeon soon. She had to be out of sight by then. Her feet propelled her forward, but she kept her eyes pointing upward

All at once, she saw the small alcove in the ceiling. Her feet landed in an abrupt stop. She took in a deep breath. For some reason, her thoughts turned to Aaden. He would say this idea was insane. Ridiculous. The craziest thing she'd ever thought of. But he also would've believed she could do it.

She tried to hold onto that thought as she straightened her arms as stiff as rods. It had been impossible to practice this exact shaping technique in her cell since guards had been watching her constantly.

But she had been through the technique many times in her head. Hopefully it would be enough. With her arms still straight, she tilted her hands up until her palms were parallel to the ground.

Then, with as much force as she could muster, she shaped the air so that it shot out of her palms and hit the ground with great force. At first it did nothing and her heart dropped.

Closing her eyes, she dug deep inside. *Air shaping comes from the lungs* she said to herself. Filling her lungs with a heavy breath, the wind coming from her palms blew faster. And then, just as she had imagined in her head, her feet started to lift off the ground.

The further she got from the ground, the easier it was to keep rising. She shaped more air from around her and shot it to the ground. Had anyone ever shaped this way before? She wasn't flying exactly. It was more like hovering. But it felt like she could take on anything.

Soon, the ceiling was almost in reach.

Her spirits lifted the same as her body did. The clattering of swords and boots came down the hall, but it didn't matter. She was almost there.

Moments later, her fingertips reached for the alcove. Using a lip around the edge, she pulled herself inside just as boots pounded over the dungeon floor. Two dozen guards rushed through the corridor, just underneath her.

They shouted and growled, but not one of them bothered to look up.

And just like that, they had passed.

She was safe again.

Fearing the wind might be too loud, she decided to jump from the alcove and only use the wind shaping at the last second. Just enough to keep her ankles from cracking on point of impact.

Once on her feet, she could see the guards had put out the flames. Lucky her.

While the guards bounded down the corridor toward the chimney, she turned the opposite direction and headed up the stairs.

In her plans, Beady was supposed to be passed out on the ground so Talise could steal her clothes and blend in with the guards. Unfortunately, nothing had worked out the way she expected.

From here on out, she'd just have to wing it.

♕

Chapter Fifty-Seven

ESCAPING WITH BARE FEET HAD to be Talise's worst idea yet.

Each time her heel found a pebble, her muscles flinched in anger, and her brain kept screaming at her to slow down. Of course, she didn't.

This was her last chance to escape. If she didn't make it out now, surely Kessoku wouldn't bother keeping her prisoner anymore. They'd just kill her.

She bounded around a corner with her arms out, ready to shape if necessary. The upstairs corridors felt like a maze. Nearby Kessoku soldiers shouted and swore but not at her. In fact, they hadn't even noticed her. Whatever battle or attack was happening kept them fully engaged. She didn't have time to find out what it was. All she could do was run.

When she tripped over a water bucket, a few of the soldiers started turning her way. She ducked behind the nearest corner, increasingly aware of her burlap tunic. The burlap must have been servant garb because none of the soldiers seemed to be wearing it.

Panting breaths escaped her as she ran down the latest corridor. She'd gotten turned around completely. All her plans to listen for noises outside that would help her find an exit were completely lost. It was too loud now. For a moment, she stopped in tracks.

The water bucket. It had been filled with water and she didn't do anything with it. She should have shaped some of the water to carry with her in case she needed a weapon. At the very least, she could have drunk some of it. She needed the strength.

With a small huff, she whirled around. Maybe her feet and her head were right about the need to slow down. She'd never escape if she moved without thinking about simple things like water. As she tiptoed down the corridor, a door flew open right in front of her.

She raised her hands to attack, but after the hovering earlier, weakness plagued her muscles.

A tall figure stepped through the doorway, his back to her. When she glimpsed the side of his goatee, she nearly slapped him across the face, just for existing. But when she looked closer, she realized. It wasn't Lucian in front of her.

Talise lunged forward, her arms around him in seconds. It didn't matter that she was holding onto him from behind. He was here and nothing could keep her back.

"Aaden," she breathed into his crisp silver uniform.

Only a second later, she realized he wasn't hugging her back. Maybe it was because she had grabbed onto him from such a strange angle, but maybe…

Immediately, she stumbled as she took several steps away. "Sorry," she said, brushing a matted strand of hair out of her face. She took another step back, unable to look up at him. "I must be filthy."

At the sound of her voice, she saw his feet turn toward her. He stepped forward until his boots brushed up against the sides of her feet. She dared to glance up. Disbelief shone bright in Aaden's eyes.

He cupped her cheek, tilting her head up. His eyes went from her cheeks to her ears, her forehead, and finally to her eyes. He kept brushing the hair out of her face even after all the strands were tucked well away.

Tears brimmed under his brown irises. He seemed to be holding his breath. When he swallowed, his jaw flexed. The scar across his eye had turned white. The pink of a fresh wound no longer colored it.

Finally, he let out a breath. He dropped his forehead until it met hers. "I was so scared." His voice was husky. He gulped again. "I thought for sure you'd be…"

His words failed him then. A single tear dropped from his lashes and onto her cheek.

Without another word, he wrapped her tight in his arms. He pulled her closer, resting her head against his chest where she could feel his heart thumping.

Before either of them could fully enjoy the embrace, the shouts of nearby Kessoku soldiers brought them back to the present moment. Aaden drew a sword from its sheath. He looked at Talise's empty hands with a frown.

"Can you shape?" he asked.

She bit her bottom lip. "My muscles are weak, and I'm dehydrated." And she was exhausted from her earlier hovering, but she'd tell him all about that when they had more time. Her head hung. "I don't know how much I can do."

Without a word, he pushed his sword into her hand while he reached into his boot. Soon, she held his sword, and he held a dagger with flames carved into the hilt. He nodded, but only took one step down the corridor before he looked down at the dagger. Then, he looked at his sword still in Talise's hands.

He looked back to his dagger again.

He seemed to be thinking the same thing as her.

She wanted to laugh, but with their enemy so near, it wasn't the best time. Without a word, they switched weapons. The weight of the dagger felt much better in her hand. Wendy had been right all along. Talise was a dagger person not a sword person.

A soft smirk lingered on Aaden's lips as they started down the corridor. It delighted her how they'd both been thinking the same thing.

Her thoughts turned again. If Aaden was here, and the base was under attack, then she'd been right. This was a rescue. But the sounds of battle raged, and now that Aaden was here, if they didn't escape, the Kessoku could have two prisoners to bargain with.

They couldn't get caught again.

♕

Chapter Fifty-Eight

Talise and Aaden raced through the corridor. With thick boots on, Aaden didn't notice when his feet crunched over broken glass. Talise realized it a moment too late.

Her feet jumped in pain as the shards cut through her skin. She fell to the ground, unable to put any pressure on her feet. She plucked a glass shard from her heel, but many more remained.

Blood seeped out of her fresh wounds. Soon, it covered her feet, making it impossible to find the rest of the glass still embedded inside.

Aaden sucked in a breath. His jaw dropped at the sight of her bare feet. When the blood dripped onto the ground, he winced.

She bit her bottom lip as she reached for the hem of her tunic. "Maybe I can get something to…" Her voice trailed off as she tried to rip a strip from the burlap. The weakened muscles in her arms couldn't manage it. Suddenly, a woozy feeling spread through her. The ground tilted under her, and she couldn't tell if she was still sitting up.

How much blood had she lost? Or maybe her dehydration had kicked in.

A new figure appeared in the corridor with them. For a moment, it looked as if the man was going to bow to Aaden. His form stiffened when his eyes met Talise's. He pulled a sword from his side and charged forward.

Aaden struck him straight through the heart. Her blood loss must have been pretty serious because it seemed like the perfect moment to pull Aaden in for a kiss.

A shiver shook through her.

The past three weeks had been torture. She knew that. She had lived them. But she had hung on just enough to escape. But now her feet? She had one last thread holding her together, and it had snapped.

Everything unraveled. She had passed the limit of what she could handle.

Her body moved, but not because of anything she did. It took a moment to realize why. Aaden had lifted her into his arms. He was running.

The shouts around them grew louder, but then abruptly, they changed. Small chirps and rustling leaves joined the clash of swords.

Outside.

Aaden shouted. Suddenly, he set her down on top of something soft and bright white. They shouldn't have set her on something so clean. She'd spoil the linens in her dust-covered skin. Was that a strange thought to have a moment like this? Maybe.

The world went black.

But then it came back again, and everything was the same.

Except stars danced in her eyes.

Black.

Then white.

Was she inside a tent?

Why was the stone so soft? Wasn't she lying on stone? Or no, that wasn't right. She'd escaped. Right?

When she blinked, she let her eyelids rest for a moment. Just a little longer.

Liquid poured over her feet and her spine shot her straight up. Her teeth clenched together as needles seemed to slice through her legs.

"Lie back down." Aaden's voice was gentle, grounding. "You can squeeze my hand if it hurts too much."

He seemed to regret those words a moment later when another wave of liquid was poured over her feet. She squeezed so hard, his hand must've nearly broke. She clenched her teeth, suddenly remembering Kessoku. It probably wouldn't be good to scream out and give away their position. A small scream still escaped. She couldn't help it.

The liquid felt like acid. It seemed to eat away her skin and muscles until only bone remained. She checked four different times to make sure it hadn't. Through it all, Aaden's calm voice reassured her like a steady drum, grounding her and keeping her present.

It felt like hours had passed before the healers finished with her feet. While still working, one of the healers asked, "Do you have any other injuries?"

After feeling their remedies firsthand, she didn't really want to reveal her possible frostbite. The fear of losing her fingers won in the end. She raised her hand unsteadily.

"I think my fingertips are frozen."

The two healers pounced on her hand, staring at it with open mouths. One of them had a glint in her eyes. Talise wanted to rip her hand away and remind them she was not a science experiment. In the end, she didn't bother.

Aaden had started running his fingers along her forearm, and it thoroughly distracted her.

"You said you were dehydrated." She could hear the ache in his voice. "Did they starve you?" It wasn't like him to ask a serious question within the earshot of others. But, considering her recent kidnapping, they probably wouldn't get an abundance of privacy any time soon.

"No," she said, taking time to enjoy how the weight in his eyes lifted slightly. "Idiots," she added with a smirk.

He squeezed her hand in response. She decided not to tell him how they planned to start starving her that very day.

"They should have known it was only a matter of time before I escaped."

Aaden stroked her cheek as he smiled. It was a dangerous look. It made her forget other people existed.

A razor-sharp blade sliced over the tip of her finger, taking off a layer of skin with it. Talise yanked her hand back. The healer holding her wrist glared. Slowly, she extended her fingers once more, letting them do their work. She tried to sit still, but when the healer pulled off the skin from another finger, the pain bled through her. Her muscles seized as she fought to bear it.

"It's okay," Aaden whispered into her ear. He was stroking her hair now. "Just squeeze my hand when it hurts."

She had momentarily forgotten her free hand was still laced in his. It did feel better when she held it tight. Or maybe it just felt nice to have Aaden at her side.

The healers sliced another layer of skin off her pointer finger. She let out an involuntary gasp.

"Is this really necessary?" He offered a polite smile with the words, but Aaden spoke them through clenched teeth.

The nearest healer grunted, apparently too engrossed in his work to form words. The other said, "We have an ointment that will promote regrowth, but we have to remove all the dead skin first."

Despite her dehydration, small tears escaped through Talise's eyelids as another layer of skin was sliced away.

"Well," the tension in Aaden's voice pulled tight, "can't you hurry?"

Both healers glared in response. The news set Talise's muscles on edge. At least she only used one hand to make the ice key and not both of them.

Aaden leaned in closer. "It will be over soon. You're doing great."

She wanted to make some witty retort about how nothing about this was great, but the pain inhibited her ability to access wit. It was all she could do to keep from ripping her hand free of the healer's grip.

Luckily, Aaden was right. Before she knew it, the healers wrapped fluffy white gauze around each of her fingers. With everything finished, the pain already began to subside. Not normal, but better. And anyway, it would probably be a long while before she felt anything near normal.

Just as the healers left the tent, an anxious voice came from outside it.

"Why didn't anyone tell me earlier?" the hurried voice shouted.

Moments later, Wendy burst through the tent flaps with her hair in a messy braid. A slight sheen of sweat adorned her plump cheekbones. Her bright, black eyes looked Talise over from head to toe. At last, she let out a breath.

"Talise, you—" Suddenly, Wendy's nose wrinkled as she tried to cough away a gag, "smell awful."

Before Talise could chuckle, Aaden pulled her good hand against his chest. "It's not that bad."

Wendy clicked her tongue. "Yes, it is. You're just biased, so you don't notice."

Aaden's eyes narrowed as he pulled Talise's hand even closer.

Again, she fought back a chuckle.

"Don't worry," Wendy said, pulling a tent flap to the side. "I have buckets of warm water, lots of soap, and a few scrubbing tools. You'll be good as new in no time."

Aaden helped Wendy carry everything inside. Now fully conscious, Talise noticed she sat on top of a cot covered in a clean, white sheet. At the other side of the tent, two large tables stood with papers on top. She couldn't see past the tent flaps, but at least a few guards were probably standing nearby. Battle sounds tainted the air, which meant she hadn't been taken too far from the Kessoku's base.

Once Wendy set everything at the edge of Talise's cot, she waved Aaden toward the exit.

His lips pressed into a thin line. He folded his arms over his chest and planted both feet on the ground. "I'm not leaving."

Wendy let out an exasperated sigh. "In order to clean her, I have to undress her. I think the emperor would strangle you if he found out you were here for that part."

The determination in Aaden's eyes wavered for half a second. He reached for his elbow, squeezing it a little too tight. "What if something happens to her?"

Wendy brought two fingers to her forehead, impatience brimming in her eyes. "Do you know how many guards are standing outside this tent? Fifty. I counted them myself. You can join them if you like, but you need to be outside."

Aaden frowned, his feet unmoving.

Wendy's hands flew into the air with another exasperated sigh. "Do you *want* the emperor to strangle you?"

When he glanced back at Talise, his shoulder seemed to lean toward her involuntarily. He gulped, indecision still plaguing him. At last, he turned away. "Just promise you'll take care of her."

Wendy plastered a strained smile on her face before blinking twice. She waved him away again. When he didn't move, she flicked her hand against his arm until he started moving. She kept hitting him, speaking a word with each slap. "I have been her best friend ten times longer than you've even known her. I will take good care of her, I promise." She gave him one last shove.

The moment he finally disappeared behind the tent flap, Wendy let out an exaggerated groan. "He has been insufferable these past three weeks. You have no idea."

The chuckle that had been building in Talise's throat spilled out all at once. Soon, they were laughing. For the first time in too long, Talise's heart felt light.

It took three washings before Wendy declared the job finished. She said the smell still lingered, but after a few spritzes of perfume, she seemed satisfied.

Wendy even thought to bring clean linens, so Talise could lie down feeling as fresh and as clean as possible.

With the washing done, Wendy's face lost the look of purpose it had while working. It absorbed a new quality that seemed much darker than usual.

Did she wonder what the prison had been like?

Talise didn't want to discuss that topic yet. Since Aaden hadn't returned, she decided to use the moment to talk to the one person she trusted most.

Once her fingers landed on her friend's arm, Wendy froze in the middle of putting away a bottle of soap. She seemed to sense she should come closer. "What is it?" she whispered.

Talise pinched a piece of fabric between her fingers. The words rolled around in her mouth before she determined how to say them. "Have you ever heard of an amulet?" she asked, pinching the fabric tighter.

"Sure," Wendy said, returning to her task of putting the soap away. "Isn't it a pendant or some other kind of jewelry? Wait." Her eyes went wide. "*Man* jewelry? Is it man jewelry that you're thinking about getting for…" She gave two meaningful glances toward the tent flaps as if pointing to them.

Talise waved her hands in front of her face while a blush crept into her cheeks. "No, it's nothing like that." She resisted the urge to fan the heat from her face. "I'm talking about a specific amulet. Something…" Her hand reached out as if trying to grasp the word she wanted from the air. When nothing came, she just said, "powerful."

Wendy shrugged as she carried the box of soaps over to the entrance of the tent. When she turned back to grab the water buckets, Talise swung her legs off the cot, so she could help.

After a heated glare from Wendy, Talise slowly moved her legs back.

Wendy moved the water buckets to the entrance before pouring something into a mug on one of the tables. With the mug in one hand, she twirled a small piece of hair through her other. "Didn't Kamdar have an amulet? He used it to give people shaping abilities or something."

Talise frowned. "I've never heard that."

Wendy pulled her lips into a tight knot as she twirled the hair even faster. "I thought I learned it in a history class, but maybe it was before I went to the elite academy in the Crown."

After several more seconds of staring off into space, Wendy shrugged. "We'll have to ask Claye when we get back to the palace. He loves doing research. And he always remembers the most obscure things. Here, drink this."

"Claye isn't here?" Talise asked as she took the mug of what turned out to be cool cider. The crisp liquid sent a flurry of cinnamon, nutmeg, and clove down her throat in a pleasant cascade. Her question suddenly seemed strange now that she thought about it. Why would Claye be there? With Aaden and Wendy nearby, maybe a part of her just felt like Claye should be there too.

Wendy showed the smallest hint of a scowl before it went back to its normal sweet look. "The emperor wouldn't let him come. He said because Claye is a *gardener* not a *soldier* and some other nonsense."

Talise let out a chuckle before leaning back into her cot. The pillow seemed even more comfortable than before. So did the cot. Or maybe they just felt nice because they weren't a stone floor. Whatever the reason, they seemed more comfortable than anything she'd ever known.

Her eyelids drifted closed for a second too long. She had to force them back open. "Can we go back to the palace now?"

Wendy shook her head. "No one knows your true identity." She let out a sweet shrug. "Except me, Claye, and Aaden, obviously. And whoever else already knew. In order to justify rescuing you, we've had to pretend the real goal was seizing control of the base. That's what the palace army is doing now."

"How can I help?" Talise's words ended in a long yawn. She'd just been racing through the corridors of Kessoku's base less than an hour before. She assumed her adrenaline wouldn't allow her to rest yet. But maybe all the exhaustion from the last three weeks had finally caught up with her.

Wendy brought a small stool over to the cot's side. Her eyes were suddenly anxious. "You didn't see Cyrus, did you?"

It felt like wading through mud as Talise brought her mind back to the conversation. These words needed her full attention, but each second it was more difficult to keep her eyes open. "I didn't see him. I didn't see anyone from the palace."

Hopefully she conveyed at least a smidgeon of the sympathy in her heart.

Wendy's expression turned indifferent. "It's fine. We know this isn't Kessoku's main base. We're still in the Crown. We know they have at least one base in the Gate. According to latest intelligence, they might have a few. The other prisoners are probably there."

Talise tried to swallow over the lump in her throat. She wanted to believe that as much as Wendy did, but she'd also seen how they treated their prisoners. The only reason Talise had been kept alive was for information. The other prisoners had been killed within hours.

The cot seemed eager to swallow her. With a heave, she tried to sit up. "Where's that dagger? Aaden gave me a dagger on our way here. I just need to get some shoes on, and I can go join the battle."

Wendy laughed as she pushed Talise back into the bed. "You're not going anywhere, especially not with your feet cut up. You are staying here until you've slept through the night. The fifty guards outside will make sure you stay put in case you get any ideas."

Her eyes were fluttering closed again, but she managed to clench her jaw and let out an angry huff.

Apparently, her effort made Wendy giggle. With a sweet smile that looked slightly devious, she said, "Besides, that sleeping draught I gave you should be kicking in right about now."

Talise didn't bother sitting up since it felt like her shoulders were filled with wet sand. She did manage to shoot an accusatory frown at her friend. "The *what* you gave me?"

"Emperor's orders," Wendy replied with a wink.

While Talise tried to arrange her sleeping face into a scowl, Aaden appeared and shooed Wendy away. He ran his fingers through Talise's hair, which felt much nicer than she expected.

She wanted to accuse him too. She wanted to use her most fiery voice and ask if he also knew about the sleeping draught. But sleep tickled at the edge of her mind making her mouth betray her. In a mumbled voice she asked, "Now that I'm all clean, don't you want to kiss me?"

Aaden let out a light chuckle. That smile could have kept her alive through any amount of starvation.

"Yes," he said, letting his fingers slide through her hair. "But not while you're falling asleep like this. Tomorrow. After you've rested."

His last words felt like a dream, beckoning her into a deep and peaceful sleep.

Chapter Fifty-Nine

THE WALL WAS COMING DOWN. Behind it, a storm raged.

Talise knew she was dreaming because the wall had a shimmery quality along with a slight blue glow. Crowds of people surrounded her, but none of them had distinct faces.

Her clothes were even more dream-like. She wore a dark purple gown with silver crescent moons threaded through the silk in a rich brocade pattern. The skirt was ridiculous. Its train trailed at least three dress lengths behind her.

The wide bell sleeves fell down past her feet. Every few seconds, she pushed the sleeves up to her elbows, but they'd fall back down almost immediately.

Most conspicuous, her head felt heavy under the weight of a crown. The thick belt around her waist had been pulled tight, making it difficult to breathe.

She was a princess.

Just as the thought came to her, a strong grip tugged her by the wrist. The folds of her gown tripped her with each step, but the tugging at her wrist only grew more insistent. Talise glanced through the crowd, trying to see where she was being pulled.

Between heads, she could barely make out a small squadron of soldiers, each wearing a tunic with a yellow hem. Her soldiers.

She gasped and glanced back at the wall. Her heart stopped at the sight of it. Danger. The word gripped her, shook her as she stared. Pieces of the wall crumbled to the ground. Some spots looked ready to burst apart.

Bad. This was bad.

Talise ached to rush toward her soldiers. They would need her protection once the wall came down. All at once, the figure pulling her along became distinct. Not just a random person from the crowd. It was… her.

Her?

She pulled herself, but this version of her wore a silk tunic and training pants. This part was the Master Shaper.

Before she could even imagine what that meant, another figure grabbed her other wrist and tugged her the opposite way. The second figure was just a child, but she dug her nails into Talise's wrist, forcing her to take a few steps in the desired direction.

The glittering tiara and orange velvet dress gave her identity away much sooner than the other. This was Princess Talise.

Master Shaper Talise tugged on the left while Princess Talise dug in her nails on the right. Each pulled her in opposite directions, turning the dream world into a hazy fog. She blinked away the tears that burned her eyes and tried to ignore the tugging.

The wall.

Didn't they understand? The wall was coming down. It didn't matter if she was a Master Shaper or a princess. She had to stop the wall from coming down.

She only managed one painful step forward before the wall crumbled before her. Exultant shouts cried out as the wall fell like dust to the earth. The storm behind it thundered and shook the ground.

Her eyes narrowed as she tried to make out who was so happy. The figures around the wall blurred, but one figure she recognized.

Lucian Sato punched a fist into the air while a wide smile split across his face. The others around him wore Kessoku's symbol on their backs.

They knocked the wall down. They had freed the storm.

The tugging at Talise's wrists grew more insistent. Master Shaper Talise wanted her to fight with the soldiers. Princess Talise wanted her to give a speech at the emperor's side.

They both seemed to think their needs were most important, but only Talise understood what was about to happen. She took a step back. Then another.

More.

She tripped over the swaths of fabric behind her, but it didn't stop her from backing away.

Even as she moved, she knew it wouldn't save her from the onslaught.

As the Kessoku cheered, figures appeared among the mist of the storm. They hardly looked like people at all.

Their teeth jutted out in long, sharp fangs. Animalistic claws grew straight from their knuckles. They didn't speak. Instead, they let out hisses and spits. They attacked everything around them without any hesitation.

Claws ripped through the Kessoku until their symbols had been painted with blood. Fangs ripped through muscles and bone.

Her soldiers were falling. Citizens were falling. Kessoku was falling.

The animal people let out growls and turned their attacks onto each other. Their eyes glowed gray and blue with flashes of white. Exactly like a storm.

Terror gripped Talise as she watched people fall on every side. The storm people frightened her the most, but then, nobody liked people from the Storm.

They were dangerous. Criminals.

She tried to run. Her feet had melded to the ground. Her heart raced.

They were coming.

She held her breath, waiting for the thrashes, the slices. The death.

Then, a new person appeared. This one didn't have a figure. She was nothing more than a voice in Talise's ear. A memory.

"You must help them, love."

A voice of honey and sparkles.

Marmie.

Who? Talise wanted to shout. Her mouth hung open, urging the word forward, but it wouldn't come. Tears streamed down her face while every muscle inside her froze.

Who do I help?

As Master Shaper, her duty belonged to her soldiers. As princess, she owed her allegiance to the emperor, to the crown.

But long ago, she'd been a citizen of the Storm. Did she owe something to them? Those people *were* dangerous, but only because they were desperate. It wasn't their fault. Was she supposed to help them?

How could she choose?

And what about Kessoku? Surely Marmie didn't think *they* deserved help. She couldn't possibly want Talise to aid her enemy.

An animal-man with stormy eyes growled as he approached her. Black coated his mouth while black veins spread out around it.

I'll help you. She tried to say it, but her throat had filled with sand.

The man howled as he took his claws to her dress. Pain dropped onto her stomach, causing her to wake with a start.

CHAPTER SIXTY

"SORRY!" A GIRL GRABBED A heavy scroll from off of Talise's stomach as more apologies spewed from her lips. "I was trying to put it away in this chest, and it slipped out of my grasp."

Sleep weighted Talise's eyelids down. Her heart still raced from the horrific dream. The edges of the room slowly came into focus as she blinked.

After rubbing her eyes, everything became easier to see.

A tent. She was inside of a tent. Sleeping on a cot.

She let out a breath of relief as memories of the day before came back to her. She'd been rescued.

Even though it had ended, the dream kept her heart pounding. She forced herself to focus on the present moment.

The girl who dropped the scroll didn't have Wendy's sweet smile or bright eyes.

Instead, she wore a soldier's tunic with a blue hem. One of the better soldiers, except still one of Talise's. In fact, it was the same soldier who had defied her in front of the emperor, but who later trusted Talise enough to tell her about the Kessoku spies in the ballroom.

"Tempest," Talise said as she sat up.

Tempest's eyebrow raised. "You remember my name?"

Laughing seemed like an appropriate response. How could she forget? Emotional memories were the easiest to remember and every interaction with Tempest always seemed to have so much emotion. But even as Talise tried to laugh, it wouldn't come.

The haunting shadow of Marmie's voice still lingered at the back of her mind. Competing allegiances fought inside her, no matter how she tried to ignore them.

"Where is Aaden?" Talise expected a protest when she swung her legs off the cot, but Tempest seemed to welcome it. "And Wendy. She's my friend. Do you know Wendy?"

A hint of a smile appeared on Tempest's face. "She's inside the base. So is Aaden. So is practically everyone." With a bit of a scowl she added, "Except me."

"Can we join them?" Talise leaned forward as she asked, gripping the side of the cot a little too tight.

For a moment, Tempest's eyes lit up. A moment later, her face fell, and she let out a groan. "No, we have orders to stay here. They said you need to recover."

Judging by the face Tempest made, she didn't seem overjoyed about being chosen to stay back.

Talise grinned. She could use that.

"Do you know where they are? What they're planning?"

Tempest hopped off the stool and showed her first real smile. Pointing to a diagram on one of the tables, she said, "It's all right here. They sent in a scout yesterday after Aaden found you. The scout created a map of the base, and he found this awesome tunnel thing that leads from the dungeon corridor down to their main strategy room. That's where all the top Kessoku members are now. We have soldiers fighting outside the base, but the real fight is going to start in about an hour. A squadron is going down the tunnel to surprise the Kessoku."

Tempest looked enormously pleased with herself as she finished the explanation.

With each of the words, Talise's heart jumped higher into her throat. She ran a finger over the tunnel and down one of the mapped corridors.

"Is this the dungeon?" Talise asked, pointing to the paper.

Tempest took the diagram into her hands and turned it sideways. She mouthed a few words while nodding at different rooms on the map. With a curt nod, she said, "Yes, it is."

Take a breath. Talise put one hand over her forehead as she forced herself to suck in air and let it out slowly.

When finished, she scanned the room. First, she needed clothes. She couldn't wear the soldier uniform Wendy had given her yesterday.

At the end of her cot, her burlap prison clothes were tossed on top of some boots.

Perfect.

She stripped down to her underclothing and went straight for the burlap.

Behind her Tempest stood eerily still. "Um, what are you doing?"

Before Tempest finished the sentence, Talise already had the prison clothes on. She reached for the boots and pulled them on in time to get a whiff of the clothes. *Blech.*

They really did smell awful.

Pain nudged through the cuts on her feet as she pulled on the boots but not too much for her to handle.

Tempest's foot began tapping on the dirt ground of the tent. "Remember when I said we have orders to stay here? I'm not supposed to let you leave."

Talise spared her a single glance. "That tunnel leads to an incinerator. Once they go down, the only way out is to go back up. By the time they realize what the tunnel is, Kessoku soldiers will be at the top waiting for them, and a bonfire will be at the bottom ready to burn them alive."

When she stood, Tempest was squeezing her forearm. She stared at the ground. "Do you think they could get hurt then?"

Talise shook the linens on her cot, hoping to find the dagger Aaden had given her the day before. "Definitely."

After shaking the linens again, Talise noticed the dagger sitting just under her cot, as if it had been placed there with care. The fluffy gauze on her fingers stretched as she plucked it up.

"But," Tempest said while squeezing her forearm again, "I have orders to keep you here."

The dagger fit perfectly in the little belt Talise fashioned from a strip of extra linen. "Do you want them to die?"

"No."

"Then you'll let me go." She marched toward the tent entrance expecting no resistance.

Tempest caught her by the wrist, which sent her back to her dream for a single frightening moment. Shaking away the memory, Talise glanced back at her soldier.

Tempest had a bit of her lip stuck between her teeth. "I don't want them to die, but I have to follow orders."

Talise pulled her wrist free and let out a sigh. Her heart started to sink, but in a flash, the world brightened. "Who gave you the orders? The emperor? General Gale?"

The soldier shook her head slowly, as an idea seemed to be sprouting in her mind. "No, it was Master Shaper Aaden who gave the order."

A smile grew on Talise's face at the same rate as her soldier's. "Well, I'm a Master Shaper, too, am I not?"

Tempest's smile continued to grow as she nodded.

With a smirk, Talise said, "As Master Shaper, I'm giving you new orders. You are to stay here while I rescue the others."

"Oh." Tempest's shoulders fell as she dropped her eyes to the ground. "I thought you would want my help." She turned around and wrapped a hand over one of her elbows.

Talise blinked. "It would require water shaping. I know the fire balls were difficult for you. I don't want to ask something of you that would be too difficult."

With a twirl, the soldier turned around, her eyes beaming. "I know my fire shaping is dismal, but water is my primary." Her chest puffed up. "I can collect rainfall for three hours before I get tired."

Excitement caught on fire inside Talise's toes. "Perfect. We just need to find you some new clothes."

♔

CHAPTER SIXTY-ONE

IN THE END, TALISE GAVE the prison clothes to Tempest. Neither of them loved the idea, especially because it meant Tempest had to endure the smell of Talise's three weeks in prison. But neither one of them could think of another way for Talise to sneak past the fifty guards outside the tent.

Talise's chin-length hair would be a problem. She braided it as well as she could, but it didn't look close to her soldier's typical long braid. Hopefully the guards would be too bored to notice. She snatched the diagram of the Kessoku's base from off the table and buried her head in it.

Her boots fell heavier than usual as she marched out of the tent. The pain from her cuts skittered across her feet with each step. If she showed the slightest sign of hesitation, the guards might recognize her. They might recognize her anyway but acting like Tempest had to count for something.

She held her breath the whole way. A few steps outside the tent, one of the guards did call after her. "Where are you going? You're supposed to stay with Master Shaper Talise."

Her throat constricted. Would they recognize her voice if she responded? Tempest had been easy to convince, but could she convince fifty other guards to defy orders and let her into the base?

"Eat flames, Phoenix. I'm just getting her a drink."

The voice came from the tent, but it was Tempest's voice. *Phoenix* apparently didn't seem to notice the odd direction. From behind her, Talise heard a soft chuckle. She squared her jaw and kept marching forward.

Once she passed the large tent, she snuck into an area of the Kessoku base that had already been seized by the palace army. Talise pulled the diagram drawn by the palace scout from her pocket. Her finger traced over a small room labeled *Servant Quarters*.

She frowned at the door in front of her.

It was a risk going into the quarters before the base had been officially seized. But Tempest insisted the army already had control of this part of the base, so there shouldn't be any servants inside.

With a deep breath, Talise pushed open the door. She let out a breath at the sight of the empty room before her. It didn't take long to find an extra pair of servant clothes to change into.

A few minutes later, Tempest burst in through the doorway with a maniacal grin on her face. "They're looking for you. But I told them you wanted to go back to the palace, so they're looking in the wrong direction."

Talise raised an eyebrow. "Remind me not to get on your bad side."

"You already did," Tempest said with a laugh. "As I recall, it didn't work out too well for you."

Wincing in pain, Talise stuffed her foot into a boot while wearing her new servant garb. She glanced up at Tempest, barely suppressing the grin on her face. For someone who so adamantly followed orders, Tempest definitely had a devious side.

"Come on," Talise said. "We need to find water buckets and get down to the strategy room."

TALISE HAD SMEARED gobs of dirt over her face, but it still felt like the Kessoku soldiers all stared at her. With each step down the tight corridor, their eyes seemed to pierce her skin. At any moment, she could pass one of the guards who had watched over her in the prison cell. They could recognize her. At any moment, she could be caught.

The balls of her feet hit the stone with each step but not her heels. Each time they got close, her heels would bounce, forcing her heart in her throat again.

"Did you hear about the princess?" one of the soldiers whispered.

Talise nearly froze. How could it be a coincidence that a guard talked about her right as she came near?

The Kessoku guard's voice didn't waver as she kept walking. He punched a fellow guard while wearing a wide grin. "The general asked if she had ever seen Emperor Kamdar's gravestone, and she said yes."

The guard next to him rolled his eyes. "She's gone, remember? What good is it if we can't even use her to find the gravestone?"

"It means the amulet is real." Hope glimmered in the guard's eyes.

Hope.

That was a word she hadn't thought about in a long time. It reminded her of a letter from Marmie, but she couldn't remember exactly why.

"Stop dreaming." The second guard jabbed his friend in the shoulder. "Just because the gravestone is real doesn't mean the amulet is."

The first guard's eyes took on another layer of hope. "It has to be. The amulet is our only chance to win this war."

The second guard looked ready to jab his friend again, but he seemed to notice how Talise's steps had slowed.

"Hey!" he shouted in a gruff voice.

Her head dropped as she shuffled forward. The guard yanked her by the wrist until she stood right in front of him. Still, she kept her head down. Her heart thumped wildly.

Tempest's boots knocked into Talise's, but the guard waved her on. "Not you. You go ahead."

The ground crunched as Tempest backed away. The guard's grasp began to burn around Talise's wrist. He scowled. "I swear, the people in Kamdaria keep getting stupider."

The lump in Talise's throat hardened. The room had too many people for her to run from. With Tempest's help, she could take on at least half the guards. Maybe after that, they'd get a chance to run.

"Look at that blank expression." The guard snarled at her as he spoke. "Do you have anything inside that brain, little servant?"

Talise blinked. She assumed he had recognized her, but now? "D… did you want something?"

Her voice wavered with each word, which seemed to prove whatever point the guard was making. He lifted her wrist higher until it hung level with his eyes. Only at that moment did she realize he had grabbed the hand that held the water bucket.

"Oh!" Talise quickly nodded and dropped the wooden ladle inside the bucket. Did the other servants usually shape the water out of the ladle?

Before she could ask, the guard snatched the ladle out of her hand and dumped the water onto his head. He let out a quiet sigh, then did it again.

Her jaw clenched. Her fingers wanted to form fists, but that would probably look a little suspicious. Instead, she curled her toes inside of her boots until they ached in pain.

She needed that water.

It took everything in her not to shape it out of the guard's hair and put it back in the bucket where she needed it.

At last, he dropped the ladle into the bucket with a sneer. "Don't forget to offer water to the other guards. He caught her wrist again. "And no more eavesdropping, or I'll tell the general to send you back to the Storm."

She couldn't get away from him fast enough. Soon, she scuttled just behind Tempest as they continued down the crowded corridor. His words stuck inside her like sap.

The Storm? That's where they got their servants? So Lucian hadn't lied about that, after all. No wonder they got away with treating their servants so badly. If the alternative was the Storm, they'd probably be willing to endure anything.

She pushed the thoughts to the back of her mind. That was yet another thing she'd have to consider once she got back to the palace. That list had almost grown too long to endure at this point.

Aaden's father worked for Kessoku. Kessoku was looking for an amulet that could supposedly give them the power to win a war. Kessoku had someone working in the palace that may or may not have been one of her friends.

Her head visibly shook side to side, and one of the guards gave her an odd look. No. It wasn't one of her friends. She had gone over the evidence enough times. The betrayer could have been anyone.

Once she caught up to Tempest, it didn't take long to reach the end the of the corridor. They slipped into the shadows without much trouble. Perhaps being a servant did have some benefits. Nobody treated her with dignity dressed as she was in these clothes, but they hardly noticed her either.

The entrance to the strategy room didn't have a door. Instead, a large archway had been cut through the stone. The room it led to had large couches and tables with simple furnishings.

There were no guards standing in the archway.

Maybe it was a message. Maybe Kessoku wanted its people to believe there were no secrets. Anyone would be welcome in the strategy room at any time.

That seemed like such a foreign concept to Talise, who had grown up smothered by lies. Thinking of a world without them felt both intriguing and terrifying.

As they inched forward, more of the room came into focus. A dozen Kessoku soldiers bent over a large table as they whispered with each other. Talise looked for Lucian first, still desperate for any kind of revenge.

He wasn't there. As one of the Kessoku guards had said earlier, he must have left long ago.

She turned to Tempest, pulling the bucket of water closer to her chest. "Are you ready?"

♔

Chapter Sixty-Two

THE ARCHWAY INTO THE STRATEGY room provided the perfect cover. Talise and Tempest crouched to one side so they could shape the water out of their buckets and onto the floor.

According to the plans Tempest had overheard, they still had a few minutes before the palace squadron arrived down the chimney.

"Is that it?" Tempest whispered as she pointed to the back corner of the room. A short wall only a few bricks high had been built to enclose the corner. Inside the short wall, stacks of wood reached almost as high as the ceiling.

A small pile of clothes and papers sat next to the wall, probably waiting to be incinerated. Maybe the clothes had worn out that was the purpose for burning them. Or maybe they were evidence of some kind. If the chance came up, she'd try to save the items to go through them.

At the moment, more pressing information stole her attention.

The bonfire wasn't lit.

Fear clenched inside of Talise at this observation. She hoped the incinerator would be burning, then the palace squadron would realize the danger before climbing all the way down. But now?

They would get to the end of the chimney, the Kessoku would light the fire, and they would burn before they had a chance to climb back up. For the few who managed to escape the flames, the Kessoku would send soldiers to meet them at the top. They'd be killed the moment they exited the chimney.

That realization only deepened Talise's resolve. Maybe she had defied orders, but that entire squadron—including Wendy and Aaden—would soon be dead if she hadn't. Princess Talise wouldn't approve. But Master Shaper Talise did.

Turning back to her soldier, Talise shaped a small ball of water from the water bucket. "They'll probably use fire shaping to light the wood as soon as they hear people coming down the chimney. Hopefully our people get down pretty far before that happens."

Tempest nodded. "And then we'll shape a water dome over the fire to protect them, and you'll turn some of it to ice, so they can slide down the side."

Talise nodded without a smile. She doubted things would work out as easily as they planned. For one thing, ice shaping concerned her. The tips of her fingers still throbbed from the healers' treatment on her frostbite. But it was too late to second guess anything. Now, she could only focus on protecting the palace squadron.

She shaped the small ball of water from the bucket and straight onto the stone floor. Before it could seep into the stone, she moved it so it would slide across the stone almost like a stream.

Except it wasn't really like a stream at all because she kept the water just above the stone so it wouldn't flow. She and Tempest needed to get their water from the buckets over to the incinerator, and they had to do it without any of the dozen Kessoku noticing.

Tempest leaned onto the balls of her feet as she watched the water glide over the stone floor.

Talise moved it slowly enough to look like a water spill, except the puddle moved.

Still on the balls of her feet, the soldier slowly raised the water out of her own bucket. It lowered to the ground in a sweeping movement, devoid of any jerkiness.

Impressive.

For the first time ever, Talise wondered if her soldier had gotten a place in the palace the same way Wendy had. Because of her shaping.

Soon, the two puddles slithered silently over the stone. Not one member of the Kessoku had noticed it yet.

When they finally got the water close enough, Talise's stomach clenched in terror. The piles of wood dwarfed their two tiny puddles. Maybe it would be better to abandon their plan and douse the wood now. Except, they didn't have enough water for that much wood.

Besides, with strong enough fire shaping, the Kessoku could dry out the wood in no time. Before she could consider any other ideas, noises trickled down from the chimney.

The Kessoku noticed at the same time she did. It only took one hurried whisper before three of them lit the wood into burning flames.

Tempest grinned wildly. "Let's do this."

Talise formed the dome with ease, especially with Tempest's help. But the fire began turning the water to steam within seconds. Still, the water must have shielded the people inside the chimney from at least some of the heat.

Shouting echoed through the room.

It wasn't clear if the shouting came from the chimney, the Kessoku or both, but there was little time to figure it out. And there was little point in hiding. The Kessoku knew the water came from somewhere. They'd find her and Tempest soon enough.

Rather than wait for the inevitable, Talise marched out from behind the archway. She kept the water dome in place with her right hand and held the flame-carved dagger in her left. When two

Kessoku came near, she sneered as she raised the dagger toward them.

"By order of the emperor, you will all surrender." She raised the dagger again as if to make her point.

Her tenacity definitely surprised them. That was something at least. But it didn't take long to begin an attack.

Five of them drew swords and another four raised their hands, ready to shape. The others scuttled to the other side of the room where Tempest stood.

Talise decided to ignore them. She couldn't fight off all twelve of them anyway. Hopefully Tempest could handle the rest.

Before she could get her bearings further, one of the Kessoku punched fire balls toward her. Another sent a wall of wind. She dodged them both, but the fire caught the hem of her tunic. A flame burned at her waist.

She dropped to the ground in a tight roll, letting the stone floor smother the flame as she moved. Keeping her right hand out, she just managed to keep the water dome in place. When she got back to her feet, she shaped a wall of wind at the Kessoku while she ran toward the chimney.

They dodged her wall as easily as she had avoided theirs. But she had no time to think about that now. More shouts rang through the room, and those ones definitely came from the chimney.

The water dome shimmered as it began to lose integrity. Fire flooded her veins as she prepared to shape ice. The moment the cold split through her, needles of pain stabbed into her fingers where the frostbite hadn't finished healing.

Without a second thought, she tossed the dagger into her right hand and tried shaping ice with her good hand instead. But her fingers shook, and her heart beat too wildly. She couldn't tell how much heat to use. She couldn't feel how much cold she needed.

With a gulp, she accepted the truth. No more ice shaping, At least for now.

She nodded to herself and began running through new ideas in her head. Considering the situation, she thought she handled the news with a fair amount of cool.

Someone jumped onto her back and held a knife to her neck, which ripped her focus from the dome for a split second.

Her knees collapsed. While the knife blade flirted with her throat, her eyes fixated on the water dome. Or where it should have been.

Nothing remained but the flames now licking high into the chimney.

She lost concentration for only a moment when the Kessoku jumped onto her back. But it had been enough. Too much. The dome of water fell into the fire, which left the palace squadron unprotected.

Her heart jumped into her throat.

That reminded her of the knife still lodged against it. *Deal with the knife first.* She couldn't do anything to help her soldiers with a blade at her throat.

Her elbow sank into the Kessoku man's gut. He grunted but didn't release the grip of his knife. Crushing the top of his foot with her boot seemed like the next logical step, though it did send a fresh slice of pain through the cuts on her feet.

It also forced a gasp from her attacker. He didn't let go, but his grip loosened just enough for her to twist around.

The heel of her hand jammed into his nose in an upward motion. Finally, the knife dropped to the ground as the man took chaotic steps backward. By the time he reached up for his nose, drips of blood already drained out of it.

More Kessoku ran toward her, but she sent another wave of wind at them. With so much desperation grinding through her insides, it wasn't difficult to create a stronger wind than before. This one knocked them all off their feet.

Tempest fought on the other side of the room. Her movements involved a sword, but Talise didn't have a spare second to look closer.

Her eyes turned back to the fire. Small flames near the top wisped upward in a strange motion before they would vanish. Suddenly, a memory of the masquerade ball came back to her. Wendy had saved her from two fire arrows by shaping the air away from them so they couldn't burn.

Now Wendy must have been doing it again.

Talise grinned. With even more force than she used on the wall of wind, she sucked the air away from the fire.

The oxygen starvation didn't work as well as she wished, but it did temper the flames greatly. For a moment, they lowered to tiny flames.

With her feet planted on the ground, she raised her hands to do it again. The second time, the flames turned to embers.

Two people jumped from the chimney onto the glowing wood, which sent sparks flying everywhere. She thought she recognized Aaden's goatee, but a moment later someone had grabbed her by the waist.

Without thinking, she swung her dagger back until it sank into flesh. She felt her mouth twist in horror as she rounded on her heel to see who she had stabbed. The Kessoku man gripped his shoulder while gnashing his teeth.

She ripped the dagger from his body, but a second later, her body slammed forward onto the stone. Twisting her body, she rolled onto her back with her face forward. A Kessoku guard with two broken teeth towered over her. He aimed his slim sword straight for her heart. His boots shoved her arms so they were pinned at her sides.

Wriggling seemed like her only available tactic, but that wouldn't get her far.

Her breath caught in her throat. This was it.

CHAPTER SIXTY-THREE

THE THIN SWORD ABOVE TALISE glinted in the light. Her shoulders moved side to side, trying to free herself from the Kessoku soldier's grasp. It wasn't enough.

As his sword dove toward her, a large stone crashed into it, forcing it off its course until the tip clanged against the stone floor. Before the soldier could react, Aaden tackled him to the ground. A palace guard Talise didn't recognize stuck a sword through the Kessoku's uniform, piercing his heart.

The palace guard turned without a second glance, already focused on his next target. Aaden jumped to his feet and offered a hand to Talise.

Her heart was still galloping like horses, but at least it didn't have a sword through it.

"You're supposed to be resting," Aaden said as he pulled her to her feet.

She glanced back at the glowing embers as she brushed the dirt off her tunic. "If I had stayed back in the tent, you'd be dead now. I think what you meant to say was *thank you*."

His grin made her heart jump, but at least it jumped in delight instead of terror. She moved closer to the chimney to get a better look inside it. "Is everyone down yet?"

Even as she asked, two more palace soldiers jumped down from the small opening. A small burst of wind kept the fire sparks from spreading too far.

"That was the last of this group. We have another group coming, but they're trying to seize one of the rooms upstairs first." Aaden had drawn his sword. His grip looked tighter than usual. Apparently, even he could forget proper grip in a dire enough situation.

For a moment, the world seemed calm. As calm as it could be under the circumstances, at least. With the arrival of the palace soldiers, most of the Kessoku were already dead. The others fought hard, but it wouldn't be long before the palace soldiers had control.

Her eyes danced around the room in a gut-wrenching panic as she saw a woman with shiny cheeks fall under a sword. After jerking toward the fight, she realized with relief that the woman wasn't Wendy. Her best friend stood in the corner fighting off a Kessoku with a clump of dirt and a small tornado.

Wendy clearly had the upper hand.

Aaden rested his hand on her back. It felt nice to lean into his touch instead of cowering from it as she had spent pointless months doing. With a growing grin, he asked, "How did you get past—"

"Duck!"

Tempest's voice cut through the stillness just as an arrow whooshed past Talise's ear. Aaden yanked her toward the ground as he drew his sword. Three more arrows shot through the air while Talise fumbled to grip her dagger.

Palace guards trampled toward the new threat, but more Kessoku archers spilled into the room from the stone archway. After a single blink, two of the palace soldiers were dead.

Even more Kessoku soldiers poured into the room, each carrying weapons poised and ready to kill. Another palace soldier fell before Talise could finally get a grip on her dagger.

On her hands and knees, she crept toward the Kessoku soldiers, ducking behind tables as she moved. Another wave of men wearing Kessoku's symbol burst into the room.

One archer pointed an arrow at Wendy and Talise moved without thinking. Her left hand shaped a circle of wind. It shook so much it was difficult to keep the wind crown steady.

When the archer pulled back the string on his bow, Talise's arm acted on its own. She threw the dagger into her wind crown. The Kessoku man collapsed to the ground the moment her dagger sank into his heart.

His bow clattered to his side with the arrow still in place. Her heart stopped.

She had used the dust trick to ensure Kessoku soldiers died back at the palace. She had been standing right next to Kessoku soldiers and palace soldiers as they met their death.

But this. This was her first kill.

It ripped her heart in two. It shred her soul to pieces. A single action but one that had changed her forever.

Aaden pulled her back behind a table. For a moment, she had forgotten about him. He took her hand and held it against his chest. "You did it for Wendy," he said.

And then her heart started again. It took one slow beat. And then another. The pulses felt too weak, but then it all changed, and they felt too strong. Too heavy.

Her head fell as she nodded.

The warmth in Aaden's hand brought her back to reality again. He squeezed gently and brought her fingers to his lips.

"For Wendy," she repeated, though the words felt like dust in her mouth. She cleared her throat. "And for Kamdaria."

Aaden's smile had vanished, his eyes were already back on the fight. No matter how her heart squeezed, they had already wasted too much time behind that table. Her jaw clenched as she jumped back into the fight.

Talise shaped walls of wind whenever she could. She blasted fire balls into as many interlocking circle uniforms as she could find. She didn't want to kill. But just like at the palace, Kessoku made the fight necessary.

She whirled around on her feet, sending fire balls all around her. She felt Aaden at her back, his sword swinging in one hand while the other he used for shaping.

A Kessoku soldier used two swords to fight. Talise slammed a wall of wind against her. When the soldier's back hit the ground, it knocked the wind out of her.

With the soldier out of the way, Talise noticed a pair of Kessoku she hadn't seen before. Two willowy Kessoku, one man and one woman, scuttled through the room on their tiptoes, just missing the blades and fireballs that sliced through the air.

But they didn't just prance around with no intent. Each of them gathered papers and maps from off the tables.

Talise shaped a large stone from a corner of the room and slammed it into the nearest Kessoku's gut. This gave her room to get a closer look at what the two Kessoku gathered. They took most of the papers from the tables, but they checked underneath before pocketing them.

Were they looking for something?

Talise blew an oncoming Kessoku soldier off his feet as she stalked even closer.

"I got the prison records," the man whispered as he tucked a leather-bound notebook into his tunic. The leather had been embossed on the front with a design that looked like a gate. But from so far away, Talise couldn't tell for sure.

"We still need the amulet research." Panic laced the woman's voice as she lifted another set of papers off a nearby table. Her eyes lit up. "*Here* it is."

Another leather-bound notebook sat in her hands. This leather looked much softer, as if old and worn from frequent use. The front didn't have a fancy embossing like the other. But it did have a symbol scratched onto its surface.

A circle with four symbols inside, one for each element. The Master Shaper symbol. According to Lucian, it was the same symbol that adorned the powerful amulet he sought.

The Kessoku woman tossed the notebook to the man just as she looked over her shoulder. When she saw Talise's eyes on her, her eyes narrowed to a glare.

The woman pulled something with a shiny blade from her tunic, but Talise had already ducked before it could hit her.

By the time she looked back up, the man and woman had neared the archway that led out of the room.

Talise needed that amulet research. She needed the other notebook too. If it really contained Kessoku prison records, then it would have information about Wendy's brother, Cyrus. The battle in the room waged, but those notebooks would be worth any risk.

She glanced around for a quick assessment. Wendy stood in one corner with a palace soldier on either side of her. Loose strands flew from her braid, but her shaping was magnificent.

Wendy didn't need help.

Glancing behind her, Talise quickly determined Aaden also didn't need help. A little more sweat than usual slid down his hairline, but other than that, he looked his usual self.

Just as Talise decided to chase after the notebooks, far too many things happened all at once.

A shrill wail cut through the air. She identified it in an instant.

Tempest teetered on one foot while a line of blood slid down her opposite leg. She had a sword in one hand, but two Kessoku soldiers fought her at the same time. Even with her palace training, Tempest struggled against two at once.

The man with the notebooks neared the archway. If he got much further, Talise would lose sight of him completely.

Talise's gut pulled in two different directions. It felt just like her dream.

Master Shaper Talise would want her to help Tempest. Princess Talise would want her to go after the notebooks.

Too many allegiances fought for her attention. Was she a Master Shaper or was she the princess? Who needed her help the most?

She took one step toward Tempest, shooting a fire ball at the attackers. But then Talise took two steps back, anxious to keep an eye on the man with the notebooks.

Everything around her moved so fast, and it felt like she couldn't breathe. She just needed a moment. Just one second while she tried to decide.

A heavy silver vase swung down and suddenly the dilemma wisped away like an afterthought.

Aaden.

One of the Kessoku soldiers had slammed the vase onto Aaden's head, knocking him out. His body hung limp as the Kessoku threw him over his shoulder.

Before Talise could shout or attack or anything, the man ran toward the archway with Aaden on his back.

The noises of the room faded to the back of her mind. The movements around her blurred into indistinct forms. With perfect clarity, her mind focused in on the only thing that mattered.

She had to get Aaden back.

Chapter Sixty-Four

Talise sped over the stone floor.

The cuts on her feet twisted and stung as she ran. The man carrying Aaden over his shoulder moved with impossible speed. He jumped over rocks and fallen bodies like they were tiny flowers in a meadow.

When he rounded a corner, something whispered at the back of her mind. *Be careful.* Where did that corridor lead?

But visions of sword-wielding Kessoku popping out from the corner weren't enough to slow her steps. If Kessoku wanted Aaden, there had to be a reason. Or a *person* who wanted him.

Her heart twisted when she remembered the moment she laid eyes on Lucian. She harbored an enormous amount of hate for that man. Every time she thought of him, she remembered when Aaden's voice broke in the treasury. He spoke of how his father had ruined his life.

But if he was given the chance, would he let his father repair their relationship? No matter how much bitterness he nurtured, could he really deny his own father?

None of that mattered. It didn't matter at all because she would rescue Aaden, and he never had to know about his father.

She rounded a corner just in time to see the Kessoku man disappear through a doorway. The wood dug into her palm as she slid the door open again. The man jumped at the sight of her, which sent Aaden to a crumpled mess on the floor.

Her heart caught in her throat when his head bounced on the stone. She didn't have time to worry. The Kessoku stood in front of her with his muscled arms at the ready.

"Get out!" the man shouted at her.

She attempted a smile. "Funny. I was about to say the same thing to you."

Apparently, he didn't care for comedy. The man balled his hands into fists. When the first one swung toward her, she let it swipe across her ear. The next hit, she took a careful step back so it would hit her in the stomach. But not too hard.

Just when the man took a confident step forward, she jammed her foot into his ankle. His arms flailed as he lost his balance. While he teetered, she slammed the side of her palm into the man's neck.

It wasn't perfect. He saw the hit coming and tilted his head away just enough that the blow didn't knock him out. But he did land hard on his backside. With his attention on dodging her blow, he did nothing to catch his fall.

The resulting hit on the stone floor caused the wind to knock out of him. He let out a few coughs, immediately following them with huge gulps of air.

Just when the man prepared to take another gulp, Talise shaped the air away from his mouth, leaving him even more oxygen starved than before. He clutched his throat and tried to take another breath.

Talise shaped the air away from him again, then delivered a more precise hit to his neck. This time, he lost consciousness.

Before his shoulder even hit stone, she had reached Aaden's side. His cheek jiggled as she patted it in quick bursts. "Wake up, wake up." Her voice felt stretched out and thin. "Please hurry, Aaden, I don't know how long he'll be out."

When he didn't move, she cradled his head in her lap and patted his cheeks even harder. "Aaden!" she said through a hiss.

Finally, his eyelids began fluttering. She let out a breath of relief as she ran her fingers through his hair.

"Well, this is a nice way to wake up," Aaden said, reaching for her face.

She held his hand against her cheek long enough to put on a smile. Then, she began to stand. "We have to get out of here. I don't know how long he'll stay unconscious."

Aaden followed her pointed finger over to the unconscious Kessoku. His eyebrows flew up to his forehead. "You knocked him out? By yourself?"

She was already hurrying toward the door as she nodded.

He grinned. "You're very impressive, do you know that?"

Heat crept into her neck and through her cheeks. "We need to go, Aaden. The fight is still going. They need our help." Her fingers curled as she gripped the hem of her tunic. "And I saw this notebook the Kessoku grabbed. Actually, there are two notebooks. One has information about Wendy's brother, and the other one…"

A knot of fear twisted inside her. But why? She had talked to Wendy about the amulet. Wendy knew even more than she did. So, why was she so hesitant to mention it to Aaden?

"We need to talk." Aaden had moved so close she could feel his breath ruffle her hair. How had he recovered so fast?

He looked afraid. Or possibly apprehensive. No, concerned. He looked concerned and that concerned her.

When he reached for her, his hands felt cold. Her eyes shot up to his, but they didn't speak to her the way they usually did.

She could only see how the skin wrinkled at the bottom corner of his eyes. It perfectly mirrored the almost frown he wore. Her heart skittered. It wasn't sure whether to speed up or stop altogether.

Just when Aaden opened his mouth again, the Kessoku let out a groan. Talise moved her hand into Aaden's grasp when he offered it. Before the man could stir again, they were already flying down the corridor hand in hand.

Talise pointed out the way back to the fight, but Aaden only shook his head. He led her down another corridor until a few empty rooms came into view. He chose the closest one and slid the door closed behind them.

Her palms felt clammy as she pulled away from his grasp. His lips had moved to form a tight line. His eyebrows knitted together.

Forget concerned, she was straight up scared now. She feared the silence, but she feared his words even more. "We have to get back to the fight," she said. "And I *need* those notebooks. We don't have time to talk."

Again, he ignored her insistence. He slid the door open a crack and glanced outside before he turned back to face her. Was he looking for someone?

Her heart decided to turn into a mallet, slamming against her chest.

"The emperor asked me to be a spy." He wouldn't look at her as he said the words. His eyes kept jumping to different corners of the room. He gulped.

Did he have to be so fidgety? Her fingers shook just from looking at him. She clasped them behind her back, desperate to regain some control. "What does that mean? He wants you to follow the Kessoku who leave this base? He wants you to sneak up on them as they travel?"

Aaden gulped again, which made her increasingly aware of the lump in her throat. His fingers ran over his normally neat hair, which sent at least four strands out of place. "He wants me to join them."

She blinked.

"To *pretend* to join them," he quickly amended.

When he reached for her, she took a step back. "No."

Thoughts went reeling inside her. A hundred and one versions of that story rushed through her mind and not one of them had a happy ending. "You can't do it. It's too dangerous. What if they find out you're lying? What if they trick you? What if they hurt you?"

Aaden sighed as he rested his forearm on the nearby wall. "I don't love the idea, but you have to admit, they're more likely to trust me than anyone else. The emperor wants me to do it today. He wants me to join the retreating Kessoku as soon as we gain control of the base."

His voice nearly broke as the words came out. His nose wrinkled as if his statement tasted like bile in his mouth.

"Don't do it. You *can't* do it. What if you start to believe…" Her voice trailed off before she said anything too incriminating, but it didn't matter.

The scar over Aaden's eye twitched as his eyebrows drew closer together. His eyes held pain. She could see how it affected him. He thought they were past this. So did she. But the truth hung between them as present as it had ever been.

She didn't trust him.

Her throat constricted when she tried to speak. She wanted to reach for him, but her arms seemed pinned at her sides. "Why did you look up my testing record?" she asked. "You found out I could shape all four elements when I was tested for the academy, but that's not what you wanted to know. What were you trying to find?"

He leaned into the wall as he let out a sigh. "Is this really the best time to ask me that?"

His words sliced through her gut. He wanted her to believe he had an innocent purpose, yet he gave no reason for her to believe otherwise. "Just tell me why." Her boots scraped the floor as she took a step forward. The reluctance in her voice had carried down to her toes. "Was it really because you wanted to know how someone from the Storm could shape?"

He gave her a single glance before staring back at the ground. His silence spoke more than words ever could. No. That wasn't the reason, and he wasn't going to tell her the real one.

She took a step back.

He reached out to her immediately. "I know you don't understand, but I have to do this. I have to be a spy."

"Why?" Tears started burning in the back of her throat. "You said the emperor *asked* you. So technically, it wasn't an order."

He curled his hand into a fist and pressed it against his forehead. "No, it wasn't an order, but I still have to do it."

She folded her arms across her chest. "What would happen if you don't? Did the emperor threaten to beat you again?"

The loose strands from Aaden's hair fluttered as he shook his head. "He didn't threaten…" His head cocked to the side. Suddenly, he stared into her eyes with a deeper intensity. "What do you mean *again*?"

A puff of air burst through her mouth as she tightened the muscles in her arms. "I know he beat you that day after you told him to stop yelling at me. You defied him, and then you left the training hall without being dismissed." She looked to the side, digging her nails into her arms as she spoke. "The next day your face was covered in bruises. You wouldn't explain what happened, but it wasn't hard to figure out."

"That wasn't the emperor." Aaden's voice came out flat. His jaw tight.

She let one hand wave through the air dismissively. "I don't mean him personally. I assumed he had one of his guards do the actual hitting. So he wouldn't injure his precious hands."

"No." Aaden stepped toward her. "It wasn't the emperor. He knew nothing about that until after it happened."

Talise narrowed her eyes. "Then who was it? How can you expect me to believe—"

"It was my grandfather."

Her eyes flew to his.

"He's the one who hit me."

Her limbs had frozen while the words trickled through her. His *grandfather*. Commander Blaise was the only person she had ever seen

Aaden give unflinching respect to. But had that respect been earned from fists?

Aaden went back to the wall. He rested his forearm on the stone and pressed his forehead into his forearm. "The emperor told my grandfather what happened in the training hall and he…" An audible gulp sounded through the room. "He wanted me to remember it is unacceptable to defy the emperor."

Her voice was still frozen. Her feet were lead. But she managed to reach out and touch his hand.

"It's fine." His hand jerked away from her. "I don't need you to. …I'm fine. I just didn't want you to think it was the emperor."

"Aaden." She wanted to talk, but what could she say? No words seemed adequate to heal the raw edges on her heart.

"Why don't you trust me?" An ache clung to his voice, but his eyes broke her. They were pleading. Hurting.

It pained her to see him like this. To know she contributed to his pain. So, she said the words that plagued her. It may have been a mistake, but when he looked at her like that, she could deny him nothing.

"Your father works for Kessoku."

A flash of fire went through his eyes. His head jerked as if shaking away an irritation. "No. He never worked for them. It wasn't like that. He—"

"I saw him."

Talise knew these words would surprise Aaden, but she didn't expect him wrap his arms around his stomach like he'd been punched in the gut. "What?"

Her fingers found the hem of her burlap tunic, and she stared down at it, unable to meet Aaden's eyes any longer. "He came to the dungeon. He questioned me." She pulled at the hem, forcing a thread loose just so she could pull it out. "The other Kessoku called him *general*."

"No." It was more an appeal than a statement. His fingers dug into his scalp, throwing his hair into complete disarray. Suddenly, his eyes shot up. "How do you know it was him? Maybe he just *said…*"

His voice trailed off when she shook her head. "You look just like him," she said under her breath.

She could practically feel his soul crushing as he pressed his forehead against the stone wall once more. She didn't want to hurt him any more, but she didn't have the luxury of time. The battle still waged in the other room and decisions needed to be made now.

"If you pretend to join Kessoku and your father is there, what would stop you from turning to their side? He's your father."

And your grandfather apparently likes to hit you is what she didn't add. She reached for him, desperate for contact. "No one could expect your allegiance to the crown to be stronger than your allegiance to family."

The moment she reached him, he wrapped his hand around her waist and pulled her a few steps closer. He used his other hand to stroke her cheek as he stared into her eyes. "Maybe my strongest allegiance isn't to the crown or to my family."

She turned her face away. "Don't say that, Aaden. Don't give me hope like that when there is so much at stake. He's your *father.*"

Heat seeped into her back as Aaden's arm got warmer. "He left me."

"This is Kamdaria," she said with a sigh. "Family lasts forever."

His hand slid around her waist until it found her spine. Without stepping forward, he moved his body closer. He gulped. While tracing small circles into the small of her back, he asked. "If I do what the emperor asks and become a spy, you won't ever trust me?"

She buried her face in his chest, relieved when he brought his arms around her tight. "I want to trust you. You have no idea how much I want to. But he's your father, I can't ignore that. And… and they do have some compelling ideas, but their methods are all wrong. If you go, I'll spend every second wondering if you've already turned. I can't do that to myself. And it isn't fair to you either."

When she pulled away, he seemed to understand. At least his eyes looked subdued rather than angry. She took a step back, and a chill spread through her. "If you go, I can't keep doing this." She gestured at the air between them. "Whatever *this* is, I can't do it if you pretend to join Kessoku. No more kisses. No more private moments. It would be over."

His signature smirk graced his face as he reached back out to her. "But if I stay?"

She obliged without a thought, stepping into his embrace. The heat of his lips felt like fire in her mouth. But the kind of fire that warmed the heart, not the kind that blistered skin.

The door crashed open.

A fist came swinging toward them before Talise could get her bearings. The fist caught her in the jaw, swinging her head back.

Her skull jarred after the hit. When she blinked the stars out of her eyes, she recognized her attacker. The same man who had knocked out Aaden earlier.

He wasn't happy.

Chapter Sixty-Five

TALISE SENT HER OWN FIST at the Kessoku soldier attacking her. She jabbed and kicked with wild abandon, not focusing enough for targeted attacks. But how could she focus when Aaden just stood there?

His hands had flown twice as if to hit the soldier, but when it came time to do so, he simply blocked the blows instead.

Was he going to do it? Was he going to leave her and become a spy?

He glanced back at her while indecision colored his every feature. After a glance into her eyes, his jaw flexed. He lurched forward, barreling into the man's chest. He sent two hard blows to the man's head.

The man didn't lose consciousness, but he paused in pain long enough for Talise to jump past him toward the door.

Aaden caught her hand before they took off down the corridor. This holding-hands-while-running thing wasn't the most practical idea in the world, but deep down she needed it. For a moment, she truly believed Aaden would abandon her.

It felt nice to feel his presence at her side.

When they reached the archway leading to the strategy room, Talise's feet planted to the ground with an abrupt stop.

An empty room sat before them. The only people left were corpses.

"*There* you two are," Wendy said from down the corridor.

Talise whirled around to see her friend with a dagger in each hand. Wendy's flushed cheeks shimmered with sweat. Her hair looked more knotted mess than braid. A tear ripped through one side of her tunic, but no blood stained the fabric at least.

Talise glanced back at the empty room. "Is the fight over?"

"Not yet." Wendy jogged toward them, her breath coming in sharp pants. "Our reinforcements came a few minutes ago. Most of the Kessoku have retreated, but a few of them are still fighting. We pushed them out to the edges of the base."

Wendy tossed one of the daggers toward Talise.

"Thanks," Talise said when she caught it. She caught a glimpse of the flame-carved hilt and bit her lip. Slowly handing it toward Aaden, she said, "Actually, I guess this is yours."

He pushed it away, letting their hands touch a little longer than necessary. "Keep it. This isn't over yet. Where is everyone?"

Without a word, Wendy beckoned them as she ran down the corridor. They turned a few times. Talise lost the last sense of direction she had in those few turns. Everything seemed unfamiliar to her now. Dirt caked the stone in this part of the base. Debris littered the ground. Everything from broken chairs to smashed ink pots and even a soft blanket covered the floor.

After a few more turns, the noises of battle became clear. Weapons clashed, but they didn't seem as loud as earlier. Just before Wendy ducked through an archway, a shadow caught Talise's eye. She glanced back and noticed two figures tiptoeing down an opposite corridor.

Without a word to the others, Talise bolted after them. Their willowy figures made them easy to recognize. These were the same two Kessoku who had snatched those notebooks. They must have been looking for a way out of the base that didn't take them through the middle of a battle.

After a few steps, the Kessoku seemed to realize they had someone on their heels. Their speed increased. Talise urged herself to run faster, but the throbbing cuts on her feet protested.

When they disappeared through a doorway, Talise growled and forced herself to run harder.

Footsteps pounded from behind her. A moment later, Wendy appeared at her side, heaving as she brushed the hair away from her face. "I know they're Kessoku, but they don't even have weapons. Just let them go."

Talise shook her head, which disoriented her more than she expected. "They have information," she said through a pant. "Notebooks."

She couldn't manage anymore while running. Wendy nodded and pushed forward.

The Kessoku tried to escape through a doorway, but a wall of fire appeared in front of it. Since Talise hadn't done it herself, it had to have been Wendy or Aaden. It looked like Aaden's work.

At last, they reached the end of the corridor. The two Kessoku found themselves facing a wall. They each turned and backed into it as if eager to disappear inside.

"Give me the notebooks," Talise said through her teeth.

The two Kessoku glanced at each other with looks of horror.

"Both of them." Talise hoped she sounded authoritative. Did other leaders do that? Did they constantly worry if their voice held enough authority, or if they were even doing the right thing? Maybe someday she'd get used to the feeling.

When Talise stepped forward, panic seemed to ignite in the female Kessoku's eyes. "Do it," she said to her companion.

The man nodded and wrenched the two notebooks from his tunic.

Talise lunged, but she couldn't get there fast enough. While she moved toward him, he threw both notebooks into the air and shot each with a fire ball. Flames engulfed the pages inside before she had a second to breathe.

No.

It couldn't be too late yet. She just had to put out the fire. There had to be something salvageable inside. There *had* to be.

Talise's mind whirled while the notebooks fell. By the time they reached the ground, she had made her decision. They fell on opposite sides of the corridor, so she couldn't put them both out by herself.

She didn't choose the notebook that fell closest to her. Instead she lunged for the notebook with the gate embossed on the cover. The notebook with information about Cyrus. Using her body, she smothered the flame, hardly noticing or caring whether it burnt her clothes in the process.

"Save the other one," she shouted as she jumped.

In a flash, Wendy had jumped over the notebook that held the amulet research.

Amidst the chaos, the two Kessoku had run. Aaden went after them, but they had moved too fast for him.

Talise dropped herself on top of the notebook a few more times before she dared lift her body completely. When she did, the brown leather had been singed black. She sucked in a breath as she lifted the corner.

The edges of the paper were blackened, but most of it had survived. She let out a breath. Her heart throbbed as she gingerly turned page after page. All of them were safe.

The paper didn't look pretty. Some pages burned more than the others, but the information remained untainted.

After closing the notebook, she held it against her heart and let out a long breath. The pulsing in her veins nearly stopped as she turned around.

Wendy held her hands outstretched, the notebook with the amulet research perched on top. She bit her lip, staring intensely, as if too afraid to open it.

Talise nodded, urging her friend to act.

Wendy reached for a small bit of hair and twirled it once before she finally grabbed the corner of the notebook. When she opened it, the pages inside crumbled to ash. Her eyebrows flew up her forehead as she forced the notebook open even wider. She looked eager to find even one page that had survived.

But not one had.

Ash fluttered to the ground in blackened heaps.

"I wasn't fast enough." Wendy's head hung with the words.

It hurt. They had needed that notebook too. But Talise merely pulled the other notebook closer to her chest. "It's okay." She had made her decision, and for once, she didn't question it.

Aaden came down the corridor toward them with heavy steps. "I lost them," he said in a dark voice.

Talise tucked the notebook into her burlap tunic as she stood. "It's okay," she said again. When she started back down the corridor, the others followed without a word. Just before rounding the corner, someone rushed around it, slamming into Talise.

The collision caused her to take several steps backward.

The person's hair flew out in a wave around her face as she fell backward. When she landed on the ground, Talise finally recognized her.

Tempest scrambled to her feet and grabbed Talise by the shoulders. "Master Shaper Talise." She rested her head in her hands as she let out a big sigh. "Oh, I'm so glad to see you. I thought you were dead." She flicked Aaden in the arm. "Aaden would have killed me." Her hand flew upward as if reaching for the ceiling. "The emperor would have killed me." She glanced to Talise's side. "*Wendy* would have killed me."

"Where is everyone?" Talise asked.

Tempest waved her hand through the air. "Oh, all over. We seized the base. All the Kessoku have been killed, been taken prisoner, or they've escaped. A group of them are retreating now, probably to their base in the Gate."

Aaden twitched at these words, but he didn't move. Apparently, his decision was final too.

Wendy continued, "Then, some of the army will stay here to maintain control, but it's time for the rest of us to go home."

Home.

For the first time in three weeks, Talise could breathe.

Chapter Sixty-Six

On her way up to the palace doors, Talise couldn't help thinking of six months earlier when she had arrived for the competition.

Aaden had hated her then. He might have already been planning a way to sabotage her demonstration. Wendy and Claye had been whispering hurriedly, both anxious to find out if their demonstrations would be enough to get them jobs inside the palace.

Things seemed simpler back then. Their lives hadn't yet been tainted by the recent attacks. Talise hadn't been broken by the difficulty of the trials. She and Aaden were still enemies.

The past six months since the competition had been anything but easy, but Talise found gratitude for every moment of them. They shaped her into someone new. Someone better. She poked her tunic, feeling through it for the notebook inside.

At last she knew who she really was.

A set of guards trailed both in front and behind Talise. Supposedly, her true identity remained secret, but being guarded this heavily everywhere she went was bound to make people suspicious.

For now though, hopefully everyone would assume her Master Shaper status afforded her the extra protection.

Even the smell of the palace felt familiar as she walked through the doors. With autumn approaching, the cherry trees had long since lost their blossoms. But the cedar walls and beams gave off a familiar scent. And the usual dinner smells of ginger and soy wafted through the air.

To her surprise, the guards didn't lead them toward the throne room. Instead, she noticed a long line of people spilling out of the throne room doors. Many of them wore scowls, and at least half had their arms crossed over their chests.

The guards took them around a few corners until they reached the hallway leading to her own living quarters. The guards left then, allowing her mind more room to think. Before she could wonder at the line of people coming from the throne room, a friendly voice came from behind her.

"You're alive." A beaming smile covered Claye's face. He nearly knocked Talise over with the force of his hug. "We received word yesterday, but I was afraid to believe it."

His presence brought her a surprising amount of comfort.

"Of course she's alive," Wendy said wearing an even bigger smile. "We'd never let her rot in some stupid dungeon."

Claye took a step back and tapped his chin as he looked Talise over from head to toe. The whole thing made her feel like a child whose parent was trying to decide if she was ready for school.

"You don't look too underfed," Claye said, still tapping his chin. Suddenly, he stopped and pointed. "What happened to your hand?"

Talise let out an embarrassed smile as she lifted her gauze covered fingers. "Frostbite."

He mouthed the word before he let out a laugh. "Well, at least we know you aren't invincible." He laughed again and pulled her in for another hug. A minty smell clung to his clothes.

"We missed you," he said in her ear before pulling away.

The moment he stepped away, Aaden reached for her hand, lacing their fingers together.

A smile grew on Claye's face when he saw their hands. He leaned forward. "Aaden's the one who found you. Did he tell you that?"

At her side, Aaden shuffled one foot across the ground. He wouldn't look her way, but the hint of a smile lingered on his lips. That didn't surprise her. Aaden never bragged.

Claye bobbed his head up and down. "Yep. After you were taken, he stayed up for two days straight trying to find you. The emperor finally had to order him to get some sleep. Aaden was…" Claye tapped his fingers together under his chin. "How do I put this lightly?"

"Not happy?" Wendy suggested.

Claye let out a snort. "Ready to murder everyone who kidnapped you is probably more accurate, but yeah, let's go with *not happy.*"

When Aaden pulled her closer, she went without hesitation. "Let's go. I'm sure the emperor wants you back in your living quarters." He looked over his shoulder, his eyes narrowing at the sounds coming from the rest of the palace.

Once they were on their way, Talise asked, "Who were all those people in the throne room? Why were they in a line?"

Aaden, Wendy, and Claye all glanced at each other while silence hung in the air. Aaden gulped. Wendy twirled a piece of her hair.

"Yeah," Claye said, elongating the syllable for several seconds. "Remember how Kessoku attacked and killed the Master Shapers and a bunch of other people, and the emperor decided not to tell anyone? And remember how Kessoku attacked at the masquerade ball in front of a bunch of citizens?" He shrugged. "Now everyone knows about the attacks. All of them."

Talise blinked.

"The people are angry," Aaden said. "They're mad the emperor lied to them."

Wendy clasped her hands in front of her chest. "We're doing damage control, but…" She pursed her lips as she looked to the side. "It's going to be awhile before the emperor gains their trust back."

When they arrived at Talise's rooms, she shoved everyone inside. She pushed Aaden and Claye over to the two chairs at her breakfast table, then sent Wendy to the chair in front of the desk.

As she pulled the notebook from her tunic, she made a mental note to get two more chairs for her breakfast table. "I heard two Kessoku talking when they found this notebook." Her voice lowered, leaning even closer to her friends. "It contains prison records." Her eyes turned to Wendy. "Kessoku's prisoners."

Claye seemed to just manage to suppress his eye roll, but he didn't drain all the sarcasm from his voice. "How *exciting*."

"Cyrus." Wendy's voice came out as a whisper. Claye's sarcasm had been forgotten. Even Aaden leaned closer to the notebook.

Talise nodded. "We need to give the notebook to the emperor. If it has information about the prisoners, it could also have information about their bases and possibly leadership, that sort of thing." Talise gulped as she handed the notebook out to her friend. "But I thought you should get a chance to look at it first."

Wendy took the notebook solemnly. Her eyes showed real hope for the first time in a long time. With the leather in the hands of her friend, Talise knew she had made the right choice saving that notebook and not the other.

Now they could know once and for all if Cyrus was alive.

CHAPTER SIXTY-SEVEN

THE WOOL CAPE AROUND TALISE'S shoulders fought the chill of the outside air.

She hadn't visited the palace graveyard at all since she won the competition. Her last time seeing it had been through the gate that separated the graveyard from the grounds of the elite academy.

But tonight, death was on her mind. So many prisoners had died. So many had been tortured and killed without reason. Without cause.

But not all of them.

Cyrus was still alive. The news had been enough to make everyone cry. Wendy had skipped around Talise's living quarters with joyful tears streaming down her face. After a few minutes of that, she had pulled them all into a group hug and even Aaden cracked a smile.

The day got even better when they had given the notebook to the emperor and discovered it named all of Kessoku's bases and even gave vague location details for a few of them. New plans had been made in a matter of hours.

They were going to find Kessoku's bases in the Gate and seize control of all of them. If things went according to plan, their enemy might be beaten by Water Festival in mid-winter.

Talise hugged the cape tighter around her shoulders.

But not all the prisoners had survived. As joyous as the day had been, a wedge had driven itself into Talise's heart when she remembered the first casualties of this war.

At last, she found the gravestone that had prompted so many of her tears. Kneeling in front of the stone, Talise read her mother's name.

Isla Tempest Malksur Ruemon

Empress of Kamdaria

Over a thousand marks adorned the grave, but Talise traced her finger over the mark carved just under the *I*.

Talise had made that mark. As a five-year-old, her shaping hadn't been advanced enough to leave a proper mark. But Marmie had helped her use a mallet and chisel to carve in a small mark. It had been night then too.

She and Marmie had left their marks in the dead of night before they ran to hide in the most unlikely place of all. The Storm.

Talise leaned her head against the stone and reached for her heart just as it seemed to splinter into pieces. She and Marmie had risked getting caught just so they could leave a mark on the graves of their family.

The marks on her brothers' and sisters' graves had been left in a hurry, but Talise had still marked them because this was Kamdaria, and family lasted forever. Even in death.

Her throat ached. Her stomach churned. The tears fell as the memory of her risks took hold. She'd been able to risk her life for the graves of her mother and her brothers and sisters, but not for Marmie.

She had made her peace with that. Or tried to anyway. But sitting in the graveyard, the pain cut through her as she imagined Marmie's grave sitting bare in the Storm. Not a single mark to honor it.

Talise swiped her wrist across her nose before she pulled a worn letter from her cloak. No matter how bare Marmie's gravestone was, Talise was still determined her sacrifice would never be forgotten.

Though technically her aunt, Marmie had become a second mother to Talise even before the Kessoku's attack. She had always been there when Talise needed her. Even in her dream at the Kessoku base.

The letter crinkled as Talise smoothed it out. She read the words that had helped her so many times.

Without hope, people have nothing. They aren't happy; they don't live. But the smallest things can change that.

Marmie had been talking about the flower she finally got growing in the Storm, but the words held so much more meaning to Talise now. Just like in her dream, Talise knew people from the Storm were dangerous and frightening. But they only needed hope, and that could change everything.

She still had to find out more about the amulet, and they still had to stop Kessoku and seize their bases. They had to find and rescue Cyrus. But more than ever, Talise knew she had more than that to do.

She would save the Storm.

In Kessoku's base, so much turmoil plagued her while she tried to decide if her role as Master Shaper or as princess was more important. She wondered if the soldiers needed her more or if the emperor did.

The notebook had changed everything. As Master Shaper, she would have let the notebooks go and focused on seizing the base. As princess, she would have saved the amulet research to ensure the emperor had everything he needed to fight his enemy.

But she had chosen something else entirely. She chose Kamdaria. The people of Kamdaria needed to know what had happened to their family members. Now, thanks to the prison records, they would be able to find out.

Clasping the letter tight in her hand, she lifted her eyes to the sky. Whispering, she spoke to the air. "You died for me, Marmie. I promise I won't let your life be lost in vain."

Talise took in a breath, squeezing the letter against her heart. "Of all the titles, I've held in my life, I finally realized which is the most important. From now on, I'm not just the princess or a Master Shaper. I will be Defender of Kamdaria."

Tears slid down her cheeks as she finished. Her throat seared from the ache. After touching her mark in her mother's grave once more, she took a few minutes in front of the other graves. She touched her mark on each grave and thought of their lives. Honored them.

When she had finished, her heart felt both full and empty all at the same time. They were gone now, but she would make things right.

While tucking the letter back into her cloak, the sound of crunching gravel made her freeze. She looked into the night for whoever had found her. Perhaps one of the emperor's guards had noticed she snuck out of bed.

A tall figure wore a cloak over their head making the face unrecognizable. But the figure didn't seem to be there for her at all. Whoever it was moved swiftly past the graveyard toward the boats that led to the Gate.

She followed without thought. When her own footsteps began crunching over the gravel, the hidden figure turned. For a moment, the light of the palace spilled onto his face. Even after he hastily dropped his head, so the hood would hide him, it didn't matter. She had already seen.

Aaden.

She clutched her chest while her throat swelled. Was it possible for her heart to break any more? Apparently, it was.

She glanced down at the boats and then back to Aaden. He turned away with his shoulders hunched, as if trying to make himself look smaller.

The boats took people to the Gate. The Gate only had one thing he would want.

Kessoku.

With her throat so tight, she had to squeeze her voice through. "I thought you weren't going to go."

He had the decency to look her in the eye. He pulled his hood back just enough that she could see how pain traced over his features. "I wasn't going to but…" His voice seemed even tighter than hers. He stared with longing in his eyes before he looked down. He dropped his head into his hand. "He's my *father.*"

The patter of her heart sent a flurry of terror through her entire body. "Please don't go."

His lip trembled before he whirled around. "I have to." His fists tightened at his side as he began stepping faster than before. When she followed after him, he flicked his hand as if shooing her away. "I'll report back in two weeks. If I'm not back by then, you have every right to distrust me."

"Aaden." Her feet had frozen in place with her arms outstretched. But he didn't see. He marched forward without a single glance back.

The tightness in her throat hardened. Her fingers formed fists. "Don't you dare leave me like this. I swear on Kamdaria, if you leave right now, I'll never forgive you."

His steps didn't waver.

"I mean it!" Her voice cracked as she spoke, but they had no effect on his retreating figure.

"Aaden." A single word had never conveyed her heartbreak so completely than in this moment.

At last, he turned. The hood shielded his face, leaving only his lips and goatee visible. The stillness lasted long enough to fill her bones with ice. When he spoke, the words ate her from the inside out.

"I'll miss you," he said.

And then he was gone. Her knees hit the gravel while his betrayal punched hole after hole into her shattered heart.

She had so much to do. So much to change.

But how could she defend Kamdaria with a heart broken in two?

ACKNOWLEDGMENTS

This series has been an absolute blast to write. It pushed me to the limit creatively and brought to life characters that I adore. Even though I have enjoyed writing this series, I could not have done it without the support of many wonderful people.

First, I have to say thank you to you. Yes, you! It brings me so much joy to share my books with others. I love knowing other people can experience this world with me. I treasure each of my readers. Even if you're a little mad at me for that ending. ;)

Second, thank you so much to my editor extraordinaire, Deborah Spencer. Your insight is always so valuable. Thank you for telling me the parts that made you laugh. And for helping me work through the inconsistent plot points. This series is truly better thanks to you.

Now I must offer heaps of gratitude onto my incredible book designer, Angel Leya. You have such a great eye and so much talent for putting together all the little details. Thanks for working with me and bringing my vision to life. Among your gorgeous design skills, you also have patience beyond measure.

I also have an amazing ARC team who deserve even more than all the praise I can give them. You all believed in this series from the start. Thank you so much for your willingness to review. Your support gave me the motivation I needed to get each of these novellas finished.

Another huge thanks goes to my awesome author buddies. You have been such a great support to me throughout the writing of this series. Thank you so much for believing in me and for celebrating with me when I reached my goals. You always make me feel much smarter than I really am. Thank you to Abby J. Reed, Alison Ingleby, Anita Kharbanda, Clarissa Gosling, Hanna Sandvig, Joanna Reeder,

Kay Cordell, Kristin J. Dawson, Renee Dugan, Rose Garcia, Shelbi Wescott, T A Chan, Tessonja Odette, and Valia Lind.

My Instagram tribe deserves a huge shout out as well. I love Instagram, especially for the incredible community in the bookstagram world. So many of you have taken me under your wing and helped me enjoy all the wonderful goodness that exists in the bookstagram world. Here is a huge, huge thanks to these friends: @a.court.of.books.and.dreamers, @adventuresthroughwonderland, @ash_cat_books, @ashleys.reading.cafe, @bookbookowl, @bookloverfairy, @bookphenom, @books_over_everything, @booksandtheblacktea, @bookswithtails, @dreamerofpages, @in_acourt_ofbooks, @_jenthebookworm, @kaysbooknook, @magic.within.pages, @mystic_fables, @pennys.books, @rachel_r._smith, @read.write.coffee, @readcommendations, @reading_dianne, @scooze_me, @tanvisreadventures, @temporary.escaper, @theheartisabook, @totallybookedandread_y, @xenatine.

And finally, the biggest thanks of all goes to my remarkable husband. There aren't enough words in the world to express my gratitude for your support and love. Just know, you are the best, and you mean the world to me.

KAY L. MOODY is proud to be a young adult fantasy author. Her books feature exciting plots with a few magical elements. They have lots of adventure, compelling characters, and sweet romantic sub-plots. Most of her books have a dystopian flair. They include a variety of technology levels and lots of diversity. Kay lives in the western United States with her husband and four sons. She enjoys summertime, learning new things, and doing her nails with fancy nail art.

www.KayLMoody.com
facebook.com/KayLMoody
instagram.com/KayLMoody
goodreads.com/KayLMoody

CHARACTER ILLUSTRATIONS

Talise

Aaden

FORCES OF KAMDARIA
INSTRUCTIONS FOR PLAY

ITEMS NEEDED

One game board with 64 squares in an 8x8 square. Two sets of 16 tablets. One set is black, and one set is white. Each set includes 8 blank tablets and 8 symbol tablets. The symbol tablets include 2 waterfall tablets, 2 tornado tablets, 2 tree tables, and 2 flame tablets.

OBJECT

Capture all your opponent's blank tablets from the gameboard.

GAME SETUP

Take 16 tablets of the same color and place them on the 16 squares in the first two rows in front of you. Your opponent does the same.

You may place your tablets in any configuration you wish. Both players must begin placing tablets at the same time. The player who finishes placing their tablets first gets to take the first turn.

HOW TO PLAY

On your first turn, you may move the tablet of your choice as many squares as you wish. After the first turn, tablets can only be moved one square (up, down, or diagonal) at a time. (See Special Rules for Symbol Tablets for Exception.)

Tablets can be placed on top of each other with no more than 6 tablets on a square at a time. If tablets from both players are on a square, either player can move the pile of tablets on their turn.

To play, move tablets across gameboard and attempt to capture all of your opponent's blank tablets. If you jump over an opponent's tablet, in any direction, you capture it. Remove it from the gameboard and set it aside.

SPECIAL RULES FOR SYMBOL TABLETS

Waterfall Tablets: When placed on top of flame tablets, it makes the flame tablets vulnerable to capture.

Air Tablets: When placed next to an opponent's tablet, it forces the opponent's tablet over one space in the opposite direction. This does not count as a turn for the opponent.

Tree Tablets: Can move up to three squares in any direction on one turn.

Flame Tablets: Invincible to capture (unless covered with a waterfall tablet).

FINAL FIGHT

When you "prompt the final fight" you must capture at least one blank tablet from your opponent on every single turn until you capture them all and win the game. If you prompt the final fight and fail to capture a blank tablet on each turn, your opponent may capture any three of your remaining tablets.

Visit kaylmoody.com/kamdaria for the complete short story.

WENDY DELICATELY CLEARED HER THROAT before folding her arms in front of her chest.

Cyrus cracked open one eye before flashing a brilliant smile. "Wendy. It's so good to see you."

Her head shook side to side. "Why do I have the feeling my day is about to get more complicated?"

As he pulled himself to a sitting position, he placed a hand over his chest and let out a scoff. "I'm offended by that. When have I ever made your life complicated?"

The chuckle she tried to suppress made them both smile. "What do you need?" Even she was surprised by how devoid of annoyance her voice sounded. But then again, she did love her brother.

Even as his cheeks turned pink, he shrugged. "I won't bother trying to pretend I don't need anything. You know me too well. But trust me, you're going to be excited this time. I have something fun for us to do."

The pens on her desk rolled as she plucked the earth shaping book from its top. She doubted very much that anything Cyrus wanted to propose would be fun. It certainly would be thrilling though, which he seemed to think was the same thing.

"Here's the thing," her brother said. That definitely sounded like trouble. "There's this man named Rein who organizes these," he looked to the side while one side of his face scrunched up in thought, "*game* nights."

Wendy raised one eyebrow.

"It's true. A bunch of people get together and play Forces. We all love Kamdaria's most popular board game. How could we not?"

She let out a sigh as she dropped the book back onto her desk. "You've been gambling again." It wasn't a question.

This time, his cheeks turned a much brighter shade of red. He scratched the back of his neck. "Normally, I'm one of the best Forces players there is, but this time…"

She massaged the bridge of her nose as the words came out. "You're deep in debt with no way out. You can't borrow money from Mother and Father because they have none. You can't borrow money from Aunt Breezy or Grandmother Skye because they're both still mad about your gambling habits. And let me guess, your weekly soldier's salary isn't enough to cover the debt either?"

"Rein said I don't have to use money pay back the debt."

A tight smile found its way onto Wendy's face because her only other option was to freak out. "This keeps getting better and better, doesn't it?"

"He just needs me to do a job that takes two air shapers. I would have asked one of my soldier friends for help except none of them is as good at air shaping as you."

"Is this job illegal?" She plopped one hand on her hip to punctuate the question.

"Wendy," Cyrus said through a laugh. "Don't you know brothers are protective? I would never ask you to do anything that could put you in danger."

"Which means *yes* otherwise you would have answered the question."

"Eh," he said while his hand shook back and forth. "It depends on how you look at the law."

Visit kaylmoody.com/kamdaria for the complete short story.

9 781954 335059